Praise for the novels of Kate Cochrane

"...A wintery women's romance perfect to cuddle up with on icy days (or between quarters at a PWHL game this season)."
—*Vulture* on *Wake Up, Nat & Darcy*

"A charming debut, perfect for readers looking for queer stories in the popular hockey romance trend or those who enjoyed Anita Kelly's *How You Get the Girl*."
—*Library Journal* on *Wake Up, Nat & Darcy*

"A fun and flirty enemies to lovers romance, *Wake Up, Nat & Darcy* is perfection on ice. A stunning, sporty sapphic debut you won't soon forget."
—Jennifer Dugan, author of *Love at First Set*

"*Wake Up, Nat & Darcy* had me kicking my feet from the start. Everything about it is delicious: the banter, the Winter Olympics hijinks, and most importantly of all, the genuine chemistry and history between Darcy and Natalie. I was rooting so hard for both of them, and for their lovers-to-enemies storyline to finally loop back to lovers. The sapphic hockey romance of my dreams!"
—Anita Kelly, author of *How You Get the Girl*

KATE COCHRANE

YOURS for the SEASON

ISBN-13: 978-1-335-08192-6

Yours for the Season

Copyright © 2025 by Kate Cochrane

All rights reserved. No part of this book may be used or reproduced in any manner whatsoever without written permission.

Without limiting the exclusive rights of any author, contributor or the publisher of this publication, any unauthorized use of this publication to train generative artificial intelligence (AI) technologies is expressly prohibited. Harlequin also exercises their rights under Article 4(3) of the Digital Single Market Directive 2019/790 and expressly reserves this publication from the text and data mining exception.

This is a work of fiction. Names, characters, places and incidents are either the product of the author's imagination or are used fictitiously. Any resemblance to actual persons, living or dead, businesses, companies, events or locales is entirely coincidental.

For questions and comments about the quality of this book, please contact us at CustomerService@Harlequin.com.

® is a trademark of Harlequin Enterprises ULC.

Carina Press
22 Adelaide St. West, 41st Floor
Toronto, Ontario M5H 4E3, Canada
www.Harlequin.com

HarperCollins Publishers
Macken House, 39/40 Mayor Street Upper,
Dublin 1, D01 C9W8, Ireland
www.HarperCollins.com

Printed in U.S.A.

For the real JT and Coxie. Thank you for lending me your names but most of all thank you for your friendship.

And for Puck, the world's most mischievous puppy.

Chapter One

JT Cox never thought that Hart's Landing would surprise her. But that was before she saw her name on the sign welcoming folks to her hometown.

Welcome to Hart's Landing.
Home of Gold Medalist JT Cox.

"What in the hell?" she said, slowing her car to gawk at the sign as she rolled down the two-lane road. The double yellow line in the center was faded and obscured by a layer of salt, sand, and snow and her car was jostled by a series of frost heaves as she tried to make sense of the new sign. When did they put her name on the welcome sign and why hadn't anyone told her they had? Man, her hometown was so weird.

The sign wasn't quite accurate. JT didn't live there; it wasn't her home. She grew up there and her parents still lived there. But if home was a place where a person could feel comfortable, embraced, and at peace, this was not JT Cox's home.

Her parents guilt-tripped her constantly about not coming home enough, but this place didn't exactly love her. Well, maybe it loved her now. But if they were only going to love her because she won gold at the Olympics, she figured they could fuck right off. Her memory was good enough to recall her entire childhood here and the way they'd treated her.

She shook her head, trying to clear the memories. She didn't need to relive this now. It was Christmas, which meant chocolate and candy canes and pine smell everywhere. She *was* happy to see her family, at least in theory. The town wasn't the only thing that didn't understand her as a child. Her family *still* didn't. She was the weird jock in a family of artists. She was also the gay one who the town had thought was weird for playing on the boys' team but maybe now they were happy to pretend they'd supported her in her quest for gold.

Yeah, right. They hadn't done a single thing to help her. Unless you counted making JT so driven by spite that she'd excelled just to shove it in their stupid faces.

She drove past the high school, a building that still looked like a converted factory. By the time JT got there they'd traded out walls that stopped two feet short of the ceiling for redone classrooms, but the feeling that the town cared so little for education that they repurposed a shoe factory remained. They tried renaming it, but no one forgot the dim lighting, the three-quarter walls, or the way the carpet smelled like metal and bleach.

Her stomach fluttered when she put her blinker on to turn down the road to her parents' house. The sand spread across the road to help with the snow and ice shifted under her tires as she slowly made the turn onto a road that hadn't been repaved for years.

The house had smoke curling from the chimney and light in all the front windows when she pulled into the driveway. She bounced along the ruts created by years of driving and parked her car next to her brother's. Either her sister, Emerson, or brother-in-law, Clark, must have popped out to run an errand, probably something super helpful her mom asked them to do. Emerson and Jonathan were always jockeying to be the favorite kid. JT didn't even try anymore.

She grabbed her duffel out of the trunk and turned around at the sound of the door springing open. She dropped the bag on the snowy ground and crouched down before her puppy Toby flew into her and knocked her on her ass.

"Oh, I missed you too, girl," she said, laughing and trying to hug the wiggling yellow Lab, who was so excited she didn't know whether to lick JT's face or to run around the yard. At least JT would always be her favorite.

Toby raced around the car only to return to JT ten seconds later, tail wagging so hard she couldn't walk straight. JT hadn't been this happy since she won the gold medal game. As she rubbed Toby's silky Lab ears, she wondered if that was true. Toby was probably better than the medal, but it was close at least.

JT's dad walked out, shrugging his barn jacket over his sweater and stamping his feet deep into his Bean boots. "Drive okay?"

JT nodded. "Yeah. Roads were fine, not too much traffic."

He wrapped her in a hug. "When was the last time there was traffic around here? There's only two thousand people in the town."

"You don't need a lot of people to have traffic, just a couple of dumbasses. Last time I checked there were plenty of those here."

He laughed.

"Jasmine Cox, you just got here and you're swearing already?" JT's mom was standing on the porch, wearing one of JT's old hoodies—now splattered with paint.

"Mom, you say that like you think she stopped swearing at any point in the past fifteen years." JT's sister, Emerson, stood in the doorway, smiling as Brooke, her toddler, gripped her leg.

JT crouched down to be at Brooke's level. "Brookie! How's my tiniest niece?"

Brooke smiled and JT felt her heart grow three sizes. Brooke was so cute with her head of red curls, unsteady feet, and determined face. Brooke squealed and did her best to run toward JT. JT scooped her up and twirled her around. It was likely that JT would be ready to kill her parents in ten minutes, but the toddler hug was great.

JT buried her face in Brooke's neck and plastered kisses all over her until she laughed so hard JT joined her. JT set her down on the porch, careful not to get her socks in the snow.

"Jaytee, Christmas."

JT nodded. "Christmas? Is that happening this year?"

Brooke giggled. "Jaytee. Santa gonna come."

JT looked up at her sister. "Oh yeah? I bet you've been wicked good this year."

Brooke nodded solemnly.

The door creaked open. "Are you interrogating a toddler?" Jonathan, JT's older brother, stood with his hands in his pockets and looked so much like their dad JT felt like her brain had glitched.

JT hugged him. "More like talking to the main draw. Where's your bunch?"

He smiled, his eyes crinkling at the corners. "Beth gave them cocoa. Sorry to have to break it to you but marshmallows are way cooler than you."

"How can I argue with that? Did she make extra?"

"Not extra, just an absolute boatload. She knew you were coming."

Toby bumped JT's leg. "That will be great, but I gotta take my girl for a walk first. I'll be back in a little bit. You wanna go for a walk, girl?" She wagged so hard her butt did a full circle.

JT's mom pursed her lips. "You just got here. It's not like we haven't been taking care of Toblerone."

"I know, Mom. I appreciate you taking her while I was at camp, but I can take her now. Then I can hang out with the little guys for a while before dinner."

Her dad put his hand on her mom's shoulder and tugged

gently. "Come on, let's get out of the freezing cold. She'll be back soon. It's too cold to walk far."

"I don't understand why she feels the need to leave so quickly. She just got here," her mom muttered as she went back inside.

Home for less than five minutes and JT had already disappointed her mom. Had to be some kind of record.

JT grabbed Toby's leash and headed down the road before it got too dark. Toby settled quickly into the walk, her tail bouncing side to side and her steps jaunty. People came to New Hampshire for the foliage or the skiing or the lakes. They didn't come for the bleak season when it was freezing and everything was gray. But JT loved it. There was a bite to the air as it skated across her face. The air was crisp, clear, and with a hint of smoke from someone's fireplace.

JT wished she could love the town as much as she loved the way the winter air snapped with cold, the way the woodsmoke-flavored air filled her nostrils and the way the promise of snow comforted her. She wished she could feel at home here. But years of not being accepted here made that an impossible dream.

JT wandered down to Ms. Grant's house. Someone had painted it a deep blue with white trim and a red door. The paint changed the entire character of the place without making it seem unfamiliar. JT hoped Ms. Grant was okay. She'd always looked out for JT at school, even when opposing fans were obnoxious or even cruel.

Toby was sniffing a pile of leaves when JT's phone dinged. She dug her phone out of her back pocket. Tommy.

Drinks. 7. Dolan's Pub.

JT had zero interest in seeing all her former classmates at a bar, but it had been too long since she'd seen Tommy in person, so she said yes.

Meet you there. You better not stand me up.

He sent back a laughing emoji. I'm bringing Ali. Don't be late.

JT's stomach flipped over at the sight of Ali's name. Tommy's older sister was JT's first crush. Looking back, it was clear Ali never thought of JT as anything other than Tommy's best buddy, but she was always kind, even when other people weren't. She even told her boyfriend, Kyle, off once for making jokes about JT. Tommy told JT that Ali and Kyle got divorced last year. JT was glad to hear it; Ali was always way too good for him.

JT's mom was going to give her a hard time for going out on her first night home, but JT hadn't seen her best friend in way too long. Leaving the house for a few hours should also keep her from getting too annoyed with the parents.

Toby pushed the door open to the kitchen, leaving JT to kick off her shoes before following her inside. The kitchen was warm and smelled like cookies and bread.

Jonathan's kids, sporting cocoa mustaches, rushed over to JT.

"Auntie JT, can we see your medal?"

JT looked over their heads at Jonathan.

He smiled. "They've been asking about it for weeks."

Something shifted inside JT's chest. She crouched to their level. "Do you think I carry my medal everywhere?"

The twins, Harrison and Mabel, looked at each other with creeping panic.

JT laughed. "Of course I do. Chicks dig it." Jonathan gave JT a look, but she ignored his horror. If he had a gold medal, he wouldn't be so prudish about using it to impress women. "Let me put my bag in my room and then I'll dig it out for you. Okay?"

They cheered and ran off screaming for Brooke.

"You're in the den," JT's mom said without looking up from the apples she was peeling.

"What?"

She sliced the apples into a bowl, her hands moving in the practiced way of a woman who had made a thousand apple pies in her lifetime. "The twins are in your room. Jonathan and Beth are in his room, and Emerson, Clark, and Brooke are in her room. We made the couch up for you and figured you'd be happy being out of the way."

"Outstanding," JT said, doing very little to disguise her annoyance at being relegated to the den.

The "den" was the name their parents gave the finished portion of their basement. It could only be accessed from a door on the other side of her parents' art studio. JT hoisted her bag over her shoulder and walked through the room where her parents did their smaller art pieces. Anything too big for the studio happened out in the barn, which had a second studio space for larger sculptures and any oversized pieces. The studio in the house smelled of paint, wood shavings, and a variety of dusts from plaster to stone, which gave it a smell JT had never found anywhere else in the world. As she walked through the room, she breathed deeply, taking in the scent that lingered on her parents and was as familiar as the smells from the kitchen.

Once she got to the cellar door, JT flicked the lights on before trudging down the stairs in semi-darkness—the bulb over the stairs was out and no one had gotten around to the annoying job of changing it. It was lighter at the bottom of the stairs but with nothing more than tiny windows, the place felt claustrophobic. The ceiling was normal height; her parents had made sure of that so her mom could do her yoga stretches down there without her hands hitting drywall. JT stepped over the yoga mat and around a small tower of dumbbells. She dropped her duffel next to the couch where she would be sleeping for however many days she could stand being there. She planned to stay until the day after Christmas, but this level of comfort did not inspire her to consider extending her stay.

As an added bonus, Toby didn't like stairs, so JT didn't know if she would even hang out in the basement at all. And they wondered why JT didn't come home more.

The door at the top of the stairs opened. "Jasmine, we're planning a movie for the kids later, so don't set up your bed yet."

She rolled her eyes. Great. She couldn't even get comfortable because of course her "bedroom" was also the movie theater, gym, and all-around romper-room. She filed this fact away for the next time someone asked how her life had changed since winning gold.

JT dropped onto the couch. At least it was comfortable. And she had the big TV at her disposal—when the kids weren't using it.

Only three hours before she'd have to leave for the bar. She could go that long without murdering anyone, right?

She dug around in her bag and grabbed the wooden box holding her medal. The kids would like it even if her parents were entirely unimpressed.

They'd come to the Olympics, but JT couldn't shake the feeling they'd come because it would have looked bad for them to have stayed home. Everyone had had some family or friends there, and if they'd stayed home, it would have been obvious to everyone how much they did not give a shit about her. Even when she was playing in the biggest tournament in the world.

Her siblings had wanted to come but couldn't wrangle time off work, and bringing a bunch of tiny kids to Switzerland during the school year would have been a nightmare. But they'd sent videos of their families watching the games and cheering and even one of the kids all getting together and watching the tape-delayed gold medal game. JT had watched them chant her name in their tiny, high-pitched voices about a million times.

By contrast, JT's parents took the opportunity to turn their trip into a European vacation. They'd taken more pictures of their travels than they had of the opening ceremony or anything related to the Olympics. It was as if being there was a chore, and the travel was the reward for having to endure it. They even left before the end of the gold medal game to fly home to make it for Jonathan's art show opening. They'd said it was important to be there to support him. JT's game had lasted three hours. His show was up for two months.

JT hauled her ass up the stairs and found the kids sitting on a couch in the living room. They leaped off the couch and ran toward her. Harrison stood solemnly in front of her, his hands clasped behind his back. Beth probably told him to be careful so he was doing his best "don't touch anything in the museum" act. Their grandparents had been taking all the kids to the MFA and other art museums since they were tiny. It was probably an attempt to ensure they all grew up sufficiently awed by the masters and underwhelmed by such trivial things as athletics.

Harrison's twin, Mabel, had zero chill and ran right into JT's leg. "Me first!" she screamed, drawing a look from her mom, but JT loved it. There was an old wooden crate next to the fireplace but it was empty—they'd probably had a fire last night and hadn't refilled it yet. JT flipped it over and held Mabel's hand as she stepped onto it.

JT opened the box and Mabel's eyes went wide in awe. "You want to wear it?"

She nodded. JT took it out of the box and slipped it over her head. She grabbed it, leaving fingerprints all over the shiny metal.

"This is so cool!" she squealed. "Can you take a picture of me, Mommy?"

Beth pulled out her phone and took a picture of Mabel and then Harrison wearing the medal, posing like they'd just won, and—after JT's encouragement—fake biting it just like the team had in their pictures.

"That's going to ruin their teeth," JT's mom said.

"Mom," she said with a sigh. "They're not actually biting it."

She pressed her lips together. "I'm surprised you'd let them do that. As precious as that is to you."

JT never figured out how her mother managed it, but she had the ability to make everything she said feel like an insult. Yes, the medal was precious. But not because it was shiny, but because she worked her ass off to earn it.

JT had foolishly thought her mom, a woman who had worked her ass off for every bit of artistic acclaim she'd received in a sexist world, would understand the satisfaction, the joy of reaching a goal. But JT had been wrong. Maybe the only goals she understood, the only accolades that mattered, were write-ups in the *New York Times* art section, features in magazines, shows with important galleries. All things she had achieved, but she couldn't possibly expand her mind enough to imagine that JT winning the gold medal on the biggest stage there was for her sport would be something to be proud of.

JT's mouth tasted bitter. She turned back to the kids. They were barely in school, but they understood how to be happy for JT. They didn't care that JT couldn't paint or sing.

Harrison waited for his turn and then stepped onto the crate after Mabel hopped down.

"JT, can you play the song?" He looked up with his gigantic brown eyes, and if he'd asked for JT's car she couldn't have said no.

JT reached for her phone. "Sure, buddy. You know what to do?"

He nodded solemnly and bent his head forward for JT to slip the medal on. Then he carefully placed his hand over his heart and stood at attention. It was almost more than JT could bear.

JT pulled up YouTube to play the anthem but wasn't ready to hear him sing along, his sweet high voice struggling with the ridiculously challenging notes. JT's mom disappeared from the room. Harrison finished the song and then thrust his fists into the air.

"I'm going to do it, too."

JT crouched down in front of him to get a picture. "What sport?"

He grinned. "Hockey." He looked at his mom. "If my parents let me."

JT chuckled. "Oh, they said no?" She raised her eyebrows at her brother. "Jonathan, you told my nephew—"

"And me!" Mabel said.

"You told my niece *and* nephew that they couldn't play hockey?"

He shrugged. "The practices are really early and, well..."

JT gestured for the twins to come toward her. "You want to go skating while you're here? I'll take you."

Jonathan and Beth exchanged a look, but it was too late. The twins screamed and jumped up and down again and again.

JT smiled and shrugged at her brother. "Do you really want to crush their dreams, Jonny?"

He put a hand on each of their little heads. "If they fall in love with the sport, I will call you from every early-morning game or practice for the rest of your life."

JT laughed. "*When* they fall in love with the best sport on the planet, I'll turn off my ringer."

The kids raced out of the room to find more cocoa, but Beth stopped on her way. "If they take after Jonathan, I don't think we have much to worry about in terms of athletics."

Jonathan laughed. "That's both rude and accurate. JT got all the athletic ability in the family."

"Hey!" Emerson trailed Brooke into the living room. "I run!"

"Yes. And we're very proud of you. But notice you picked the one sport that doesn't involve throwing, catching, any form of contact, or a need for hand-eye coordination?"

JT laughed. "I may have gotten most of the athletic ability, but you two got the only talent that matters around here."

"That's not true."

"Come on, Em, you know Mom and Dad barely care that I won the gold medal. They weren't even excited that I got invited to the White House."

Jonathan protested. "Of course they're proud. You're an Olympian. That's first-line-of-your-obituary stuff! How could they not be proud?"

JT shrugged and turned toward the kitchen. "I ask myself that five times a week."

Emerson frowned. "They're proud. They're just weird."

JT let it drop in favor of moving into the kitchen, where she hoped to find something to spike her cocoa with.

Chapter Two

From the outside, the house looked absolutely perfect. The painters had done a great job. It was too bad that when Ali Porter walked into it, she had to wonder if every box she'd packed had spawned four more. If it were more organized, it would look like the storeroom at the hardware store where she worked as a teenager. This disaster would have gotten her fired.

If one of her students had tried to use such a heavy-handed metaphor—perfect from the outside, total mess inside—she would have asked them to try again. But after her divorce finally became official a year ago, things were looking pretty messy everywhere. Now everyone in town knew she was a mess.

Not a mess, a work in progress.

Part of that progress was divorcing Kyle. There was nothing wrong with Kyle. He was fine. He was a fine husband and a fine friend and everything about him—about them as a couple—was fine. But along the way, Ali stopped wanting to stay the same couple they had been since high school and Kyle didn't want anything to change. He wanted people in town to look at them like they were still the prom king and queen, and he wanted to talk about his glory days as the captain of the football team. Ali stopped wanting to go along with whatever Kyle wanted.

Ali wanted more than simply fine.

Ali wanted to be herself at twenty-eight, not remain who she was at eighteen. She wanted to choose new things and he didn't and if she stayed, she was going to keep letting him convince her to be the girl he loved at eighteen instead of herself.

Right now, she was a woman standing in her own living room, surrounded by boxes she should've unpacked months ago in a house that would impress the people who drove by as long as they didn't slow down long enough to see the woman inside losing her goddamned mind.

But the holiday lights looked nice in the windows. Ali always liked the ones that looked like candles, but Kyle wanted to do the over-the-top multi-color flashing lights extravaganza and told her the candle lights were for old people.

You can bet your ass the first thing Ali did after Halloween was put those suckers in every window she could find.

Take that, Kyle.

Ali dropped onto the couch she hated. It reminded her of her old life. It was fine. Sturdy, well-reviewed, but beige. It had been a sensible purchase she had made with Kyle. When she moved out, they divvied up everything and he told her to take the couch so she would have at least one thing to sit on. Maybe it was a nice gesture, but sitting on it reminded her how much she hated beige and how she should have pushed for the couch she really wanted. It was a deep teal and had a weird mid-century vibe that Kyle hated. So, Ali caved, as per usual.

Ali wondered if she could get some new stuff over the winter break. That would mean unpacking enough boxes to make room for it. She looked around at the boxes and felt the creeping, overwhelming dread seep into her bones.

No.

Ali told herself she could do this. She was going to unpack five boxes before dinner. And then another five before she went to bed. She did a quick count and realized that even ten boxes wasn't going to be enough to clear the room, but it would be a start. She could make a start.

Ali Canterbury might not be able to tackle that, but Ali Porter could. And after the divorce Ali was back to her old last name, the name that fit so much better. She never should have changed it in the first place, but her mom and Kyle had talked her into that, too. And now she was going to have to deal with her mom asking when she changed her name back.

At least her brother, Tommy, was home for Christmas and could back her up with their family. Her phone vibrated so hard it fell off the box it was sitting on. She really needed to unpack these boxes so she could set up an actual coffee table.

It was Tommy.

Drinks tonight. Don't argue. We're going out. Pick you up at seven.

Ali considered leaving him on Read and letting him stew, but that wouldn't stop him from pulling into her driveway in a few hours.

Fine. I'll come but if it sucks, I'm leaving.

He sent a shrug emoji. It's not going to suck.

Ali looked at the boxes. Now she had ten boxes to unpack before seven. She should have told him no.

Chapter Three

Dolan's was the only real bar around. It was decorated with sports memorabilia, including a jersey from the high school hockey team and photos of the year they won the state championship. The other décor was from around the state and included the local colleges as well as some items dedicated to New Hampshire landmarks like the Man in the Mountain.

The bar was already crowded when JT got there around seven fifteen. She didn't want to be early, but she also didn't want to listen to her mom gush over her siblings and how amazing they were for one second longer. Thankfully, even with the place packed, she quickly found Tommy standing by the bar. JT weaved through pockets of old friends hugging and talking loudly to reach him as the bartender slid a beer and a cocktail toward him.

Tommy wrapped her in a hug as soon as she got close enough. "Hey, superstar."

JT squeezed his shoulder. "Good to see you."

He nodded to the bar. "What do you want?"

"Allagash, please." She looked around the room at way too many semi-familiar faces. "Didn't you say your sister was coming?"

He nodded in the direction of some booths off to the side. "She went to find a seat. Here, you can take this to her. And here, I already got an Allagash. You take it, and I'll get the next one."

"You sure?"

"Go on, I'll be there in a second."

JT carefully worked her way through the crowd, avoiding gesturing arms and people hugging. As she approached the booth, she could hear someone talking to Ali. She slowed, not wanting to interrupt the conversation.

"Oh hey, Ali. I wasn't sure we'd see you here this year." Marisa Michelson. Apparently, some girls who sucked in high school never grew out of it.

Ali blinked and smiled. "Really? Why not?"

JT could spot Ali's fake smile from a mile away.

"Well, I thought you might not want to come since Kyle is going to be here." She squirmed a little as she said it, and JT tried not to relish her discomfort too much.

Ali gave her a smile JT could imagine she'd given to her students many times over the years. "Kyle and I are perfectly fine seeing each other out and about. We're adults."

Marisa patted the table. "Well, that's good then! I think he's bringing Sharon, so if you haven't met, you'll get a chance. Jeremy and I met her last week and she couldn't be nicer."

When she'd heard enough, JT stepped toward the booth. "Excuse me," JT said, stepping in front of Marisa and angling her out of the way. JT set a drink in front of Ali. "Tommy said that's what you'd want." JT turned to Marisa, beer in hand. "Mary, right?" She held out her hand, damp from the glass.

"Marisa." Marisa took her hand with obvious discomfort.

JT shook her head. "Gosh, I'm so sorry. I've met so many people lately, I've gotten terrible with names."

JT caught Ali taking a sip of her drink and stifling a grin. Marisa made some excuse to leave. Mission accomplished.

JT slid into the booth opposite Ali. Part of her wished she'd sat next to her, but that would have been weird, right? Ali looked great. JT hadn't been sure how she would look after all the divorce gossip she'd heard. Twelve-year-old JT had thought Ali Porter was the prettiest girl on the planet, and twenty-five-year-old JT wondered how it was possible that Ali was even hotter now. She had long bangs, swept to one side, and her long dirty-blond hair fell in gentle waves around her shoulders. If they'd been dating, JT would have happily reached across the table to tuck it behind Ali's ears. But in what world would Ali Porter date her?

Ali's eye sparkled. "Oh my god, Tommy didn't tell me you were coming! How are you?"

For a second, JT wondered if she should give Ali a hug. Instead, she smiled across the table, trying to fight the nervousness bubbling inside her. "Hi. Tommy got that for you so if it sucks, it's his fault." JT kicked herself for being so awkward.

Ali took another sip. "Thanks for..." She trailed off, her eyes flicking to where Marisa and her buddies were clustered.

JT shrugged. "No problem." She paused. "So, you're divorced."

Ali laughed and nearly spit her drink across the table. "Oh my god."

"What?" JT asked, playing dumb.

"Everyone here pretends someone died or avoids talking about my divorce at all. But not you. It's refreshing."

JT shrugged. "Figured I'd get that shit out of the way. Besides, you've always been out of that boy's league. Glad you finally realized it." JT looked to where Marisa was standing. "She hasn't changed since high school, has she?" she asked, making a disgusted face before holding her beer out toward Ali.

Ali tapped her glass against JT's. "Yeah. She's always been fake nice to me while making it very clear that she hates my guts." She leaned against the booth cushions, looking effortlessly, unobtainably hot.

"If you want me to kick her ass, just say the word."

Ali sighed. "She's not worth the trouble, but thanks. Most people have been fine, I guess. But she seems really offended that Kyle and I got divorced."

"It's probably freaking her out that now she doesn't have an excuse to keep her feelings for you a secret."

Ali snorted, nearly shooting her drink out her nose. Her eyes watered as she swallowed. "JT!"

JT laughed, and it came out higher than she would have liked. It was hard to seem cool when her laugh made her sound like a teenager. But it must have been contagious. Ali joined her, and they both started fresh waves of laughter that only built the more they looked at each other.

"I cannot believe you just insinuated Marisa has a thing for me. Oh my god." Ali wiped her eyes.

JT shrugged again. "It would make sense. You're awesome, single, and hot so why wouldn't she?"

"Because she's been trying to get with Kyle since we were in high school." Ali looked toward the bar where Tommy was laughing with some of his friends. "How come you're sitting here with me instead of with Tommy?"

JT ran a finger through the condensation on her glass. "Bros aren't really my thing. Your brother is possibly my favorite person on the planet but those guys he's talking to are definitely not."

Ali squinted through the dark as if she was trying to figure out who JT was talking about.

"You're probably too old to remember but those guys liked to show off by taking runs at me on the ice. A few of them got some good hits in, but mostly they hated that I was good and leaned hard into being toxic assholes to prove their masculinity." JT tried to wash the taste of that memory away with a sip of beer.

"Didn't stop you from winning the state championship," Ali said with a soft smile. She nodded toward the picture of JT on the wall hoisting the trophy. "Isn't that you, superstar?"

JT blushed. "I know. But it would have been nice to have a team where I didn't have to get dressed by myself. Or where opposing fans didn't scream at me for being a girl." JT got lost for a second in the bitter memories of people questioning why she was on the team or insinuating she was both sleeping with her teammates and a raging lesbian with no thought about how those two things conflicted.

Three women stopped at the booth to say hi. "JT! Congratulations! We watched every game. You guys were awesome."

"I told everyone at work that we went to school together," another one said.

JT's face shifted into a practiced smile. "Thank you so much. We really appreciate all the support we got from folks back home."

The women asked her for a picture. "This way my boss won't be able to say I don't know you," a woman with curly red hair said. Her eyes lingered on JT's mouth. She wasn't the first woman to do that, but she wasn't her type.

JT got up and the redhead handed Ali her phone. "Do you mind?"

She flashed her an apologetic smile. Ali smiled back and JT was fourteen all over again, her stomach fluttering at the sight of Ali's perfect lips curving into a smile. "Of course. Get together," she said.

The redhead took the opportunity to put her arm around her waist. She was a little too friendly for JT's taste but not quite inappropriate. She could handle it, but Ali's eyes flashed with something JT would have said was jealousy if she didn't know better. Ali snapped half a dozen pictures before handing the phone back.

JT talked to them for another minute or so before sitting down. "It was really nice of you to come say hi. If you don't mind, I'd like to catch up with Ali. I haven't seen her in forever." The women lingered for a second. Finally, the redhead gave JT's shoulder another squeeze and took a quick selfie with her cheek smashed against JT's.

Ali laughed. "Are you blushing?"

JT shook her head, but her cheeks were on fire. "No. I mean that woman tried to give me her number but... I don't know."

"Did you want to go with her?"

"What? No. Not at all. I'm happy here." She looked across the room. "Unless you want me to leave you alone. I can go if..."

Ali reached across the table and grabbed JT's wrist. "I don't want you to go. But I don't want you to feel like you have to stay here with Tommy's boring older sister. I'll be fine if you want to go flirt or whatever."

JT dipped her head to keep Ali from seeing her cheeks turning pink. She pulled off a strip of label from her beer bottle. "I'm good. I promise."

While it was notable that there was a woman in her hometown flirting with her, it had not been JT's experience that there *were* other queer women her age in town. But why on earth would she want to talk to any other woman in this place when she could talk to Ali? JT didn't say all of that. Ali still was Tommy's sister and JT still felt like the silly kid with a crush.

The silence stretched between them. They filled it by sipping their drinks and staring into the crowd. JT glanced over to the bar, wondering what was taking Tommy so long, when she saw someone walk in.

"Shit."

"What's wrong?"

"Okay, I have to ask. When you told Marisa you were fine with Kyle, was that true?"

"Yeah, of course."

"Okay, because he just walked in with a woman who looks..." JT paused. Ali followed her gaze toward the door.

She laughed. "Oh my god. You're seeing this, right? She looks...?"

"Exactly like you," JT said. "Yeah. I mean, she's less hot but—"

JT froze. How could she be so fucking stupid? Why did she call Ali hot, again? Her face burned hotter than before.

Ali bit her lip but it didn't keep her from laughing. "I'm sorry, did you say I'm hot?"

Oh god. JT looked at Ali, who looked absolutely delighted.

Okay, JT could fix this. She leaned back against the booth cushions and gave Ali her best smile. "Look, you can't argue with facts. The earth is round, the sun is hot, and so are you."

Ali blushed and JT liked it too much. "JT Cox, are you flirting with me?"

JT laughed. "If I were flirting with you, you wouldn't have to ask."

She finished her drink and slid out of the booth to get a refill. "Why aren't you?"

JT's mouth dropped open. "What? You're Tommy's sister!"

"So? You lowkey flirted with those hockey groupies who were just here. We all saw you on *Wake Up, USA* flirting with that woman who is engaged to the other host now. But you won't flirt with me. What's up with that?"

JT opened her mouth but couldn't think of what to say. She closed it, sure she now looked like some kind of deranged fish. When she looked at Ali, she had a smile playing at the corner of her lips. "Wait, do you want me to?"

Ali leaned forward, her hair falling around her face. She tucked one side of it behind her ear. "I'm divorced, not dead."

"Flirting with straight women never ends well for me."

"Who says I'm straight?" She grinned, like she was enjoying seeing JT this flustered. JT's stomach dropped through the floor. Holy shit. Ali Porter was flirting with her. What on earth?

JT leaned forward. "Are you telling me…?"

"Bi, bi, bi," she sang, complete with hand gestures.

JT sat back. "Well, in that case," she said, unable to keep from smiling. "Can I buy you a drink?"

Ali bit her bottom lip. "Thought you'd never ask."

Chapter Four

Ali watched JT go up to the bar and return with another round of drinks. She set Ali's drink in front of her and waited to clink glasses before sipping her own. It looked like JT had switched to seltzer water, but it could have been something else.

"So, are you going to tell me the truth or just some bullshit about why you never flirt with me?"

JT laughed and looked toward the bar. Tommy was still surrounded by his former jock friends. She sighed and looked at Ali. "Fine. I'll admit that since leaving this town I've been called a flirt from time to time."

Ali laughed. "If people didn't know before, they do now. Flirting on national television…"

She grimaced. "Not my best move. But I take your point. Yes, I like flirting with women. It's fun. Sometimes it gets me a date, sometimes it's just fun to banter a little."

"Yes, JT, I am aware of the fun and side effects of flirting."

She looked at the table between them. "But when I do it, it's nothing serious. It's fun, I see where it goes, and that's it. But you…" She looked away.

Ali watched her face change with every thought going through her head. If only Ali could tell what she was thinking.

"Scoot in, dude." Tommy slid across the booth seat, knocking into JT and forcing her to the inside. "Sorry I left you guys here for so long." He leaned forward and lowered his voice. "I saw Kyle come in, are you okay?"

Ali waved a hand dismissively. She knew why he was asking but everyone's concern was getting boring. "Yes, I'm fine. We both still live in this town. If I wasn't fine running into him at least a couple times a week I'd have to move."

Tommy nodded. "Okay, but how weird is it that his date is basically you?"

Ali looked at JT over the rim of her glass. "I'm hotter."

Tommy laughed and high-fived Ali across the table. "Okay, but if you need me to pull some protective brother shit, I can."

She shook her head. "Really, it's fine. I've been having a good time grilling JT."

"Oh yeah?" Tommy leaned back and threw his arm over the back of the booth so he could look at JT. "Anything good?"

JT shook her head with a slightly panicked look on her face.

Ali smirked at her, letting her squirm a little. "I was just getting to the good stuff when you arrived. So go on, get out of here so I can talk to her. I see you all the time. I want my chance with the gold medalist."

"I invited both of you to the bar and it turns out neither of you want to hang out with me? Wow…" He shook his head but didn't seem too offended when he walked away.

JT took a swig of her seltzer. "So, what did you mean, 'your chance'?" Pink climbed up JT's neck toward her cheeks, and she worked hard to meet Ali's eye.

"What do you think I mean? No. Better question…what do you want me to mean?" Okay, maybe Ali was going too far, but she hadn't had this much fun flirting in a long time. Even if she was Tommy's best friend, it didn't take away from the fact that JT was hot. Hell, even the straight women in the bar were staring at her. And Ali's fingers were dying to know if the buzz of her undercut was soft or bristly.

"Ali," she said, her voice low. So low Ali felt it more than heard it.

"JT. Or do you prefer Coxie?" Ali smiled around her straw and ran her foot up her calf under the table.

"Jesus." JT's voice escaped in a breath.

Before either of them could say anything, Tommy returned. "So, I know I'm your ride, but would you mind if JT drove you home?" He looked at Ali and then at JT. "Do you mind giving Ali a ride? She's on your way…"

"Two seconds ago you're pouting because we want to talk and now you're pawning me off?" Ali said, giving Tommy a look.

Tommy shrugged and looked across the bar at a pretty woman standing by a high-top table.

"I see," Ali said with a laugh.

"Of course. I'm happy to drive you if you don't mind."

JT's eyes were locked on Ali's, and Ali hadn't wanted to kiss anyone this badly since she first started dating Kyle. Ali nodded, not taking her eyes off JT. "If she doesn't mind taking me home, I'm in." Ali forced herself to look at Tommy. He was confused, but judging by the fact it looked like he was ditching them to hook up with some woman he only met that night, he didn't seem inclined to argue.

Tommy gave JT an appraising look. "You're okay to drive?"

She nodded. "This is water. I'm good."

He patted JT on the shoulder. "Thanks. And I'll see you tomorrow, right? Mom wants us to…"

"Shut up about Mom and get out of here," Ali said. The last thing she wanted was thoughts of her mom and her annoying expectations. Ali could hear her mom telling her that Kyle would take her back, that she should really think about it, that they were so good together... Ali ran a hand through her hair hoping it would push her mom's voice out of her head.

JT cocked her head to one side. "So, do you want another drink or...?"

Ali had an idea for how to get her mom out of her head. She looked JT in the eyes. Goddamn, she had gorgeous eyes. She let her eyes move to JT's lips and wondered if they would feel as soft as they looked if Ali leaned forward to kiss her. Someone laughed loudly close by, reminding Ali they were in public. Ali reluctantly dragged her eyes from JT's mouth, back to her eyes.

In a town of very few queer people, and even fewer her age, Ali didn't have many options to indulge her curiosity about kissing a woman. Two drinks into her night, she was facing a very hot single woman, and it dawned on her that JT might be willing to be the answer to some of Ali's curiosity. The thought of kissing JT intrigued her. She'd been a teenager the last time she kissed someone new, and the anticipation, the uncertainty about whether JT would reciprocate, the question of how it would feel, how JT would taste, all of it made Ali deliciously, tantalizingly nervous.

She licked her lips, tasting the sweetness of her drink lingering at the corner of her mouth. She didn't miss the way JT's eyes tracked her tongue or the look in her eyes as she held Ali's gaze. Game. On.

"I want you to take me home."

JT's eyes went wide like a cartoon. She quickly recovered and leaned forward, her sculpted forearms resting on the table. "Ali." Ali didn't know eyes could spark, but hers looked ready to combust. "Did I hear you right?"

JT was giving her an out. Part of her wanted to take it. It was JT, Tommy's best friend. Ali had known her forever. There were so many reasons to say, *Yes, you heard me wrong.* So many reasons to chicken out.

"Yes." Ali swallowed and fought the urge to break eye contact. "Unless the only thing you want is to drive me, you heard me right the first time."

JT exhaled and looked over toward Tommy. Pink crept up her neck. She was flustered. Ali knew she should feel bad, but all she could think about was how cute it was when JT blushed and how Ali wanted to touch her cheek to see if it was hot from all that blood rushing into it.

"Tommy—"

Ali wrapped her hand around JT's wrist. "My baby brother has nothing to do with who I..." It was Ali's turn to be flustered. "It's none of his business."

JT didn't look convinced, but when her eyes dropped to where Ali's fingers were curled around her arm, she bit the inside of her cheek like she was trying to suppress a smile. "Okay." She slid out of the booth and then held out her hand to help Ali up.

Ali took it, her fingers lingering a beat longer than necessary on JT's palm. JT moved to the side, her hand finding the small of Ali's back to guide her through the crowd. When JT reached to open the door, Ali pressed back into her hand. They didn't speak as they walked to her car, but Ali stopped her when JT tried to open the passenger door for her.

"I appreciate the chivalry, but I am perfectly capable."

She was taller than Ali and she looked down as she reached around Ali to grab the door handle. Her chest was deliciously close to Ali. "I know." She looked around the empty parking lot, before leaning forward and brushing her lips against Ali's cheek. "But maybe I *want* to take care of you." She moved back but Ali would still feel JT's breath ghosting across her ear. JT gave her a wicked smile over her shoulder as she walked to the driver's side.

JT turned the heat up and then looked at Ali. "Where do you live now?"

Ali giggled. "No one told you?"

JT frowned. "Why would they?"

"I live next door to your parents. Ms. Grant's old house."

JT put the car back into Park. "What? You bought that place?"

Ali nodded, a proud smile catching the light from the streetlights.

JT's hand rested on the shifter. "Toby and I walked past it earlier. I really like the paint you chose."

"Thanks," Ali said, her hand hovering over JT's. "Wait, is Toby your girlfriend? Should I not be flirting with you?" The moment of panic cut through some of her buzz from the alcohol and from the flirting.

JT's laugh startled Ali. "No. Toby is my puppy. I definitely do not have a girlfriend. I would be a complete dirtbag if I had a girlfriend and was flirting with you like this." Her eyes held Ali's gaze.

A car beeped near them, breaking whatever moment they'd been having. Ali looked out the window at several people piling into a car in the next row and giggled at her nervousness.

Ali leaned against the headrest to watch JT. Her hands gripped the wheel, but she made no move to put the car in gear. She stared into the rearview mirror. Either she was an exceptionally cautious driver or she was avoiding looking at Ali. Could she be nervous?

"Okay, so why don't you have a girlfriend?"

JT shook her head. "Too good-looking."

Ali laughed.

"Oh, so you think I'm *not* good-looking?" JT glanced at Ali long enough to offer a wink.

Ali paused, deciding how to respond. She could tease her, she could placate her, or she could call her out for whatever it was she was trying to hide. Ali really wanted to kiss her when they got to her house, so she contemplated which approach was least likely to screw that up.

"I think you know exactly how hot you are, and I think it's a dangerous thing for you to be aware of. I also think you're full of shit and there's something you're not telling me, but for tonight, I'm perfectly happy to focus on how hot you are and ignore everything else."

JT grinned. "You think I'm hot?"

Ali swatted JT's leg. "How did you put it? The sky is blue, the earth is round, and you, JT Cox, are really fucking hot."

Ali liked the way JT's mouth curved up at the corner like she was holding on to a secret. She liked it so much she wished she could crawl into JT's lap and kiss those lips. Except, she didn't really like the idea of one of her students or their parents seeing her straddling JT in the parking lot of the local bar.

Instead, she reached across the car and let her fingers find out how soft JT's hair was. Ali kept her eyes locked on JT's.

"I really want to kiss you," Ali said, her mouth hovering inches from JT's.

"So kiss me, then."

JT's kissable smile was too much for Ali to resist. She'd waited twenty-eight years to kiss a woman; she wasn't going to wait a second more. Her hands found JT's hair, and her lips brushed JT's. After a moment, Ali pulled JT closer, her lips moving hungrily against JT's. JT matched her intensity, her tongue sliding out to tease along Ali's lip. The second it touched her, Ali thought she'd been struck by electricity.

She surged forward, annoyed that the interior of the car wasn't designed for this. She wanted more, and to get it she was going to have to wait until they drove home. But she wasn't ready to stop, not yet. Her hands wandered from JT's hair to her shoulders, down to her waist and finally to the belt loops of her jeans. Ali gave them a firm tug and was rewarded with a guttural sound in the back of JT's throat.

"Ali."

Ali smiled, leaning her forehead against JT's. "Yes?" She asked innocently.

JT looked out the windshield, slightly fogged from their breathing. "I think I should take you home."

Ali nodded enthusiastically. "Yes, please."

Chapter Five

JT drove home, hoping Ali couldn't tell that she had a tornado of thoughts swirling in her head. This was Tommy's sister asking JT to take her home and not in a "hey can you give me a ride" kind of way. Her best friend's sister felt like someone she should not be kissing in a parking lot. But, on the other hand, Ali was an adult and Tommy didn't get to decide who her sister kissed. That would be weird and gross.

JT paused at the only stoplight in town, almost relieved to have a second to think. The drive to Ali's house wasn't long enough for her to sort all this out. She still didn't have it figured out when she pulled into Ali's driveway.

She left the engine running, not wanting to seem presumptuous. "So, I—"

"Do you want to come in?" Ali asked before JT could even attempt to put her thoughts into any kind of coherent sentence.

"Yes, but…" JT gripped the steering wheel. Her teenage self was screaming at her to shut up and walk into that house. "Are you sure?"

Ali leaned away, almost imperceptibly. "If you don't want to—"

JT shook her head. "No. That's definitely not it. I really, really do. But it's more important that you one hundred percent want me to." She looked at Ali, whose face was lit on one side from the porch lights. In this light, she looked like the best version of a dream JT had been too scared to have.

Ali reached across the car and took JT's face in her hands. Her lips brushed against JT's before pulling back half an inch. So tantalizingly close. "I one hundred percent want you."

JT didn't think. She crashed her lips into Ali's. Her hand found the key to turn off the car without breaking the kiss, which was rapidly escalating to not safe for the driveway.

JT pulled back and reached for the door handle.

Ali cocked her head. "I swear to god if you ask if I'm sure again, I'm going to make you pay for it."

JT's mouth dropped open. "Oh yeah?" She smiled. "Depending on what you have in mind, that could be fun."

Ali laughed, full and throaty. She led the way to the door, unlocking it and turning on the light before JT caught up to her. JT reached for Ali, spinning her around to face her. She stepped forward pinning Ali against the wall. Ali gasped into her mouth. JT's hand found her waist, while Ali ran her hands up JT's face, brushing her fingers through her hair. JT leaned forward, relishing the feel of Ali's boobs pressing against hers.

"Shit," Ali said, pulling away.

JT immediately dropped her hands to her side. "What? Did I do something wrong?"

Ali shook her head and laughed. "No. Not at all. I just forgot about that." She pointed behind JT.

JT turned expecting to see a house guest or someone Ali forgot she'd invited over. She didn't expect to see an empty room full of boxes. "You forgot you have boxes in your living room?" JT had been with women who had decided they didn't want to hook up after all but never because of some cardboard. "If you don't want to do this, that's really okay. You can say so."

"No, it's not that." Ali's face turned pink. "I'm sorry. It's embarrassing that this place is such a mess. I got caught up talking to you and kissing you and I forgot that my house is a disaster."

JT took her hand. "If it helps, I didn't notice until you pointed it out. And I don't think having moving boxes when you just moved is weird or embarrassing."

Ali squeezed JT's hand. "It's been over six months. It's embarrassing. I'm sorry." Her tone made it clear that whatever had been going so well was over, at least for that night.

Feeling a bit confused, JT leaned forward to kiss Ali's cheek. "You have nothing to apologize for. I'm around for the holidays. If you need help unpacking or anything else, let me know. I'm sure I'll be dying for an excuse to get out of the house."

"You don't have to do that. It's my mess to clean up." Ali let her head fall forward onto JT's shoulder. "I really am sorry that all this ruined our night."

JT pulled her into a hug. "You didn't ruin anything. I'm serious about helping. I've moved a lot and I'm more than happy to help you finish up." She paused, unsure of how to leave gracefully. "I should go. I'm sure my nieces and nephew will be up at the crack of dawn." She kissed Ali on the cheek one more time before opening the door and walking back to her car.

The night had not gone at all how she'd expected, and at that moment she wasn't sure whether that was a good thing or not. Kissing Ali was more incredible than every teenage fantasy she'd ever had, but it was overridden by her fear that Ali wouldn't feel the same way. She sighed as she climbed into her still-warm car. Staring at the door, she hoped Ali wasn't standing on the other side regretting kissing her.

Chapter Six

Ali closed the door behind JT and leaned her back against it. How could she have brought JT back to her house with boxes everywhere? How did she forget what it looked like inside?

She'd been having too much fun existing outside her normal life and forgotten the reality that she was a divorcée who still hadn't put all her belongings away despite moving in well before the school year started. When she divorced Kyle, she knew she was taking a hatchet to the perfect image folks in town had of her, and of them as the high school sweethearts who'd gotten married and settled in town. But even though she'd known they would see her differently, it hadn't quieted the voice in her head telling her she had to always appear perfect.

Coming home to a house filled with reminders that whatever perfection she wanted the world to see was a lie deflated her. She'd been in the house for far too long for there to be any excuse for it to look the way it did. JT didn't judge her, but she felt like such a loser.

In all her mortification she'd forgotten that after so many years of wondering what it would be like to kiss a woman, she'd found out. She'd kissed a woman and she'd liked it. Screw Katy Perry for ruining that phrase forever. Kissing JT was better than any stupid pop song more concerned about what a boy might think of two girls kissing. Ali didn't care what any boy thought. One of the many perks of being single for the first time since she was a teenager was that she didn't have to consider what Kyle might think. She could kiss as many women as she wanted.

She hadn't gone into the night thinking she was going to kiss anyone, let alone the woman who'd spent most of her time in middle and high school hanging out with Tommy. She could picture the two of them sitting side by side on the couch in their basement playing Nintendo for hours. They'd yell at the TV and laugh but JT always stopped when Ali walked in. She'd say hi and ask how Ali was doing. Ali smiled at the memory. JT had grown up, but she hadn't grown out of that soft kindness.

Ali walked to the kitchen for a glass of water to stave off the hangover she was bound to have. Did she want to kiss a whole bunch of women? She didn't know. But she liked kissing JT, and she would have happily kept their night going if not for her inability to unpack her shit. Maybe if she were a different person, someone who didn't care so much about what other people thought she would have been able to keep kissing JT even with the boxes everywhere.

But that wasn't her. She did care what other people thought of her. She often wished she didn't, but so far she hadn't found a way.

She chugged the first glass of water and refilled it before climbing the stairs to her bedroom. She paused in the doorway and considered it from the perspective of a guest. From JT's perspective. What would she have seen if Ali had the courage to drag her up the stairs? The bed was made. There were a few pieces of clothes—worn once but clean enough to wear again— draped over a chair in the corner. Her closet door was open and she could see two small boxes, opened on the floor. The walls were a pale pink. Ms. Grant had liked flowers, and Ali had been glad there wasn't any flower wallpaper in the bedrooms, but the pink wasn't her choice. She'd been meaning to paint.

She slumped onto the bed. She had a little over a week before school started again. She swore to herself that she would have her house in order before she went back. She wasn't sure she wanted to sleep with JT that night, but she knew she wasn't going to spend the rest of her life not getting laid. And when the right person appeared, she wanted her bedroom to reflect who she was.

Now all she had to do was figure out what that looked like. Easy peasy.

Chapter Seven

Lying in the dark, on the couch her family hadn't bothered to make into a bed for her, JT stared at the ceiling. Where had she gone wrong? She'd thought things were going well with Ali. She had kissed Ali Porter. It was a literal teenage dream come true. Ali's lips felt like the world's most perfect pillows and tasted like heaven. But then everything went sideways, and JT couldn't decide if Ali really cared that much about the state of her house or was simply looking for a gentle way to tell JT to get out.

Had she taken it too far when she backed Ali against the wall? She'd been careful to give her space and not to make her feel trapped, but maybe that was it. Or maybe kissing JT had been a massive disappointment. JT sighed and put one of the pillows over her mouth so she could scream without waking up the house. Why was she such a fuckup? Tommy was going to kill her for kissing his sister, and Ali was going to avoid her like the plague.

Nice going, Coxie. Home for twelve hours and she'd royally fucked up. What was it about coming home that made her more of a mess than her normal life? It was like the scrutiny of her family turned her back into a stupid teenager.

She eventually fell asleep but only after remembering that her siblings were, for sure, going to enter the annual town couples contest and she'd be left out. Because she was single with absolutely no prospects in sight.

Gold medal loser.

JT woke up to the sounds of footsteps above her head. There were quick running feet and the heavy footsteps of several adults. She stared at the ceiling, wondering how long she could stay hidden.

"Jasmine," her mother's voice called from the top of the stairs.

JT groaned. She had been perceived.

"I need you to get the paper from the store. Your father says he can get it, but I need him here."

Normal people who read the newspaper in print every day would have arranged to have it delivered. It was the twenty-first century, and they had the technology to have a paper delivered even in rural New Hampshire. But not JT's dad. JT knew that what he really liked was having a reason to get the hell out of the house for a few minutes every day and because he'd developed a taste for the mochas they made at the store. When he discovered that he could sneak in a little treat every day if he told his wife he was going to get the paper, he'd suddenly become devoted to the crossword.

And if he ran into some folks at the store, so much the better. He could kill the better part of an hour gossiping with the other men who had their own reasons they gave their families for having to zip into town.

JT didn't know why her mom wasn't letting him go this morning, but she was happy to have an excuse to take a drive.

"Wanna go for a ride, girl?" JT asked an excited Toby when she got upstairs. Toby wagged her tail and followed JT to the door. "Just the paper or do you need other stuff too?"

JT's mom handed her an envelope with a short list scribbled

on it. "We need more milk and eggs, and a loaf of bread if the bakery delivered this morning but if not, skip it."

JT took the list and swiped her keys from the rack by the door. "Be back in a bit." Toby hopped in the back seat and lay down. JT wondered if Ali was awake or if she was sleeping in. She hoped she wasn't too hungover from the drinks or from their kissing. Nothing about Ali's little house answered those questions when she passed it on the way to town.

She'd made the drive to town so many times her body anticipated the curves in the road and the dips that made her stomach drop. She passed the town green, complete with bandstand, and rolled onto Main Street. The center of town boasted a post office, town hall, the inn, the general store, the café and a few other shops, interspersed with beautifully maintained two-hundred-year-old houses. It was something out of a postcard.

As she drove down Main Street, she stayed well under the speed limit. She didn't want a ticket, and the old folks who frequented the store had a terrible habit of pulling into traffic without looking. She waited for one of them to back out of the space before pulling in and cracking the windows for Toby. It was cold but she liked to sniff the breeze.

"I'll be right back, okay?" JT said, patting Toby.

The general store was red with white trim on its front porch. The newspapers were set out in piles on the porch, so JT grabbed one before walking in. She passed the wall of fliers advertising everything from snow shoveling to pottery classes and paused in front of the flier for the town's annual holiday festival competition.

It was for couples to enter a variety of events, with prizes along the way and a grand prize for whichever couple was judged best. The general idea was to get folks to visit all the shops in town and to drum up business and maybe even attract a few tourists, who came to Hart's to enjoy the holiday postcard vibes.

JT stared at the flier, which proudly stated that this year any two people could enter together, couple or not. She thought of Tommy and wondered if he would be up for it. Emerson and Jonathan had been entering with their spouses since before any of them had gotten married, but JT had never had someone important enough to bring home for Christmas. She would relish the chance to kick her brother's and sister's asses at something. And it would be a reason to get out of the house.

"The prizes look good this year," the person next to her said.

JT turned to find Ali. She couldn't help but smile. "Dinner for two and a night at the Hart's Inn for New Year's. Seems like a great prize." She pointed at the flier. "But do you think they came up with the prizes before they decided noncouples could enter?"

Ali laughed. "I'm sure there are rooms at the inn with more than one bed."

JT nodded. "Sure, but how many of those are called the honeymoon suite?"

Ali put her hand over her mouth to cover her laugh. "Oh my god, you're right."

"Hi, Ali," a deep voice said behind them.

They turned and found Kyle standing next to Ali's doppelgänger from the night before. "Hi Kyle." Ali stuck out her hand to the woman. "I'm Ali."

The woman extended her fingers in what looked like her best impression of wilted lettuce. "Sharon."

"Nice to meet you," Ali said, her smile tight. JT could tell she was trying, but it was possible the effort was killing her.

"Sharon and I are entering the contest. The prizes look sick."

Oh my god, how had Ali endured this ding-dong for so long? "Totally," JT said, sarcastically.

Kyle put an arm around Sharon. "Having a good partner makes all the difference."

JT saw anger and hurt flicker across Ali's face. Fuck it. "That's just what I was saying. Wasn't it? That's why Ali asked me to be her teammate. Winning is kind of my thing, you know."

Kyle blinked. "Who are you?"

Ali interjected. "This is JT Cox. She won gold in the Olympics. But I'm sure you knew that. Her picture has been up all over town. I don't know how you could have missed it."

JT stared at Ali and tried to stifle the smile threatening to split her face apart.

"That was you?" Sharon asked, her voice sounding giddy. "I thought you looked familiar. I follow you on social media, you're hilarious."

JT smiled. "Thanks."

"We watched you guys win that final. That was amazing!"

Kyle looked annoyed. "Oh right. Congrats or whatever." Kyle steered Sharon toward the deli. "See you around, Ali."

JT waited for them to make it past the cereal aisle. "You all right?"

Ali shrugged. "Thanks for covering for me. It's going to suck to miss the competition this year. Especially if he's entering with Sharon."

"Why would you miss it? I think I just told him you and I are teammates." She smiled, hoping Ali couldn't sense how nervous she was.

"It was sweet of you to say that, but you don't have to enter with me. It's fine."

JT placed her hand on Ali's arm. "If you don't want to do it or you don't want to do it with me, that's fine. But if you want to enter, I would be psyched to kick his ass with you."

Ali narrowed her eyes. "Really?"

JT grinned. "I've been wanting to kick Jonathan's and Emerson's asses in this thing for years, but I've always been single. But now that they've changed the rules... If you're in, I am." Partway through her sentence she realized how that might sound to Ali. "Not that I... Shit. I am not making assumptions… Last night was fun…" Someone squeezed behind JT, bumping her forward toward Ali.

"Sorry. I'm making a mess of this." She held up the paper. "Give me a second to get all this stuff for my parents and then maybe we can talk outside."

Ali nodded. "Yeah, okay." She hurried down the aisle away from JT.

Perfect. This was why JT was perennially single. She was a complete disaster when it came to talking to women instead of just flirting.

JT grabbed everything on her list, paid, and then found a seat on the porch to wait for Ali. What was she going to say? There was no way Ali wanted to do this very public competition as a couple. Not after one night of a little bit of kissing. But would it be weird for JT to make it clear that they were doing this as friends? Would Ali be offended because they *had* kissed the night before and had maybe been on their way to more? JT didn't live here and she wasn't the kind of person women were interested in seeing long distance unless it was for a hookup here and there.

She still had no idea what she was going to say when Ali walked onto the porch and stood next to JT.

"So…"

JT opened her mouth, hoping that she'd figure out the right thing to say as she spoke.

"I'm in," Ali said before JT could speak. "I love this competition, and I was so sad about not getting to do it this year after the divorce."

"But?" JT asked.

"But I think we should enter as friends. Is that okay?"

JT smiled and patted the seat next to her. Ali sat, balancing her bag of groceries on her lap like protective armor. "Totally okay. I wasn't trying to imply we were anything else. I was too caught up with Kyle's bullshit. I would be very happy to compete as friends. And my offer to help you with your house stands. If you want help moving boxes or unpacking or anything else, give me a call."

Ali handed her phone to JT. "Well, you better give me your number, then. Because I would love some help. Honestly, just having someone to keep me company would be nice." She gave JT a shy smile. "I love living on my own, but…"

"…sometimes you want a buddy. I get it. Why do you think I got Toby?" JT pointed to the car where Toby had her nose poking out the top of the window, sniffing the air.

"Oh my god, she's adorable. Can I meet her?" Ali asked.

JT smiled and led her to the car, where she rolled down the window so Ali could greet Toby without the dog hopping onto the sidewalk. She was pleased to see Ali wasn't shy about the dog greeting her with kisses. Ali reached her hands into the car to rub Toby's ears.

"I love her."

JT laughed. "It's hard not to."

Ali continued to pat the dog but turned back to JT. "Okay, so we're good?"

"Ready to kick some serious ass. You should know that if you enter this thing with me, we're going to have to win. I am a terrible loser."

Ali laughed. "Kyle and I never won in the years we entered."

"Well, that's because you didn't have me as your partner. This is our year."

Ali adjusted her grocery bag. "I expect nothing less from our resident Olympic champion. See you later, JT."

JT watched her walk away, enjoying the way Ali said her name too much for a couple of friends. She was in dangerous territory, but if they were going to be nothing more than friends that was fine. As long as they kicked the ever-living shit out of Kyle and her siblings in this competition.

Chapter Eight

Ali took a deep breath before knocking on her mom's front door. She didn't wait for a response before opening it, but despite her mom telling her she didn't need to knock, Ali felt strongly that it was inappropriate to barge into anyone's house without knocking.

Her mom, a slight woman with dyed-blond hair cut in a neat bob, hovered over the island in the small kitchen. "Glad you're here. I need your help."

"Hi, Mom." Ali placed the grocery bag on the counter and reached for an apron.

"No, I don't need you in here. Your brother is helping me already."

Ali looked around for any sign of Tommy.

"I need you to set the table. Use the red napkins."

Ali closed her eyes. She hated those stupid napkins. They were scratchy and made of some synthetic material that did not absorb anything. But her mom insisted.

"Anne said she saw you and Kyle talking at the store. How is he doing?"

This town and the busybodies with nothing better to do were going to be the death of her. Most of what she owned was still in boxes; maybe she could load it all on a truck and just drive as far from here as possible.

"Mom, are you serious? I ran into Kyle at the store getting the things you asked me to pick up. How is that newsworthy in any way?" She folded the napkins the way her mom liked as she moved around the table setting one at each place. "Anne needs to get some hobbies," she said under her breath.

Her mom pulled a casserole dish out of the oven. "You two were so good together. I'm sure he'd give you another chance if you just talked to him."

"Mom." Ali forced herself to take a deep breath. Where the fuck was Tommy? "I have zero interest in being married to Kyle. Which is why we got divorced."

Her mom tutted.

"Mom, leave her alone. Kyle's a douche."

"Thomas! Language."

Tommy smiled at Ali. "You taught me the power of using descriptive language. It's not my fault that the best adjectives to describe Kyle are douche and canoe."

Ali snorted. She caught Tommy's eye and mouthed *Thank you*.

"I do not understand what went wrong between you two. You have so much history."

Ali walked to the china cabinet to get the plates they only used at Christmas. She gave herself a moment to take several deep breaths before returning. "Mom, you don't have to understand why Kyle and I aren't married anymore, but you do have to stop meddling."

Her mom held up her hands as if surrendering. "I'm sure he'd enter the holiday contest with him if you asked."

Ali laughed. "He's entering with his new girlfriend and, actually, JT and I are going to compete together."

"Tommy's JT?" Their mom's face looked like she was trying to do complex math in her head.

"You are?" Tommy asked. "That's great! She's always wanted

to beat her siblings. You guys are going to have fun." His grin spread. "I can't wait to see Kyle's face when you two mop the floor with him."

Ali was grateful for a baby brother who was always on her side, especially when her mom was up to her usual matchmaking shenanigans. She felt a pang knowing that Tommy had no idea that JT didn't simply drive her home the night before, but she quickly pushed it out of her head. They were competing as friends. Nothing more.

If she'd spent too much time this morning lingering over their series of heated kisses, Tommy didn't need to know that. Neither did her mom. But it also didn't mean she wouldn't spend some more time later thinking about JT's lips and her tongue in Ali's mouth and the way her hands ached to touch JT. She flexed her hands, willing them not to tingle at the mere thought of JT's hair wrapped around her fingers and the soft skin of her neck when Ali pulled their lips together. No. She'd let her daydreams flood back in later.

Ali's mom startled her out of her thoughts with a hand on Ali's shoulder. "I did hear Kyle's dating again. But I'm sure if you called him—"

"Mom. I am not getting back together with Kyle. He's moved on, and I have no interest in a repeat of the last decade."

Her mom opened her mouth, but Ali shook her head to silence her. "No, Mom. I am not ever going to be Mrs. Kyle Canterbury ever again."

Her mom walked back to the stove, but Ali heard her mutter, "Never say never."

Ali deserved a medal for not throwing one of the very special Christmas plates at the wall. Her phone buzzed in her back pocket.

It's JT. I know you're with your family but text me when you're ready for me to come help you. Any time. I'm going to need an escape from these people.

Ali turned toward the china cupboard to hide her smile. She scanned the room. Her mom had asked her to come over that morning to help set up for Christmas Eve dinner, but there was no way she was going to hang around all day. She had a house to put together, and spending that many hours listening to her mom harp on her failed marriage wasn't going to be good for anyone.

She typed out a reply and smiled when the reply came almost instantly.

Ali finished setting the table feeling much lighter knowing that she was going to see JT in a couple hours.

That was normal friend stuff, right?

Chapter Nine

The kitchen smelled amazing when JT walked in with the paper. Her siblings had made French toast for their kids and the whole room smelled of vanilla and cinnamon and sweetness. JT's stomach growled loudly.

"Any left for me?" She craned her neck to see the plate warming on the stove.

Clark, Emerson's husband, turned away from the stove. "Yes. There's enough to eat it for dinner and maybe for breakfast tomorrow. Please eat some. My wife insisted I make like ten loaves' worth."

All three kids ran through the kitchen followed by Toby. They disappeared into the living room.

JT raised her eyebrows. "Everything okay?"

"The twins showed Brooke how to get Toby to lick the syrup off their fingers yesterday. It's kind of gross, but it makes them all laugh so we gave up trying to make them wash their hands."

"Of course." JT grabbed a few slices of French toast and took the syrup over to the table. "Thanks for this. I'll take Toby for a walk in a minute, but I'm starving."

Clark followed her to the table and slid a cup of coffee toward her. "So, I hear we've got some competition this year?"

"Jesus, the rumor mill is fast. Yes, I'm entering the contest this year with Tommy's sister."

"Oh really?"

JT frowned. "What's that supposed to mean?"

Emerson joined them at the table. "It means we all remember how you mooned over her as a teenager. That's what."

"I did not moon over her or anyone else!"

Emerson raised her eyebrows. "Mmm-hmm. I seem to remember you making a lot of excuses to go to the girls' soccer games."

"And basketball games and softball games," Jonathan added.

JT sighed. "She is Tommy's sister. Of course we were going to support her teams!"

"Oh yeah, you were definitely there to cheer on the entire team," Emerson said, unable to contain her laughter.

Jonathan joined them at the table. "Oh yes, you were definitely there to hone your knowledge of basketball. Not to ogle the point guard."

"I hate you both," JT said, her head in her hands.

Their mom walked in, carrying a massive dish. "I heard you're entering the contest with Tommy's sister. I hope you know what you're doing."

JT gaped. "What on earth is that supposed to mean?"

"I can't imagine it's been easy to be divorced and still living here with her ex and her meddling mother."

JT widened her eyes at her siblings. "A meddling mother? What's that like?"

Her mom picked up a tiny potato and held it like she might launch it at JT. "Careful, Jasmine. All I'm saying is Jean Porter has been trying to finagle the two of them back together since they broke up. I don't imagine she's going to be pleased with Ali entering the contest with anyone who isn't Kyle."

JT took a bite of her breakfast while she thought about what her family had said. She hadn't realized anyone had caught on to her schoolgirl crush on Ali. At the time, JT didn't really understand it either. She'd thought Ali was the coolest girl in town but so had a lot of people. She wouldn't have been homecoming and prom queen if they hadn't. It was only once she understood she was gay that her feelings about Ali became more obviously a crush instead of simple hero worship.

Her family didn't know that they'd hooked up last night. They didn't even know that she'd driven Ali home.

"Did you know she bought Ms. Grant's house?"

JT's mom nodded as she cut the eyes out of the potatoes.

"She lives next door?" Emerson asked. "Since when?"

"Six months ago. Give or take. She bought the place when she got divorced. I like the paint she chose," JT's mom said.

Well, there was one thing JT and her mom agreed about. "Why didn't you tell me?"

Her mom didn't look up from her work. "Didn't know you'd care. It was in the middle of all the Olympic preparations. Must have slipped my mind." She wiped her hands on a towel. "If I had told you, would you have come to visit sooner?" Her mom's lips twitched into a smile.

"Mom, oh my god. It would have been nice to know that before Tommy asked me to give her a ride last night. It was a little surprising to find out that she'd been living in Ms. Grant's house and no one bothered to tell me." JT immediately wished she hadn't mentioned driving Ali home. Emerson looked ready to burst.

"What do you mean you drove her home?"

JT shoved a bite into her mouth, purposefully picking a massive piece of toast. Emerson drummed her fingers on the table and gave her husband a look that made it seem like they'd had a conversation about JT and Ali before.

"Tommy drove her to the bar. He met someone there who he wanted to spend a little extra time with, so I said I would give Ali a ride. It's not a big deal."

Jonathan stood up to investigate a crash in the other room. "I think the lady doth protest a wee bit much." He swiped a piece of bacon from the stove on his way out.

JT took three more bites, annoyed but unable to respond in any way without sounding like she was protesting. They didn't need to know what happened between her and Ali. They didn't need to know anything at all. It wasn't their business and, honestly, there wasn't much to tell beyond the ride home and the contest. It wasn't her place to tell them she and Ali made out. She had no idea if Ali was out around town, and she wasn't going to be the one to make that choice for her.

Emerson and Clark followed once it became clear the crash involved multiple kids and possibly some smashed toys. That left JT alone with her French toast and her mom.

"I'm glad you have someone to enter the contest with."

JT looked at her mom like she was an alien.

"Don't make that face, Jasmine."

God, why would she not call her by anything but her godawful first name?

"I know you've wanted to enter in the past and I'm glad you found a friend to enter with."

Good to know that her mom thought she was a pathetic loser who couldn't find a date. JT almost wanted to rattle off a list of the women she'd hooked up with in the Olympic village, but that was gross and not her style. She wasn't incapable of finding women to date, regardless of what her mom thought.

A voice in her head reminded her that hooking up in the Olympic village was not the same as having a real relationship. Instead of thinking about that, JT shoved the remainder of her breakfast into her mouth.

"I'm going to take Toby for a walk." She put her plate in the dishwasher.

Her mom put a hand on her arm. "Ali is a great girl. Just be careful. Her mom is dead set on getting Ali and Kyle back together, and I would hate for you to get caught in the center of a Jean Porter tornado. That woman is *a lot*."

JT couldn't stop the laugh from flying out of her mouth. "Wow, the pot is really talking shit about the kettle, huh?"

Her mom swatted her on the leg. "You don't have to listen to me. But don't be surprised if Jean tries to meddle."

"We're just friends, Mom."

"If you say so, honey." She walked into the laundry room and let the conversation drop.

JT grabbed a tennis ball and a leash, unsure if Toby wanted a walk or was more in the mood to chase a ball. Toby spun on the porch at the sight of the ball and took off like a shot when JT launched it as far as she could into the field. She wasn't shocked that Ali's mom wanted her back with Kyle, but her mom's words made her second-guess whether she wanted to be in the middle of that mess. Then her mind drifted back to Ali's lips against hers and she thought if a mess was the price of kissing that woman, that was a fair price for a little bit of heaven.

Chapter Ten

Ali understood that the point of having JT come over was to empty the boxes and put away all her stuff. But she hated looking around her house and feeling embarrassed by the boxes and the mess. It wouldn't get better until after they put things away, broke down boxes, and probably bought a bunch of new furniture, but that didn't stop her from wanting it to look better now. Before JT arrived.

In the spare moments she'd had since the night before, Ali's mind had drifted to kissing JT. The way it'd felt to lean across the center of the car and touch her lips to JT's that first time. The way she could barely contain herself on the drive home, even though it had only been a few minutes. The way JT's body had felt pressed against hers in the entryway.

And then her mind always found its way to the screeching halt when Ali remembered she'd invited a woman back to her house that was in no shape to receive guests.

Ugh, this was so stupid. She wasn't someone obsessed with having a clean house. She knew people who freaked out if they had anything in the sink or clutter on counters. She wasn't one of those people.

But last night she'd felt embarrassed. The more she thought

about it the more she realized it was because she was embarrassed that she'd let her house look like this for so long. She hadn't moved in a week ago. It had been months without her completely unpacking. That was the thing she hated anyone to see.

But not just anyone. She had to admit that having JT see her messy house, and her messier life, bothered her more than she'd thought it would. Before last night, she wouldn't have been able to articulate it, but it occurred to her that she liked the way JT looked up to her when they were kids. JT had been a kid who was genuine and kind even when the people at school or in town weren't. She'd always put Ali on a bit of a pedestal, and Ali tried not to ruin that. Last night, she was afraid if JT saw that she wasn't the picture-perfect girl that people expected, Ali might lose that respect.

To have JT bring her home, where Ali had every intention of keeping their night going as long as possible, only for Ali to look around and imagine what JT would think of her had been awful.

Not that JT had given her any indication that she'd judged her at all.

JT was lovely. And her lips…

No. Ali couldn't keep getting distracted by JT's mouth and strong hands. Fuck. She needed to get her house in order, literally, if she was ever going to get laid again. And after making out with JT, she was sure she wanted to get laid. Soon, if possible.

She shifted a few boxes to the side to make a walkway through her living room. She might as well have been rearranging deck chairs on the Titanic. JT knocked on the door. Ali found her standing on the step looking hopeful and pink-cheeked.

"I'm taking Toby for a little walk. You want to come? I just have to take her back home and then I can help you get all your stuff put away."

Ali crouched to rub Toby behind the ears and was greeted with kisses all over her face.

"Toby, no! I'm sorry."

Ali laughed. "I quite literally was asking for her to do it. God she's sweet." The puppy wiggled and turned on the spot, unable to control her enthusiasm.

"We're working on her manners," JT said, crouching to try to corral Toby. Instead, Toby ran through Ali's legs and into the house, pulling the leash enough to knock JT off balance. She fell forward, unable to catch herself, and landed on Ali.

Stunned, she looked down at Ali. "Oh my god, I'm so sorry. Here, let me…" She reached down, her hand grazing Ali's boob before reaching the floor. "I'm sorry. Jesus. Toby, no!"

Ali cackled. JT was so flustered her cheeks had gone from pink to crimson. Ali lay on the floor laughing while JT scrambled to get up. She helped Ali up and then raced to find the dog. Ali was still trying to catch her breath when JT returned with the puppy in her arms.

The dog wasn't small. JT must have very strong arms to be able to carry this puppy. Ali allowed herself a moment to imagine what JT's arms might look like under her coat.

"Are you okay? I'm so sorry. Did I crush you?"

Ali smiled. "I'm fine. You didn't crush me. That wasn't the first time I was flat on my back under someone, you know." Ali had a momentary thought that she'd gone too far, but the way JT's face, ears, and neck reddened and her eyes bugged out told her she'd gone just far enough.

JT stood, holding Toby, her mouth opening and closing. Finally, she said, "I don't remember you being this…"

"Forward?"

JT nodded. "Yeah, when we were in high school you were definitely not making sexual innuendos when I was around."

Ali tilted her head to one side and let her hand find Toby's soft ears. "Maybe if I had been I wouldn't have wasted a decade on Kyle."

JT gently put Toby on the floor. "Do you want a little walk, or do you want me to take her home and come back?"

Ali grabbed her coat and boots. "I would love a few minutes outside. How could I say no to that face?"

Toby wagged.

They walked her back to JT's parents' house in relative silence, watching Toby wander through the clumps of snow and leaves.

"So, this contest," JT said on the way back to Ali's house after dropping off Toby. "How badly do you want to win?"

"Chickening out already?"

JT shook her head and looked offended. "Hell no! I want to kick everyone's ass, but if you're not into that I can dial it back to a normal-person level of competitiveness. At least I think I can do that. I've been told I take stuff like this a bit too seriously."

"Good. Because after Kyle was such a smug goober earlier, I want to win this thing without him."

"A goober? Seriously?"

Ali opened the door and let JT in. "I'm a teacher. Sometimes you have to come up with more creative and descriptive ways to talk about people so the kids don't hear you dropping f-bombs."

"May I never get on your bad side. I'm not sure I could recover from being called a goober. The horror." JT stepped out of her boots and hung her coat on the hooks by the door. She carefully stepped between the boxes and into the living room.

Ali lifted her arms and turned. "So this is room one of my disaster house. Welcome."

JT laughed. "It's not a disaster. You own a house! No matter how many boxes you have to unpack, you are way further along on the being a grown-up scale than I am."

Ali smiled. She'd forgotten how kind JT was. It surprised her that JT never got mean even when the people in town weren't always kind about her. Ali wondered how she did it. "Thank you, but this place is embarrassing. It's been months, I should be way more put together."

JT shrugged. "That's what I'm here for. That, and strategizing about how we're going to smoke my siblings."

"And Kyle," Ali added.

"And Kyle, obviously." JT looked at the stacks of boxes. "Where do you want me to start?"

Ali shrugged. "Anywhere, really. I guess just open a box and then we can figure out where to put everything."

JT nodded and used her keys to slice open the tape on the top box.

"I do have knives for that."

"Do you? Or are they buried in the bottom of one of the boxes?" JT asked with a grin.

Ali swatted her arm. "Oh my god. Did you come to help me or roast me?"

"Both," JT said, taking three throw pillows out of the box and placing them on the couch. Sadly, none of the rest of the boxes were so easy to empty.

They got into a rhythm where JT opened the boxes and removed items and Ali directed her where to put them. When they ran into something tough, or something that required a table or other furniture to be its home, Ali made a list of what they needed and set the knickknacks aside.

After two hours, the room was cleared of boxes, leaving small piles around the room.

"You need a trip to Ikea," JT said, scanning the space.

Ali nodded. "Yeah, I kind of knew that. But I don't want to have to go eight times so for now we should make a list of how many bookcases and stuff we need." She sighed. "Not that I can fit much in my car. Kyle has his truck but I don't imagine he'd want to lend it to me."

"No problem. My parents have that van they use to move art and shit. We can borrow that. I'll even drive you." JT met Ali's gaze and mistook Ali's surprise at her offer for displeasure. "Unless you don't want that. I'm sure they'd let you take it if you don't want me to come or you were looking forward to going alone."

Ali thought JT's uncertain rambling was cute. She shouldn't, but she did. If they were going to do this thing as friends, she couldn't find all the things JT did so goddamned cute.

"I would love it if you came with me. And borrowing the van would make it a lot easier. I don't want to have to make multiple trips if I can help it. How long are you staying?"

JT sliced the tape on the boxes so she could flatten them into the growing stack. "I was going to stay a couple days but the contest is all week, right? So at least until New Year's, I guess."

She bent to pick up the stack of cardboard and carry it to the garage. Ali snuck a peek at JT's ass. This competing-as-friends thing would be hard if she kept thinking about their kiss and wondering what JT's muscles looked like under her clothes.

JT walked through to the garage door, being so careful about not hitting the walls Ali could have kissed her. Again. She waited for Ali to open the door for her so she could add five more boxes to the heap.

"Why are you smiling?" JT asked when she walked back inside.

Ali shrugged but couldn't help but smile. "You're cute."

JT stopped a few feet away from Ali. "Thanks." She paused. "I might regret this, but should we talk about last night? I feel like we kinda glossed right over it when we decided to do the contest."

Ali took a deep breath. "You're right." She stalled by walking into the living room, now blissfully empty of boxes, and taking a seat on one end of the beige couch.

JT hovered near the other end. From the way she kept looking at the couch and Ali, it appeared that she was having trouble deciding if she should sit, too.

Ali patted the cushions. "I'm not going to bite."

JT sat and rested her elbows on her knees. Ali must have really made her nervous. Gone was the relaxed woman who had met her at the bar last night. Last night, JT lounged. She took up space in the booth at the bar. This version of JT was different. She looked more like the shy teenager Ali remembered when she rubbed her palms together, adjusted the legs of her pants.

"Why are you so nervous all of a sudden? I'm the one who kissed a woman for the first time!"

JT leaned back to look at Ali. "Sorry. Now that I've brought it up, I'm not sure what to say. Are you okay after last night? Do you regret it? Was it okay?"

Ali scooted closer and put a hand on JT's leg. She ticked off each point on her fingers. "I'm more than okay. I don't regret it. You're a really good kisser."

JT exhaled. "I'm not annoyingly needy, I promise. But you're Ali freaking Porter. There's a little bit of pressure not to suck when it comes to you." JT sat up. "I mean, first of all, Tommy would kill me."

Ali laughed. "My baby brother doesn't need to protect me from anything, let alone you. But I understand what you're saying. Think about how I feel. I kissed Tommy's best friend." She waited for JT to look at her. "And I really fucking liked it."

Chapter Eleven

Hearing Ali Porter say she really liked kissing her was the best Christmas present JT could have received. Her inner teenager celebrated while she tried to remain looking calm and normal. It was really hard not to grin like a fool but JT did her best.

"Okay, so the kissing was good. Does that mean you want to do it again or it was a onetime thing?" JT wasn't sure what she wanted Ali to say. If she said they could keep hooking up or even dating JT would like that on the one hand, but even the idea of it scared the crap out of her. She was sure the bro code had a lot to say about dating your best friend's older sister, and she was going to be leaving at the end of the week. She didn't even know yet where she would be going.

The new women's hockey league hadn't given her any indication of where she would be playing, and she had made a point of saying she didn't want to be in Boston. It was too close to her family. The only thing worse than not being supported by your family was knowing they were close enough to come support you and decided not to. She decided for her own sanity she would ask to be placed on a team as far away from New Hampshire as possible. That way she could at least pretend that the reason they never came to see her was distance and not disinterest.

"Is it okay if I say I don't know?" Ali asked, looking nervous for the first time. "I'm not sure if I want to get into it with everyone in town. Can we still do the contest as friends?"

JT nodded. "Of course! The contest is kind of its own thing, right? I meant apart from the contest. But maybe that's too complicated and it would be better for us to avoid mixing kissing fun with the fun of crushing everyone in the various absurd tasks they have made up for us."

Ali stood up and walked to the kitchen.

Shit, did JT say something wrong?

She came back with two cups of water and noticed the concern on JT's face. "I was thirsty and thought you might be, too. You're leaving after New Year's, right?" JT nodded. "I don't know whether that makes us hooking up a better or worse idea."

JT laughed. "Me neither. What if we keep it light, casual? I'm happy to help you with your house. I'm great at putting together Ikea furniture and painting and anything else you might want help with. And if you decide you find me irresistible, that's fine. But if you're more comfortable simply using me for my handywoman skills, that's okay, too."

Ali smiled, her lips damp from the water. Entirely lickable. But not when JT had just finished saying that all of this was up to Ali. Maybe that had been stupid because she really wanted to kiss Ali. But it was the right thing to do. The ball had to be in Ali's court.

"Light and casual sounds nice. It would be new for me. Marrying the guy you met in high school is the complete opposite of light and casual. And I would appreciate your help with this place. I know I can ask my brother, but I feel bad and it's embarrassing that this place isn't more put together and I don't want to have to explain to him that his older sister is a big old mess."

JT took her hand. "You're not a mess. You're figuring out

your design aesthetic. It takes time to figure out what you like, and I bet you had to compromise when you were married. Time to unlearn that shit! You can make this place anything you want! And I'm happy to help you with anything you need while I'm home."

Ali leaned in to kiss JT on the cheek. It wasn't anything other than a friend kiss but JT loved the way Ali's lips felt on her skin. Even a chaste kiss made her feel all warm inside. Sure, she could do light, casual, friendly. But what she really wanted was light, casual, and naked in Ali's bed.

JT swallowed her lustful feelings and hopped up. "We have another hour before I have to be home for Christmas Eve dinner. What should we do before I leave?"

Chapter Twelve

JT Cox must be magic because Ali hadn't thought of how much she was dreading her own Christmas Eve dinner until she arrived at her mom's house. It would have been a whole lot less painful if Ali's mom didn't spend most of it asking her about Kyle and lamenting the fact that she had no grandchildren to dote on.

"Tommy, what are you doing to make sure Mom has grandkids to play with?" Ali asked, only to be met with a glare from her brother.

"Your brother has plenty of time to be a dad. But you really should have thought about your age when you decided to throw away your marriage."

Ali forced herself to take a deep breath. "Mom, you are acting like I am ancient. I'm not even thirty and you're acting like my life is over because I'm not a mom yet."

"Seriously. Mom, Ali and Kyle weren't meant to be. It's not a tragedy. Ali is an amazing success! She bought a house, she's the head of the English department at school. You should be grateful she still lives in Hart's Landing."

"You're leaving!" her mom said, shocked.

Ali sighed. "No, Mom. I'm not leaving. I bought a house and have no plans to leave."

Tommy was undeterred. "But if you don't stop giving her a hard time, she might stop coming over."

Ali gave him a look. Why was he stirring the pot? She'd been listening to this crap from her mom for months. She didn't need him to intervene.

"All I'm saying is you're lucky to have her close by. You should be grateful and not give her all this grief, okay?"

Their mom sipped her wine and let the topic drop. Ali didn't want to keep having this argument. The reason she wasn't married to Kyle was because she didn't want to be. It wasn't the universe conspiring against them or whatever her mom imagined. Ali no longer wanted to do things his way or contort herself into ever-smaller versions of herself. Her mom didn't want to hear that or didn't want to understand that. Ali wasn't sure which. But no matter what her mom thought she didn't want to be his wife. She wanted to be herself. And the longer they were married, the less like herself she became.

"Did you and JT put your name in for the contest, officially?" Tommy asked.

Ali relaxed at the change of topic. "Not yet. We have to go in person on the twenty-sixth. The online form closed but if we go early they'll let us sign up together."

Tommy smiled. "She's been texting me about how excited she is to compete. You sure you're ready for the full JT Cox competition experience? She can be a bit much."

Ali nodded. "I'm counting on it." She looked at her mom who wasn't looking at her. "Kyle was so smug and obnoxious. I can't wait to kick his stupid butt."

Jean scowled and finished her wine. She held out her glass toward Ali's grandmother. "Mom, can you top me up?"

She lifted the wine bottle and passed it down the table to Ali to pour. Ali's grandma caught her eye. "Who's his teammate?"

Ali poured her mom the wine. "Woman named Sharon. Seems nice enough."

Tommy snorted. "She's a clone of Ali."

Ali smacked his arm.

"What? She looks just like you."

Jean's eyes snapped to Ali's face. "See, that man's not over you. If he's dating someone who looks like you, that's a sign."

"A sign he has a type, Mom. Clearly blonde and short is his thing." She paused. "I don't know how many ways I can explain that I don't *want* to be with him."

"You don't know what you want." Jean shook her head. "No, this is excellent. Think of all the time you'll spend together in the contest. You can talk, and he'll remember what he's missing. If there's a chance of reconciling, you want to take it." She stared at her plate; hanging in the air was the feeling that she wished she'd had a chance to get back together with Ali's dad.

Ali got the feeling her presence wasn't necessary for her mom's musings. Maybe her mom would like to be married to Kyle. She looked at her grandmother, wishing she'd say something. But she was concentrating on cutting her food and not looking at anyone else. She reminded Ali of the students in her class who thought she wouldn't call on them if they never looked up. It was a terrible strategy, especially when she found that many of the kids who didn't want to talk had the most interesting things to say. But at this table, she was a daughter not the teacher. She had no power to call on her grandmother, to force her into this conversation.

Instead she sighed, stared at her dinner and waited for the night to end. It hadn't always been like this. Christmas Eve used to be fun when they were kids. There were even times when it was fun with Kyle. They'd sometimes have dinner with his family or hers. Sometimes they'd drive between the two to spend a little of the day with each family. It was one convenient thing about being from the same town.

But since things got to the point of separation and then divorce, coming home felt like being bathed in disappointment. She had to fortify herself before she walked in the door. Even with Tommy there, it felt like a heavy blanket descending over her whenever her mom talked about her plans for Ali and Kyle to reconcile.

She looked at Tommy wishing they could go back to being little kids in footed pajamas waiting for Santa to come.

Chapter Thirteen

After a Christmas day spent unwrapping presents with her nieces and nephews, sledding, and napping during the afternoon, JT couldn't wait to see Ali again. She was ready to get out of the house, and they agreed to meet up in the center of town at nine to make sure they were able to sign up for the competition.

She drove toward the center of town, around the town green, and parked in front of town hall. Ali looked cute, but freezing, leaning against the side of her car. JT hopped out and Ali gave her a hug.

"What was that for?"

Ali shrugged. "Let's just say Christmas with my family was exhausting. I'm glad to see you."

JT laughed. "I think I can relate. Is anyone here?"

Ali looked at the building. "Yeah, I saw some folks walk in a few minutes ago."

"Then why on earth are you freezing your ass off out here?"

Ali tucked her arm through JT's and tugged her toward the door. "I didn't want to go in alone. I didn't want any of them thinking I was pathetic."

JT stuffed her hands in her pockets. "No one thinks you're pathetic. And did you really think I would stand you up? Come on."

"No." Her voice was low, like she knew she was supposed to say no but didn't entirely believe it.

JT held the door open for Ali. "I won't stand you up. I know I can be a bit of a ding-dong, but I won't leave you hanging. I promise."

"Thanks," Ali said, but JT didn't know if it was for holding the door or for what she'd said.

Inside, it was noticeably warmer. It smelled faintly of warm dust. Ali led the way toward the counter where a woman sat, her head almost invisible.

Ali propped her elbows on the counter and peered down. "Hi, we're here to sign up for the holiday contest."

The woman put her glasses on and looked up. "Ali, dear! I wasn't sure we'd be seeing you this year." She made a face. "Kyle came in a few days ago. But I'm glad to see you. Who are you entering with?"

"Hi, Ms. Button, I'm entering with JT Cox."

"The gold medalist?" Ms. Button stood up. "Oh, there you are. We're so proud of you, dearie. My wife and I were screaming at the TV so loud, I thought the neighbors might come check on us."

JT couldn't mask her surprise. "Wow, that's so kind of you. Thank you."

Ms. Button sat down. "Now, let me get you to sign the forms. Waivers and such. In case you get injured in any of the events, you promise not to sue us or the businesses putting on each task."

Ali looked at JT. "Will you get in trouble with your team for doing this?"

JT laughed. "There are no clauses in any contracts preventing me from doing such dangerous activities as decorating gingerbread houses. It'll be fine."

They signed the forms and took the packet of information on all the tasks and the rules and the prizes.

Ms. Button stood up. "It's none of my business, of course, but are you two...?"

Ali smiled at JT. "We're entering as friends, Ms. Button."

JT nodded and hoped the twinge she felt didn't show on her face. "Ali's brother and I have been best friends forever, so when Ali asked me to do the contest with her, it was easy to say yes."

Ms. Button looked confused. "You didn't want to enter with Tommy?"

JT laughed. "No. I wanted a chance to win."

Ali snorted a laugh and slapped her hand over her mouth and nose. It was too late. All three of them cracked up.

"I love Tommy like a brother, but from what I understand, Ali is a ringer and I want a chance to beat my siblings this year."

Ms. Button smiled and waved them away. "Good luck, ladies. I'll be keeping an eye out for your scores." She shook her head. "My wife is never going to believe I got to meet you. She'll be so jealous."

JT blushed. "You tell her I say hi, okay? It means a lot to know you were rooting for me."

"Do you want a picture?" Ali asked.

JT would never have said anything. She didn't want to seem arrogant or full of herself.

Ms. Button's whole face lit up. "I would love that!" She came around the desk to stand next to JT. She handed her phone to Ali, who happily snapped half a dozen pictures.

Ali walked out to the cars with her but stopped when they reached the parking lot. "See, I told you people around here love you."

JT's first instinct was to push away Ali's statement. One lady didn't mean everyone. One lady didn't erase years of feeling like a misfit. She resisted the urge to minimize it. "That was nice."

"You have fans here."

"I should hope you and Tommy were rooting for me."

Ali bumped her with her shoulder. "Stop being modest. It's

not every day that someone from here, or even this state, wins a gold medal. Try to soak in the love."

JT unlocked her car. "I'll try. Hopefully, they'll still love me when you and I destroy the competition."

"Everyone loves a winner, baby!" She laughed. "See you later?"

"Text me when you're ready for another pair of hands." The look on Ali's face told JT she'd broken her with her unintentional innuendo. "I mean. Text me when you need help moving stuff, or whatever."

Ali looked at the paper Ms. Button had handed them. "We have our first event this afternoon. Why don't we meet up at my house an hour before that? We can strategize, and if I need another set of hands, that will give us a few minutes to take care of whatever I need."

If JT had been eating anything, she would have choked. Forget her accidental innuendo, Ali was not messing around. Ali held the door open for JT. "See you later," she said, her lips looking too delicious when she smiled.

JT climbed into the car, thinking she was in way over her head.

Chapter Fourteen

Ali knew she shouldn't flirt so hard with JT, but it was too easy to make her blush. And even after only a few days, Ali really liked the way JT's face looked when she blushed. It was cute and sweet and unexpected. Ali assumed JT had many women fawning all over her. She probably could have just about any woman she wanted. But here she was, in her hometown, single and entering a ridiculous contest with Ali, simply because Ali had asked her to.

It made her feel strong, and a little powerful. Not that she'd use that power for anything nefarious, but it had been a long time since she felt like she had the power to draw someone in, and she hadn't realized how much she missed that feeling.

She spent a couple hours at home, tidying the remains of boxes. Most of the boxes she opened made sense. Items from the bathroom were in several boxes together. But then she'd open a kitchen box and find her hairbrush, or a pair of slippers. She had a vague memory of things getting a bit wonky toward the end of her packing, but this was like a drunk chipmunk had been in charge of getting it packed away.

She hated past her. She was a mess and present Ali was paying the price. It had taken a long time to decide that things with

Kyle weren't going to get better. Once she realized she wasn't prepared to sacrifice her happiness to keep up their perfect image, she rushed to sever any remaining connection. Which meant the boxes strewn around her house were occasionally filled with items she'd grabbed at random as she ran through her old house.

She swore she would get through half a dozen boxes before JT showed up. JT knocked as she was finishing her fifth. She looked into the next one and saw there were only a few things left, so she dumped them into another box so she could say she'd finished six. This was clearly how she ended up with those disaster boxes full of random items. She was going to suffer later but now she hurried to the door.

"Hi, come in." Ali struggled with whether she should hug JT or not, but JT covered whatever awkward moment they were about to have by taking off her coat.

"It looks great in here. You must have been working nonstop!"

Ali appreciated JT lying to her. Things hardly looked different, but the encouragement felt great anyway.

Ali led her into the kitchen. "Do you want some tea before we go?"

JT shook her head. "No. I'd hate to have to pee in the middle of the task."

Ali clicked the kettle on for herself. She'd found the tea earlier and decided she was going to have it as a reward. "I like to live dangerously. And I think we are allowed to go to the bathroom. This isn't *Survivor*."

JT shrugged. "Still. I wouldn't want to let the team down by having to run out during...wait, what are we doing today?"

"Cocoa." Ali grabbed the paper off the refrigerator—the one place she knew she couldn't lose it. "Our task for today is going to be at the bakery on Main Street. We are supposed to concoct the most delicious and enticing cups of cocoa possible. It says we will be given access to a variety of items from the bakery, including marshmallow, caramel, fudge sauce, et cetera. And we have to combine it to make the best-looking and best-tasting mugs of cocoa."

JT grinned. "I fucking love cocoa. This should be fun."

"How are your presentation skills?"

JT shrugged. "If you're comparing them to my siblings', not too good. If you're comparing them to, like, a kindergartner's... still not too good."

Ali laughed. "Well, that doesn't give me much hope. Good thing I've been decorating classrooms for years. We should make an okay team, I think."

JT made a face. "My stupid siblings are professional artists. We're screwed. But ours will taste good at least. How's Kyle at this stuff?"

Ali made a face. "*Artistic* isn't a word I would use to describe him. But I don't know about my doppelgänger. She could be a culinary whiz."

JT frowned. "Well, does it say if anyone gets eliminated in the first round? That would be super embarrassing."

Ali scanned the sheet with the events and rules on it. "Good news. No one gets knocked out on the first day." Ali poured the water into her mug. "You sure?"

JT shook her head. "What's our game plan, then? You decorate and I taste?" She drummed her fingers nervously on the counter.

"No way. I want to drink cocoa, too. I'm not letting you have all the delicious fun."

JT held up her hands. "I didn't mean it like that. I should have said you're in charge of making it look pretty and I'll try not to screw it up."

Ali considered JT. For someone with incredible swagger in the bar, on the ice, talking about hockey, she was surprisingly unsure of herself in this silly competition. Was she worried about losing? Letting Ali down? Failing publicly? What was making her nervous?

Ali reached for JT's hand. "Don't take this the wrong way, but you played in the Olympics, so why are you nervous about this silly little contest? You know this isn't on TV, right?"

JT laughed. "Sorry. I like to know what to expect." She swallowed and gave Ali's hand a little squeeze. "I don't want to let you down." Ali watched her closely until JT met her eyes. "And, honestly, you know how much I want to crush the competition."

Ali laughed. "Me too. But it's not worth worrying about. Today is the first event. No one gets eliminated, so let's go have fun and drink way too much cocoa." She looked up at JT and thought how easy it would be to rise up on her toes and kiss her. It would be so easy, and she wanted it so badly, but it wouldn't make things any less complicated.

"Come on, golden girl, let's go kick some ass." She grabbed JT's hand and dragged her toward the door.

Chapter Fifteen

The bell over the door tinkled cheerily when JT and Ali stepped into the café. Inside the air smelled of warm chocolate, coffee, and flour. JT steered Ali along the exposed brick wall to an open space to listen to the owners.

"Welcome, contestants. We're so glad to have you at Hart's Bread & Pastries. And thank you to the town council for picking us to be the first stop for the competition this year." Tim, a tall, thin Black man with close-crapped hair, and one half of the couple who owned the bakery, spoke to the crowd. His wife, Patty, a short white woman with a beaky nose and a dyed-blond bob, stood next to him, clutching a piece of paper and appearing ready to interrupt him at any second.

"For this first event, we want you all to make two perfect mugs of cocoa." Patty put on her reading glasses as she went over the rules. One mug could be any flavor and one had to be a take on a classic cocoa. This one had to avoid any "auxiliary" flavors and had to showcase the chocolate the store was so well-known for. "I spend hours perfecting that chocolate, so don't screw it up," Patty said with a smile that came across more menacing than kind.

"Jesus, don't mess with Patty's chocolate," JT said, leaning down to whisper in Ali's ear.

Ali giggled but stopped quickly when people looked their way.

"You will have fifteen minutes to familiarize yourself with the ingredients we've provided and another hour to make your cocoa. You have all been given a standard recipe so we don't end up with anything inedible," Tim said with a laugh.

Ali covered her mouth.

"What?" JT asked, feeling curious to be let in on the joke but also a little nervous.

Ali shook her head. "I'll tell you in a minute."

They were dismissed to workstations set up at the tables in the bakery and café. Each had a hot plate and a jumble of ingredients laid out for each pair.

"Why are you laughing?"

Ali inspected the ingredients on their table. "Kyle added salt instead of sugar two years ago. Patty was so mad at us I thought we were going to get disqualified. We laughed so hard all the way home." She looked across the room at Kyle, and JT fought the twinge of jealousy blooming in her chest.

They had history. They'd entered this contest together. Of course Ali would have some memories and even nostalgia, but that didn't mean JT liked it.

"So you're saying the bar for me is so low it's in the basement?"

Ali smiled. "Yeah, don't poison the judges with a quarter cup of salt and you'll be a massive improvement. Also don't be a gigantic tool and you'll be an upgrade."

JT took a spoon to taste the various add-ons. "Don't be a tool. Well, that sounds like something I can handle." She liked the caramel and the fudge but wasn't sold on the peppermint-infused cream. She made a face Ali caught.

Ali tried a bite. "Oooh, that's good."

JT shook her head. "Crap, now I know you have terrible taste. How is that supposed to make me feel?" She made a disgusted face. "That shit tastes like toothpaste. You cannot put that in the cocoa."

"Peppermint cocoa is like the number-one drink at Starbucks starting in November. What are you even talking about?"

"Maybe, but it doesn't make it less gross!" JT moved the bowl of cream to the side. "I cannot, in good conscience, serve that."

Ali rolled her eyes. "You're kind of a big baby, you know?"

JT looked at her siblings, who were tasting everything like they were freaking cocoa sommeliers. Beth and Jonathan had their heads bent close together like they were sharing secrets about the ingredients. Emerson and Clark held up containers to the light like the color of the ingredients mattered. "I *am* the youngest, but I am not a baby. I like what I like. How is that a bad thing?"

Ali sighed but gave up the argument. JT felt momentarily triumphant.

"What flavors do you like?"

JT pointed to little pots around the table. "Caramel, fudge, not those fruit flavors though. Orange and chocolate is an abomination."

"You're wrong, but fine. I can go with no fruit flavors. I hate cherry flavor. So, salted caramel, maybe? How do you feel about peanut butter, or Nutella?"

JT moaned. "Fucking love them. Both of them, all of them. What about a caramel peanut butter cocoa? Or is that too much?"

Ali shrugged. "Maybe, but why not give it a try?"

Patty's voice cut through the room. "All right, everyone. You have one hour. Your time starts now."

JT picked up the recipe and measured ingredients to hand to Ali. "Here, why don't we make a double batch of the cocoa and then we can add the flavors to each batch? That way we can get the base right before we try to make it fancy."

Ali nodded and warmed the milk as JT handed her sugar and cocoa. She whisked like a boss while JT organized the table into the two possible flavors.

"Wait, can we put booze in these?"

Ali shook her head. "No. The bakery doesn't have a liquor license and Tim's too much of a stickler for rules."

JT sighed. "Fine, but I maintain that the best way to make amazing cocoa is a little whisky. Or maybe some bourbon."

Ali looked over the pot to catch JT's eye. "Maybe you can make me some of that later?"

"Oh, you want to hang out with me later?" JT asked, her smile creeping up at one corner of her mouth. "I don't make boozy cocoa for just anyone." She shook her head. "Very presumptuous."

Ali added the dry ingredients and whisked them together until the pot steamed and the smell wafted toward JT. "Silly me. I bet you have a date later."

"Nah, the girl I have my eye on only wants to be friends. But maybe if I tell her how cute she is, she'll change her mind one of these days," JT said, her lips curving up on one side. Ali's eyes found JT's.

"Oh, you might be too smooth for your own good."

The time passed so quickly. They tasted the concoctions so many times that by the end, JT wasn't sure if they were any good because all she tasted was sweet. As the time ticked away, Ali hurried to decorate the mugs to make them look as good as possible. There wasn't much to work with, though. She ladled the cocoa into each mug, then put some extra fudge in one and a drizzle of caramel and peanut butter sauce on the other.

"Marshmallows?" JT asked, tossing a handful into her mouth.

Ali held out her hand for the bag. "Yes, we need those, so

stop eating them." JT looked chastened but held out a marshmallow to Ali.

Ali looked at her hand and then JT's face. Holding eye contact, she opened her mouth and allowed JT to place the mini marshmallow on her tongue. JT didn't break eye contact as she watched Ali lick the sugar off her lips.

Okay, this just-friends thing was a bit harder than she'd expected. Her current status was jealous of a freaking marshmallow.

"Feeding each other? How *friendly* of you."

JT spun around. Kyle. She rolled her eyes right in his stupid face.

Ali swallowed the marshmallow. "What are you doing over here, Kyle? Your station is on the other side of the room." She nodded in the direction of his partner. "Leaving your partner to do all the work is a classic move from you, though."

He scowled. "I came to say hi but got a bit of a show from you two. Surprised you're making such a public display, Ali. There are some parents of your students here, aren't there?"

Ali blushed and looked around the room.

"Dude. The only difference between me giving Ali a marshmallow and how I would have given one to her brother is I would have whipped half a dozen at Tommy. She and I aren't at the 'bombard me' level yet. But maybe friendship is a concept beyond your understanding."

Kyle crossed his arms over his chest. JT had had her fair share of run-ins with dudes who thought they were tough and intimidating because they were big. Usually, these happened on the rink where she could skate circles around them. It was less comfortable in a café.

"Kyle, your date is looking for you." Ali pointed to the woman scanning the crowd with a bit of marshmallow fluff on her cheek.

"I'm just looking out for you, Al. You know how people are."

Ali rolled her eyes this time as he left to stomp across the room to his own counter.

JT used a rag to wipe up a bit of spilled sauce. "He's a bit of an ass."

Ali nodded, adding a dash of chocolate shavings to the whipped cream. "He's gotten worse over the years. His insecurity has made him unbearable. But my mom still thinks we belong together."

Sure enough, within a minute of Kyle walking away, Mrs. Porter arrived at their station.

"What did Kyle want?"

Ali's body tensed.

"Hi, Mrs. Porter. Do you want to try our concoction? We have a little extra if you want a sample." JT poured a small mug of the cocoa and held it out to Ali's mom.

"No, thanks. Ali, why did you send Kyle away? Honestly, I don't understand why you aren't doing this competition with him. You know, what starts out as friendship can often lead to more."

JT, who had taken a sip of the cocoa Mrs. Porter had rejected, nearly snorted it with surprise at what Ali's mom said. Clearly, the concept that she and Ali might be more than friends, or might develop into more, had never crossed her mind. Heterogoggles were very powerful.

"Mom, if you like Kyle so much, please feel free to visit his station. I'm not sure he's single but, again, you have my blessing if you want to date him. Grandma might have opinions, though."

Mrs. Porter made a sour face. "Joke all you want, but I'm right about this. You two belong together." She walked away as the café owners stepped up to the microphone to tell all the contestants they had three minutes to finish.

"God, why does she have to come in and throw me off my game? Get it together, Ali."

JT grabbed for the mug, gently taking it from Ali and setting it on the display tray. "Ali, this looks amazing. You did a great job." She wiped the tray with a cloth where some of the cocoa had dripped. "Don't worry about your mom, she's full of shit."

Ali laughed, but her eyes had a red tinge to them. JT held the cloth out. "You have a little bit of sugar that must be irritating your eyes. Do you want me to get it for you?"

Ali closed her eyes, her shoulders relaxing down.

JT gently wiped her skin, making any hint of a tear disappear before anyone could see it. JT would have given anything to remove Ali's pain, but for now she had to settle for this. Wanting more was dangerous.

Chapter Sixteen

Ali was mortified to have spent even a single stupid tear on her mom's ridiculousness. She wasn't getting back together with Kyle. It didn't matter if he blustered around and acted like a jealous ass or if her mom tried to push them together. He could become the world's greatest guy and she wouldn't want him back.

She didn't want to go back to anything. She had a new house and a new life. Sure, it was a work in progress, but it was hers. And every time her mom or Kyle or anyone else tried to throw doubt on that, she got so angry and upset. God, she hated crying. Especially in public.

JT was so sweet to give her an out. Of course she could tell the tears were threatening to fall, but she gave Ali an excuse for why her eyes might be watering that had nothing to do with her mom or her ex-husband. It had been a while since Ali had felt so cared for by a person. Was this what friends did for each other? Or was there something else?

Their kiss and flirting were a little confusing because she really enjoyed them, and it had been her who'd said they should compete as friends. She'd shut all that down. Or she thought she had. But clearly her emotions hadn't caught up. Her thoughts were interrupted by a sudden announcement.

"Stop what you're doing! The judges will now sample your cocoas. Please be patient, there're only two of us and we're old as hell!"

Everyone in the room laughed. The café owners and a few other judges trailed behind them going from station to station.

JT craned her neck to try to see her siblings' offerings.

"Remember, no one gets eliminated on this one," Ali said.

JT gave a tight smile. "Will you be satisfied with being in last place?"

Ali laughed but covered her mouth when a couple people turned their way. "Of course not. But no one wins or loses the competition tonight. The prize is a gift card to this store. Which is great, but..."

"We're here to win it all," JT whispered. "Let's fucking go, Porter."

A warmth spread through Ali's chest. It was weird of JT to call her by her last name. Weirder, maybe, because Ali had only recently gone back to it from her married name. But hearing JT say it made her feel like she'd been enveloped in a bear hug. It was friendly in a way that made her feel like they'd been best friends for ages instead of little more than acquaintances. JT made her feel like they were teammates. Ali internally rolled her eyes at herself. Yes, they were literally teammates at that moment, but having JT speak about her like they were on the same sports team, like they were completely in this thing together, made her emotional.

She'd missed having a teammate, both on actual teams, like her soccer team in high school, but also that person who was always there for her. She'd lost that when she and Kyle drifted apart. Having that feeling back, even for a few hours, was incredible.

"Mrs. Canterbury, Miss Cox," one of the judges said, stopping at their station.

"Hello, please call me JT. And this is the talent on this team, Ali Porter."

The judge blinked as if he was surprised to be corrected. He looked at his sheet. "Oh, yes. I see. Ali Porter." The other judges moved closer to the table to get a better look at the mugs.

"What have you made for us?"

Ali smiled, relieved to move on. "We made a classic cocoa with fudge, whipped cream and chocolate shavings. And this one is salted caramel and peanut butter."

"Both have marshmallows, too," JT added with a grin. "Can't have cocoa without marshmallows, if you ask me."

"Interesting." Tim gave her a skeptical look. "You don't think marshmallows are only for children?"

JT feigned shock. "Of course not! Is joy only for children? Happiness? Of course not. I know my partner in cocoa agrees with me, right, Ali?" JT waited for the judges to look at Ali before giving her a wink.

Ali schooled her features to keep from laughing. "Marshmallows are essential. Now, some folks like the tiny ones that melt into the drink, and other folks prefer the big ones that float on top. I like them both."

JT grabbed a few out of the jar. "And these, I don't know who made them, but they are heaven. Best marshmallows I've ever had, and I've tried them all."

One of the judges, a middle-aged woman with long dark hair, smiled up at JT. "Really? Those are from my shop."

JT turned her full attention to the judge. "Well, not to risk getting in trouble with the Swiss, but I drank a lot of cocoa when I was in St. Moritz, and your marshmallows would win the gold medal for sure."

"I'm Hannah," the judge said, her voice bubbling with a giggle.

"Pleasure to meet you, Hannah. I hope you all enjoy the cocoa we've made. Ali gets credit for all the artistic ability. I'm just here for the food." JT gave them all a smile, landing last on Hannah.

They sampled the mugs and then left for the next table. When they were out of earshot, Ali smacked JT on the arm. "You are incorrigible! I can't believe you were flirting with the judges!"

JT shrugged, looking quite pleased with herself. It wasn't flirting to tell the truth about the marshmallows, which were very good. She'd eaten at least a quarter of the jar. If she played up her excitement a little to get the judges' attention, that wasn't a crime.

"Jealous?" JT asked, not even trying to keep from flirting with Ali.

Ali scowled, or tried to. "No. Hannah Elmsworth is married and one of my co-workers."

"So?"

"So, I'm not jealous of her, I just can't believe you are such a brazen flirt! I guess I shouldn't be since you flirted with Darcy LaCroix on national TV when her girlfriend was right there!" Ali could say she wasn't jealous, but under her laughter she could feel the tug of it. Friends or not, she liked it best when JT flirted with her.

"There's nothing wrong with flirting. I don't flirt with people who don't want me to. Hannah didn't seem to mind. And I told you, I'm in it to win it." She looked around the room. "I don't think this is going to be our best event, but maybe if I compliment the ingredients, the judges decide they like us a bit more than Kyle or my brother and sister." She shrugged. "It's not a big deal. Unless you're jealous. Come on, you can tell me."

JT's grin suggested she knew she was pushing it, but Ali liked it. Sure, it went against her request that they be nothing more than friends, but dammit, she liked the flirting. She liked it a lot.

Chapter Seventeen

Ali was jealous. She didn't like the feeling. She didn't like watching JT flirt harmlessly with Hannah, but she liked the way it affected her even less. What kind of childish nonsense was it to be irritated by someone she wasn't even dating being flirty with someone else? It was frankly embarrassing, and her annoyance was much more directed at herself than at JT. JT was, as far as Ali could tell, simply being herself. JT was a flirt, and it didn't really mean anything.

Except Ali was still annoyed about it.

She *was* jealous and embarrassed about it. So, there was no way she was going to admit it. "No, I'm not jealous. You can flirt with anyone you want."

JT cocked her head to the side. "That's not true." She lowered her voice and bent closer to Ali's ear. "I can't flirt with you."

Ali turned, her face way too close to JT's. She could smell the sugar and chocolate on JT's breath. She was desperate to know if JT tasted like fudge or caramel or, more likely, one of the hundred marshmallows she'd eaten.

Instead, she wet her lips. "Who says you can't?"

JT gave a wicked grin. "I believe you were the one intent on keeping us 'friendly' in public. Or am I mistaken?"

God she was annoyingly cocky, but it worked for her. Ali suspected JT knew exactly how charming she was. She wanted to lean forward, run her tongue along JT's lips and taste every last bit of sweetness she knew she'd find.

Instead, she straightened up, pulling her face a reasonable distance from JT's. There were too many people here who knew her. Too many people who would ask questions she didn't want to answer. Not because she was ashamed of being into JT, but because answering people's questions, absorbing their shock or whatever other emotions they would express was exhausting. Ali dealt with other people's emotions all the time at work. She was a teacher of teenagers, after all. And on her vacation, she didn't want to have to deal with Hannah or her mom or her stupid ex-husband talking at her, expressing their feelings about her to her face.

She simply wanted to kiss a cute girl and run her fingers through her fuzzy undercut.

So, she took a step back to a safe distance where she could trust herself to banter without climbing JT like a fucking tree.

"Contestants!" The mic screeched, bringing everyone's attention to the front counter of the café. "Our judges have come to a decision. First, we want to thank all of you for your hard work and inventive flavor combinations. We enjoyed sampling everything you all made."

There was a round of applause from the assembled crowd.

"We have prizes for best traditional, best nontraditional, best decoration, and best all-around team. Each winning team will receive a small prize. As a reminder, all teams will compete tomorrow, so the stakes for this round are just bragging rights."

Ali didn't think they were going to win anything. Their cocoa was fine but there was nothing about it that stood out. The only thing that stood out at their booth was JT. She was warm and made everyone feel welcomed. Ali was busy watching her when the judges called their names.

"Ali, come on!" JT said, her voice filled with excitement. She reached for Ali's hand, and Ali, bewildered, gave it to her. JT pulled her to the front of the crowd.

"We have a special shout out to JT Cox and Ali Porter for their spectacular use of marshmallows in their nontraditional offering. Not all the judges agreed with your liberal use of them," the woman said, looking at the grumpy older judge who clearly hated joy. "But we were impressed with your ability to balance the flavors in your caramel, peanut butter cocoa. Congratulations!"

Ali blinked in surprise but allowed Hannah to hand her an envelope.

"We won?" Ali asked on their way back to their counter.

"Yes! Did you think they called us up there to say we sucked? They liked our over-the-top mug! We did it!" JT hugged her and picked her up off the floor. Normally, Ali would have hated this. She generally hated feeling small or insubstantial. But from JT, it was just an extra-amazing hug with their bodies pressed together from their chests practically down to their toes. Ali was more than a little disappointed when JT set her down.

JT leaned down. "Open it!"

Ali slipped the envelope to show JT the gift card they knew was inside. "Do you want this? I can come here anytime."

JT put her hand on Ali's, ostensibly to push the gift card back to her. "You live here, so you'll actually have a chance to use it."

"Maybe we can come for coffee later this week? That way we both get to use it."

JT nodded. "If you can stand to be seen in public with me."

Ali swatted her with the envelope. "You are kind of high-maintenance, you know? But look, if what you really want is to buy—" she checked the amount "—twenty-five dollars' worth of marshmallows to eat all by yourself, I won't stop you."

"That's a great idea. Yeah, gimme that." JT laughed. "It will be much better to share with you. Depending on the rest of the schedule, maybe we can come one morning? I can pick you up."

"Can Toby pick me up?"

JT rolled her eyes. "Do you only like me for my puppy? Here I thought you would like me for my gold medal, but instead you're just using me for my sweet Toby girl."

Ali nodded. "I mean, she's very handsome."

JT leaned closer. "Are you telling me you prefer her kisses to mine?"

Ali's eyes widened in surprise. "JT!"

"I'll have to up my game, Porter." She glanced around the room. "Looks like my siblings left already. Probably pissed we won a prize. May I give you a ride home?"

Ali raised an eyebrow. "Sounds a bit dangerous. But, considering you drove me here and it appears everyone else in my family left, I have few options."

"You flatter me. But I'm happy to drive you even if you only want me to because otherwise you'd have to sleep in the café."

Ali looked up at her with her eyes blazing. "I think you know exactly why I want you to take me home." She rested a hand on JT's forearm where she'd pushed her sleeves up for the contest, trying to make sure there was no mistaking her meaning.

Chapter Eighteen

JT was determined to be a perfectly well-behaved driver until the moment they parked and Ali leaned across the center of the front seats.

"Ali, what happened to friends?"

"Some friends make out."

JT laughed. "No. Name one couple you know who has successfully stayed just friends while hooking up." She kept her tone playful, but she had real concerns that blurring the lines wouldn't end well for them. She'd had relationships that were purely based on hooking up, but not with someone who was as important as her best friend's sister. She never wanted to screw things up with any of the women she dated, but the stakes with Ali were higher.

"You and me. That's one."

JT shook her head, too charmed by Ali's adorable face to mount any kind of argument. "Do I need to remind you that you were the one who said just friends?"

Ali waved her hand dismissively. "I meant we shouldn't hook up in public."

JT narrowed her eyes. "I don't know why I'm arguing with you about this, except I think it's really important that you're sure about being in this contest together where everyone thinks we're friends and nothing more all while making out every time we're out of sight. Do I have this right?"

Ali sighed. "God, you're annoying. I don't know what I want. I know I want to kiss you. I know I want to spend time with you. And I know I definitely don't want to be married to Kyle. That's about it. Whether you and I are destined to be anything more than winners of the contest who make out is beyond me. But don't you want to have some fun? With me?" She batted her eyelashes at JT in such an absurdly over-the-top way, JT had to laugh.

JT leaned forward and kissed Ali. It was little more than a peck. "You're impossible, Ali Porter. Unfortunately, I like impossible."

JT's phone dinged.

She looked at the messages. "Dammit. My siblings are asking what the hell happened to me after the event. So unless we want to tell them about this, I better get home."

Ali kissed her and got out of the car. "Don't get in trouble on my account. Your mom is way too scary for that."

JT waited until Ali walked into her house before driving the short distance home. She liked the proximity but it didn't give her much time to deal with her thoughts and emotions. She walked in the door to her parents and siblings sitting in the kitchen.

"Please don't tell me you're drinking cocoa," JT said.

"Oh, I'm sorry, I thought you were little miss 'you can never have too many marshmallows.' Or was that just to give you a chance to bat your eyes at the judge?" Emerson raised her glass, thankfully filled with wine. "Cheers to you and Ali on your victory."

Everyone else joined her in raising their glasses. JT kicked off her boots and joined them at the table.

"Thanks! I was super surprised. I figured caramel and peanut butter might be a bit much for the judges."

"The only thing that was a bit much was your flirting. Is that your plan for winning this thing?"

Their mom whipped her head around. "Who were you flirting with? Jasmine, I have to live in this town." But even her mom couldn't make it through the sentence without laughing.

"Mom, why do you have to call me Jasmine? I'm not a Disney princess."

Her dad handed her a glass and offered her wine. She shook her head and walked to the fridge for a beer.

"That's true. I don't remember any movies where the princesses drank beer. Gaston drank beer."

"Oh my god. I am not Gaston!" JT sounded annoyed but she wasn't. If they were going to tease her for something, drinking beer was the least of it.

"That's true, you're more of a Robin Hood. A way with the ladies, finding a way to swoop in and win the day." Clark looked pleased with his assessment.

Emerson shoved his shoulder playfully. "Nah, more of a Flynn from *Tangled*."

"Oh my god. How did this turn into roast JT? Watch out or I'll give your kids all the candy they can eat and then leave them with you. You'll regret giving me shit when you're scraping them off the ceiling."

Jonathan held up his hands. "Whoa, whoa, whoa. No need to escalate. We all know you have the most game of anyone in this family."

"True," Beth and Clark said simultaneously, drawing indignant protests from their spouses and laughter from everyone else.

JT smiled, trying to take the compliment without also feeling like it was a bit of a backhanded one. Maybe she was a good flirt, but it wasn't like any of the women she casually dated had been interested in more from her. Her siblings had successful marriages with kids and houses and everything else. They had real careers, and JT was in the middle of a low-paying "career" with no guarantees that she'd even stay in one city long enough to need a full-year lease let alone have a house. And as much as she loved being a professional athlete, and she really did, she knew it was temporary. Her siblings could make art for a long, long time. They could teach practically forever if they wanted to. But being an athlete had a short shelf life. She might be at the start of it, but there was every chance it would be gone in an instant.

She took a healthy sip from her beer.

As if reading her mind, her mother said, "There's nothing wrong with stability. And even if you have no game, you both did very well in the spouse department. So maybe being able to flirt isn't everything."

"That's my cue. Good night. I'll take my sorry, single ass downstairs."

Beth and Jonathan protested. "You just got home! Come on, stay and hang out with us."

JT shook her head. "Thanks, but I don't need to stick around for the rest of this roast. See you all in the morning."

Emerson and Clark stood up when she left and Jonathan and Beth moved for the door, too. JT felt bad to break up the party, but there was no way she wanted to listen to them list every one of her insecurities for laughs. Besides, she was exhausted.

She might be a massive flirt but talking to people when she had to be JT Cox, Olympian, was exhausting. And then there was everything with Ali. *Confusing* felt like an understatement. She clearly liked JT and wanted to add some benefits to their friendship, but JT didn't want to read the wrong thing into all her mixed signals.

She descended to the basement and flopped onto the couch. Ali wasn't a random woman JT had met at a bar and might have a nice little fling with. She was Tommy's sister who recently ended her marriage to the guy she'd been dating since they were teenagers.

But Ali was an adult, more than capable of making decisions for herself. So why did it feel so confusing? Were the signals truly mixed or was JT simply being a chicken?

JT woke to find her nieces and nephew out of their minds in the kitchen. Brooke and Mabel were running around the island at full speed, looking like a crash waiting to happen. Harrison ran to her.

"Snow! JT, it snowed!"

She looked out the window to find the snow coming down in big flakes and the ground completely covered. Pure magic. She and Harrison pressed their faces to the window and scanned the field.

"When are we going sledding?"

"Grandma says we have to have breakfast first." He didn't whine, but the disappointment was evident in his voice.

JT caught her mom's eye. "Your Grandma is right. We need fuel if we're going to sled all day. Come on, have some food with me."

JT hoisted him onto a stool at the counter and scanned the room. "Bagel?"

Harrison nodded and was joined by his sister and Brooke. "With cream cheese!"

"Please." Mabel reached for Brooke's hand. "You have to say please when you ask."

JT couldn't handle how cute they were in their pj's and with their hair all messy from sleep. "Three cream cheese bagels coming right up. Now, how do you three take your coffee? Black, I assume."

Harrison and Mabel cackled. "JT, coffee is for grown-ups!" Somehow Harrison made "grown-ups" sound like an affliction.

"Oh, you're right. Can't be stunting your growth with all that caffeine. How about some milk?"

Brooke held out her sippy cup.

She slid two cups across the counter and filled them for the older kids. "So, how big of a hill are we taking on today?"

"The biggest," Mabel said in a whisper. God she was a cute, fierce little creature. JT loved her spunk.

"You know who has never been sledding? Toby. Should we bring her?"

The kids cheered loud enough that JT's mom turned to see what was happening.

"Okay, then I need to take her out and get her ready. But then let's find a giant hill and maybe, if we're lucky, there will be treats afterward."

JT took Toby on her usual walk but nothing about it felt like every other walk they'd gone on that week. The snow made everything so quiet and peaceful. Even when Toby got zoomies and ran around the yard and chased snowballs JT threw for her, everything felt like someone had turned down the volume.

They got to Ali's and found her shoveling her walkway. JT watched her push the snow aside, and how she seemed happy to be doing such a boring task. She cleared the walk and pushed the snow to the side before stamping her feet to get it off her boots.

"Good morning!" JT called, not wanting to startle her.

Ali beamed. "I love snow!"

JT bent down to scoop a handful into a snowball. She gently lobbed it in Ali's direction. Toby tugged at the leash trying to go catch it.

"Toby, you handsome girl. Come here."

JT dropped the leash and followed Toby as she bounded to Ali's steps. Ali bent down and let Toby plaster her face with kisses.

"I guess you meant what you said about preferring her kisses."

Ali looked up at JT, her eyelashes catching snowflakes. She looked so incredibly beautiful in the morning light filtered through the snow. JT sucked in a breath.

"Jesus," she said as she exhaled.

Ali looked puzzled.

"Nothing. The snow suits you, that's all." JT recovered. "We're all going sledding in a minute. Do you want to come?"

Ali rubbed Toby behind her ears. "I would love to, but I have some work to do on this house before the next competition."

JT shoved her hands into her pockets. She should have offered to come help instead of sledding. "I can come over after if you want some help."

Ali smiled up at her. "I'd love that if you don't mind. But I don't want to take you away from your family."

"After a couple hours of sledding, those kids will all pass out in front of a movie. I would love to come help you instead of listening to my parents ramble on and on about art and museums. I'll text you before I come, okay?"

JT had the urge to tell Ali about the teasing she received the night before. She wanted to tell her everything about her siblings teasing her and how she thought about Ali's laugh and smile and the way her hair fell out of her messy bun while she mixed cocoa. She wanted to say so many things she shouldn't.

Toby tugged her glove off and pulled on the leash. "Toby! I need that." Toby wagged so hard her entire body wiggled from side to side like a worm.

Ali giggled and JT lost her breath looking at the way her face lit up when she smiled. Snowflakes dotted Ali's hair and the top of her beanie.

"What?" Ali asked, catching JT staring.

JT shook her head. "You're just really fucking gorgeous. But I'm sure you know that."

Ali blinked and then smiled. "I don't know how you do it, but you always make me feel so good."

JT dipped her head, a little embarrassed but proud. Toby tugged the leash. "I should get her back home, I'm sure the kids are screaming to get sledding. See you later?"

Ali nodded. "Can't wait."

Chapter Nineteen

Ali spent the morning staring out the window at the snow and wishing she'd taken JT up on the offer to go sledding. Surely it would have been more fun than unpacking more boxes and creating an ever-larger tower of cardboard in her garage. She could be flying down the hill with JT snuggled into the sled with her, her arms around Ali's middle as they whizzed past the little kids. Or they would be in their own sleds racing or going over jumps.

She picked up the utility knife to slice open yet another box. The box was mislabeled and should have been in her back bedroom that she was setting up as a home office. She carted it to the room, where she was confronted with a pastel lavender on the walls. She hated it. It made her think of babies and old ladies. It was dated, and there were spots of deeper color where there had been pictures hanging. She set the box down and wiped a hand across her eyes in frustration.

She wanted to put everything away. She wanted the boxes gone, but she should paint first. But that meant picking a paint color. On her phone, she found the paint store's app and flicked through what felt like a thousand colors. It was overwhelming to have so many choices.

When she was with Kyle, he always had strong feelings about decisions they had to make, and she always just agreed with him. It was easier that way. But now she had choices to make all by herself and she was not going to end up with whatever the paint equivalent of a beige couch was. She was going to pick something she loved. And no one could stop her.

The box was left on the floor, ignored, while she grabbed a cup of coffee and sat on the horrid beige couch scrolling through colors. There were so many to choose from, but she wanted to see every single one of her options.

She texted her brother and three of her teacher friends. What's your favorite color?

The answers trickled in. She didn't care what colors they liked best; it simply helped her decide which part of the palette to jump to next.

By the time she got a text from JT saying she would be over after lunch, she'd narrowed the choices down to a few grayish blues. She stared at the screen of her phone, wondering if the color was too dark. She tried picturing it on the walls, but it was hard to see with all that gross pastel staring back at her. Would it feel depressing and drab or cozy? She'd ask JT for her opinion when she arrived.

JT arrived covered in a dusting of snow from her walk and with cheery pink cheeks. "Sledding was awesome!" She shook off the snow on the steps before hanging up her coat and taking off her boots. "The kids had so much fun."

"And you didn't?"

JT smiled. "It was the best. But I'm ready to work! What are we tackling next?"

Ali beckoned for her to follow to the office. "What do you think about this color in here?"

JT made a face. "Lavender isn't really my color, but if you like it…"

"I don't. I'm thinking of this one." Ali handed JT her phone.

JT held it in front of her so she could picture it on the walls. "I like it."

Her voice didn't sound like she liked it. "Are you sure? It sounds like you don't think it will look good."

JT shook her head. "No, no, no. It's your house and you should choose what you like."

"But..."

"I would choose something brighter. But it's not my space! You should pick what you want. Do you want to go to the store to look at those little things..." She searched for the right word. "What are they called?"

"Swatches. Sure." Ali felt a bit thrown off. "What color would you pick?"

"Ali, it's your space. Who cares what I think?"

Ali raised her hand.

"Fine. I like yellow."

Ali took this in. She wasn't a person who gravitated toward yellow, but she tried to picture it on the walls. It would be cheery and bright even in the dead of winter when things often felt dreary. She pulled up a few colors on her phone and contemplated how they'd look.

JT had a point. It wouldn't have been her first instinct, but maybe something bright would be good for her. "Want to go to the paint store?"

"Now?" JT asked, looking a bit confused.

"Yeah, why not? You up for a little painting before our next challenge?"

JT nodded. "I'm just here to help."

They made their way to the next town over to buy the paint. They pulled out a lot of swatches to consider before JT showed Ali one with a yellow that seemed bright and cheery without being either pastel or too much like an egg yolk.

After paying what seemed like a bonkers amount for the paint and the supplies, they returned to Ali's house.

"Okay, so I haven't ever painted a room before," JT admitted. "I've only lived in rentals, so I've never been allowed."

Ali grinned. It was sweet to see confident JT acting unsure. She liked being the one with the expertise. "Well, it's not that hard, really. First, we're going to tape around the trim so we don't get yellow on the baseboards and ceiling. And then we're going to use the rollers on the walls and the brushes to get the corners and around the tape so we don't make a mess. I promise, if Kyle and I could do it, you can."

JT grabbed the tape. "Show me what to do."

Chapter Twenty

JT's arms ached from painting. It turned out that even all the lifting she did for hockey hadn't prepared her for the extremely specific way she had to hold a paint brush and roller.

The yellow was a huge improvement over the purple, but she couldn't tell if Ali was happy with her choice. She said she liked it, but JT wasn't entirely convinced. Before she could spend too much energy on whether Ali truly liked the yellow, it was time for her surprise.

"Since we don't have an event tomorrow, I thought we could do a little road trip. You up for that?"

Ali looked confused. "Road trip? What about painting and unpacking?" Her voice climbed higher with each question.

JT stepped closer and placed her hands on Ali's shoulders. "I'm not suggesting we blow off working on all this. But I asked to borrow my dad's van, and I thought you might be ready for a trip to Ikea for a few things, like bookcases, and you might want to try out a few couches to see what you like. But if tomorrow's not good…"

Ali's smile spread across her face like a sunrise, slowly turning into the brightest, most beautiful thing JT had ever seen. "That sounds amazing! Thank you! When you said road trip

I thought you meant taking a break from all this, and there's not much time before the winter break is over."

JT nodded. "I know, but I'm here and can help you get at least some of the stuff. I know you wanted bookcases for the office and—" The wind was crushed out of her by a semi-flying Ali, who hugged JT so tightly and so suddenly she couldn't speak.

Ali let her go and stepped back. "Okay, so after breakfast tomorrow morning?"

JT nodded. "I'll drive over in the van and we can spend the day in the Swedish wonderland."

Ali grinned. "I can't wait."

The next morning, Ali opened the door to the house and motion JT inside. "I started a list," Ali said, hurrying to the kitchen. "Let me grab it and some snacks and then we can go!"

"You don't need snacks! Ikea is a dreamland of Swedish food! The whole point is eating a bunch of stuff that only sort of makes a meal while you're there."

Ali returned from the kitchen with her crossbody bag, a list, and a bag of clementines. "I'm still hungry now, so I need snacks. But don't worry, I've been dreaming about cinnamon rolls for ages."

Ali fiddled with the radio while JT drove. "It would be better if I could plug my phone in."

"Sorry, my dad likes the radio. He thinks there's serendipity at play when a great song comes on while he's driving. He says using a playlist removes all the magic."

Ali stared at JT. "That's a weird thing to believe but I kind of like it."

JT smiled. "My dad and I don't agree on too much, but I like his idea about the universe serving up songs when you need them." She held up one hand. "I still think there's magic in a perfect playlist, but I've come around to his idea of finding a station and letting it choose the perfect song."

Ali fiddled with the dial. "Too bad most of the serendipity here is static."

It took another fifteen minutes before they were out of the woods enough to find a steady station that played anything other than the worst of country music. JT sneaked a look at Ali, who was relaxing in her seat, mouthing the words to a song.

"You can sing along, if you want."

Ali shook her head. "No way. I screw up the lyrics so much Tommy makes fun of me constantly and my voice is awful."

JT turned the volume up. "I don't mind if you get the words wrong, and I like your voice. So don't be shy about singing on my account." She belted out the chorus, which left Ali in a fit of giggles. "Being a shitty singer never stopped me!"

The drive was long but pleasant. At some point, after some very badly sung songs, Ali drifted off and JT let her sleep. She must have been worn out.

JT gently woke her up when they parked in the garage. "We're here."

Ali startled awake and then quickly wiped her face. "I'm so sorry. I didn't mean to sleep. What a terrible passenger."

JT smiled at her sleepy face, with a crease on one cheek from the seat belt. "It's fine. You're cute when you sleep, and you said all kinds of stuff about how hot you think I am."

Ali looked stricken.

"Oh my god, I'm kidding. You didn't talk in your sleep at all."

Ali punched her on the shoulder. "Jerk." She laughed along with JT, who playfully rubbed her shoulder.

"Okay, slugger. No more joking with you." She nodded toward the entrance. "You ready for this?"

Ali took a deep breath. "Honestly, I'm excited and a little

nervous. I've never had a space that was only mine. It's freeing but a little daunting."

JT nodded. "That makes sense. Think of me as your personal assistant. I'm here to give you opinions or not and to carry the heavy shit or push the cart or run and grab you a cinnamon bun. Whatever you need."

"Thanks. Let's go get lost in the Swedish labyrinth."

They started by wandering through all the room setups. In this store, they started in the kids' section. JT loved everything about the rooms.

"Man, look at those bunks and that chair. I would have loved it if my room looked like this. It's so cozy."

"Don't tell my mom, but I love all this stuff." Ali picked up a toy alligator from a bin. "I mean, look at this cute little guy."

"Why shouldn't I tell your mom?" JT teased, grabbing one of each stuffed animal and lining them up.

Ali shrugged. "She's obsessed with grandkids and thinks that me breaking up with Kyle means she'll never have any."

JT fiddled with the stuffies nervously. "Okay, this might be too personal, and you definitely don't have to answer, but do you want kids? Or does your mom want you to want kids?"

Ali sucked in a breath. "Maybe. Kyle really wanted kids and wanted to have them soon. I wasn't ready." She looked at JT. "It's not why we broke up, but it didn't help. I really love kids. It's one reason I'm a teacher. But honestly, being a teacher might be enough kids for me."

JT nodded.

"They're not mine, of course, but I spend so much time with them over the year, sometimes several years, that I think of them as my kids. I worry that by the time I come home from work I might not have what it takes to be a parent. I spend so much energy and empathy on my students that I don't know what I'll have left for my own kids. Does that make sense?"

"Yeah. I couldn't do your job. I mean, I love my nieces and

nephew. They're funny and fun, but they're definitely not my responsibility. At this point, Toby is about all the responsibility I care to have." She held up two more stuffed animals. "But these are really freaking cute."

Ali stepped closer. "You have plenty of time to decide."

"You say that like you're so much older. Whether you want kids or not, I think you'd be a kick-ass mom."

Ali considered the toys on display in front of them, grabbing for a cape designed for a toddler. "What makes you say that? You don't really know me."

JT put a cape on the bear she was holding and whooshed it through the air like a superhero. "I know you're kind and also nice. I know you care about other people. I know you were nice to me in high school when a lot of other people weren't. I know that if you have enough empathy for every kid in your class, you probably have more than enough for a kid of your own. And also, look at how cute your face is. Any kid would be lucky to get those genes."

Ali pressed her lips together. "I don't know about that but thank you." She replaced the toys she'd been holding and strolled to the next room. It was set up with a loft bed with a desk underneath and green stripes painted on the faux walls. "There are so many ways to screw up as a parent. It's scary to know how much you can fuck up a kid without being evil."

JT followed her, trying to get a look at her face so she could better understand what Ali was feeling.

"My mom isn't a bad person or evil, but she talks all the time about how I should take Kyle back and how we belong together. I don't think she understands how much it sucks to hear that from her over and over."

"Do you want to get back together with him?" JT asked, her heart suddenly pounding.

"Hell no. He and I should never have gotten married. If we hadn't gone to college together too, I don't think we would have. He would have met someone else, and I would have, too. I would have gotten to date and find out who and what I like. Instead, we stayed together because it was easy and what people expected us to do. When graduation came around, everyone figured we'd get married which made it hard to imagine doing anything else."

JT stepped closer so she could put a hand on Ali's shoulder. "I'm sorry. That really sucks, and also you don't have to talk about this. I mean, what kind of weirdo asks personal questions at Ikea?"

Ali smiled, her green eyes sparkling. "It's fine. It's not a secret but no one ever asks. It's kind of a relief to talk about, honestly. There's nothing wrong with Kyle, but we were a high school couple who never should have been more than that. If we'd won prom king and queen and then gone our separate ways, I think it would be easy to think of all of that fondly, you know?"

Ali pointed where to go next and JT pushed the cart slowly, not wanting to miss a single thing Ali was telling her.

"But now, it's so weird with my mom rooting for us to get back together, living in the same town and seeing him out with whatever that woman's name is, and now competing against him in the contest we used to do together. It's all weird. But I wouldn't change my choices. I like my life, mostly, and not being married to Kyle is a big part of that." Ali spun around to leave the room. "Being a twenty-eight-year-old divorcée is fucking weird though."

It was a lot to think about, but JT really liked this version of Ali. Away from their hometown, she seemed freer, more apt to be honest and share her feelings. And JT really liked this Ali. She maybe liked her too much.

Chapter Twenty-One

Ali watched JT's face, worrying that she'd said way too much. Something about being away from home in a giant store made her feel like she didn't have to hold back. She wasn't going to run into any of her students here, or their parents or, even worse, her own parents. No one knew her and that was freeing.

But JT wore an unreadable expression, and it made Ali worry she'd shared too much for people who were friends and kind of more than friends. She looked around for a way to change the subject. She found it in the next faux room.

"Okay, who is the person who lives here?"

"No one lives here, Ali, it's a store."

Ali shoved her playfully. "I know that, but looking at the way it's decorated, who would you imagine living here?"

JT flopped down on the couch and put her feet on the ottoman. The room was painted a deep blue-gray. It had the vibe of a cozy mahogany-walled office or library. "A professor or a lawyer. Someone serious who watches PBS mysteries and documentaries and talks about nonfiction at dinner parties."

Ali blinked. "That's very specific."

JT laughed. "You don't get that vibe? It's Ikea but it also feels like somebody who reads two hundred books every year and is like 'oh I don't own a TV' would live here."

Ali chuckled. "Okay, so if I tell you I like it you're going to think I'm an insufferably pretentious person?"

"Oh my god, was this a trap? You showed me a room you love and then waited for me to say something offensive? Rude. If this is what you love, I think it's great. And you are kind of a professional nerd. Your job is knowledge, so…"

Ali plopped onto the couch next to her. "My job is molding young minds, or something. But I do like this room. It's so cozy. If it had a couple of comfy chairs instead of a couch, I could curl up with a book and a heavy blanket and read until I fell asleep. I think I could take some epic naps in a room like this."

JT scanned the room. "Okay, I can see that. But your room preference makes it clear you are way smarter than I am. But I share your love for a good nap."

Ali rested her head on JT's shoulder for a second before tugging JT to the next room. "Okay, what about this one?"

JT looked at the room with a wall of bookshelves and a desk. There was a lamp that curved overhead like a flower stem bending toward the sun. The walls were a pale gray. "It's fine. I don't know. What do you think? You're the one with a house to furnish, not me."

Ali thought about it for a minute. "I need a desk for my office but I don't know that I like that one. It's a little bland." She reached for the chair. "I like the way this looks, though. It's kind of mid-century modern." She sat in it. "Oh, no." She popped up. "It looks great, but I couldn't sit in that for more than ten minutes. The person who lives in this room cares more about how things look than how they function, and that is not for me."

JT tried the chair. "Hmm, I see what you mean. It doesn't have a great butt feel."

"A what?" Ali asked through a laugh.

"Butt feel. You know, they talk about wines having like a nice mouth feel. This does not have a good butt feel." JT looked so serious Ali laughed harder. How did she not know how funny she was? But then JT cracked a smile. Oh, she knew exactly what she was doing.

"I think you just like saying 'butt feel.'"

JT shrugged. "Maybe. But I'm not wrong. That chair is just off. Do you want to go try some more and see if we can find one to suit your butt?"

"Yeah, but I need a snack. I'm starting to get crabby."

JT pumped her fist. "Yes! I was already hungry, but I didn't want to stop whatever momentum we had. Cinnamon rolls, here we come!" She walked ahead of Ali and then turned back so she could face her. "Are you a meatball person? Do you get the salmon? Or are you strictly a breakfast person?"

Ali shook her head. "Watch out!" She grabbed JT's arm before she crashed into an older woman who was perusing the linens.

"Excuse me, sorry," JT said, looking embarrassed.

Ali tucked her arm into JT's and dragged her to the center of the aisle. "You almost killed that lady. I'll have to keep a tight hold on you, I guess, so you don't run over any small children."

"That's fine with me. You can drag me anywhere you want." Her eyes met Ali's and Ali felt a jolt of electricity from JT's cocky smile. "I'm all yours," JT said in a lower voice.

Ali took a breath. "Okay, you big flirt. To answer your question from before you almost bulldozed that woman, I'm all about breakfast food. I could eat it at any point in the day. It's the best meal. Although I also really love soup and that's not a breakfast food."

They sat at a table that JT insisted on wiping down before they ate. Ali found it sweet that JT found some napkins and wiped the crumbs and smeared icing off the table before pulling Ali's chair out for her.

"Thank you."

JT handed Ali a plate with a cinnamon bun on it and a cup of coffee. "I can't vouch for the coffee, but I know the rolls are amazing."

Ali tapped her cup to JT's. "Cheers." The cinnamon roll was enormous, and she got icing on her cheeks when she took a bite. But it was so good, sweet and full of sugar and cinnamon, and oh lord, Ali could eat about a thousand of them.

"This is my favorite thing about Christmas," JT said, staring lovingly at the cinnamon roll in her hands.

"Ikea?"

"No. I love that everything is cinnamon. Cinnamon rolls and coffee cake, cinnamon swirl bread and apple crisp. Half of every meal has something made with it. And I love it. More than anything, it's the thing I associate with the holidays."

Ali stared at her plate. "Probably the only thing I miss about Christmas with Kyle is his mom's cinnamon rolls. I don't know what Deb put in those things, but they were incredible." Ali smiled at JT. "But don't tell my mom that either."

"What's your mom's problem anyway?"

Ali smiled bitterly. "I'm not sure I know. For a while I thought it was her being disappointed by my failure of a marriage, but Christmas day was so weird it makes me wonder if there's something else going on. But who knows what it is."

"I'm sorry, that must suck." JT sat quietly for a moment, taking a bit of her food. "Maybe seeing you all settled into your place, with furniture and everything will make it clear to her that you're happy on your own."

Ali bit the inside of her lip. God, she hoped that would do the trick.

JT misunderstood her expression. "I mean, if you *are* happy. If you're not..."

Ali shook her head. "I'm definitely happy to be on my own. I know this town and my mom can't understand that, but I really am. But if having my house together is what it's going to take to convince her, we better get our asses back to picking stuff out. The faster my house is finished, the faster she'll be off my back."

They wandered through the store, jotting down notes on what items they needed to grab from the warehouse before checking out. It was a good thing they had the van, because they absolutely packed it with bookcases, side tables, a new dresser for Ali's room and her guest room, and one cozy chair.

"I'm sorry, I know you wanted a couch, but I don't think we can fit one in today."

Ali shrugged it off. "It's fine. This is going to keep me plenty busy. But once we get the books and stuff put on shelves, we can finally clear out so many of those boxes. Then maybe it will be time for a couch or two."

"I don't know if I mentioned it, but I'm really good at putting all this stuff together. I'm happy to help assemble everything and get it into the right places in your house. You know, if you want."

Ali laughed and gave JT a hug. "I don't know where you got the idea that I was considering doing this on my own. You are the biggest part of my plan. If that's still okay."

"I'm a master with an Allen wrench. Just you wait."

Ali climbed into the passenger seat, trying not to think of all the other ways JT might be good with her hands. The trip was fun and flirty, and Ali liked the idea of setting up a house with JT a little bit too much.

Not that she wanted to have a house with JT—it was just that she liked having someone to do it with. She was fine on her own, she really was. It was only that some things were meant for teamwork. Carrying heavy flat-packed furniture was one of those things.

And if Ali wanted to spend a lot more time with JT, she could pretend it was so she wasn't alone putting all those bookcases together. Sure, that was it.

Chapter Twenty-Two

They got back to Ali's house late in the afternoon, and JT had vague plans for dinner with her family. They unloaded all the boxes into the living room.

JT looked at the pile. "Kind of demoralizing to fill the space we cleared, huh?"

Ali shrugged. JT thought she looked exhausted. "It's fine. The bookcases will help with all my books, and having dressers will mean I can empty some other boxes..." She trailed off.

JT rested a hand on her shoulder. "Hey, you should get some rest."

Ali shook her head. "It's never going to get done if I take a rest."

"If you don't rest, you're going to exhaust yourself, and then what? There won't be anyone to tell me where to put all this furniture I'm going to build tomorrow."

Ali gave her a tired smile. "Thanks. That sounds like the lazy way out, but for tonight I think I'll take your advice."

JT wrapped Ali in a hug, her chin resting on Ali's head. She breathed in. "I really liked spending the day with you." She looked down. "Thank you."

Ali shook her head and squeezed JT. "Thank *you* for helping me with all this and for making me laugh." She smiled, and it just about cracked JT's heart in two.

"Promise me you'll get some sleep?" JT raised her eyebrows, trying to look like a stern teacher. "I can't have my teammate exhausted for our next event. We've got asses to kick."

Ali nodded and placed a soft kiss on JT's cheek when they reached the front door. "See you tomorrow, Coxie."

JT parked her dad's van in the barn and took Toby for a short walk before grabbing a seltzer from the fridge and sitting on the couch in the family room. Her parents were both reading and her siblings were nowhere to be seen.

"Where is everybody?"

Her dad looked at her over his book. "They took the kids out to run them around. They're all going out to dinner later and kindly offered to tire the kids out before leaving them with us."

"How was the shopping?" her mom asked. She set her book in her lap and peered over her glasses at JT. It gave JT the vague sense of being interrogated.

"Good. I brought home a couple trays of frozen cinnamon rolls for everyone. Ali got a lot of stuff for her house. Thanks for letting me use the van. She had a lot she needed."

Her mom pressed her lips into a line. "I bet that Canterbury boy kept most of their things. He always was a tool."

"Mom!" JT said, shocked and laughing.

Her mom made a dismissive gesture. "Am I wrong?"

JT shook her head. "Half the time I think you're not paying attention to something as mundane town gossip but then you give a wicked opinion. You're a mystery, lady."

Her mom did not seem to take the sentiment in the spirit JT offered it. "No, the mystery is what Ali saw in that boy in the first place."

JT had never been so surprised in her life. Of course her mom knew who Ali was, but she never expected her to have spent more than a moment thinking about Ali, her marriage, or frankly anyone else's business in their town. Her mom focused on art, almost to the exclusion of everything else going on. Or so JT had thought.

"What other opinions do you have tucked under there, Mom? You're holding out on me."

"Dear god, don't ask her that," JT's dad said. "She's full of opinions!"

Her mom glared at him but there was a twinkle in her eye. "I have the perfectly correct amount of opinions. I may not always choose to share them with my children."

JT laughed. "Mom, when have you ever not shared an opinion about me or my siblings? Name one time."

Her dad stood up. "If you're going to goad her into sharing her opinions, we're going to need beer. You want one?" He left and returned with a beer for each of them.

"All I said was that Ali Porter can do better than Kyle Canterbury. He was always full of himself because his dad runs that landscaping business. I always thought she probably wanted more out of her life than a couple kids and a husband who thinks too highly of himself because he drives a pickup truck."

JT sipped her beer. She tried to decide if her mom was being classist or if this was a personal thing with the Canterburys.

"Don't misunderstand me, driving a snowplow, mowing people's lawns and making their gardens look nice is a good way to make a living around here. I just don't personally think it makes you as special as Kyle and his dad seem to think."

JT's dad smirked to himself before taking a sip of his beer. "What she's not telling you is one time, Kyle senior made a comment about how your mom's hydrangeas looked bad and she's never forgiven him."

"Gordon, that is not true." Her mom looked indignant. "It was the lilacs, and that fool thought they needed to be trimmed. My bushes cannot be tamed!"

JT snorted beer into her nose, groaning at the pain of the fizz in her sinuses. "Jesus, Mom!"

Her mom's eyes crinkled when she laughed, and JT was struck by how rare it was to sit with her parents and not feel on edge. Usually, she felt left out of all the talk about artists and color theory or whatever else they talked about. This was nice, even if their bonding was over taking shots at Ali's ex and her mom making cringey bush jokes.

"What your mom is trying to say is we think it's very nice that you're helping Ali with her house."

"Jean Porter is probably too busy scheming to get her back with Kyle to be useful."

JT shrugged. "Yeah, I get the sense her mom is being a real piece of work. She'll be all right though. Once we get some shelves built for all her books."

Her dad smiled. "Nice to hear that young people still read."

JT stood. "Oh my god, Dad. I read! I just don't have seven rooms dedicated to books about art." She sighed, only then realizing her dad and mom were cracking up.

"You're messing with me? Seriously?" JT's anger fizzled, but it was replaced with annoyance. Even when they were joking, it all felt the same as the criticism they felt free to share. It hit exactly the same, regardless of the intent.

"Jasmine, we know you do. But it's so easy to set you off, and we old folks have so few ways to keep amused these days."

JT narrowed her eyes at her mom. "You're impossible. Anyway, we all agree Ali deserves better." JT started walking to the door. "You're babysitting so Beth and Jonny can have a double date and no one thought to invite me to dinner?" JT didn't wait for an answer. "I'm calling Tommy. Don't wait up."

Within an hour, JT was sitting at Dolan's nursing a beer and waiting for Tommy to show up. She found herself feeling nervous to see him. If he asked her about Ali, would he be able to tell that they'd kissed? What would he think? Would he be mad?

There wasn't really a guidebook for this other than you weren't really supposed to hook up with your best friend's sister. Even if the sister was the one who initiated it. She couldn't imagine saying *Don't be mad, dude your sister kissed* me! Yeah, that wasn't going to fly.

She took a couple large sips from her beer and hoped she could find whatever the right words were when the time came.

A few minutes later, Tommy dropped into the booth across from her. "Sorry, got caught up carrying stuff to the attic for my mom."

JT clinked her beer to his. "No worries. I know how moms are. Before I left my mom was going off about Ali could do better than Kyle. It was fucking weird."

Tommy nodded. "She's right, though. Ali was too good for that dumbass."

"Ali said your mom wants them back together, though."

Tommy sighed. "My mom is also a dumbass sometimes." They both laughed. "You drove her home the other night. Did she seem okay? She seemed fine on Christmas, but it's not like she was going to have a full breakdown in front of our family."

JT considered her words. She hated keeping secrets from Tommy. She hated it so much she hadn't done it since she was a teenager trying to work up the nerve to tell him she was gay. She'd made such a big thing out of it in her head, but when she told him he gave her a hug, told her he'd suspected she was gay and then asked her who she thought was hot. Since then, she'd never kept a secret from him bigger than what she was getting him for his birthday. And half the time she couldn't even keep that a secret.

JT took a deep breath. "She seemed fine, honestly." She picked at the label on her beer. "I'm not sure exactly how to say this but when I drove her home we kissed."

"I'm sorry, what? You kissed my sister?" His cheeks had a red tinge, and his tone an angry one.

JT held up her hands. "Dude. Your sister made the first move."

Tommy's jaw bulged as he clenched his teeth. JT watched as it relaxed back to normal. Tommy sighed. "Okay."

"Okay?"

Tommy emptied half his beer into his mouth. "My sister can do whatever she wants. But I swear to god, if you take advantage of her or fuck her over I will never forgive you."

JT blinked. His tone was harsh, but she was surprised by how fast he'd gone from anger to resignation. "You're serious?"

Tommy shrugged. "My sister is an adult. She can do whatever she wants with her life. She can make her own mistakes."

"Mistakes? You think kissing me is a mistake?" Now JT was pissed. How fucking dare he talk about her like that?

"Come on, JT. You're not known for being a long-term, stable relationship kind of girl."

Anger flared inside JT.

He looked at her. "You know I'm right. All I'm saying is if you and my sister are having a fling or whatever, fine. Just make sure she knows you're not a serious relationship person. Because I mean it, if you hurt her, I will never forgive you."

"And if she hurts me?"

Tommy stilled. "JT, she's my sister. I have every right to be pissed at you for hooking up with her, but I'm not. Of course I don't want either of you to get hurt, but she's my sister."

JT nodded. "Got it. I have no intention of hurting your sister. In fact, I've been running around helping her get her stuff put away so her house can feel like a home. Where have you been? Hooking up with that chick you met the other night? Not a lot of concern for the fact that your sister has been living with boxes in every room because maybe divorce is hard, and especially when your mom is constantly reminding her that she was better off with dipshit Kyle. But you weren't so concerned about your sister until you found out she was spending time with me."

JT stood.

"Look. I love you like a brother. And I like you more than my actual brother most of the time. But right now, you're being a dick. I didn't have to tell you about Ali. It's really none of your business, but I did because we're best friends. But apparently you think I'm a massive flake. Good to know." She tossed some money on the table for a tip, grabbed her coat and stomped out the door ignoring Tommy's calls to come back.

She sat in her car, seething. Fucking Tommy. His lack of faith in her hurt. But worse than that, a piece of her couldn't shake the idea that maybe he was right. She wasn't someone who had long-term girlfriends. She had girlfriends who were fun for a little while and who got bored of her, or she got bored of them. It was fine. She was young and meeting new people and having fun was what she wanted. Mostly.

But to hear Tommy throw that back in her face as evidence of the fact that she shouldn't be trusted with his sister hurt more than she wanted to admit to anyone. Too bad she couldn't hide those feelings from herself.

She pulled out her phone.

Saw your brother. He asked about driving you home the other night. I told him we kissed

She sent it and waited for the fallout. Ali was going to be mad at her. But she owed it to her to be honest. Tommy was her brother and if he knew that they kissed, Ali should know so she wouldn't be blindsided if he asked about it.

Three dots appeared and JT's nerves cranked to eleven.

How did he take it?

Oh he took it great. Basically called me a fuckboy

The three dots were back almost immediately but then they disappeared and her phone was ringing in her hand.

"He said what? I'm going to kill him."

JT laughed. "Thank you." The sound of Ali's voice and her anger on her behalf soothed JT more than she could have imagined.

"Seriously. What the fuck is wrong with him? He scuttles off to hook up with some random woman and then has the audacity to question who I kiss? I'm going to murder his stupid ass."

"No, it's fine. He wasn't talking shit about you."

"JT, it's not okay for him to talk shit about you either. What did he say, exactly?"

JT paused. She didn't want to say it out loud. She didn't want to tell Ali that Tommy had laid out all the ways she was a terrible girlfriend, an unserious person, not someone who would be a good choice for anyone, let alone his sister.

"It's fine. I shouldn't get between you two. I just wanted you to know he knows we kissed so if he asks about it you won't be surprised."

Ali huffed a frustrated breath. "Where are you? I can come to you."

JT shook her head and then realized Ali couldn't see her. "I'm fine. It's fine."

"If you say *fine* one more time..."

JT laughed. "Okay. Maybe it's not fine. But I'll be okay. It's not like it's the first time someone has told me I'm a joke." JT paused. "Look, I'm going to head home. I'll see you tomorrow? We'll build some bookshelves before our next competition?"

Ali made a noise JT couldn't decipher. "Would you stop here on your way?"

JT wanted to see Ali so badly, but she wasn't sure it was a good idea. She might fall apart if she saw Ali. If Ali was sweet to her, if she gave her a hug and took care of her, JT might dissolve. If she went home and crawled into bed, she could try to ignore everything that happened.

"Please?"

How was JT going to say no to that? To this woman? "Okay. But only if you really want me to. I'm fine—"

"No, you're not. My brother was an asshole and I will deal with him, but tonight let me deal with you."

"Okay," JT said, her voice barely a whisper.

The drive was too short and too long all at once. She knew she wanted and needed to see Ali, but she also knew that the second she did, she wasn't going to be able to shove her feelings away anymore.

Ali was waiting for her in the doorway when she pulled into the driveway. "Come here," she said and wrapped JT in a hug. She pulled her inside out of the cold. "I'm sorry, JT. I really am. This is all my fault."

"What are you talking about?"

"If I hadn't kissed you, you wouldn't have been having that conversation with my stupid little brother and you wouldn't be hurting right now."

JT tried to wave it all away. "I'm fine."

Ali pulled out of the hug to look at her. "I swear to god if you say that word one more time…"

JT forced a smile and then made herself ask the question she was terrified to have answered. "Ali. Do you regret kissing me?" JT braced for the answer. Of course, Ali regretted it. How could she not?

"Not for one second."

"Really?" JT didn't mean to say it out loud, but the thought escaped her head through her mouth before she could stop it. "Sorry. Forget I asked." JT wasn't a needy person. She didn't cling to women or ask them to constantly reassure her. This was embarrassing for her. She hated feeling so unsure of herself and now she'd shown that to Ali. Ugh. How was it possible that she kept making this worse?

Ali's eyes blazed fiercely. "No. I won't forget it. I understand that my brother was completely out of line tonight, but please try to ignore him. I know he's your best friend, which only makes it worse if you ask me, but he doesn't speak for me. I don't regret kissing you. I don't regret spending time with you. I'll regret it if me kissing you has fucked up your life." She smiled. "But honestly, as much as I don't want your life fucked up, I really like kissing you. I would like to do a lot more of it. But I also understand how important Tommy is to you. I know you two have a forever bond. But I'm still going to kill him for making you feel like this. How dare he?"

JT rested her head against Ali's shoulder. "He cares about you and he's afraid I'm a flake. Also, I told him he should be helping you with your house and he probably didn't like that either." Ali wrapped her arms around JT and squeezed her. JT turned her face into Ali's neck, breathing in the scent of her shampoo and skin. Her heart slowed, and her anger dimmed from a blaze to a few embers. Tommy wasn't wrong about her, but he wasn't right either. That didn't change how shitty she felt, but knowing Ali didn't regret her choices when it came to kissing JT helped more than she could express.

She stepped back. "I should go. You're already in your pj's and I busted in here to ruin your night."

Ali shook her head. "You didn't ruin anything. I was having a cup of tea and reading because someone told me to take a night off and not give in to the temptation to unpack more boxes. Honestly, it felt luxurious."

"You deserve it. I'll let you get back to your book. See you tomorrow?"

Ali nodded and squeezed JT's hand. "Yeah. Promise me you'll put Tommy out of your mind."

JT didn't want to lie so she tried to make the truth sound as good as possible. "I'll do my best."

She drove the short distance to her parents' house feeling slightly reassured that at least some of the things Tommy had said weren't true. She couldn't change the kind of girlfriend she'd been in the past, but when it came to Ali, she knew she'd do better. The person she had to convince was not Tommy—it was herself. She could work on that.

Chapter Twenty-Three

The moment JT left the driveway, Ali was on her phone. Tommy picked up almost immediately and she didn't waste a second before laying into him.

"Who the fuck do you think you are?"

"Ali? Are you okay?"

"Oh, I'm fine, but you're not going to be if you don't apologize to me and to JT for being the biggest fuckwit the world has ever seen. And remember, this is a world in which Kyle exists."

"What are you talking about?"

"You told JT that she was an unserious person. You implied that she took advantage of me, your older sister, who not only got married and divorced, but also holds down a full professional job and owns a house? Which one of those things signals damsel in distress who needs your protection or even your opinion?"

Tommy groaned. "She came crying to you? God, what a drama qu—"

"I'm going to stop you before you make this worse for yourself, baby brother. She isn't a drama queen. She didn't come running to me. She simply informed me that she'd told you that we kissed, and I was able to discern through my powers of being a reasonable human being that someone had hurt her feelings, and imagine my shock when that person turned out to be her best friend and my baby brother."

Tommy sputtered.

"I'm not done. It's bad enough that every time I see Mom she tells me how amazing Kyle is and what a fool I was to divorce him. I don't need you and your misguided protective brother shit when it comes to my love life. I will kiss any person I damn well please, and if that's JT Cox, you don't have the right to say two words about it, okay?"

"Ali, I wasn't trying to be an asshole. But come on, you know how she is."

Ali stared at the ceiling, willing herself to find some bit of calm. "Yeah, I know how she is. She's sweet, caring, funny, and she has been helping me get my house put together even though she has no obligation to do so and there's literally nothing in it for her. So, if that's what you meant, then yes, I do know what she's like. If you were going to tell me a bunch of stories about her love life, I would be happy to tell you again how it's none of your fucking business."

"Okay, I'm sorry. Geez."

He sounded like such a teenager she almost laughed. But that would give him the wrong impression that she had forgiven him. "I'm not the only one you need to apologize to. She bailed you out the other night when you decided to leave to hook up with some random chick, and then you decided to yell at her instead of just saying thank you. So, yeah. You better apologize and it better be good. Not one of your dumbass bro apologies where you're all 'you know man I'm whatever, we good?' and then you move on like nothing happened. You hurt her feelings, and she might not dwell on it, but I will. I will set up shop next to you and tell every girl who thinks you look fun the worst, most embarrassing stories from our childhood until you never get laid again. Do you understand me?"

"Ali, oh my god, you are unhinged. I'll apologize. I get it! I was out of line. I'll call her now." She could almost hear the wince in his voice. "She's going to think it's so weird if I call. Can't I text her?"

Ali sighed. "You do what you think is best. But you better make the apology good enough to make up for you running your mouth about her 'taking advantage of me' like you think she's some kind of creepy predator. That was way out of bounds, and I think you know it. If it freaks you out that your sister likes kissing women, that's a 'you' problem. Do not make it hers and do not make it mine. Figure your shit out. And do it fast. Good night." Ali hung up, feeling exhilarated by her anger. It felt good to unleash it for once instead of swallowing it and letting it fester.

If the voice in her head told her she was never this fierce on her own behalf, she ignored it. She was mad and she'd done something about it. And it felt fucking amazing. She rode the high through half a chapter of her book before it subsided, leaving her exhausted and a little emotionally hungover.

She crawled into bed feeling proud. And that was worth whatever kind of hangover. She'd earned it.

Chapter Twenty-Four

JT slipped out of the house with Toby before her siblings were awake. She threw a tennis ball in the snow until Toby seemed plenty tired out to rest while she went to help Ali. She didn't know what to expect when she got there. They'd had a pretty intense conversation the night before. JT's feelings had been raw, and now she felt a little embarrassed that she'd gone running to Ali with them.

She shouldn't have said anything. She could have taken what Tommy had said and not shared with Ali. But Ali deserved to know her brother knew about them. Or about them kissing. Because she didn't really know what they were to each other beside teammates in this silly contest and friends who liked kissing sometimes.

She tucked Toby back in her crate, grabbed a bagel and headed to Ali's. She'd been an emotional whirlwind, but at least she could make herself useful today. Ali had furniture to put together and JT was a fucking wizard with an Allen wrench.

JT knocked and Ali opened the door, her hair up in a messy bun, a sweatshirt from their high school on over her pj's, and the cutest nerdy glasses JT had ever seen.

"I didn't know you wore those," she said with a grin.

Ali held the door open wider. "Come inside before you make fun of me."

"I'm not! They're super cute."

Ali rolled her eyes. "They're super thick, but necessary. I can't see much without my contacts, but sometimes it's just too damn early to stick my finger in my eye. You know?"

JT shook her head. "I wouldn't know. I have perfect vision." She laughed.

Ali swatted her with the back of her hand. "Oh my god, you're the worst. Not all of us were born to be elite athletes and fighter pilots."

"True. Because some of us were born to be an entire town's favorite teacher and inspire crushes from the time they hit puberty."

"What are you talking about? I'm not a favorite teacher and no one crushes on me."

JT shook her head and laughed. "I guarantee you that there is a huge bunch of kids at that high school who adore you and probably more who have massive crushes on you. You just don't know it. And I know it's not 'no one' because I had a crush on you from the time I was like twelve."

"Oh really? Well, I want to hear all about that while we build some shelves." She pointed to the pile of flat-packed boxes. "I think we need two or three in the office. Do you want to build them in the room or carry them in after?"

JT looked at the hallway. "Oh, build them in place, for sure. Then we won't ding the walls." She lifted one box off the ground like she was going to carry it herself.

"What are you doing?"

"Taking it to your office?" JT raised her eyebrows. How was this not obvious?

"It's a two-person job. See the little people on the box showing that it's a 'team lift'? Let me lift one end." JT protested. "Just because you *can* carry it on your own doesn't mean you have to. Come on, let's do this together so no one ends up injured."

JT shrugged. "Whatever you want." She waited for Ali to lift the other end of the box before walking toward the back of the house. "I can walk backwards if that's easier for you."

Ali followed her to the back room. It took them a few minutes to get all three boxes to the office. "Do you think we can get all these put together before the contest?"

JT nodded. "I think so. Bookcases don't have too many pieces to put together"

Ali stood in the doorway. "Do you want coffee?"

"Yes, please."

"Cinnamon rolls?"

JT laughed. "You didn't get enough of them yesterday?"

Ali made a face. "No way. I could eat them all day every day. These ones are homemade. One of my students gave me them as a holiday gift."

JT made a suspicious face. "Does this student like you or..."

"You're the one who claims I'm everyone's favorite teacher, but now you're questioning if my student might be trying to kill me?"

JT laughed. "Fine, you got me. But seriously, this isn't the one student who hates you or something, is it?"

Ali shook her head. "No, but I like that you're nervous to find out. This kid's dad is the baker at the inn. These things are going to be amazing."

"Why didn't you lead with that? Yes, I'll take ten."

They settled into the office and its newly yellow walls. JT thought it was cheerful but maybe a touch overpowering. Thankfully, the three bookcases were white and would break up the yellow a little bit. She thought it was going to look amazing.

Ali kept looking at the walls thoughtfully. JT couldn't tell what was going on in Ali's head.

"Okay, why do you keep looking around and making a face?

I can't tell if you hate it in here but refuse to say anything or those cinnamon rolls aren't sitting right in your tummy."

Ali sighed. "It wasn't the cinnamon rolls. I could eat a dozen and want more." She looked around. "It's a weird thing to be in charge of a whole house. Growing up in my family, there was always compromises and agreeing to things we weren't psyched on. Same when I was married to Kyle. Usually he won out, like with that ugly ass couch in the other room. But now I'm in charge of everything, I don't know, it's not always easy to know if I'm doing the right thing or if something is really what I want or if it's a voice in my head telling me what I *should* want. Does that make sense?"

JT nodded. "My parents let me choose the colors in my room when I was a kid. They made it pretty clear that they weren't impressed with the choices, but they kept their word and painted it how I liked. When I left for college, they painted over everything before my first trip back home." She shook her head and forced a laugh. "My artistic inabilities are well-known."

Ali cocked her head to the side as if trying to imagine how bad it could have been. "What did you pick?"

JT smiled. "I had them paint it in the school colors. I was going through a phase of idolizing the high school kids and told myself I'd make the hockey team one day and wear those colors." She rolled her eyes. "Kind of pathetic if you think about it."

"Not at all! That's so badass. Not only that you wanted to be on the team but that you did it. So many of those kid dreams never come true. But yours did."

"And what a dream it turned out to be. Half the town thought I didn't belong on the team, the other half agreed but didn't say anything, at least not to my face, so long as we kept winning. And that's just the folks from town. Our opponents were way worse."

Ali scooted across the floor and wrapped JT in a hug. "I'm

sorry it was like that for you. I remember you being an absolute badass. Flying down the ice, Cox on your jersey and your ponytail flying."

JT laughed. "Stupid to leave my ponytail out. Made me a target." She paused to tighten the final bolt on the bookcase. "But it reached a point where I was like fuck it. They're going to try to kill me anyway, why give them the satisfaction of looking like I was hiding."

Ali shook her head. "You've always been such a badass."

"Thanks. I'm not sure if that's true or if I had no choice." She stood. "Where do you want this one? Next to that one or on a different wall?"

Ali appraised her options. "There, next to that one. If we put them all on that wall it will look like a library with built-in bookcases. I've always wanted one of those rooms filled with books and maybe a secret door or something."

"I don't know about the secret room, but the bookcases I can do."

Once they moved it into position, they started unloading Ali's many boxes of books onto the shelves. "For now, put them anywhere, I'll organize them later. But I want these boxes the hell out of here."

They worked until it was time for them to go to their next event. They left the room looking nearly done. It needed a desk and a few odds and ends, but when school started again, Ali would have a place to work.

The assignment for the night was a gingerbread house. Or, more accurately, decorating a house someone else had already put together. JT was sure her siblings were going to kill her in this competition. Emerson and Jonathan were professional artists, and even if their usual works weren't done in sugar and candy, she was sure the skills would translate. She, on the other hand, wasn't known for her skill with anything so delicate as a paint brush, so she was hoping that Ali could save their team.

Ali climbed into the passenger seat of JT's car when it was time to leave. "You sure you want to be stuck driving my ass home after the competition?"

JT told herself not to make the wildly inappropriate remarks about Ali's ass flooding her brain. "I'm more than happy to drive you home. It's stupid for us to take two cars when my parents live so close to you."

"You're sure you don't want to ride home with them?"

JT laughed. "You're hilarious. Imagine that ride where they discuss the subtle brilliance of their technique while treating me like a kid who hasn't learned to hold her crayon correctly." JT shook her head, imagining how annoying they were all going to be.

"Maybe they'll surprise you."

"Yeah, and maybe Toby will cook me dinner." Her tone didn't betray her annoyance. She'd learned not to expect too much from her family. She hadn't learned not to care, but she'd figured out that going in with low expectations helped keep her from being disappointed.

They drove to the candy store in the next town over. Its town center was slightly larger and would host a couple of the events in an attempt to get folks to check out everything there was to offer in the area. JT used to ride her bike to the store as a kid. She used to ride her bike pretty much everywhere before she got her license. Most roads had no shoulder, let alone a sidewalk, and everything was too far away for walking to make much sense, anyway.

She'd climb on her bike and pedal the five miles each way for the promise of a bag of penny candy. Walking through the doors, she was transported by the smell to those years when she would spend most of her lawn mowing money on sugar. She and Tommy would buy candy by the paper bagful before Little League and then eat enough to power them through practice.

Her pregame meals had gotten considerably healthier, but she kept the routine of eating a handful of candy before warm-ups.

Ali said hi to everyone she saw as they walked in. People said hi to JT, but it was a different vibe because Ali was one of them. An old friend, teacher, staple of the area, and JT was someone they claimed because she'd won a gold medal. At least that's how it felt as people told her how proud they were of watching her put Hart's Landing on a map.

She took her spot at a table while Ali talked to a woman around her age near the Red Hots. JT fought the urge to pull out her phone to kill the time. Two teens came to her table. One was taller than the other and in that gangly stage where she'd gotten taller but didn't look at home in her body yet. Her friend was shorter with a mouthful of braces.

"Are you the Olympian?"

JT smiled, oddly charmed by only being semi-recognized. "Depends. Who do you think I am?"

The taller girl nudged the other with her elbow. "I told you it was her." She shoved her hands deep into her pockets and rounded her shoulders forward. "Don't mind Emma, she never believes me. I'm Margot. We play on the Wreckers."

JT didn't know what she was talking about.

The smaller one pointed to her sweatshirt. "Hart's Wreckers. It's our last year before we can try out for the high school team. Would you come to one of our games sometime?"

"I'd love to if it works with my schedule. Do you have any coming up?"

Margot handed her a little magnetic schedule. "Here. But don't tell my mom I took it off the fridge."

JT laughed. "How about I take a picture of it and then you can put it back without getting in trouble. I'd hate for you to get grounded and miss a game." She snapped a picture with her phone and handed it back.

"You were awesome in the Olympics," Emma said, seemingly overcoming her skepticism. "Those Canucks never stood a chance."

JT laughed. "We were lucky to get the win. Thanks for watching."

The girls left as Ali arrived at the table. "Fan club?"

"Something like that. You know them?"

"Of course. There aren't many kids in town who I don't know. Emma and Margot are the little sisters of my students. I've seen a few of their games. They're pretty good." Ali shrugged out of her coat and hung it on the chair behind their table. "You better watch out, they're coming for your job one of these days."

"I don't doubt it. Margot's tall. If she grows into her height, she'll be able to hold her own. The other one better be fast."

Ali shook her head. "Don't tell me you're worried about a couple kids."

"I had to take someone's job to make the Olympic team. Someone will try to take it from me next time. Someday it might be one of those kids. You never know."

Ali scanned the table. "This says there should be a set of rules for us. Do you see it?"

JT pulled a piece of paper out from under jars of candies. "Will you check to see if there are rules against me eating all of this? Because I swear they picked all my favorites." She made a face. "Except for those. I hate gum drops. They're all weirdly spiced. They taste like old people."

Ali gave her a quizzical look. "Spend a lot of time nibbling on old people?"

JT rolled her eyes. "You know what I mean. Don't tell me you're one of those weirdos who likes the black licorice ones."

Ali read the rules. "I do not like black licorice but lots of people do. It says here we don't have to take taste into account. All that matters is that it looks good. So we can mix any flavors together."

JT lifted the jars and gave a few full of candies she didn't recognize a sniff. She could feel herself getting more anxious about the competition. This was the first event where a team would be eliminated, and she would rather eat a pound of black licorice than get bounced from the contest at this early stage. Hating to lose was an asset on the ice. Her inability to phone it in when it came to sports and competition worked in her favor most of the time. But when it came to competitions she knew she wasn't going to dominate, it made her anxious and cranky. She needed to get some perspective, but when her parents walked in, beaming at her siblings, it made her anxiety spike and her feeling of doom a thousand times worse.

Ali placed her hand on JT's arm. "You okay?"

JT nodded. "Yeah, it's fine."

"You are an atrocious liar. What's going on?"

JT gritted her teeth. "I suck at this stuff." She sounded like a petulant teenager. She could hear it, but she couldn't stop herself.

"Okay," Ali said, drawing the word out. "So what?" She followed JT's eyes to the rest of her family. "Oh my god, are you this worked up over competing against them? Who cares? They're the ones who should be nervous. They're the professional artists. We're a couple amateurs at best. If they don't win it's embarrassing for them. We have nothing to lose."

JT grunted. "Tell that to my parents. I promise you they'll be fawning all over them and talking about how brilliant and gifted they are."

"So? Neither of them has a gold medal the last I checked. And Holden's Candy Emporium isn't handing out Olympic medals for gingerbread decorating."

JT forced herself to look at Ali. "Thank you." She didn't

know what else to say. The only thing her family valued was art. Her inability to do what they did with paint and clay left her feeling like an outsider. She was never going to measure up, but she was too stupid and too stubborn to stop trying to beat them at their game.

Ali squeezed JT's hand. "Let's have some fun, okay? And if they kick our asses, who cares? It's just a candy house."

Chapter Twenty-Five

They had two and a half hours to decorate the gingerbread house. It was not enough time but, as Ali looked around the room, it wasn't enough time for any of the teams. JT had fallen into the role of her assistant, which involved finding the roundest candies or breaking them into smaller pieces or hunting down something that could pass for snow in the many, many jars on the shelves set up for them to browse. Turned out coconut flakes worked pretty well.

Ali focused on getting everything to look as good as possible in the short time they had, but JT's anxiousness and insecurity came back to her at random intervals. It was a side of her Ali hadn't seen before. She'd been accustomed to the brash, slightly cocky persona JT usually wore. She had no idea how much her family messed with her head.

"Contestants! Please pause your decorating!" A voice broke through the murmuring among the teams. "We want to let you know you have thirty minutes left to decorate and we are adding a task!"

The crowd cheered. Sadistic bastards.

"We will be handing out sheets of gingerbread to each team

and we would like you all to make a second structure in the time you have remaining."

JT groaned next to Ali.

"We don't expect perfection. We know this is a bit mean, but frankly, it's too much fun not to ask you to do something wacky." They spent another few seconds explaining the rules before releasing them to continue.

"This is why I don't come home," JT muttered under her breath.

"Auxiliary gingerbread structures are what keeps you from visiting?" Ali asked, unable to finish the sentence without laughing.

JT caught the giggles and shook with the effort of controlling her laughter. "I'll have you know that it was the great gingerbread building catastrophe of '08 that first made me want to leave here forever."

Now Ali couldn't help her case of the giggles. "You're going to have to build it. I've still got about a billion shingles to add, and I don't get the sense you want to take over."

JT shook her head. "I don't want to do either." A volunteer walked to their table and dropped off a stack of gingerbread. "Thanks," JT said, eyeing it suspiciously.

"It's not going to bite you. Just make a little house or something and then decorate it. We don't have much time."

JT sighed. "Fine. But this all seems very unfair." She took two pieces and leaned them against each other in a tiny triangle.

"A house, JT, a house."

"It's an A-frame, Alexandra."

Ali looked shocked.

"What?" JT said, her face all scrunched and grumpy.

"You called me Alexandra."

"So? It's your name."

Ali smiled, her heart warm in her chest. "Yes, but most people assume it's Alison. You got it right."

"Ali, I may be a big dumb hockey player, but I've known your brother and you my entire life. If I couldn't remember your name, it would be embarrassing."

Ali nodded and focused on the Smarties she was using to shingle the house. Kyle had called her Alison once when they'd been arguing. He hadn't remembered her real name. After a decade together, he'd called her Alison. But here was JT, her brother's best friend, remembering the name she rarely used. How many times had she even heard it?

JT had all this warmth and kindness and kept acting like it was nothing, like everyone did what she did. Maybe JT expected too much from people, but Ali wanted to live in that world where no one, especially not your husband, called you the wrong name. She liked JT's world where people weren't just nice but were genuinely kind.

She focused on the Smarties and the frosting that held them in place while her brain did cartwheels and shot off fireworks about what a lovely person she'd found in JT.

JT, meanwhile, struggled with the new gingerbread task. She'd succeeded in getting two pieces to form a tent-like structure, but Ali was skeptical it was what the judges had in mind. JT's face was twisted with concentration. She bit her lower lip and the crease between her eyebrows was impressively deep.

"How's it going?"

JT grunted. "In terms of what? It's standing, so that's good. But it looks worse than the lean-to I made with Jonny in the woods when we were younger. At least then I had the excuse of being five." She stepped back from the table and wiped her frosting covered hands on a cloth. "There's no excuse for this." She looked at Ali. "Sorry your partner sucks."

Ali shook her head. "You don't suck. Your A-frame looks amazing. Do you want to add some decoration? Maybe you could make it look like we made a cute little house for Toby?"

The mention of her puppy snapped JT back into focus. "Definitely. I can do that." She grabbed a piping bag and scoured the table for the right candies to decorate. "No chocolate, obviously, because dogs can't eat it."

"Obviously," Ali said, trying not to laugh. JT's serious face was too cute.

Ten minutes passed and then the announcers had the whole crowd count down. Ali and JT set their tools and supplies down. Ali hugged JT, letting her head find JT's shoulder.

"You did great," Ali whispered into her ear.

JT hugged her but Ali could feel that she was keeping her hands away from her back. "I'm all sticky. Don't want to ruin your sweater," JT said, looking down.

Ali stepped back. "Let's get cleaned up so you can hug me properly when we win."

JT laughed. "Do you need your glasses? That shit is a train wreck. There's no way we're winning, but I can take a hint. I'll get cleaned up."

Chapter Twenty-Six

They did not win. But they didn't get eliminated either. As far as an afternoon of decorating could go, it wasn't the worst. Emerson and Clark won, which was predictable. Clark was an architect and Emerson's entire job was based on her impeccable artistic skills. Their only real competition came from Jonathan and Beth.

JT was gracious when she complimented both of her siblings on their incredible, and they really were incredible, houses. She stared in disbelief at Clark's pergola. The man made a goddamned pergola out of gingerbread in the same amount of time she made a dilapidated A-frame doghouse thing. He'd figured out how to make it look even more amazing by stringing candies like fairy lights.

Beth had managed to make a child-sized playhouse complete with window boxes. Window boxes with icing flowers! JT had known this event wasn't going to play to her strengths and would be perfect for her siblings, but this felt worse than she'd imagined. Their creations looked professional while the parts of their house that she'd helped with looked like an uncoordinated preschooler had done them.

At least when they walked around the room to admire the

other houses, she saw that Kyle and Sharon's was nothing more than fine. Getting her ass handed to her by her professional artist siblings was one thing; being worse than Kyle was another.

Back at their table, she looked down at their house. Ali had done a great job with the Smarties as shingles and the decorations made of icing. There was even a walkway leading up to the house made with brown M&M's. JT's contributions were mainly picking out the brown M&M's from the rest of the pack and trying not to screw up Ali's work.

"Sorry you got the worst of the Coxes." She sighed and shook her head.

Ali gave her a confused look. "Are you apologizing because you're not a professional artist? Geez, yeah that's a shame. If only you'd been able to excel at literally anything in your life." She feigned reaching for JT's chest. "Oh, I'm sorry, is that a fucking Olympic gold medal you're wearing? Yeah, real shame you're such an underachiever."

JT managed a chuckle. "You know what I mean. My hockey skills mean fuck all in this competition. You would have been better off with anyone else."

Ali pointed to the team that had been eliminated. Their house had fallen in on itself, they'd spilled candy all over their table and floor, and both seemed to have icing in their hair. "False. Dale and Carol are a hot mess."

JT followed Ali's finger and found the couple laughing and feeding each other candy. "Fine, but they look very happy."

Ali reached into a bowl of Red Hots. "I can shove these in your mouth if that would make you feel better."

JT laughed, her shoulders shaking. "No! I'm just trying to say I'm sorry I suck at art."

Ali shrugged. "I'm not." When JT looked confused, she continued. "You're going to kick ass at other stuff. It's nice to be the one who's good at this."

JT smiled. Ali was too adorable. She should stop that, or JT was going to have even more of a problem keeping everything between them friends only. She liked seeing Ali so proud of herself. She deserved that feeling. Honestly, everyone should have it at some point.

Except for Kyle. He could go fuck himself.

"Come on, we should congratulate your sister." Ali dragged JT across the room to where JT's parents and brother were standing around Emerson's table.

JT did not want to join this conversation. She didn't care that Emerson had won. She was happy for her and would happily congratulate her, but she knew what she'd hear when they got there. Sure enough, as soon as they got close enough to hear her mom's voice, it was everything she'd been dreading.

"The way you used the candy canes to make a striped pattern across the sides of the house to mimic shutters is genius."

Her dad pointed to the roof. "I like what you did with the gelt, it looks so much like wood shingles. What made you think of that?" He crouched to look closer at every angle of the house. "Clark, the pergola! How did you make that stay up? This whole thing has such a wonderfully artistic feel. It's not kitschy at all."

Her mom shook her head. "No, I'm seeing a little bit of kitsch, and I love how you play with that sense of nostalgia and tackiness. It's such an interesting commentary." She turned to Jonathan. "Yours is so wonderful, too. I'm not sure the judges understood that yours had elements of Van Gogh's style. But I think it was a bold choice to try to bring his style into your work."

JT stiffened when she approached the table. She shrugged her shoulders to try to loosen up but hearing her parents shift into art professor mode always stressed her out.

"You okay?" Ali whispered, her breath tickling JT's ear.

JT nodded. "Yeah, this is normal for them. I'll congratulate Emerson and then we can get the hell out of here." She stepped forward to give Emerson a hug and Clark a high five. "Putting us all to shame, once again. Congrats, Em. Clark, a pergola? Really?"

Clark laughed. "Honestly? I broke a couple of the pieces and had to improvise."

JT shook her head. "You're a liar but I appreciate it."

"Jasmine, did you have fun?"

JT told herself not to start an argument with her mom. She wouldn't do it. She didn't want to take away from Emerson's win. She didn't want to. But goddammit, why did her mom refuse to call her JT?

"JT and I had a great time!" Ali said with a bright smile. "The late addition to the requirements threw us a little, but I think JT's A-frame doghouse is super cute."

"It certainly is…cute," JT's mom said, completely failing to keep disdain out of her tone.

"Mom," JT said, hoping she could stop this train before it got started.

"Oh honey, you shouldn't feel bad. Art was never your thing."

JT looked down at Ali and gave her a look that she hoped conveyed how annoyed she was but also that she wanted to leave without getting further into this argument.

Ali wasn't having it. "Mrs. Cox, I think JT did a great job. She made sure I had everything I needed exactly when I needed it. She's such a great teammate." Ali smiled, but it was the kind of smile JT could picture her giving to a difficult parent who had come to her classroom to complain.

"Of course she is! That's her whole life." JT's dad's voice was even, but somehow the statement felt like an insult.

Ali stepped toward him, but JT put her hand on Ali's arm. "It's not worth it," she said in a quiet voice. Ali could argue with her parents forever and they were never going to value her work the same way they valued her siblings'. She gave up on that a long time ago.

"Jonathan, your house looks amazing. Emerson, congrats on your win. Ali and I are going to take off. I'll see you back at home." JT kept her hand on Ali's forearm and gave it a gentle tug. "Let's grab our coats."

Ali walked half a step behind her back to their table. When they got there, JT held Ali's coat up for her to put on.

"Why do you let them talk about you that way?" Ali's eyes flicked between JT's like she was searching for something.

JT shrugged. "It's not worth it. They're never going to change." She looked over Ali's head to her family, still gathered around the winning house, gesticulating wildly and pointing out their favorite parts of the scene.

She walked toward the car, and Ali fell into step behind her. "JT…"

JT ignored her until they got to the car. When they slid into their seats, JT started the car and turned the heaters up to full blast.

"JT, you are a fierce woman. You kick ass on the ice and off. Why the fuck do you let them treat you like that?"

JT gripped the steering wheel. "Because they aren't wrong."

"What?"

"Ali, I am a terrible artist. They're not wrong about that. It's not my strength."

Ali made sputtering noises of protest. "You're not a bad artist! And even if you were the worst artist on the planet, they still don't have any right to treat you like that."

JT shrugged. She didn't know how to make Ali understand. She'd been the golden girl all through childhood. She was the prom queen and the homecoming queen and everyone in town loved her. JT would bet anything that she was the most beloved teacher at their old school.

On top of all that, she was beautiful in a way that made people stop and look at her without feeling threatened. Ali Porter was *the* dream girl and JT wasn't.

Outside her house, she was too big, too strong, too weird, too gay, too everything to be beloved. At home, she wasn't enough. The things that her family valued weren't the things she could do. She couldn't paint or draw or make beautiful things. That wasn't her. The only place she knew she was good was on the ice. Give her a sport and she was in her element.

"They don't understand me. They never have. It's not their fault they don't get me. Their whole world is art. It's what they talk about at dinner, it's the subject of every book they read—they eat, sleep and breathe art and the art world. I'm the weirdo in the family. I'm the alien. And I don't think they know how to know me. I might as well be speaking a foreign language that uses a different alphabet. They have no way in." She sighed. "I gave up trying to make them understand a long time ago."

Ali leaned against the door, her head resting on the window. "JT. Will you look at me?" JT turned her head, embarrassed by her outburst. She'd said too much and didn't want to meet Ali's eyes. "It's not for you to convince your parents you're worthy. You don't have to be enough for your parents. You just have to be you. It's *their* job to love you, no matter who you are and whether you want to discuss the Impressionist movement or not. If they can't see how incredible you are, that is *their* failure, not yours."

JT's eyes burned. Fuck. She never cried. Okay, that was a lie, she cried regularly at cute commercials and videos of dogs and all kinds of stuff. But the tears pricked at the corners of her eyes and one slid down her cheek before she could stop it. Ali's hand was on her cheek in an instant. It was warm and soft and JT leaned into it without thinking.

"Sorry," she breathed.

"Honey, you have nothing to be sorry for. I'm sorry they can't see how incredible you are. I'm so sorry they ever make you feel less than how incredible you are. JT, you are possibly the kindest person I have ever met." Ali paused to smile. "Have you always been this kind?"

JT gave a shrug.

"You show up at my house and help me put it all together on your vacation week. Who does that?"

"You needed help."

Ali laughed. "I sure do. But I've needed help for a while and you're the one who has shown up for me. You're absolutely remarkable."

Now JT had tears rushing down her cheeks and there was nothing she could do to stop them. "Thank you," she breathed, swiping a hand across her face. "Anyone would do the same."

Ali laughed and placed a gentle kiss on JT's cheek. "I'm going to kill your family for letting you live this long thinking you are anything other than a spectacular miracle. Not everyone would show up and help someone they haven't seen in years. But you have. You're one of one, JT Cox."

For a second, JT thought Ali was going to say more. Instead, she rubbed her thumb across JT's cheek and then sat back against the door.

JT wiped her face and reached for the gearshift. "Ready to get out of here?"

Ali nodded. "Yeah, I'd like a glass of wine the size of a bathtub."

JT pulled out of the spot and steered onto the road. "Do you need me to make a stop on the way home?"

Ali shook her head. "My house is a complete mess, but I have plenty to drink."

Chapter Twenty-Seven

Ali turned on the lights as she walked through her hallway to the kitchen. She heard JT taking off her boots and hanging her coat on the hook. It was good she was behind Ali because Ali was pissed. Not at JT—she was anything but angry with JT. It might have been helpful for her to be angry with her instead of feeling whatever was going on inside her.

Ali pulled a couple glasses out of the cabinet, a bit embarrassed they were regular cups and not wineglasses. "Sorry, I'll unpack the wineglasses soon."

JT stood in the doorway, leaning against the doorframe looking so hot Ali almost dropped her cup. "It doesn't matter."

Ali stepped closer. "Wine snobs would disagree."

"Are you one of them?" JT's mouth quirked up at one corner.

Ali shook her head, her eyes burning a hole in JT's lips. "No. I'm sure a lot of people care about the shape of the glass, but sometimes I'm just thirsty." She was laying it on a bit thick, but JT didn't seem to be noticing her flirting, or if she was, she was either not interested or holding back. And judging by the way she was tracking Ali's every move, she didn't think she was uninterested.

The way JT leaned against the doorframe was killing Ali.

Her shoulder resting on the molding, her arms crossed in front of her with her shirtsleeves rolled up, showing off her forearms. She was the perfect image of a romance novel cover model, adorable and rugged. Ali stepped closer, giving JT a chance to stop her but making her intentions clear.

"Ali," JT said in a low voice. "Again, you wanted us to be friends."

Ali shrugged. "I still want to be friends. But I also want to kiss you until I'm drunk on you."

JT shifted. "Ali."

Ali grew frustrated with JT's restraint. "If I were some woman in a bar, would you kiss me?"

"You know I would."

"Then why are you holding back?"

JT dropped her hands to her sides. "Because you're not some random woman in a bar who has a thing for hockey players, or whatever. You're Ali. I've known you my whole life. I had a painfully awkward crush on you for years. You're not just anybody. Which means I can't fuck this up. You're too important and I'm way too good at making messes."

Ali wrapped her hands around fistfuls of JT's shirt. She gave a gentle tug. "Look around. Do I look like someone afraid of a little mess?" JT smiled and a laugh escaped from her lips. "JT, I know I said we should stay just friends, but I can't stop thinking about kissing you."

JT looked down and gently placed her hands on Ali's hips. "Are you sure? I'm only visiting and your brother..."

"Oh my god, I do not give a flying fuck what my little brother thinks," Ali said with a cackle. "Do you?"

JT shrugged. "He's my best friend. I really like you but...I can't imagine not having him in my life."

Ali was confused. "Do you think that my brother is going to stop being your friend because you fucked his sister?"

JT's eyes widened. "You didn't say anything about more than kissing."

Ali pressed her body against JT's and bringing her mouth as close to JT's face as she could without touching. "I didn't realize I had to spell it out."

JT's lips curled into the sexiest smile Ali had ever seen. "Maybe I need you to be *very* specific about what you want from me."

Ali surged up on her tiptoes, capturing JT's lips. She tugged at JT's shirt, drawing her closer as she kissed JT as hard as she could. "I want to get you naked so I can touch every inch of you. And I want you to fuck me until I beg for mercy." She lowered herself back to flat feet. "Is that clear enough for you?"

Without hesitating, JT lifted Ali up, wrapping her legs around her waist and carrying her to the counter. She put Ali down without taking her hands off her. She kissed Ali, hard at first, like she was desperate for her. But then she slowed down. Frantic kisses turned softer but no less insistent. She brought her hands to Ali's face, cradling her cheeks in her hands and using her fingers to keep Ali's blond hair out of her way.

"Is this okay?" JT asked, her breath hot on Ali's ear.

Ali breathed. "Yes."

JT ran her tongue across Ali's lips, tracing them, tasting them before replacing her tongue with her lips. Ali sighed, her mouth falling open and her tongue finding JT's. It didn't take long before these sweet kisses became more heated again. JT's hands found Ali's thighs and squeezed and JT leaned her hips forward pulling them closer together.

Ali's fingers were in JT's hair, her palm on her undercut and her fingers threaded through her hair. She was thankful JT didn't have her hair up in a ponytail because her hair felt so good, so different from Kyle's.

Ugh she didn't want to think about Kyle. She didn't want to compare them. But if she were comparing, JT would win, hands down. Ali moved her hand to JT's chest, cupping one of her breasts and letting her thumb trace JT's hardened nipple. Even through her shirt and flannel, Ali could feel it, hard and sensitive. JT sucked a breath through her teeth when Ali ran her thumb back and forth across it.

"Ali," JT growled. The rumble of her voice shot straight to Ali's core.

She was already so wet but hearing JT so turned on was unbearable. She felt powerful and she fucking loved it. This woman who she had known her whole life and who was now an international hockey star with a gold medal and possibly the kindest heart she'd ever known, was in her kitchen with her hands all over her and Ali was loving every second of it.

She took her other hand out of JT's hair and grabbed her ass. Holy hell. JT arched into her and Ali let her head fall back against the cabinet. JT looked down at her, her pupils dark, her breath ragged. She leaned forward and nipped at Ali's swollen bottom lip, taking it between her teeth and tugging. It didn't hurt but made Ali want that mouth on her skin.

As if reading her mind, JT pressed kisses across her neck and pulled her sweater to the side to allow access to Ali's collar bones. She ran her tongue along the length of her clavicle. Ali squeezed her legs together, or tried to, but squeezing them around JT only made her want more.

"JT, hold on." Ali ripped off her sweater and shirt and threw them across the kitchen. This was a mess she was happy to make.

JT leaned down farther, tugged Ali's bra to the side and devoured Ali's nipple, her tongue flicking over it, her lips sucking until Ali thought she might black out. She pushed JT's flannel off her shoulders and made a noise she hoped JT would understand as *Take off your shirt*. JT laughed, her mouth vibrating against Ali's skin, before stripping her shirt off and leaving her in a sports bra and jeans.

"You can't be real," Ali said, her fingers gripping JT's abs. "Your body is like a freaking superhero."

JT laughed and brought her mouth to Ali's belly, placing kisses ever closer to the top of her jeans. "Nothing super, I promise." She ran her tongue over Ali's hip bones. "I want to taste you. Can I do that?"

Ali laughed. "You can do anything you want to me. Just make me come."

JT unzipped Ali's pants, slowly tugging them off her ass before she knelt on the floor and pulled them off completely. "You okay up there?"

Ali nodded, suddenly feeling a little chilly and exposed. JT handed her the flannel she'd recently removed. She waited for Ali to slide it on, leaving it open across her chest while JT ran her tongue the length of Ali's leg from ankle to thigh. Ali shuddered. It felt so good, but she was squirming with impatience.

JT smiled up at her. "I want to make you feel so good."

"You do, but I'm fucking dying. Please. Touch me or I'm going to explode."

JT slid her fingers into Ali's underpants and moaned. "Fuck, you're wet." She waited a moment, looking up at Ali from where she knelt between her legs. "Tell me what you like."

Ali rested her head on the cabinet behind her and let out a sigh. She stared at the ceiling, not sure how to explain what she was feeling or what she wanted. Her body screamed for JT but her head was having a little freakout over such a simple question.

"I don't know." She said it quietly, not looking at JT. She swallowed and forced herself to look down. "Kyle wasn't very good at getting me off."

JT stood up and wrapped Ali in a hug. She placed gentle kisses on her cheek and whispered in her ear. "I'm sorry. That's super shitty. I swear to god I'm going to make you come if it takes all week." She leaned back and searched Ali's face. "All you have to do is tell me when I'm doing something that you like, okay?"

Ali smiled, her heart pounding. JT hadn't laughed at her. She hadn't made her feel bad or embarrassed. Something about her gentle confidence made Ali melt even more. "You'd do that for me?"

JT nodded. "I'm very coachable."

"Well, then. Show me what you got, Coxie."

Chapter Twenty-Eight

JT tried not to get distracted by her homicidal thoughts toward Kyle. He and Ali had been together for like a decade and that motherfucker hadn't been making this woman, this absolute goddess, come regularly? What a jackass.

JT focused on one thing and one thing only: making sure Ali had an amazing time. "If it feels good, let me know, and if I do something you don't like, tell me and I'll stop. Okay?"

Ali nodded, her face flushed, JT's flannel dropping open, exposing Ali's torso. JT couldn't get enough of looking at her soft belly, her perfect breasts, her delicious nipples. JT began again, slowly, trying to bring Ali back to the place where she was begging for JT to touch her. It didn't take long.

As she placed a line of kisses down past Ali's belly button to the top of her underpants, Ali's hips thrust up toward JT's face. Fuck yes. JT made eye contact with Ali as she pulled her underpants down enough to expose her hip bones. "This okay?"

Ali nodded. "Yes," she breathed.

JT placed a gentle bite on Ali's hip bones and smoothed it with the flat of her tongue. Ali bucked again. JT smiled and repeated the action until Ali was panting and pulling at her hair.

"JT, please. Stop teasing me."

JT hooked her fingers in the elastic and tugged Ali's underwear off. She let her tongue wander from her hip bones closer and closer to Ali's core. JT relished the way Ali's body reacted, the way her thighs clenched, the sounds that came with her ragged breathing.

JT knelt on the floor. Sure, it was hard as hell on her knees, but she would stay there all night if that was how long it took to make Ali lose control. She ran her tongue up the inside of Ali's thigh before flattening it across Ali's clit.

"Fuck," Ali husked as her hips moved against JT's mouth.

JT used her hands to hold Ali against her, her fingers splayed across Ali's ass, gripping it tighter and tighter. As she sucked and licked, Ali moved harder against her. Her breath grew more ragged, and JT was more and more turned on from the sounds coming from Ali's mouth.

"Don't stop. I'm almost there," Ali panted.

JT hummed in response. Ali's breathing changed and JT sucked harder while pressing her tongue against Ali. In an instant, Ali tensed and then released, her body relaxing as she let out a string of expletives. It was super hot.

JT relaxed, sitting on her heels to take some of the pressure off her knees, which she now noticed were screaming at her. Ali's floor wasn't soft or forgiving, and JT was sure she'd have bruises on her knees in the morning. She didn't care. It was worth every ache.

JT rubbed her hands over Ali's legs, which were chilly under the heat of her palms. "You're cold."

Ali smiled down at her, looking blissfully happy. "Then come warm me up."

JT stood and wrapped her arms around Ali. Ali's bare chest against her skin threatened to turn a sweet hug into JT wanting more. She told herself to relax, she wasn't going to rush Ali into anything more. No matter how much she was dying to have Ali's hands on her. She could wait. She *would* wait. Ali deserved to enjoy what they'd done without thinking for one second about JT's wants.

"My ass is numb," Ali said with a giggle. "I think the counter put it to sleep and now I can't feel it."

JT looked down. "We can't have that." She scooped Ali off the counter and held her as she walked them through Ali's house. "Where to?"

Ali nodded in the direction of the living room. "Couch. I hate that thing, but I think knowing you carried me to it like some hot firefighter might make me hate it a lot less."

JT maneuvered through the few boxes remaining in the room and gently put Ali on the couch. "Blankets?"

Ali pointed to an ottoman, fake leather with cracks all over the top. JT pulled the top off to find a soft fleecy blanket she used to cover Ali. "Better?"

Ali gave her a sleepy, satisfied smile. "Literally never been better in my life. You're really fucking good at that."

JT blushed but didn't take her eyes off Ali. "I do my best." She shivered and realized she'd left her T-shirt in the kitchen.

"Come in here with me," Ali said, holding up the blanket.

JT looked at the couch and shook her head. "I'm too big."

Ali shook her head. "Don't be silly. I want you in here with me." She scooted to one side, leaving a sliver of couch.

JT let her hand rest on Ali's cheek. "You underestimate my sheer massiveness. There's no way I can fit there without squishing you."

Ali tugged at JT's belt. "Are you always this difficult when a hot, naked woman asks you to come lie on top of her?"

JT knew she was blushing. Her face was on fire even with the top half of her body exposed to the chill. She took a deep breath. She crouched next to the couch. "Fine, but if you're getting smashed, you have to promise to tell me."

"Get in, Cox."

JT did as she was told, and lay next to Ali, with one leg barely on the couch. She was not going to hurt this woman. Even if it meant falling off the couch or freezing her ass off.

Ali immediately wrapped her in the blanket with her and kissed the tip of JT's nose. "So, that was amazing."

JT couldn't stop the grin on her face, not that she wanted to. Okay, maybe part of her wanted to play it cool but too much of her was giddy from the fact that she'd just had sex with Ali Porter, her all-time dream girl and first devastating crush.

"Do you need anything? Water? A snack?"

Ali shook her head. "You're very sweet but right now all I want is you."

JT protested. "It's okay. I'm fine."

"Shut up and let me touch you."

Electricity shot through JT when Ali grabbed her ass. She was trying to keep the focus on Ali but it was getting harder to concentrate on what Ali might need when all the blood in her body was rushing to her center.

Ali kissed her, her tongue sliding into JT's mouth and teasing her. Her hands raked down JT's stomach, bumping over each set of ab muscles as she worked her way to her jeans. "May I?" Ali whispered into JT's mouth.

JT nodded. "But you don't have to if you don't want. I'm—"

"I have been wanting to fuck you since you sat across from me at the bar. Please don't make me wait any longer."

"Okay," JT said, her voice rough with want.

Ali undid her belt and moved to unzip her jeans, but JT got there first and pulled them off, leaving her in her underwear and sports bra. Lying face-to-face on a narrow couch made it really awkward for Ali to touch her, so she spun JT around, so they were spooning. Ali reached under JT's bra and wiggled it up and off to give her access to JT's chest. JT arched her back, sending her ass to press against Ali.

Their bare skin together burned as JT reached behind her

to pull Ali into her. Ali responded by moving her hips against JT's ass as her fingers flicked across JT's stiff nipples.

"Ali, holy fuck."

Ali's hand moved lower until she paused at the waistband of JTs underwear.

"Ali, I swear to god. Touch me."

Ali laughed. Her fingers found JT soaking wet. Ali sucked in a breath. Her hips bucked into JT from behind causing her to arch back into the pressure. Ali's fingers slid along JT's slick folds, moving slowly but with urgent pressure. They rocked together, Ali's hips coming forward into JT's ass and JT pressing back against her, and Ali's fingers worked JT into a frenzy.

"Fuck, Ali. I'm so close," JT said between raspy breaths. "Don't stop."

Ali didn't until JT came hard and shuddering against her fingers. Then she let her fingers ride out JT's delicious aftershocks and then wrapped her arms and a leg around JT. Ali held her from behind like the sweetest, hottest spoon on the planet.

JT rolled toward her, bringing their faces back to being mere inches apart. "Okay, that was fucking hot."

Ali beamed. "Yeah?"

JT leaned her forehead against Ali's. "Either you had a lot of girlfriends during your time after Kyle or you're a natural, because damn, Porter."

Ali let her head fall against the couch. "I was nervous."

JT adjusted her position on the couch, nearly falling off in the process, so she could look down at Ali. "You didn't seem nervous when you told me to fuck you," JT said with a wicked grin. "But I'm sorry if I make you nervous. You don't need to be nervous around me, ever." She kissed Ali on the cheek, then the tip of her nose, then quickly on her lips.

Ali smiled and ducked her head into the crook of JT's neck. JT felt her lips against her skin as Ali placed sweet, delicate kisses.

JT sighed. She could so easily fall asleep here. It would be so easy to spend the night wrapped around Ali. But then there would be questions she wasn't sure she wanted to answer. She looked over Ali's head to the clock propped on some boxes. Shit.

"I'm sorry to do this, but I think I better go home, unless you want me to have to explain to my parents where I was all night." She threaded her fingers with Ali's. "I wouldn't mind letting them know I got to have sex with the hottest woman in the state, but you might not want your business out there like that."

Ali sighed. "When you put it that way, I don't really want to have my run-ins with your mom being any more awkward than they already are. And I think if she knows I was busy fucking her daughter, things might get super weird."

JT laughed at the thought. Her mom wasn't a prude. They'd been looking at classical art, much of it nudes, for her whole life. Her mom was never weird about the human body or sexuality. But how she would feel about JT and Ali, she was less sure. It wasn't a problem for them that JT was gay. It might raise an eyebrow—momentarily—for them to learn Ali was also interested in women after having been married to Kyle for years. But her parents would shrug that off. But none of that meant Ali, or JT, wanted the awkwardness of running into either of their parents at the supermarket or the post office with them knowing about this.

JT kissed her on her way to put her clothes on. "If they ask, I can say I was helping you with some boxes."

Ali cackled and gave her a wicked smile. "Yeah, you go ahead and tell her you were helping me with my box."

JT blushed crimson and stammered an explanation before giving up. "I will not be saying the word *box* to my family for the rest of my life." She leaned down and placed a kiss on Ali's lips. "See you tomorrow?"

Ali nodded and watched JT leave. She knew JT had to go

home, but that didn't stop her from wishing they could have spent the night wrapped up in each other. She rolled onto her back and stared at the ceiling reliving every kiss, every touch. Although if JT had stayed, she wasn't sure either of them would've slept at all...

Chapter Twenty-Nine

Emerson and Clark were sitting in the kitchen when JT got back to the house. She reached for the leash but Emerson stopped her.

"We took her for a walk when we got home. Hope you don't mind. Brooke wants a dog so badly so we borrowed her for a test drive."

JT hung up her coat and leaned against the counter. "Thanks for walking her. I'm sure she loved it. What's the verdict? Is Brookie getting a puppy?"

Clark laughed. "Not yet. A toddler is enough of a handful for now. Can you imagine her with a puppy? Adorable but pure mischief."

"So, I figured you two would be out celebrating your big win. Did you shame Beth and Jonathan into going to bed early?" She checked her watch. It wasn't even eight.

Emerson looked at Clark before responding. "No. Mom and Dad were being so weird, we didn't want to go out with them."

JT waited for her to explain more.

Emerson sighed. "I don't want to sound ungrateful, but they're so over the top about the stupidest things. This is a small-town holiday contest and they're talking about how they can see that our 'work' derived from great art movements. I'm like, 'Mom, it's candy and icing.'"

JT laughed. "Can I be here when you tell her that? It can be my birthday present for the next decade." JT couldn't believe that her sister was complaining about the things her parents did that drove JT crazy, too. She always thought Emerson and Jonathan basked in the attention.

"You think it's weird, too?" Clark asked.

"Of course I do. Imagine what it's like to be me—with zero artistic talent—in a family where that is the one thing that matters."

"But you're a superstar," Emerson said, like she'd never considered how much this might bother JT.

"No, you and Jonathan are superstars. I'm your artistically inept little sister who plays sports." JT hadn't meant for her voice to sound angry, or for her words to come out with such force, but it was hard to talk about this without the hurt creeping in.

Emerson pushed her chair away from the table, walked across the kitchen and gave JT a hug. She was tiny next to JT. JT was almost six feet tall and built for power and speed, while Emerson was barely five foot five and slight. Even though she was five years older, people sometimes thought she was JT's younger sister based on the size difference alone.

She squeezed JT tight and muttered an apology into her shoulder. "I didn't think you cared. You're always rolling your eyes at them, and I thought you had an okay relationship with their bullshit."

JT nodded. "I'm doing my best to let it go, but it's hard when all they care about is your career and Jonathan's and they act like the Olympics were some cute thing they could skip to see museums and Jonathan's show. Not like the culmination of all my hard work and the hours they spent driving me to rinks."

Clark walked over. "Can I join?"

JT laughed and opened her arms. He joined the hug. He

wasn't a big guy. Taller and bigger than Emerson but that wasn't saying much.

"I'm sorry, JT. Being in the Olympics, everything you've accomplished as an athlete, it's amazing."

Emerson stepped out of the hug. "You took the boys' team to the state championships in high school. Do you have any clue how badass that is?"

JT shrugged. "I think I'm really fucking badass but...imagine if you were like this art show is the best thing I have ever done. I have worked so hard to get here and then Mom and Dad missed it because they wanted to go to a Red Sox game or something." JT paused. "I know that's not fair. But they skipped my gold medal game to make it back for Jonathan's show. That thing was going to be open for months! My game was only a few hours long!" Her voice cracked with emotion, and she fought to get back under control. "Look, it's fine. But it wears on me, you know?"

Clark and Emerson shared a look. "I'm sorry that my pergola brought out the worst in them today," Clark said.

Emerson bumped him with her hip, but JT laughed. "Clark, never apologize for your truly majestic pergola. It looked amazing and delicious and I would have taken a giant bite out of it if we'd been allowed to sabotage our competitors."

He laughed. "I don't know how good it tasted after I slathered all that icing on it. But for what it's worth, Em and I tell everyone we know that her sister and my sister-in-law is a gold medalist. Even if your parents are...whatever, we're super proud of you."

Emerson squeezed her arm. "What he said. And also, we had to win tonight because you're going to kick everyone's ass in the human dogsled." She looked at Clark. "I mean, do you think this guy is going to be able to pull me around that track very fast?"

Clark feigned indignation. "Wow, way to assume I'd be the

one pulling. I was planning to lounge in the sled while you showed off those running skills you were bragging about the other day."

Emerson made a face. "Can your fragile male ego handle being the one in the sled when all the other pullers are dudes?"

"Ahem? Did you forget about me?"

Emerson shook her head. "You're not a dude, obviously, but you're the biggest stud athlete this town has ever seen. You're in a category all your own. Honestly, they should give you a time penalty to even out the field."

"Like they gave you and Jonathan a disadvantage in the contest today? I don't think so. If you get to use your professional art skills, I get to use my speed and power. May the best sled puller win."

After another hug, Clark and Emerson said good-night, and JT spent a few minutes sitting with Toby and giving her belly rubs before going to her "room" in the cellar. She was struck, again, by the glamour of her current surroundings. It was annoying when she was going be there for maybe two or three nights but agreeing to the contest meant staying longer and her parents had made no move to upgrade her accommodations.

But the couch and the cobwebs in the corners of the cellar couldn't dent her happiness when her thoughts drifted back to Ali. The way she sounded, the way she tasted, the way she wrapped herself around JT. Every bit of it brought her so much happiness that it felt like her chest was filled with sunshine.

There was clearly no way this was going to last. Not as long as Ali lived in Hart's Landing and JT lived anywhere but Hart's Landing. JT was set to play professional hockey for any team that wasn't in Boston. She didn't have anything against the city, but it would be much better to play in Minnesota or Montreal if it meant not feeling like she should check the stands for the family who would never come.

But now this thing with Ali, whatever it was, made her question if maybe it would be good to be close to Hart's. Maybe if she were nearby, that hot blonde woman would come watch her play. She drifted off to sleep thinking of the way it would feel to look up and see Ali waving at her and, even better, what it would be like to have Ali waiting to take her home afterward.

Chapter Thirty

The next morning Ali woke up feeling amazing. She'd slept like a rock after the best sex she could ever remember having. When she'd dragged herself off the couch and up to her bedroom, she'd spent an hour wide awake thinking about JT telling her how unappreciated she felt and planning how she could change that.

She double-checked the calendar while she waited for her coffee to brew and made a few calls to some of her teacher friends to see if they could make her plan work on short notice.

After five years of always saying yes to every request for help, every time her principal asked someone to volunteer, and taking every crappy chaperoning job known to the world of Hart's Landing High School, she had enough goodwill that folks were thrilled to make her vision happen, even with less than half a day to prepare.

Next, she called Tommy and, after yelling at him for a solid ten minutes, told him what he needed to do to get back into her good graces and make it up to JT. He agreed immediately.

"I'll make sure she's there," he said. "I promise."

The only thing she was unsure about was JT's family. A big part of her wanted to invite them, to give them a chance to show up this time for their daughter. But, in the end, she decided against it. The possibility that they would let JT down again was too much. This was JT's day and Ali wasn't going to give anyone a chance to ruin it.

Ali spent the rest of the morning running errands to get everything they needed to make her plan a success. She stopped by the venue two hours early to talk to the guy in charge.

"You want me to take that down?"

Ali nodded. "Yeah, I need you to take it down so we can do a ceremony and put it back up."

Charlie, the rink manager, Zamboni driver and "ice guy," rubbed the stubble on his chin. "What's all this for?"

Ali smiled. "You know why we have that banner in the first place?"

Charlie nodded slowly. "Yeah. But I don't get why I have to take it down just to put it back up. You know that's stupid and a pain in the ass, right?"

"How about we don't take it down but just cover it? Then we can take off the cover during the ceremony."

"That sounds good. I have some tarps in the back that should do the trick."

"Thanks."

Charlie cocked his head and squinted at the banner hanging on the wall. "You do know it's really high up there."

"Mmm-hmm. That's why Jill is going to bring over the lift we have at the high school. No one has to get on a ladder, just the lift. Easy peasy."

"Lemon squeezy," Charlie said without thinking. Then he blushed. "Damn, my kid says that. Fine. I can do all that. The free skate guys have a Spotify account if you want music or anything like that."

Ali made a note on her phone. "Good idea. Thanks, Charlie. See you in about an hour, okay?"

As Ali walked to the parking lot, a busload of teens arrived carrying massive bags of equipment. Ali spotted their coach and ran through the plan. The coach, a gruff sweetheart of a man named Ben, nodded along.

"The girls are super excited. They loved the idea when I told them. This is going to be great. Think JT will stick around to watch us play?"

Ali considered the possibility that this could all go horribly wrong. But she wouldn't let it.

"I'm sure she will."

Ali mentally added to her list to figure out a way to make sure JT wanted to stay for the game. Hopefully, the rest of her plan would go so well JT would be happy to stick around. Otherwise Ali was going to need to improvise.

Ali checked her texts. The group chat she had going with her teacher friends was a steady stream of people telling her who they'd convinced to show up and what they were bringing. The school administrator had gotten permission to use the school email lists to send a message to all the parents in town about the game. The head of the PTO had posted about it all over social media, including in all the parent groups. Maybe they would pull this off after all. She took a minute to chastise herself for not coming up with this plan with more than a few hours to make it work, but then moved on. No time to dwell on it. She had streamers to hang and T-shirts to pick up from the guy in town who owned a custom printing place. She was going to owe him big-time.

She hopped in her car and drove through town as quickly as she dared. When she arrived at the shop, Greg was waiting for her with two giant boxes.

"If you pop your trunk I'll load them up for you."

Ali shoved a few bags to the side to make room and let him drop the boxes in the car. "I can't thank you enough for this, Greg. I know it was a bonkers request and I appreciate it so much that you could make this happen."

Greg paused with his hands in his jacket pockets. "I told you I'd do anything to repay what you did for my kids. They're both in college now and doing great." He scuffed his boot over the gravel driveway. "If I'd had more time with the shirts…"

Ali shook her head. "I called you like four hours ago. This is amazing. I hope you'll come to the rink to see your handiwork in person."

He nodded, a small smile playing at the corner of his mouth. "I'll do my best. The kids are home but maybe they'll come with me if they know you organized all this."

Ali drove back to the rink, her mind racing with all the things she needed to do.

She had just pulled into the rink parking lot when Tommy texted her to say he would be arriving with JT in ten minutes.

Ali rushed to unload the box of T-shirts onto a table one of the parents had brought for a bake sale but agreed to share with her.

"Miss Porter, over here! Maddy is so excited that she is going to get to meet JT! She could barely contain herself. I told her to get her head in the game."

Ali smiled. "Thank you so much. Please call me Ali." She set out the shirts in piles. "Can you help me hand these out to people as they come in?"

The moms nodded vigorously. "Can we have one?"

"Of course! I was hoping we could get everyone wearing them, but I don't know if I have enough."

Ali had already put one of the blue-and-yellow shirts on. It had "Hart's Landing Loves Our Olympian!" on it with JT's number on the front. She handed shirts to the moms and busied herself with any last-minute things she could think of to burn off her nervous energy.

Townspeople filed into the rink and grabbed shirts along

the way. Aside from a couple of confused people, everyone was there to see JT and was excited to put the shirts on.

"Thank you for coming early! Be sure to cheer loud!" Ali called after them as they found seats on the bleachers in the rink. The closer it got to the ceremony, the more nervous Ali got.

What if JT wasn't happy with all this nonsense? What if she didn't want all this attention? After last night, Ali felt like she needed to make JT understand that even if her parents didn't get it, everyone else was so proud of everything she accomplished.

Ali had a vague understanding of JT's complicated relationship with the town and her time living there. She made a mental note to ask JT about it later, and she hoped that maybe JT would be able to change that a little bit. Even if all she could do was adjust the story in her mind about how the town felt about her now, even if people had sucked when she was a kid.

That was a lot to ask of a fifteen-minute ceremony. But Ali wanted to try. JT made her want to try, and that was something new.

After Kyle, she'd had a while where she wondered if any of what she did mattered. She'd been a good wife, at least she thought she had, and it hadn't been enough for her. She was a good teacher, that she knew for certain, but she wondered if all of her going above and beyond for her students mattered. Or if it mattered enough. Because there was always another kid who would need her, and as much as she relished being needed, she wondered if there ever was a time when the needs would be smaller, less acute, or if she was one person trying to stem an impossible tide.

Ali's phone buzzed in her back pocket. A text from Tommy.

In the parking lot. Coming in now.

"She's coming!" Ali squealed. The moms at the table went into a flurry of activity. Ali was a little embarrassed by the way she'd shouted, but it was important they got this right. She scurried to the door and opened it as JT approached. JT looked at Tommy when Ali opened the door.

"Hi? What's going on?" JT hovered by the door, seemingly unsure if she wanted to come in,

Ali pulled open her coat, revealing the T-shirt she and the other moms were all wearing. "Surprise! It's JT Cox day at the rink!"

JT stepped inside. "I'm sorry, what are you talking about?"

Ali waved her arm toward the women working the bake sale booth. "We're celebrating you today! Surprise!" Ali smiled, but the longer she waited for a response the more unsure she was.

JT smiled at the mom and pulled Ali aside. "Ali, what is going on? It's not JT Cox day. What are you doing?"

Ali's smile faltered. "Everyone wanted to celebrate you, but you're not home very often so I took a chance that we could pull this off today. It's the only game the girls have while you're home…" Ali had a terrible sinking feeling in her gut. JT did not look pleased, and Ali was starting to see that this surprise might be a total disaster.

Chapter Thirty-One

Starting with Tommy coming to her house to pick her up, JT felt unsettled. He apologized thoroughly for being a tool about her and Ali, but JT couldn't tell why he was lingering at her house. He asked her to come to the girls' hockey game with him. She agreed even though she wasn't sure how she'd feel walking into the rink and watching a girls' team that didn't exist when she was in high school.

On the one hand she was thrilled for the girls. It had to be easier to play on a team of girls than to do the combat it took to get a spot on the boys' team the way she'd had to do. But all that fighting and scraping to get her roster spot only to suffer ugly cheers and sexist and homophobic behavior from opposing fans (as well as a few from her own town) left her with a lot of conflicting feelings about her high school hockey career. She didn't know what emotions to expect when she walked into the rink.

Her senior year, she'd been voted captain by her teammates, and she'd led the team to the state championship. But they never had a ceremony for the state championship banner. Or, more accurately, they didn't have her at the ceremony. She'd been invited, they hadn't been that cruel, but they'd made no effort to accommodate her college hockey schedule. So, she'd missed it. And she hadn't returned to the rink since then. It was too painful.

So when she saw where they were, she was flooded with anxiety and discomfort. "Tommy, what's going on?"

He put a hand on her shoulder. "I promise it will be good."

JT didn't feel like his promises were worth a hell of a lot at the moment, but she walked into the rink lobby anyway. She was transported by the smell, a mix of the scents of the rubber floor mats, sweat, and whatever they were heating up in the snack bar. When Ali met her at the door, she got suspicious and her emotions threatened to overwhelm her.

"Ali, what is going on?"

Ali showed her the T-shirt she was wearing. "It's your day!"

After asking Ali what was going on, she allowed Ali to bring her into the rink, mostly out of politeness and a desire not to cause a fuss.

"Ali, really, what is all of this?"

Ali looked scared for a fleeting second. "Everyone in this town is proud of you. And we all wanted to show it. So, I asked around, and we made today's game the JT Cox game and, well, come with me."

Ali pulled JT by the arm to the glass doors leading to the rink. "See?"

JT peered through and saw the stands full of people in blue T-shirts with her name and jersey number on them. She looked to the end of the rink where the banners hung and saw one covered in a tarp.

"It's not perfect, but we want to give you the recognition you deserve. Is that okay?"

JT's eyes hurt from the pressure of the tears that surprised her by appearing. She looked at the stands. She didn't know most of the people. There were a few familiar faces, but so many people she didn't know or didn't recognize anymore. She didn't know what to say to Ali. She felt anger and anxiety, and she couldn't tell where one ended and the other started. She was angry to have been tricked into this, and anxious that she'd had no time to prepare, and angry that Ali had done all this without asking, and so scared it would go horribly and she would embarrass herself in front of most of the town.

When she'd been on the team, people had laughed and pointed and yelled rude things. She'd hated it. She'd played through it because she'd wanted to prove them wrong and because she loved playing more than anything else in the world. That spite, her all-consuming drive to prove them wrong, had gotten her all the way to the gold medal stand at the Olympics. And now this town that had been so cruel wanted to celebrate her? Fuck that. For a second, she thought about running out of there.

But then she looked at Ali, whose face was all concern for her, and who had the kindest eyes JT had ever seen, and she let herself relax for a second and let herself believe that this time it would be different. So, instead of running, she did the brave thing and opened the door.

Ali led her to the door to the ice. "I'm sorry if you hate me for all of this, but please give it a try."

JT clenched her jaw and shoved her hands in the pockets of her coat.

Ali waved to someone and music started playing. It was the Olympic theme, the song she used to sing at the top of her lungs when she was a kid dreaming of making the team. It never failed to make her emotional. But that was only the beginning. Once the music started, the crowd erupted. They screamed their cheers and chanted her name. She heard loud whistles and screams and the squeals of little girls wearing her jersey. It was too much.

She waved and let Ali lead her onto the ice, where her old coach, Mr. Hannings, was standing on the center dot waiting for her. "What are you doing here?" She hugged him, not realizing until she saw him how much she'd missed him. Mr. Hannings had been her coach for four years. He'd been the one to take a chance on putting a girl on the boys' team, and he'd done what he could to protect her, even getting thrown out of a game for screaming at the refs for failing to call penalties when the other team took cheap shots at her. Seeing him brought a wave of emotions.

He smiled. "Waiting for you. I didn't realize old age would make you so damn slow. You know I have a game to coach after this, right?"

JT laughed. His voice, gravelly from years of yelling on the bench, was still the same. Still rough and easy to mistake for harsh, but he was an absolute marshmallow of a man who cared for his players more than he cared about winning.

"Since when do you coach girls?" she asked.

"You started it. Once I coached you, I thought, 'What am I doing coaching these boys?' As soon as they made a team, I told them I wanted to coach it."

JT looked around at the stands. People shouted louder. She gave a nervous wave. Was this really happening?

Ali handed her coach a mic.

"Good afternoon and welcome to the long-overdue JT Cox celebration! I am going to read off a bunch of JT's accomplishments in a second, but before I do, I want to say a few words about what an incredible player and person she is. When she came to try out for our team, I was skeptical. I wasn't sure what having a girl on the team would mean, but she showed me that having JT on the team would mean we were good for a change."

The crowd roared as JT laughed. The team hadn't been bad before she made it, but she appreciated the sentiment.

"From the beginning no one worked harder, played more shifts, or took more cheap shots from the other team and their fans. JT endured a lot over those four years." His voice softened. "I hope I helped, but I'm sure I didn't do nearly enough. JT took all of it with more courage and strength than folks twice her age. And in her senior year, she led our team to its first, and so far only, state championship."

JT's eyes were streaming now. She wiped at her cheeks, mad that she was crying in front of all these people.

Her coach clapped for her along with the screaming crowd. "Now, we should have had her here years ago for this, but she was too busy being the best damn hockey player ever to come out of the state of New Hampshire. So, to honor you, JT, we want to unveil the championship banner you brought to this team and this town and give you your due."

JT hadn't noticed, but Ali had made her way onto the lift at the end of the rink, and she and Charlie pulled down the tarp covering their banner. When it dropped to the floor of the lift, JT could see the words only through a curtain of tears. She never imagined this day, with this many people cheering for her, in this rink, all for playing on a team no one had seemed to want her to be on. She wiped her face and waved to the crowd as she tried to compose herself. Her coach gave her a hug.

"JT, I hope you'll come back to visit us again. We'd like to retire your jersey, but maybe we can give you a little more notice of that one."

JT nodded, completely overcome.

He handed her the mic and she laughed. "God, I don't know if I'm going to be able to talk. I can't put into words what this means to me. It wasn't always easy being the only girl in the league." She paused to collect herself. "But it was worth it. The support I got from coach and the guys on the team."

"Eventually," her coach said into the mic.

She laughed. "The guys were quicker to embrace me than you might have thought. But a lot of the teams we played weren't happy to see me. But being here, knowing that girls have a team of their own now, it makes me so happy. I hope some of these girls will be my teammates one day. It would be nice to have another kid from Hart's Landing out there with me. Thank you, everyone. This means the world to me."

After the ceremony, JT and her coach walked off the ice together. "You okay, kid?" he asked with his gruff voice.

"Yeah. I'm all right. This was really nice."

He nodded in Ali's direction. "She put it all together. You probably know this but when Ali Porter gets an idea in her head, you better get on board. She's only been at the school a little while, but we all figured that out."

JT smiled and tried to keep her feelings about Ali off her face.

"Something tells me you already knew that, though," he said with a gravelly laugh. "Stick around after the game if you can. I know my players will want to meet you and I want to hear where you're playing this season. I'll travel if I have to, but I hope you put in your preference for Boston."

JT had not, in fact, put in her preference for Boston. She didn't speak French, so she was hoping for New York or maybe Toronto. "I'm not sure how much pull I have, but as soon as I know where I'm playing, I'll let you know and get you a game schedule. If you ever want to come to a game, let me know and I'll be sure to leave tickets for you."

"I can buy my own damn ticket, JT."

She laughed. "I'm sure you can, Coach. But think of it as a long-overdue thank-you gift from me."

He patted her shoulder and walked toward the home team locker room. "You want to talk to the players?"

JT shook her head. "I would never want to deprive anyone of your trademark pep speeches." She cleared her throat and tried to lower her voice in imitation. "You've had a terrible week of practice and warm-ups looked embarrassing, but maybe you'll surprise me by not sucking today, boys."

He laughed. "I've mellowed. And I'm not that mean to the girls. They don't need it."

JT didn't stand alone for long once he left. She was swarmed by a team of girls, all wearing matching jerseys and asking her to sign them.

JT bent down and talked to each girl as the teams warmed up for the game in the background. There were a couple of kids who were clearly the ringleaders of the gaggle. JT asked them about their season and what positions they played. Once she'd signed their jerseys, a few of them skittered off to find their parents.

One girl lingered after the others had gone.

"Hi, what's your name?"

The girl smiled, showing a few missing front teeth. "Hazel."

"Nice to meet you. What position do you play?"

Hazel, wearing a very serious expression, said, "Goalie."

JT lit up. "You must be very brave! Do you like being goalie?"

"Not at first. I got stuck playing because no one else wanted to. But now I really like it. I never have to come off the ice. I get to play the whole game!"

JT nodded solemnly. "That's pretty great. I never want to get off the ice either. And you know, the goalie is the most important position."

Hazel shook her head. "The other kids say it's where they put kids who suck at everything else."

JT laughed. "Well, don't listen to them. It's where they put the smartest, bravest, quickest players. If anyone says otherwise, we'll know the truth."

Hazel narrowed her eyes and clutched the photocopied program for the game. "If it's the best position, how come you play forward?"

JT thought for a second. "I'm only pretty smart, and a little quick, and I'm not the bravest. So, I had to play somewhere else."

Hazel nodded like this made sense to her. "We watched you score in the Olympics. That was really cool."

JT grinned. "Thanks. The Olympics are cool, but so is being here. Thanks for coming over to say hi. I hope you'll come to one of my games this season if you can."

Hazel nodded and then hurried to catch up with her teammates. JT watched her. She wished she'd had that as a kid, a team full of other girls, instead of boys who were hit-or-miss and parents who often despised seeing her on the ice against their sons.

"Will you sign my program?"

JT turned to find Ali staring up at her with a pen clenched in her teeth, her lips curled into a smile around it. "For you? Of course." JT took the paper and waited for Ali to hand over the pen. "I can't believe you did all this." She blinked and stared at the paper. "I was scared when I walked in, but this is amazing. Thank you." JT's voice fell to a gruff whisper as her words trailed off.

Ali put her hand on JT's arm. "You deserve it. It shouldn't have taken this long to celebrate you but, honestly, you don't come home much."

JT sniffed. "Didn't have much reason to come home." She held Ali's eyes with hers, not saying the words in her head. Now she did have a reason. A reason who was only supposed to be a friend. A reason no one knew was more than that. A reason who JT knew never would be. Not as long as JT lived somewhere else and Ali lived in the cute house near the Coxes.

Chapter Thirty-Two

Ali wasn't a gambler. She thought it was stupid to risk losing something valuable for fun. But that didn't mean she didn't take chances on things that mattered. It had been a leap to divorce Kyle, to buy a house of her own, to stay in the town she'd grown up in even if it meant being haunted by her past at every turn. Taking a risk that JT would be angry with her or unhappy to have this surprise thrust on her was one of the bigger risks she'd ever taken. But seeing JT's face, her happy tears, and the dawning realization that the town she'd had a rocky relationship with was full of people who adored her was worth every minute of planning and worrying and calling in every favor she had in town.

"I hope you understand how much everyone here loves you." Ali said it before her brain could tell her to stop. She wasn't telling JT she loved her. That's not what this was. How could it be? They were something that wasn't quite friends but it wasn't love. That was silly. It had been a few days.

Well, a lifetime of knowing each other, and a few days of spending time together doing silly couple things. Before this week, her relationship with JT had been an add-on to JT's friendship with Tommy. Ali was like a free-gift-with-purchase who drove them around before they got their licenses and told them which high school teachers were mean and which ones were easy graders.

When Ali thought back, she didn't remember JT talking much around her, which made more sense now, knowing that JT had harbored a crush on Ali as a preteen. When she thought back on JT's shy smiles and small kindnesses—like bringing Ali ice cream when she and Tommy had gone out for cones— she saw the seedlings of the kind, thoughtful woman JT had become.

But that history and a few amazing days together couldn't be love. JT lived somewhere far away. And she might never live nearby, and Ali had her own complicated relationship with her mom and Kyle and the way the town expected her to be, but she loved it here. She'd come back because this town needed teachers who cared deeply about kids who grew up in all kinds of circumstances in rural New Hampshire. Kids who fit in and were prom queen and kids who barely made it to class because home was a disaster. Kids who fit nowhere but in her classroom and kids who didn't know who they were and kids who didn't know if they could be who they were in rural New Hampshire. Those were her kids. Every single one of them was a reason to stay even when Kyle's stupid face and her mom's stupid questions made her want to start over somewhere else. The kids kept her there.

"So, how many of these kids do you know?" JT asked, nodding toward the ice.

Ali smiled. "All of them, obviously. They aren't all in my classes but it's hard not to know the kids in a town this small. You know that."

JT smiled and watched warm-ups. "So, did you pick out a place for us to watch the game? And do they serve cocoa here?"

Ali tucked her arm through JT's. "I thought we could sit up

there so people can talk to you if they want to. And yes, they make terrible cocoa mix with hot water in the lobby."

"Marshmallows?"

Ali smiled. How was this woman so cute all the time? "Of course. The packets come with them, but those melt with the hot water. But if you play your cards right, I'll get the moms to hook us up."

"I'd like that. You know how I feel about marshmallows."

"After the first contest, I think I have a pretty good sense of your feelings about them."

JT took a step toward the stands, her foot paused on the first wooden bleacher. "What you don't know is I have a real soft spot for crappy rink cocoa. It tastes like my childhood. Of course, my tastes have gotten slightly more sophisticated. I appreciate bougie cocoa and fancy marshmallows, but there's something about a Swiss Miss packet and a scoop of grocery store marshmallows."

Ali followed JT to a space on the bleachers near the top. "You're a woman who appreciates the simple things."

JT stared at the ice. "I know what I like." She turned her head to look at Ali. "And when I find something I like, I stick with it."

"Oh yeah?"

JT nodded, a tiny smile playing at the corner of her lips. She didn't have a chance to say more because a gaggle of kids swarmed her and asked her to sign their shirts.

"Is this okay with your grown-ups? I don't want to get anyone in trouble for writing on your clothes." JT searched the stands to find the adults who were with the kids. She mimed writing in the air and got a round of thumbs-ups. "Okay, if your folks say it's fine. Why don't you all tell me your names."

It took the rest of warm-ups for her to sign and talk to all the kids. One girl, who had to be about five, sat next to her and stared up at her until all the other kids left. Only then did she speak.

"My name's Gretel and I love playing hockey but my brothers tell me I'm too little. But I don't care. I'm going to be big like you someday and then I'm going to beat them both." Her high voice was hard to understand because it was so squeaky, but JT followed every single word.

"You tell your brothers that it doesn't matter how big you are if you have enough heart. And I think you have plenty of heart, Gretel. If they don't let you play, you let me know and you can be on my team, okay?"

Gretel grinned and pushed a strand of hair out of her face. "Bye, JT. You're my favorite." She wrapped her arms around JT and gave her a tight hug before hopping off the seat and hurrying back to her family.

JT looked at Ali. "God, how do you deal with all these kids and not have you heart explode?"

Ali laughed. "For starters, I have the high schoolers who aren't so earnest or forthright. But some days it's hard not to explode. They're so amazing, even the real stinkers will usually have a moment now and again that makes you realize they're not totally rotten. The kids are the best thing about teaching."

"And the worst?"

Ali laughed. "Everything but the kids. Administration, lack of funding, living in a state that thinks education is unnecessary, the parents. But I still wouldn't trade it for another job. At least at this point. Talk to me in a decade."

JT nodded and watched the teams line up for a faceoff. "Hopefully, I have time to figure it out, but I will have to come up with a real job at some point." She watched the action on the ice. "Hey, these kids are good."

"You sound surprised."

"It wasn't that long ago that there was no girls' team at all."

Ali pointed to the banner. "Yeah, six years. But these girls always had someone to look up to. That can make a big difference, don't you think?"

JT blushed. Ali loved that she could do it so easily. "Come on. None of these kids knew who I was back then."

Ali waved her hand around the crowd. "See all those little girls who came up to you, they know who you are. Do you think these kids out there didn't? You were the captain of the boys' team and you won the state championship. Everyone knew who you were."

JT's expression darkened. No more cute blushing. "Yeah, I heard what everyone said about me back then." Her tone was hurt, bitter, nothing like the light banter they'd been having.

Ali leaned her shoulder against JT's. "Yeah, people around here sure can suck. But it's only been six years and anyone who didn't love you then, because they were too stupid or small-minded, they do now."

Before JT could acknowledge the sentiment, she leaped out of her seat and startled the crap out of Ali. The rink exploded in cheers. Hart's Landing had scored, and the girls on the ice mobbed the scorer before skating the length of the ice to tap gloves with the bench and then their own goalie. She turned to Ali and hugged her while lifting her off the stands.

Ali held on for dear life. JT gently put her down. "Sorry. But that was awesome!"

Ali sighed happily. She'd been to a lot of games over the years. Tommy and JT had been teammates in high school so her family always went to the games. Although, to be fair, Tommy had been on the third line and hadn't played nearly as much as JT. But he'd be the first to jump to her defense if the other team tried to take any cheap shots at her.

Ali thought warmly of her brother, who'd been capable, even as a teenager, of being proud of his best friend and not jealous of all the attention she got. He was her biggest fan. It was sweet. It made what he'd pulled the other night with her so much worse. Ali knew he'd been trying to protect her, but it still wasn't fair to JT.

"Hey, did my brother talk to you?" Ali nodded to the far side of the stands where Tommy was talking to someone Ali didn't recognize.

JT nodded. "Oh yeah. Grovel city. He apologized for like ten minutes before I cut him off." JT laughed and shook her head. "It was pretty pathetic. Did you scream at him or something?"

Ali shrugged. "Let's just say I was very clear about my thoughts and feelings about his behavior and I have every expectation that he will not disappoint me in the future."

JT's jaw dropped. "Oh my god, is that your teacher voice?" Ali saw her throat bob as she swallowed. "That was... Oh my god, I can't believe I'm hot for teacher, but damn, Porter."

Ali felt her face blush hot. "I can neither confirm nor deny but you better believe that if someone steps out of line in my classroom, I know how to deal with it."

Ali didn't have long to appreciate the lust in JT's eyes because she was interrupted by an unpleasant voice.

"Ali, was that ceremony your doing?" Kyle asked from a step below them. "So nice of you to help your new *friend* in such a public way." He raised his eyebrows in a way he probably thought looked cool, but instead he looked like a creep.

"Hi Kyle. Nice of you to stop by. I swear, any time I go anywhere in this town, there you are. Almost makes me wonder..." Ali said before returning her gaze to the game, hopefully giving him the hint to leave her alone.

"Funny how that happens in a town this small. How long are you sticking around for, Cox? I heard you hated it here."

JT gave him a bored expression, but Ali could tell it was fake. "I'm here for the rest of the contest, obviously." She looked at Ali. "But after that, who knows."

Ali watched Kyle's face change from cocky douche to shades

of anger. Thankfully, his date showed up and took his arm and greeted them both.

"My niece plays on varsity this year, so we thought we'd come cheer for her." She looked at JT. "She thinks you're the coolest. Would you sign my program for her?"

JT smiled. "Of course. That's so nice of you to say. What's her name?"

"Molly."

JT signed the program and handed it back to Sharon. "Here you go. But I'll be here until the end, so if she wants to come say hi, please tell her I'd love to meet her."

Kyle's gaze never left Ali. "We gotta go get some food before the rush between periods. Come on, Sharon."

They left but Ali seethed. "How on earth was I with that dipshit for a decade?"

JT didn't say anything. She leaned her weight against Ali's side. "I'm sure he wasn't such a jackass the whole time."

Ali considered her words. "Maybe. But he's always had that side to him. I wish I'd seen it sooner. Or that he'd pull that in front of my mom. Maybe then she'd stop trying to get us back together."

JT put an arm around Ali's shoulder. "I cannot wait to kick his ass in the dogsled. He's going to be such a shitty loser. Guys like that always are." She dropped her arm and Ali wished for it back. She missed the warmth and the feeling that someone was on her side. But looking around the rink, maybe it wasn't a terrible idea to keep things between them at least looking like they were only friends.

Ugh, she hated herself for thinking it. But it was so much less complicated if people didn't ask her a million invasive questions about them. She knew how it felt to have a town invested in her relationship, and it was nice to have whatever was going on with JT be only for the two of them. At least for now.

Chapter Thirty-Three

It was a beautiful, clear, sunny day for the human dogsled race. It was also fucking freezing, but JT was not about to let a little cold stop her from demolishing the competition. She might be terrible at icing and art and every delicate thing the contest had asked her to do, but she was going to crush this task.

There had been another fresh snowfall last night, so she checked how slippery and deep the snow was when she took Toby for her morning walk. The old snow packed pretty well but, because it was so cold, the new snow was really powdery and light. It kept getting blown around by the wind. She tried making snowballs to throw for Toby, but the snow just disappeared from her hands like a cloud.

She needed a plan for how to use the conditions. She'd been ready for packed snow that would be rock-hard and would make pulling the sled somewhat easy because it would glide over the snow. This powdery stuff was a different story.

She pulled out her snow boots and a pair of sneakers.

"It's freezing out there, Jasmine. You need boots."

JT sucked in a deep breath and willed herself not to yell at her mom at 7:00 a.m. "It is cold, but I don't know how I'm going to get any traction with these. Do you have those Yaktrax things? Can I borrow them?"

"Ask your father. My feet are too small. Wait, is this for the competition? We can't give you an advantage over your siblings."

Emerson wandered into the kitchen and headed straight for the coffeepot. "I think the advantage is that she's an Olympic gold medalist with muscles on top of her muscles and I'm an art prof. You could tie a stone to her back and she'd still kick our asses."

JT smiled. She wasn't sure she'd ever loved her sister as much as she did right then. Emerson waggled the coffeepot in JT's direction.

"Thanks, I'd love some."

Emerson handed her a cup. "You know, I'd wear boots if you can stand them. I think there are multiple heats, and if you wear sneakers your feet will be ice blocks. Actually, never mind. Maybe you should show up barefoot. That might give the rest of us a fighting chance."

"Are spikes off-limits?"

Emerson nodded. "Last year some dummy wiped out and cut himself with them. They changed the rules to try to keep anyone from needing stitches. I actually think it's more to ensure that everyone wipes out. The spectators like a good laugh."

JT felt stupid for not knowing the rules. She should have asked Ali or even her siblings. She hated feeling like she was the only one who didn't know something. It was how she felt at all her family dinners when the rest of the group started talking about museums and the shows currently touring the country. Half the time she didn't even know what city they were talking about because she didn't know all the museums by name.

"How did you know this?" JT asked with more annoyance creeping into her voice than she'd intended.

Emerson rolled her eyes. "It's on the contest website. Did you do zero research before signing up?"

"Whatever," JT said before slurping a too large sip of her too hot coffee and burning the shit out of her tongue. She made a strangled groaning noise in her throat and knew instantly that everything was going to taste like nothing for a few days. She was such a dumbass sometimes.

Emerson watched the entire display of impatience and petulance with an air of amusement. "Why are you so worked up over an event you know you're going to win? Jonathan and I are the ones who should be anxious. Our lack of athletic talent could end our time on *Survivor: Hart's Landing Edition*."

JT shook her head. "I don't know. I suck at the delicate little tasks that you guys are good at. This feels like my only shot to contribute, you know?"

Emerson sipped her coffee while keeping her eyes on JT. "You really like this woman, don't you?"

JT jerked her head up, spilling coffee on her shirt. "What? No. Who told you that?"

Emerson laughed. "Oh my god, you've got it bad. I thought you were just having a little fling or something, but this makes so much more sense. If it was just a fling you wouldn't be over there at seven a.m. to put her furniture together or whatever you claim you're doing."

JT scowled. "Are you saying you don't think I would go help someone unpack and fix up their house if I wasn't getting something in return? That's what you think of me?"

Emerson shook her head. "No, I'm saying I think you've had a crush on Tommy's big sister since you first discovered girls and it makes sense that if you got the chance to date her or whatever you claim you're doing, you'd take it. Hell, if I were single and my first and best crush walked in and asked for my help, I probably wouldn't say no."

JT shrugged. "I don't really know what this is but it's fun and I like her."

Emerson pushed herself away from the counter and walked toward the door. "Anyone who organizes an entire event to celebrate you as the badass hockey player you are is all right with me."

JT smiled. "You heard about that?"

"Yeah. After the fact, or we would have been there. But I get why she didn't tell us. Maybe if they do another one, we can all go."

Once she was gone, JT wandered down to the basement to get dressed for the event. It was cold outside but she didn't want to wear so many layers that she wouldn't be able to run. If the price for winning was a little cold, she could handle it.

She settled on her team warm-up pants over a pair of leggings and several layers on top. That way she could easily take them off if it got warmer or if the "dogsled" rigging was bulky or annoying. She left for Ali's house half an hour before they needed to be on the green and was greeted with a sweet kiss and a mug of cocoa.

"Rumor has it you like cheap cocoa and marshmallows."

JT grinned and took a sip of cocoa out of the cap of the thermos. "I do, but this is not the cheap shit. You made the good stuff."

Ali looked proud. "Yes. I tried to re-create the kind we made in the first contest. But I made sure to get the tiny marshmallows you like from the supermarket. Those things were on sale so I promise there's nothing bougie about them."

When JT kissed her, Ali tasted like cocoa and sugar with just a hint of vanilla. "This was so nice of you. And probably necessary since it's like ten below out there."

Ali made a face. "I think you've gotten soft, Cox. It's in the twenties. It's barely below freezing, let alone below zero."

JT pulled out her phone to check. "You're right. In my defense it was colder earlier when I took Toby out."

"Mmm-hmm." Ali didn't sound convinced, but her sexy smile was worth the skepticism.

JT drank the rest of the cocoa and then handed the cap back to Ali. "Ready to go?"

Ali nodded. "The car is all warmed up, so your muscles will be ready to go when we get there. Can't have the Olympian pulling something in our little town contest."

JT laughed but nodded. "Getting injured because I tried too hard in the human dogsled race is definitely something I would do. And then my teammates would tease me about it forever."

Ali climbed into the driver's seat. "Teammates, huh? Does that mean you know where you're playing next season? Your fans are curious. They have merch to buy and jerseys to wear in your honor."

JT looked at the footwell. "Uh, no. I don't know where I'm going to be next year. The league is so new they're figuring out how to divide the national team players to make the teams as equal as possible."

JT could feel Ali looking at her. She braced for the question she didn't want to answer. But Ali let her off the hook.

"Well, I hope it's somewhere close by, but even if it's not, I'll figure out how to watch all your games."

"Thanks," JT said, her voice low. How could she ask the league to put her on a team far away from Ali? But they weren't exactly serious enough that she should be asking for a spot close to home. They were just messing around, right? Asking for a different team when they were basically friends with benefits was insane. Ali would think she was a weirdo clinger for sure.

JT watched Ali's face as she drove. She really liked that face and Ali's laugh and this time together. But Ali wasn't serious about her—how could she be? No one was ever serious about

JT. She was fun, that was it. Good for a laugh and a short-term thing, nothing more.

As they drove to town, JT stared out at the beautiful scenery with the snow dusted on the trees, fence posts and houses. When they got to the center of town, the green was set up with flags and barriers denoting the sled track. A couple volunteers had set up a table by the bandstand with coffeepots and carafes that steamed in the cold.

Ali parked in one of the designated spots for contest participants. "This is a nice touch. Although I'm not sure how many people are going to brave these 'subzero' temps to watch us be silly in the snow." Ali grinned at her.

"It's cold out! You sound like a Boomer telling me how much colder it was in your day."

Ali laughed. "God, it's too easy to tweak you."

JT crossed her arms over her chest and faked pouting. "If this is your way of antagonizing me into performing better, you should know it's absolutely going to work."

Ali leaned against the headrest. "I want to win, but I'm not going to try to manipulate you. I don't do that." Ali stared out the windshield. "Besides, if I'm right, Kyle being a jackass will be more than enough motivation for both of us." She pointed to Kyle climbing out of his giant truck with "Canterbury Landscaping" painted on the side.

JT found the display annoying but had to admit that he drove a truck for a reason and not simply to mask his insecurities. Probably the truck helped with that, too, but at least it was legitimate for his kind of work.

Sharon hopped out of the passenger's side without Kyle offering her a hand. She landed in a snowbank that was deeper than she'd expected and yelped at the snow falling into the tops of her boots.

"So nice of him to help her avoid having frozen feet all day."

Ali rolled her eyes. "Care for others isn't high on his priority list." She rested a hand on JT's. "You ready to set a track record?"

JT's eyes lit up. "They keep track of the times? Oh my god. Yes." She tied her boots. "Do you know the fastest? Who has the record?"

Ali laughed. "You'll just have to be the fastest ever to find out."

"Oh my god, you're messing with me again. I promise I'll do my best, but be honest, are there all-time records?"

Ali leaned across the center of the car, brought her mouth an inch from JT's ear and whispered. "I know how you like to be on top. Maybe we can celebrate together later?"

JT's mouth dropped open. "Ali!"

Ali laughed and opened her door. "I told you I wouldn't manipulate you, but I didn't promise not to offer incentives for winning."

JT hopped out of the car and followed Ali to the table with the volunteers to check in. She told herself not to get distracted by how cute Ali looked in her hat and mittens or by what she'd said in the car. They needed to win this thing. Then she could worry about spending the day with Ali, naked.

Chapter Thirty-Four

"Ali Porter and JT Cox checking in," Ali told the woman holding a clipboard. She took the number and safety pins and handed them to JT.

"Those go on whoever is pulling the sled." She reached behind the table. "And this goes on whoever is sitting in the sled. Everyone has to wear a helmet."

Ali nodded. "Of course. Anything else we need to do before our turn?"

Dolly, according to her nametag, pointed to the starting line. "When you're ready, go over there. They're going to announce the order and the rules before the start. But you can help yourself to coffee and cocoa if you want." She lowered her voice. "But there's only porta pots and they're wicked cold so you might want to wait."

"Thanks for the tip, Dolly," JT said, and Ali could have sworn she winked but maybe that's the way JT's charm worked. She didn't even have to wink, and women would feel like she was flirting with them.

JT walked away from the table. "You wanna risk it?"

Ali made a face. "Nope. No coffee is worth having to use one of those things in, what did you say it was, ten below?"

JT slumped. "Oh my god, you're never going to let me live this down, are you?" She handed Ali the safety pins. "If you're going to give me shit, can you at least help me with these while you do it?"

Ali pulled off her gloves, exposing her hands to the wind and cold. She couldn't complain, though, after giving JT grief about whining about the cold. She opened the safety pins and then waited for JT to position the number across the front of her coat.

"Pin me," JT said with a sly grin.

"Later if you give me the chance."

JT's eyes sparkled with mischief when Ali looked up at her. "You know, you send a lot of mixed signals to people who you're friends with. Almost like you're not sure how you feel about me."

Ali fastened the pins to JT's jacket, her hands pressing into her torso a little more than strictly necessary. "I know how I feel about you, but I also know how you feel about Hart's Landing. I'm not sure if those two things can coexist."

Ali looked up at JT, squinting into the sun peeking out over the trees. JT's mouth curved into a tiny smile. "And how do you feel about me?"

Ali fiddled with her gloves for a moment, buying time to consider whether holding JT's hand was something she wanted to do in this public place. She settled for holding JT's arms and pushing her back so she could look at the number. Anyone seeing them from a distance would think Ali was making sure the bib wasn't crooked.

"I like you a lot. I like you as a person and would want to be your friend even if I didn't think you were the hottest woman I have ever seen in real life."

JT grinned, pink creeping onto her cheeks. "So there are hotter women you haven't met?"

"If Zendaya showed up here and asked me on a date, I

wouldn't say no." Ali tugged at JT's sleeves, pulling her closer. "But in terms of women I know, have met and have even a remote chance with, you're the hottest."

JT laughed. "I want to be offended by all those qualifiers, but honestly, I can't compete with Zendaya. I wouldn't even try. I'd offer to drive the two of you on the date."

Ali really liked JT like this. She was light and carefree and so quick to laugh it made Ali feel like anything was possible.

"I don't know how you think two girls have any chance of winning this."

Ali knew the voice behind her. She spun with her best teacher-on-the-edge-of-losing-her-temper smile. "Kyle, good morning. So nice of you to barge into our conversation with your toxic masculinity."

"It's not toxic, it's nature."

Ali stepped toward him, but JT stopped her. "Kyle, the number of guys who have thought so much of their skills that they told me, to my face, that they could kick my ass on the ice is pretty fucking high. The number of guys who actually could, zero. I don't see any reason why today should be different."

Kyle puffed up his chest and spit in the snow. "I don't know if you're aware, but I'm not some guy who sits at a desk all day."

JT nodded along. "Yeah, I know how driving your daddy's truck from job to job is pretty strenuous."

Kyle sneered and looked at Ali. "Is that what you told her I do?"

Ali laughed. "Kyle, I don't talk about you at all."

His face burned a deep crimson. "Maybe you don't remember, but I was captain of the football team."

JT covered her mouth.

"Yes, you were, and JT just won a fucking gold medal at the Olympics this year, so forgive me if I take my chances with the only world-class athlete in the contest." Ali grabbed JT's arm. "See you on the starting line."

Ali pulled JT along with her. She was pissed and ready to kick Kyle's ass. JT didn't seem nearly as worked up, though.

"Ali, do you know how many times some high school hero has tried to take a run at me during a pickup game? Or how many guys think that they can beat me because they 'played a little' back in the day? It's fine. It only makes kicking their asses more fun." JT threw her arm around Ali's shoulder like they were teammates.

Ali liked the weight of JT's arm and the way it made her feel like they belonged together. Not necessarily in a romantic way, but as a team. They were a pair and together they were going to destroy the competition. If it was going to be Ali against the world, she was happy to have JT by her side.

They waited at the starting line for the rest of the teams to assemble. Emerson and Jonathan stood off to the side talking with their spouses, but they both waved to Ali and JT. JT looked over Ali's head and scanned the crowd.

"Looking for someone?"

JT shrugged. "Thought my parents might come to watch. But maybe they only come to the art events they know I'll lose spectacularly." She had her hands shoved deep into her coat pockets, her shoulders rounded forward, and with the sad air of a teenager forgotten at school pickup. Like she knew she was too old to be this bummed out but it still bothered her.

"Maybe they're watching the kids?" Ali asked, hoping she was helping by injecting an alternate possibility for the lack of parental support. "I mean, it's pretty early still."

JT nodded but looked unconvinced.

"Contestants, please make your way to the starting area for your instructions," the announcer said into a megaphone so everyone in the crowd could hear. "Each team will have one turn around the track on their own to get a baseline score. Then you will be placed in heats. The top finisher for each heat moves on until we have two teams racing each other. The winning team earns a gift certificate to Watson's Hardware Store, and the team in last place will not continue to the next task. Any questions?"

Kyle raised his hand. "Do the girls get a head start? You know, to be able to compete with us?"

"All teams compete on an even footing in all of our events. This is no different." The announcer looked at Kyle. "I will say, in the past, there were some male contestants who would have done well to understand their limitations and not gotten overly cocky prior to the races."

Ali laughed but covered her mouth to muffle the sound. "Man, Kyle's going to be so pissed."

JT's face was stoic. Ali wondered what she was thinking but didn't want to ask in case this was the way she was getting prepared for the races. It made her wonder what JT was like in the locker room before games. Was she serious, or the fun, goofy woman Ali was enjoying spending time with? She had seen a little of JT's serious side and she knew how competitive she was, but this locked-in version was something new.

Ali thought it was kind of hot.

Chapter Thirty-Five

Did the women get a special head start? JT couldn't believe that Kyle'd had the audacity to ask if she was going to get special treatment. She stood, staring a hole in the back of his head, visualizing all the ways she was going to crush him.

"You okay?" Ali asked, tucking her arm into JT's and giving a gentle tug.

JT looked down at her. She was so cute with snow dusted on her hair. "I'm fine. Just imagining all the ways I am going to kick the ever-loving shit out of your ex-husband." Ali looked surprised and a little alarmed. "On the course, obviously. I don't want to actually kick his ass. I just want to beat him so badly he considers moving to the woods, becoming a hermit and never showing his face in public again."

Ali's laugh erupted with a cackle and JT loved the sound so much she wanted to make Ali laugh that hard all the time. "Well, if that's all."

JT felt herself blush. "I'll settle for winning. But if I manage to crush his spirit in the process, would that be such a bad thing?"

"No. Especially after that bullshit question." Ali pulled JT to the side to inspect the sleds. "Okay, how can I help you with this? I know you're doing most of the work, but there has to be something I can do, or not do, to make this easier to pull."

JT pulled one of the sleds toward them. "Climb in." Ali sat in the back of the sled while JT pulled. "Hmm, hold the sides." JT walked backward to pull and then turned to walk forward. She leaned forward into the rope. "Okay, do they give us a harness or anything for this?"

Ali blinked and then a sly, sexy smile spread across her lips. "You want a what?"

JT held up the rope. "A harness. It would be much easier to do this with the proper equipment." When she saw Ali's face, she realized that Ali was not thinking about a harness for pulling a sled. JT blushed bright red, her face so hot she wanted to lay it against the snow. "Oh my god! I was talking about the competition...not, whatever filthy thing is going on in your brain."

Ali laughed, her head tipping back with a giant whoop. "Come on, you're talking about harnesses and the right equipment, what's a girl supposed to think?"

JT walked toward her, wrapping the rope around itself. "I'm thinking that teachers are much more...multifaceted than I could have ever imagined."

Ali shrugged. "Teachers are people, JT. And some of us like to have sex with hot Olympians. We can't be blamed for our vivid imaginations."

"Can you be a reasonable adult for a moment?"

Ali shrugged. "I doubt it."

JT held up the rope. "Do they have some kind of mechanism for me to pull this rope that won't cause it to chafe all my skin off, or is this also some kind of puritanical masochistic thing?"

Ali pointed to the table. "I think they do have vests you can wear and attach the rope to instead of destroying your incredibly hot skin."

"Ali." JT looked down at her, her voice a low warning growl. "If you keep flirting with me it will be much harder for me to crush the competition, including your misogynistic ex. So, leave the flirting for when we win?"

Ali rolled her eyes in the cutest way possible. "Fine, but if you look cute in that thing, I'm going to steal it."

JT had no idea what had gotten into Ali, but she liked it. She liked feeling wanted, not just liked or tolerated but having this woman who she was obsessed with as a teenager look at her and think she looked hot enough in snow pants and a parka to flirt with on a freezing-cold morning. Her brain kept telling her to question it, but she kept telling her brain to shut up and leave her alone.

There were obstacles in their future. JT could see them clearly, but she could also pretend they weren't there for long enough to thank her lucky stars that Ali Porter thought she was hot and was making jokes about sex toys. She trudged to the table and asked for a vest. They handed it to her, and she realized she was supposed to pin the bib to it. She pulled off her gloves but Ali was there, ready to help.

"Need me?"

JT looked down at Ali's sparkling eyes, delicious lips, and tried to act normal. "Always," she said in a low voice.

Ali made quick work of the safety pins and then helped JT get the vest adjusted correctly. "Is this an excuse for you to touch me?"

"Obviously," Ali said, her eyes trained on JT's chest. "Too bad you're wearing so many layers you're like one of those nesting dolls." She huffed out a breath. "I can't even feel you under there."

"Yes, I am actually a very tiny lesbian in seventeen coats. And I don't think the point of this competition is for you to feel me up in public."

Ali shrugged. "Shows what you know. I signed up for this solely so I could cop a feel with an audience." She tugged at the vest one last time. "Turn around." JT complied. She would have done anything Ali asked.

"Wait, are you checking out my ass now?"

Ali laughed and gave the vest a sharp tug. "I wasn't, but I am now." She tugged again. "How does that feel?"

"Fine. Why?"

"There's a spot to hook the rope with a carabiner. I assume they're going to attach it to you when it's our turn to race. You want to practice?"

JT nodded. Ali grabbed the sled and attached it to JT. JT waited for Ali to climb onto the sled and then walked to get used to how it felt to pull. The angle of the sled was a little weird, as the rope pulled it up in the front and almost made Ali topple out of the back.

"You okay back there? Do you need me to try to run crouched over? Like this?" JT took a few hard steps with her legs bent and her chest as low and she could manage without falling over.

"Stop!" Ali yelled. "I don't need you to do that. It looks awful. Try pulling with your normal running form and see how we do. I'll hold on tight."

After a couple minutes, they figured out the method that worked the best. JT's job was to go as fast and as hard as she could while Ali held on for dear life.

"You have to trust me!" Ali said. "You're doing all the hard work. I will find a way to stay in the sled, I promise."

JT tried to turn around, but the way the sled was clipped to her back made it very difficult to face Ali. She looked around and confirmed no one was near them. "I don't want to hurt you." She said it in a low voice, so they wouldn't be overheard.

"What?" Ali yelled from the sled.

JT tried turning again and made it about halfway, the rope wrapping her up like a mummy. "I don't want you to get hurt.

If you fall out, you could get hurt on the hard snow. I—I don't want to hurt you."

Ali climbed out of the sled. "Do you think I'm made of glass?"

JT thought she sounded annoyed so she shook her head. "No! Of course not!"

Ali leaned closer. "Seriously, do you think I'm some fragile person?"

JT shook her head again, feeling like she was in the principal's office. "No. I—"

Ali held up her hand. "Then run this race as fast as you fucking can and leave it to me to stay in the goddamned sled. I will not break if I fall out. I may be little but I am fierce."

JT grinned. She loved this Ali, the fiery, fierce, powerful woman standing in front of her. No, she didn't love her. That wasn't right. She couldn't, not this fast. She really liked her and admired her fire. Yeah, that was better, saner.

JT looked down at Ali. "Fine. I don't think I've ever had a coach quote Shakespeare during a pep talk, but it worked. Next time I get nervous before a game, I'm calling you."

Ali smiled and wrapped her hands around the straps of JT's vest. She gave a tug. "And I will provide one anytime you need it. I'd love to be your secret weapon. But first, we have a silly hometown competition to win."

They walked to the starting line, JT resisting the urge to grab Ali's hand. Ali didn't seem shy about her affection, but holding hands, in front of Kyle and the rest of the town, seemed like a bigger declaration than JT was willing to make without talking to Ali first. But her hand seemed to drift toward Ali as they walked, and it was only by stuffing it in her pocket that JT managed to resist.

"First up, we have two of the three Cox siblings who have entered. Jonathan and Emerson will be racing each other accompanied by their partners Clark and Beth."

JT clapped her gloved hands together and whooped. She definitely wanted to win this, but she also knew that familial bragging rights were on the line and her money was on Emerson. She had that steely competitive fire and honestly, Clark looked more like he'd seen the inside of a gym in the last five years. Jonathan, by contrast, looked like he spent a lot of time in the studio.

They didn't have a starting gun, which was not very on-brand for New Hampshire, but JT was happy not to have to hear one fired over and over. Instead, they had a whistle. When Jonathan and Clark took off around the track, the crowd cheered. They got to the first turn with Jonathan shockingly in the lead, but then it all went sideways. Jonathan slipped and fell, which should have given Clark a path to victory, except when he fell, he blocked the track. Clark tried to pull his sled, with Emerson shouting at him to go faster, over the Jonathan's rope, but he got stuck.

The result, two tangled sleds and two brothers-in-law sprawled on the snow while their wives shouted at them to get up and move, causing a gasp to come from the crowd half a second before everyone, including Jonathan and Clark, laughed. They looked at each other and lay down on the snow while their wives laughed but climbed out of the sleds.

"If you two are going to lie there, at least lie in the sleds."

"Oh my god," JT said to Ali, laugh tears covering her cheeks. "Em and Beth are going to fight it out."

Ali pointed to the track. "Did Emerson just kick Clark?"

JT shook her head. "No, she wouldn't. That was a nudge. She's offering encouragement. Believe me, I was on the receiving end of that kind of encouragement many times as a kid, and my mom always said it wasn't a kick."

Ali was shaking with laughter. "He doesn't look encouraged. He looks pissed!"

Jonathan wasn't moving any faster, until he saw Clark in the back of the other sled and Emerson throwing all her weight against the rope. Then he hurried his scrawny butt into the sled and told Beth to pull.

Beth was no bigger than Emerson, but she was intent on not losing. JT wondered if they had some kind of side bet that involved having to babysit all the kids if they lost. That was the only thing she thought would motivate them all to try this hard.

Halfway around the track, the women gave up and swapped with their husbands again. It was honestly embarrassing to watch, but possibly the funniest thing JT had ever seen. Her sides hurt from laughing.

"And time!" The timekeepers showed their stopwatches to the officials, who dutifully wrote down the times.

Clark and Jonathan stood next to each other trying to catch their breath while laughing. JT walked over to them.

"Guys, that was amazing!"

"Shut it, baby sister. We don't need your sarcasm." Jonathan spoke but all four of them laughed.

JT held up her hands. "Who says I was being sarcastic? You gave us so much time to cheer you on."

Emerson popped out of the sled and tried to tackle JT into the snowbank, but JT simply picked her up.

"God, this is so unfair. You're a physical specimen, and we ran around looking like the kids picked last in gym class."

JT laughed and put Emerson back on the ground. "The important thing is that you tried. Isn't that what you said to me after the gingerbread houses? Congrats on giving a good effort." She held her hands up for high fives, but none of them bothered.

Beth stomped over to the timekeepers and returned looking grim. "Jonathan, I'm sorry to say you and I will be in charge of the children this evening."

Emerson and Clark high-fived each other as if they'd set a world record. JT shook her head. "I knew you had a side bet going."

Ali had made her way over to them. "What was the bet?"

"Losers have to do dinner and bedtime for all the kids tonight while the others get to go out for a date."

Clark put his arm around Emerson. "We didn't want to have to ask their parents to do it again, so we made a bet." He sniffed the air. "I can almost smell it now."

"We can do it," Ali said.

JT gave her a look of surprise. "What?"

Ali smiled at JT's siblings. "Why don't you all go out and JT and I can take care of your kids for the night."

"What are you doing?" JT said, her voice urgent and slightly panicked.

Ali rolled her eyes. "I'm offering to babysit so your siblings can go out on a date."

JT scowled. Now there was nothing she could do but go along with Ali's offer. Otherwise, she was going to look like an asshole to Ali and to her siblings. "Yeah, sure we'll take your kids. But if you give them a bunch of sugar this afternoon I will murder all of you."

The four of them exchanged a look. "Are you sure?" Emerson asked. "They're kind of a lot."

"Are you implying I can't handle three kids for a couple hours?" JT asked, annoyed at being underestimated.

Clark smiled. "Not at all! The two of you definitely can handle them, we just want to make sure you actually know what you're agreeing to."

Ali looked at JT. "I'm a high school teacher, I can handle almost anything. We got this."

Before JT could add anything else, the announcer called the next teams to the starting line and called for JT and Ali to line up next.

"Gotta go," JT said, pulling Ali toward the start line. "Why on earth would you volunteer to take care of all those kids?"

Ali gave her a questioning look. "Seriously? Your siblings

were so desperate for a night out they nearly killed each other in the race. Why wouldn't I offer to help them?"

JT grunted. Now she felt like an asshole. And asshole who was annoyed that she'd been bamboozled into babysitting when she could have been doing anything else. Being reminded that she should have been offering to babysit without being coerced made her feel bad. She was being a shitty sister and aunt. She didn't like feeling this way at all.

She looked at Ali, who was smiling like she had a secret. "What?"

Ali grinned. "You done feeling like a crappy aunt?"

JT harrumphed. "Yes. No. Whatever."

Ali bumped her shoulder into JT. "We'll have fun, I promise. I'm good with kids, and I bet you are too even if you're being a giant grumpy baby about it right now."

"I'm not being a baby."

Ali laughed. "You are. You're whiny and grumpy and I'm surprised you are not stomping your boots in the snow because you didn't get your way."

"Shut up," JT said, unable to keep the laugh out of her voice. "It's annoying that you can read me so well."

They watched the race before theirs. It had Kyle and Sharon matched up against a middle-aged couple who were doing their best but who couldn't keep up with Kyle. He was annoyingly good at this. JT had hoped he would fall on his face or pass out from exertion, but it appeared that working in a manual labor profession had kept him in decent shape. It was going to be harder to kick his ass than she'd thought.

"What's the time to beat?" JT asked the timekeepers.

They told her the lowest score so far, and she calculated how fast she would have to make it through each of the four sides. She knew she could do it, but it didn't stop a few butterflies from flapping around in her stomach.

"We've got this. You don't have to beat that time now. Just do well enough to move on. Remember, we can't win it all here."

"Survive and advance," JT said, staring at the track.

"Survive and advance," Ali repeated, and put the helmet on over her hat. JT looked at her. "My brain is kind of important to me."

"You don't trust me not to crash?" JT asked with a grin.

"I trust you, but just like I wear a helmet on my bike, I'm wearing one now." She nodded at their competition. "I might trust you, but not them."

JT looked at the competition, which was a guy wearing outerwear that was way too stylish for him to be from New Hampshire. His partner also had on an outfit that looked like it was put together by a stylist and not the folks who worked in the LL Bean store.

"What do you think? Connecticut?"

Ali looked at the couple. "Maybe. Or New York."

JT grinned. "Let's give them a proper welcome."

When the whistle blew, JT lunged forward, the vest and rope trying to pull her back. Fortunately, years of weight training and sprinting made this easy for her. She sprinted forward, zipping past the bewildered Greenwich types, and was making the first turn before they really got started. Ali slid a bit wide in the turn, which almost threw JT off balance, but she recovered and was ready for the swing on the last turns. She crossed the finish line panting, her lungs and quads burning.

"Holy smokes," she heard the timekeeper say when she looked at her stopwatch.

JT waited for Ali to unhitch her from the rope. "How was that?"

Ali grinned. "So fun. You were flying. I'm surprised I was able to hold on. I almost slid off the back at the start, and the turns were crazy."

JT hugged her. She'd had fun showing off. She was already

thinking about how to improve for the next run but she wanted to know how well she'd done this time. The timekeeper showed her the time.

Ali asked the question JT wanted to. "Is that the fastest so far?"

The timekeeper laughed. "I would say so! It's the fastest time I've ever seen."

JT blinked. "Seriously?"

Ali grabbed her in a hug and squeezed like she was going to try to lift JT off the ground.

JT responded by lifting Ali. "Don't hurt yourself. I'm too big for you to lift, tiny." If they weren't in public where they were supposed to be 'just friends' JT would have kissed her. But there were so many people, including JT's siblings and Ali's ex watching them they didn't need to make a scene.

"I knew you could do it," Ali said with a laugh. "So much for survive and advance, though."

"I wasn't trying to set any records, I promise." JT felt a little sheepish. She really hadn't been.

Ali shook her head. "Of course you weren't. Only you could half-ass it and set a course record. You're an athletic freak."

JT pushed her hair out of her face where it had fallen out of her winter hat. She scanned the crowd and lifted her eyebrows. "He doesn't appreciate my effort."

Ali turned. "Oh man, he looks so grumpy. Think how pissed he's going to be after we beat him in the final."

JT looked at him warily. She'd been around enough guys who were bad losers to know that things might get ugly. "If we're racing him, you have to be extra careful, okay? It's not worth getting hurt."

"Kyle isn't going to hurt me."

JT sighed. "I'm not saying he'd do it on purpose. Some guys get really aggressive when they think they might lose to a girl. If we pull ahead, he might not take it very well." JT shrugged.

"Don't get me wrong, I want to win, but not if it means either of us gets hurt in the process."

JT wanted to kick Kyle's ass. She wanted to make him sorry he'd entered the contest and to beat him so badly it made him rethink his entire life. But not if it meant Ali getting hurt. As much as she hated to lose, she would never forgive herself if she let something happen to Ali. She looked down at Ali's beautiful face, her cheeks pink from the cold and her eyes sparkling, and JT knew she would do anything to protect her.

Chapter Thirty-Six

Ali thought JT was overreacting. Kyle was a dope who would definitely hate losing to them, but she didn't think he would get out of control. She watched the next few races, which only cemented the fact that JT was the best athlete the town had ever seen.

While she watched, JT talked to her siblings and their spouses and then lingered at the coffee and refreshment table talking to the women who were running it. Ali watched her smile at each person she met as if they were the first person she was seeing that day. Ali knew JT wasn't always happy or in a good mood, but when she talked to people, she had a way of lighting up as if she were delighted by them and their attention. Maybe it came with the territory. Maybe she'd had a million hours of interview and publicity prep, but however it'd happened, JT was good with people. Even the people who had once questioned whether she should be on the ice with the boys, even when she brought home the state championship trophy.

She heard footsteps approaching and turned expecting to see JT holding two cups of cocoa. Instead, she found her mom.

"Hi, Mom. Did you see our run? Set the course record, apparently."

Her mom made a face. "Yes, very impressive if you want to remain single."

"What is that supposed to mean?" Ali looked over her mom's head, willing JT to come back.

"Ali, I know something about divorce in this town. When your father left me with you and Tommy, I lost so much. All those couples' evenings, friends who stopped inviting me over because I didn't have anyone to watch you two? We didn't have much and certainly not enough for me to get a babysitter."

Ali blinked. "What?"

Jean sighed. "Being divorced here isn't easy. The dating prospects are few and far between. Most importantly, Kyle owns a business. He will keep you secure. You won't have to worry about how you're going to afford groceries or heat your house. Trust me, doing this on your own is hard."

This was the first time anything her mom said regarding the end of her marriage had made any kind of sense. Ali hadn't realized how hard things had been after her dad left. She and Tommy had been too little to remember him being around. She felt bad for her mom and for not knowing how hard it had been for her. But she wasn't her mom. She had friends, she had a good job, she had her own house. She was going to be fine.

"Trust me, Kyle is not going to want you back if you embarrass him in front of everyone."

Ali sighed. "Mom, I want you to listen to me. I don't want Kyle back. I was the one who divorced him, remember?"

"Come on, Alexandra. You know he was the best thing to ever happen to you. And if you're to have any chance of winning him back, you can't beat him in the final."

Ali took a deep breath. She wanted to scream at her mom, but this wasn't the place for that, no matter how good it would feel. "Mom, I want you to listen to me. I never want anything to do with Kyle Canterbury ever again. I know I am stuck living in the same town as him, probably for the rest of my life, but trust me when I tell you I have no intention of ever getting back together with him. I'm sorry for everything you went through to take care of Tommy and me, I truly am. But that doesn't mean I need to be with Kyle. Honestly, you should be ashamed to suggest it. I'm too good for him and I always was."

JT stood behind Ali's mom, her hands wrapped around two paper cups. "Cocoa? Oh hi, Mrs. Porter. Did you want cocoa? You can have mine, and I can get another if you want."

Ali's chest ached with what she could only imagine was her heart expanding. JT was just so *good*. When she was younger, she didn't understand why anyone would settle for someone decent and kind, but now she got it. Not that JT would mean settling. JT was everything she could have ever wanted in a person. Ali smiled at her, unable to keep the happiness she felt from rushing out.

"No, thank you. I was just trying to talk some sense into my daughter. But I can see she'll never listen to me." She made a face like she'd bitten into a lemon. "Someday you'll regret not listening to me."

JT looked entirely bewildered, her golden retriever energy scrambled by Ali's mom's bitter outburst. "Do I want to know?" she asked, handing over the cup.

Ali sighed. "She warned me that if we kick Kyle's ass in the final, he's never going to take me back. I mean, she has her reasons. Things were really hard for her when she and my dad split up, but..." Ali sighed. "She refuses to listen when I tell her there is no universe in which I want Kyle back." Ali's anger rose inside her, threatening to bubble out. She decided to focus on the woman in front of her. "Thank you for this. And for being you. My mom might not have the ability to imagine something better than being married to the owner of the biggest landscaping company in the county, but I can."

JT frowned for an instant. "Wait, that douche owns the biggest—"

"That's what you took from what I just said? JT, I want to be with someone who makes me happy, who listens to me, who makes me laugh, and who for some reason thinks a good time is helping me make my house livable." She sipped her cocoa and tried to remember they were in a public place with half the people she worked with. It was the only way she was going to stop herself from declaring her undying affection to this woman. "How could anyone choose the Kyles of the world when you exist?"

JT blinked. "Are you serious?"

Ali nodded and watched a grin break across JT's face like a perfect sunrise. "Ali, there have to be hundreds of reasons not to choose me."

"Shut up," Ali said, wrapping her mittened hand around JT's. "I know you don't live here… Come to think of it, I have no idea where you actually live. But I want you to know how I feel about you."

"And that is?" JT asked, hiding a massive smile behind her cup.

"I really, really like you. And I think we should kick the ever-loving shit out of Kyle in the finals. You know if that's okay with you."

"Let's fucking go, Porter."

Of course it was Kyle against JT in the final. How could it have gone any other way? Ali buckled her helmet and noted that Sharon had opted not to wear one until the folks running the event told her she had to for liability purposes. Sharon protested but as one older woman stated, "We're not going to bankrupt the town because you're too stupid to wear a goddamned helmet."

Ali smothered a laugh when JT bent down to check on her. "I'm going to win, obviously, but if he starts to act like a douche, I'll stop before I let you get hurt. Do you understand?"

Ali grabbed JT's vest in her mittened hands and gave it a

tug. "What the fuck are you talking about? He's not going to get close enough to us to hurt anyone but himself. You're JT motherfucking Cox, and you are going to mop the floor with him." It killed Ali not to kiss JT right there on her neon green sled in front of the entire town.

JT grinned. "You better hold on tight, then."

"Let's fucking go, Coxie." It came out before Ali could think twice. Coxie was what JT's teammates called her. She'd heard them on the Olympic broadcast. Ali wasn't sure it was right for her to use it, but it felt good in her mouth. She liked the idea that they were teammates. It might only be for this competition, for this silly sled race, but maybe it could be for more, for longer. Maybe, if she played her cards right, they could be teammates for a lot longer than one week.

Chapter Thirty-Seven

After all that buildup, the race was over in the blink of an eye. Kyle puffed out his chest and tried to talk shit, but JT didn't listen. She focused on the track and her footing, and in the end all her worries that Ali might get hurt if the race was close were pointless. Kyle kept it close until the first turn, but after that JT left him behind with every stride she took.

He was half a length back by the second turn, and then she was finishing before he hit the third turn. No one in town had seen anything like it before. But, then again, they'd never seen anything like JT Cox before either. But they hadn't appreciated what they had, a shooting star, Halley's comet, the northern lights, something rare and fleeting and beautiful. Awe-inspiring.

Ali jumped out of the sled the moment they crossed the finish line and threw herself into JT's arms.

"Easy there." JT panted and gulped air to catch her breath, her heart hammering and her legs burning.

"You did it!"

JT laughed. "*We* did it. It's a team sport, remember?"

Ali shook her head. "My only job was to hold on for dear life. You're a marvel, you know that?"

JT gave her a stern look. "If the other events were team efforts, then so was this. I know I didn't contribute much to the gingerbread house, so I'm glad I could do better today, but whatever we do in this contest, it's as a team."

Ali hugged her. "I really want to kiss you right now." She said it into JT's ear, so low JT wondered if she'd heard her correctly.

"Really?"

Ali squeezed her harder. "Yes, but I don't really want to have to talk to my mom about it. Or Kyle or any of my fellow teachers who are standing around watching."

JT pulled back. "Totally get it. I feel the same. I mean, I'm less worried about your teacher colleagues, but I don't really want your mom murdering me or your ex throwing a fit."

Ali looked past her. "He doesn't look like he has enough energy to pitch a fit." She giggled. "I thought beating him would be fun, but I never imagined it would be this fun."

JT heard footsteps and turned.

Ali's mom stood in front of them. "Well, I hope you're happy. Look at him! You've broken his spirit."

Kyle, who was being consoled by Sharon, did not look like a broken man so much as a guy who'd overestimated his physical capabilities and had maybe pulled a muscle.

"Mom, come on. Kyle's fine. And even if he's not, why on earth would I give a shit?"

"Alexandra! Language!"

Ali rolled her eyes. "Mom, I'm twenty-eight years old. I swear. Get over it."

JT snorted and then tried to cover her laugh with a cough.

Mrs. Porter glared at her. "I suppose this is all your idea of fun? You come here for a few days, cause a bunch of mess and then leave, right?"

JT felt like she'd been punched in the gut. "What? No."

"You come home maybe once a year and then you're gone, avoiding your folks and this town. But now you're here causing trouble and then you're going to leave again."

JT opened her mouth but couldn't think of a thing to say. She was going to leave. She didn't live here. She'd asked the league to put her on a team far away from home because it hurt too much to have her family ignore her career. It was too much to know they didn't think anything of her hard work. And now Ali's mom, Tommy's mom, was screaming at her for protecting herself from the pain of having parents who couldn't be bothered to watch her win a gold medal.

"Mom, leave her alone. You're not mad at her. You're mad at me."

Mrs. Porter stepped toward Ali. "You're right, I am. You're throwing away your future for some fun? A laugh at Kyle's expense?"

Ali closed her eyes and took a deep breath. For a second, JT thought she was going to cry. Instead, she opened her eyes and looked at her mom. "Mom, I don't know why you think Kyle is in my future. I have been very clear that I have no intention of ever getting back together with him. I'm not interested in him. Not for a date, not for a minute of my time. He and I are done. If that's a tragedy for you, I suggest you find someone else to talk to about it." She grabbed JT by the elbow and dragged her toward the judge's table.

JT sputtered as she tried to keep up with Ali. "Ali, what is going on?"

Ali stopped in front of the announcer's table. "You and I are getting our prize, and then we are getting the hell out of here before I say something to my mom that she regrets."

JT shifted uncomfortably. She'd had plenty of unpleasant run-ins with her own parents and random people but never with Tommy's mom. She'd always been nice to JT, even when the rest of the town had thought a girl shouldn't be the captain of the boy's hockey team or shouldn't be on the team at all. She'd never seen this side of her.

The announcer took the bullhorn and let everyone know

that JT and Ali were the winners, then presented them with their gift certificates to the hardware store.

"These will come in handy with your new place," JT said, trying her hardest to lighten things up.

Ali still looked ready to do a murder, so JT shepherded her toward the car and then back home. The drive was too short for her to come up with anything to say, let alone the right thing. She didn't know how to reassure Ali that she wasn't a flake, especially because she didn't have an intention of sticking around their hometown.

Or she hadn't when she first came home for Christmas. After spending this much time with Ali, she got the feeling that home might not be as bad as it had been in the past. Maybe Hart's Landing had changed. Or maybe JT had.

Chapter Thirty-Eight

Ali never wanted her mother's voice in her head but especially not now. She didn't want her voice telling her that JT wasn't going to stick around. Especially because Ali knew she was right. JT didn't stick around Hart's Landing. Ever since she'd left for college, she'd been home a handful of times, and each time she'd stayed only as long as was necessary to be a reasonable daughter. Then she was gone again.

Ali invited JT to come into the house with her. She wasn't sure what to say, but she had questions she should ask before they spiraled out of control in her head. She walked to the back of the house and offered JT a drink.

"I have water, seltzer, tea, and I can make some coffee." Ali spread her arms to gesture at her cabinets.

"Water sounds good, thanks," JT said, her voice quiet.

Ali handed her a glass but didn't let go until JT met her eyes. "I'm sorry my mom ruined our win."

JT shrugged. "It's fine."

"No, it's not. I'm sorry I let her get to me. But can I ask you a question?"

JT nodded.

"Do you already know where you're playing this season?"

JT shook her head. "No."

Ali considered her face; there was something she wasn't saying. "But?"

JT sighed and set her glass down. "But I asked the league to put me anywhere but Boston."

"What? Why?"

JT rested against the counter. "Because being that close to home is too hard." Ali shook her head, unable to understand. "My family doesn't care about my career. I know that. I knew that before my parents skipped out on my gold medal game. I knew it, but it still hurt more than I expected when they weren't there."

Ali took her hand, wishing she could take away her pain.

"So, when the league asked us to give them our preferences, I told them to put me as far away from home as possible. Because if I play in Boston and they never come, it will hurt a thousand times worse than if I'm in Minnesota and they never come. At least then I can tell myself it's the distance. If I'm playing an hour from home and they never come..."

Ali wrapped her arms around JT and wished she weren't so damn small. If she were bigger, she could scoop JT up and comfort her. Instead, the best she could do was a hug around her middle.

"I'd come, you know? I'd come and cheer you on."

JT kissed the top of her head. "You would?"

Ali pulled back to look up. "Of course. I'd be the most embarrassing fan in the world. I'd wear your jersey and make a big dumb sign." She sighed. "I'd do everything I could to make up for your stupid-ass parents who don't deserve to have a kid as great and as sweet as you."

JT chuckled, her chest vibrating with the sound. "So, when your mom said I would leave and never come back, she was right."

Ali nodded and leaned her head against JT's chest. At the

end of the week JT would be gone. She'd be living a thousand miles away, only visiting the East Coast a few times during the season. She'd be off being a hockey superstar with her pick of women who would be happy to cheer her on and share her bed.

And Ali would be in Hart's Landing, teaching high schoolers, trying to avoid Kyle, and fighting off her mother's attempts to get them back together. It all sounded so bleak. Ali looked around the room. Thanks to JT, the house was looking more like a place where she actually lived. It had furniture and fewer boxes filled with her crap. She had a whole office with beautiful bookshelves filled with novels and books about teaching and even books people had given her because they'd thought she might like them.

She had a home and a job she loved. She loved the teachers she worked with, and she loved the kids she had in class, even the ones who drove her crazy. She loved the satisfaction of seeing a kid get it or find a passion, even when it wasn't a passion for her class. She could leave but she didn't want to. She wanted to stay here and teach these kids because she knew what it was like to live in a small town and to think that was all there was in life.

She knew what it was like to dare to dream of more even when no one around you thought more was possible. Even when your own mom thought the best you could do was the boy you met when you were a teenager. The guy who stole ten years of your life being "fine" because you didn't think you could have more.

She wanted to be the teacher that made sure her kids knew there was more and they deserved everything they could find in the big wide world, even when that big wide world was Hart's Landing.

"I'm sorry," JT said, her voice full of emotion. "I know you love it here. I don't want to ruin that for you."

Ali managed a weak smile. "You're not ruining it. No more

than you telling me you don't like peanut butter and chocolate would ruin Reese's for me."

JT pushed away from the counter. "I really am sorry, though. I—" Her voice cracked and she rushed to clear her throat. "I like you a lot. I never expected there to be anything that could make me reconsider this town, but you have." She paused. "Seeing all those people showing up for the hockey game, I don't know how to describe it, but it felt amazing. I never expected it."

Ali's heart broke for JT. She'd changed the town when she brought the first state championship to it. She'd changed women's hockey when she played in college. She'd won a gold medal for Team USA, and yet she was overcome thinking about a bunch of people she barely knew coming to a hockey game. How could she not know what she meant to everyone in Hart's Landing? How was it possible for someone to change a place for the better and to have no idea of her impact?

"I know it wasn't always easy to be you in Hart's Landing. I'm sure I don't know the half of it, but I got a sense from Tommy of some of the bullshit you went through in middle school and high school."

JT shook her head. "You didn't need to know. I'm not looking for sympathy, I swear."

Ali took JT's hands. "I know you aren't. But I want you to understand that even if it was awful for you when you were here—and I'm sure it was—it's not as bad for the kids now. This isn't some big 'it gets better' ad or anything, but you should know that this place changed because of you."

JT hunched her shoulders forward, her hands buried deep in her pockets, and stared out the kitchen window. Ali couldn't read her mind or her expression, but it looked wistful. "I'm glad," she said, finally. "But my parents haven't changed." She looked at Ali, her face fighting for a smile. "Look at today. They were there for the artsy challenges. They oohed and ahhed over gingerbread houses, but they couldn't be bothered to show up and watch the one competition I might be good at. We set a record for the fastest time! Of course it's silly. The whole point is to make us fall and slip and slide around a track pulling neon sleds. But this is the stuff I'm good at. And when it's my time to shine, they're nowhere to be found."

Ali stepped forward and wrapped JT in a hug. "I'm sorry," she said into JT's shoulder.

"It's not your fault. If it weren't for you, I would have left the day after Christmas. The problem is me hoping that this time will be different, this time they'll show up. It's the hoping over and over only to be let down that kills me."

Ali placed a kiss on JT's cheek. "I'm so sorry." She felt JT relax against her. "Not to put this on you, but have you tried talking to them about this? Do they know how much they're hurting you?"

JT shook her head. "It feels so hopeless. Even talking to them feels like just giving them another chance to disappoint me."

Ali nodded. "I get it, but maybe it's worth trying. I know it's selfish to want you to be nearby. You should play for whatever team is going to make you the happiest, but I want you to know that if that happened to be the team in Boston, I wouldn't hate it."

JT sighed. "I feel so stuck. If I end up far away, I don't give them the chance to hurt me. But then I'll be far away from my nieces and nephew, I won't be able to come cheer on those girls we saw the other day and…" She pulled back so she could look down at Ali.

"And?" Ali said with a sweet, expectant smile. She knew what she wanted JT to say, but she'd been the one to say they were friends and nothing more. And here she was, hoping for more.

"It wouldn't suck to be able to visit you, too. Someone is going to have to check on all this furniture I built."

Ali laughed. "You could always FaceTime with the bookcases. I'm sure they'd love to hear from you even when you're on the road being a hockey star." Ali put a hand on each of JT's cheeks. "I know I said friends, but I'd like that, too."

JT's lips flattened into a line. They fought against a quivering building in the center. A tear slid down her cheek. "I know this is impossible, I really do. But I really like you. Not because I had a thing for you when I was a teenager who had just discovered how hot girls are. Okay, maybe a little because of that. But mostly because of how you make me feel. I really…"

Ali kissed her and then rested her forehead against JT's. "I really, too."

"Yeah?"

Ali nodded. "At least we have one more event before we find out who wins the whole thing."

JT nodded sadly. "Yeah, we're guaranteed one more ridiculous contest. What is it?"

Ali shrugged. "They always keep the final one a secret. No one knows."

JT frowned. "That's annoying. But whatever. As long as Kyle doesn't have some secret in with the contest committee or whatever. I don't want to lose because he plows their driveway or something."

Ali shook her head. "We'll get a text telling us where to go and when and maybe a few instructions. How do you not know this?"

JT smiled. "I've never stuck around long enough to watch the whole competition. And maybe I like it when you explain things to me."

"Oh yeah?" Ali pulled them closer together.

JT kissed her. "Mmm-hmm. Maybe now you can explain how we can get out of these clothes?"

Chapter Thirty-Nine

JT was exhausted when she got home. Between the cold and the several races around the track in the snow, she was worn out. So, when she walked into the kitchen and found her mom and dad sitting at the table doing the crossword puzzle, she didn't mean to pick a fight.

Her mom didn't look up when she spoke. "There's coffee in the pot if you want it. Your siblings got home a while ago and took the kids out."

JT's dad looked up from the paper. "You look tired."

JT turned her back on him and walked to the pot to pour herself a cup of coffee. With each step she got more annoyed. "Thanks, Dad."

Her mom popped her head up. "Don't be snippy. He's just pointing out a fact. You look tired."

JT sucked in a breath. She should not fight with this woman. It never ended well. "Maybe if I wasn't on a couch I would sleep better."

"What? Are you complaining about the free accommodations?" her mom said, her voice with an edge.

"Of course not. It's great that you gave my room away and put me in the cellar. Totally great."

Her dad shared a look with her mom, which only infuriated JT further. Something about being home turned her back into a teenager with rage coursing through her veins.

"Emerson said something about the contest this morning, how did it go?"

The coffee in JT's mug rippled as she shook with anger. She set the mug down on the counter. "How did it go? Ali and I set the fastest time on the course, twice."

"Oh? That's nice."

JT couldn't hold in her anger any longer. "Know what would have been nice? You two being there to see it. But I know, you will literally fly halfway around the world to go to some show but you can't be bothered to come to an event where I might do something amazing. You couldn't do it for the final goddamned Olympics so I don't know why I would think you would bother to come watch me this morning. Except maybe because you came to the stupid gingerbread decorating contest so you could ooh and ahh about Emerson's design skills with icing!"

"Jasmine…"

"Stop calling me Jasmine!"

Her mom blinked. "It's your name."

"And you know I hate it. I have asked you, for my entire lifetime, to call me JT. But you insist on calling me by that stupid Disney princess name that I have hated for my entire life."

"But I love your name."

JT sighed. "Yes, you love the name and you love art and you love people who are good at art. But do you love me? Because you never show up for me. You leave the Olympics early. You only come to contests involving artistic ability—which you know I don't have. You skip the event that you had to know I was most likely to excel in. Why? Why do you hate watching me do things I enjoy so much?"

Her parents exchanged a mystified look. "You think we don't support you?"

JT felt like she was going insane. "Of course you don't! You missed most of my games in high school. Once I was old enough to be on the team and get bused to games, you stopped coming. You weren't there when I won the National Championship in college. You weren't there when I won the Kazmaier. You are never there! What am I supposed to think?"

JT took a deep breath.

"And then when I'm here you make all kinds of cracks about how I never come home. Do you have any idea why that might be true?"

Her mom looked close to either ripping JT's head off or crying. It was hard to tell.

"If you had come to my games in high school, you would have heard the shit I heard. You would have heard opposing players and their parents calling me slurs, trying to kill me out on the ice, saying the most vile stuff you can think of. You would have known what I was going through if you had bothered to come out of your bubble."

JT's dad swallowed before standing up. He took off his glasses to wipe his face. "We did come to your games. Maybe you don't remember, but we came."

JT tried to remember. She was sure he was wrong, sure he was lying.

"We came to the game you had against Valley Regional. We sat in the stands and heard what they were saying about you. We hoped you couldn't hear them. We hoped the glass was thick enough to send their words reflecting back into the crowd."

JT's mom put a hand on his arm. "It was too hard, honey. It was too hard for us to sit there and listen to what people were saying about you."

"What?" JT's voice came out a whisper.

Her dad sighed. "People were saying awful stuff and there

was nothing we could do about it. We didn't want to walk out in the middle of the game. So, from then on, we made excuses."

JT leaned against the counter feeling like she had whiplash. She never knew why they skipped her games. "But why didn't you say something? You could have told me instead of letting me assume you didn't care about my sport. Or me."

Her mom pressed her lips together. "Maybe we should have told you, but it would have meant we'd have to say what people were saying in the stands. We didn't want you to know."

"I knew!" JT said, almost shouting. "I knew the shit people were saying about me. They said it in the stands and to my face. One lady yelled at me when I was getting on our team bus!" The memories flooded back so fast that she was hit by a wave of emotion. "I had to deal with it alone because you two thought it was too hard for *you* to hear?"

"I'm sorry," her dad said in a low voice.

"It was our job to protect you, and every time we were there it felt like we were failing you. We didn't want to make you not play; you loved it so much…but it was so painful to listen to people say those things."

JT's head was spinning. "I don't understand. That was ten years ago. Why not come to the home games where you could sit with people you knew? And why not come to my college games? Once I was on a women's team, why didn't you come then?"

Her mom crossed her arms over her chest, making her look less defiant than small and cold. "It was your place, not ours. We didn't understand the game. We didn't understand sports or your passion for it."

"Then fake it! I've spent enough time with little kids to know you have to fake being interested in a shitload of things! Bugs and dirt and whatever god-awful book they want you to read for the four thousandth time! But you fake it. You pretend to be interested in the bug or the terrible book. It matters to you because they matter to you! You couldn't even do that for me. Instead, you gave all your time and attention to Jonny and Emerson. There was nothing left for me!"

Her parents were quiet. They sat at the table and fiddled with the paper. Finally, JT's dad spoke. "I'm sorry. I'm sorry we weren't there when you needed us."

JT appreciated the apology, but she wasn't finished being pissed off. "You know, somebody told me that it's not the kid's job to make their parents care about them. It wasn't my job to make you understand sports or the fact that I'm really fucking good at them. That was your job."

Her mom looked up, her eyes wet. "You're right. It was our job." She cleared her throat. "It still is."

JT deflated. Her anger wasn't gone, but some of her willingness to fight with her parents had dissipated. "If you know that, why didn't you come this morning?"

Her parents shared a look but couldn't do anything more than shrug. "I don't know, honey. I don't think it occurred to us to come."

JT pushed herself away from the counter. There was nothing to say. Her parents didn't even think that they should come to watch her. Yes, it was a stupid little competition. But they came for Emerson and Jonathan. They came to watch their first two kids kick ass at the gingerbread event. Maybe they came because they knew how well they would do or maybe they came because they understood art. But for whatever reason, they showed up for her siblings but not for her. She wished it didn't hurt. She wished she could brush it off the way she brushed off opposing players talking shit in the middle of the game.

But in a game, she could do something about the trash talk. She could make them shut up by scoring a goal or kicking their asses up and down the ice. With her parents, there was nothing to do to show them they were wrong. They weren't there to see her kick ass, and talking trash didn't seem like the right way to deal with her parents or their disinterest.

It left her feeling powerless, and she hated feeling that way. She was strong, confident and one of the best athletes on the planet. After the Olympics, people stopped her in the airport and congratulated her. People asked to see her medal. Little kids stared at her with their big eyes filled with wonder at the sight of her. But not her parents. They weren't even in the country to see her dip her head to receive her medal. They weren't there to listen to the national anthem while they raised the flag. They missed all of that. And she wished it hurt them half as much as it hurt her. But until that morning she had never seen them express an ounce of regret for missing her successes. It was like they didn't think about her at all unless she was at home. And then it was all comments about her lack of artistic talents and how infrequently she visited.

"I'm tired," JT said, walking toward the cellar door. "I'll be napping in the dungeon if anyone needs me."

Chapter Forty

Ali walked through her house, relishing the progress she'd made with JT's help. There were still boxes, but a lot fewer. The bookshelves in her office looked amazing, but something was off. She stood in the doorway and cast her eyes around the room, trying to put her finger on what the issue was.

The white bookcases filled with her collection of books looked great, but she kept snagging on something. Yes, she needed a desk and a chair and probably a couple of lamps to make the office a place she could do work, but that wasn't the problem.

As she turned, scanning every inch of the room for what was bothering her, it dawned on her. She hated the walls. She hated the yellow. Once she realized it, the hatred came flooding in. She really fucking hated the color they'd chosen to paint the room.

She thought back to standing in the paint store with JT, lifting swatches off the wall, comparing them, and landing on this one. She hadn't liked it in the store. She wasn't a person who liked yellow. What had she been thinking?

She wanted something deeper, cooler, something bold. Instead, she'd gotten the kind of bland color people chose for a gender-neutral nursery. She leaned against the doorframe. It wasn't even that JT had tried to convince her to choose the color. She wanted to be mad at someone, but JT hadn't done anything more than suggest she go with something neutral. It wasn't her fault that Ali was so set on not inconveniencing anyone, not rocking the boat by saying *No, I don't like that color*, that she'd ended up spending hours painting the room a color she hated.

She looked around at everything she'd done with JT to put the room back together. The bookcases were filled with books. They weren't organized very well, but they were full. If she was going to repaint the room, she would have to dismantle so many things. She sat on the floor, her back against the wall as she estimated how long it would take her to do it. She didn't feel like she could ask JT to help. JT had put together all the shelves, painted the walls and filled the shelves with what felt like a million books. How on earth could Ali ask her to do it all again? She would think Ali was flighty and indecisive.

Ali dropped her head back against the wall, allowing herself a moment to feel bad about all the work ahead of her. If only she had said something earlier. JT didn't care about the color. She wasn't invested in Ali having a yellow office. Ali wouldn't have hurt her feelings saying she didn't like it. But Ali had gone along with the choice because it was easy and she thought it would make JT happy, instead of thinking about what would make her happy. What she wanted was a deep blue-green. She wanted that jewel-tone office she'd seen in a magazine. She fucking knew what she wanted but she didn't get it because she'd been too busy worrying about what other people might want or think.

This was how she'd ended up marrying Kyle. She'd ignored the part of her that'd said she didn't want to and gone along with what everyone else wanted and expected of her. It wasn't like she'd been tricked or trapped into marrying him—she simply hadn't said *No, this isn't what I want* when the time came. And now, a decade later, in a house she bought all on her own, she'd done the same thing. Granted, paint colors were much easier to change than marriages, but how had she not learned her lesson?

She thought back to that morning, to Kyle talking shit about how JT could never measure up to him and how her mom had pleaded with her to let Kyle win to preserve her chance to be with him again.

The anger returned. It burned in her chest. She was pissed at her mom but she was pissed at herself, too. It shouldn't have taken her so long to tell her mom, and Kyle, to fuck off. She hoped she'd been clear enough that morning. She hoped her mom finally understood that Ali didn't want Kyle. She didn't want him or a chance that they might be together again in the future. Her mom may have wanted something different because it had been so hard for her to be a single parent, and Ali could understand that. But she didn't want the safety and security her mom thought Kyle and his landscaping company represented. She didn't want Kyle at all.

She wanted her own damn house and her own money and she wanted a room that didn't look like a generic baby nursery. She wanted her home office to be hers, and if no one else on earth liked the color she chose, who cared? They weren't the ones who were going to use it every day.

It was a daunting task. Undoing all the work she'd done to get the room painted and put together in the first place was a little scary. But after telling off her mom that morning, she felt like maybe she could do this. She wasn't going to ask JT to help, though. She wanted to surprise her with the result. But she also didn't really want to do it on her own and she wasn't sure she could move the bookcases by herself without risking getting crushed by them in the process.

She took out her phone and dialed. "Hey baby brother. Can

you meet me at my house in an hour or so? Wear shitty clothes. I need your help and it's going to be messy."

Tommy didn't miss a beat. "I'll grab a six-pack and be over in an hour. Let me know if you need me to grab anything else on the way."

An hour later, Ali was standing in her office with a new gallon of paint courtesy of one of the gift cards she and JT had won that morning. Might as well put it to use. The guy at the store had told her he liked the color, and she was annoyed with herself for how happy that had made her. It didn't matter what he thought because she liked the color. But it also didn't suck to have someone confirm she'd made a good choice.

She wasn't as confident about Tommy. But when she showed him the color smear on the top of the can he surprised her.

"Oh, that looks amazing! Mom's going to hate it, but it's going to look so good in here with all the white bookcases." He paused, understanding dawning on him. "Shit, that means we have to move them all out, doesn't it?"

"Oh, so you *are* more than just a pretty face," Ali said, cracking up.

Tommy scowled for a second before joining her. "How come you didn't ask your girlfriend to help with this?"

Ali's heart stuttered at the sound of the word *girlfriend*. JT wasn't her girlfriend. They weren't even a couple or publicly acknowledging that they were more than friends. Ali decided not to get into it. "Who do you think put all those together in the first place? And helped paint the room this god-awful yellow? I didn't want to ask her to do it all over again. I wanted to surprise her with it when it's done."

Tommy nodded but his lips twitched at the corners.

"And she's not my girlfriend."

"There it is! I was waiting for you to object."

Ali smacked his shoulder with her dry paintbrush. "If I'm

not mistaken, you're the one who called her a flake and told her to stay away from me."

Tommy hung his head dramatically. "Not my finest moment." He straightened up and looked at her. "I was wrong. I was trying to protect you, and honestly, she doesn't have the best track record when it comes to long-term relationships—"

"This is the worst apology in the history of the world, Thomas."

"I was wrong! I'm sorry. I was trying to look out for you, and I screwed up. Ali, she's my best friend for a reason. If I ever needed something I know she'd be there for me. She would do anything she could to help me." He looked around the room. "I mean, she's obviously shown up for you this week. That's who she is. She will go to the ends of the earth for the people she loves."

Ali's heart lurched again. She tried to keep her face neutral, but Tommy's face made it clear she'd done a terrible job.

"Do you love her?"

Ali froze. Did she? She didn't know. How could she? It had been less than a week. God, was she that much of a cliché that she'd fallen for a woman instantly? "Maybe. But it doesn't matter. She's not going to stay here. Not with the way she feels about this town and her parents. It's too complicated. And I could never ask her to, it hurts her too much to be reminded of all the ways this place treated her like shit." She swallowed. "I would never want to hurt her."

"Have you told her how you feel?"

Ali shrugged. "Tommy, how can I tell her when she doesn't want to be here? She asked the hockey league to put her on any team except for Boston, that's how much she hates it here. If I tell her how I feel, that puts her in a terrible spot. Even if she feels the same way, especially if she feels the same way, she would have to choose between those feelings and the way being here makes her miserable."

Tommy gave her a hug. "Do you think she's been miserable this week? Because I've never seen her happier."

Ali let her head rest on her baby brother's chest. "You think?"

He laughed and his chest rumbled against her ear. "Ali, from the looks of your house you two have been working day and night, and I have truly never seen her happier or more full of joy when she was home. Usually, she's miserable unless I rescue her from her family and we go out for drinks or to skate on the pond. This year, she hasn't called me once for a rescue."

Ali sighed. "Well, I've been keeping her away from her family probably more than they are happy with."

Tommy let his arms drop. "I don't know what's going on with the two of you, only you guys do, but I do know that my best friend has never been like this before. I'm sorry I almost fucked everything up. I've apologized to her, but not to you. I'm so sorry. She's not a flake. She's the best person I know—except you, of course—and I think the two of you could make each other wicked happy."

"And would that be okay with you? Your big sister dating your best friend?"

Tommy laughed. "As long as you don't tell me any details about your sex life, I will be the happiest guy on the planet if the two of you are together."

Ali grinned. "Thank you," she said, surprised by the tear sliding down her cheek. "That means a lot to me, and I know it will mean the world to her. Now, enough of this chitchatting. We have a room to transform."

Tommy pried the top off the paint and poured it into the tray. "You get started on that wall while I carry these books out of here."

"I fucking love this color." Ali dipped her brush into the paint. "Thank you for helping me."

Tommy nodded and filled his arms with books. "Least I

could do after you made JT help you with the rest of it. If I didn't do something she'd never let me forget how useless I am."

Ali rolled the first bit of the new color across the wall and paused. "How pissed is she going to be that I changed everything in here?"

Tommy returned for another load of books. "Not at all." He grabbed for more books before setting them down on the floor out of the way. "Okay, she might be mad, but only because you didn't call her to help you do it."

Ali grabbed for a small brush to do the edges. "Really?"

Tommy shook his head. "No. She'll have wanted to help but she'll understand why you didn't call her to redo it."

"And you don't think she's going to be annoyed I changed colors?"

Tommy set his stack of books down. "Ali, with all due respect to you and the very important choices you're making, I don't think JT gives a rat's ass what color you paint the room in your own house. She'll only care that it makes you happy." Ali looked at him, disbelieving. "Ali, I swear, the only thing JT is going to care about—after she gets over you not asking her to help—is that you are one-hundred-percent happy."

Ali smiled and went back to painting. Even with only half the wall done, she loved it. She believed Tommy, but the prospect of being with someone who only cared about her happiness was something she would have to get used to. She hoped she got a chance.

Chapter Forty-One

JT received a text message from the contest committee that afternoon and a phone call from Ali about three seconds after the text.

"Did you see it? We have to do the final today! What the hell?"

JT was half asleep, still cocooned in her cozy couch bed. "What do you mean? I thought the final was tomorrow?"

"They moved it up. The contest website says something about adjusting due to weather. What the hell does that mean?"

JT sat up, squinting into the dark. "Maybe they want to take advantage of the snow?"

Ali made a noise into the phone. "Can you come over? Or should I pick you up?"

JT grabbed her hoodie. "Sure. You can come get me if you want. I'll take Toby out for a minute and then I'll be ready." JT was supposed to have more time to sleep and hang out with her family. After the argument she'd had with her parents, not hanging out with them might be a blessing in disguise. She grabbed her boots and headed into the snow with Toby, who chased a tennis ball into the deep snow for a few minutes and then flopped at JT's feet.

The snow was thick and had switched over from the light fluffy stuff that morning to something stickier. So when JT threw a snowball for Toby, she was able to catch it with her mouth before making it explode by biting down.

Headlights appeared at the end of the driveway. It was afternoon, but between it being the end of December and the snow falling, the sky was gray, and the lack of sun made it seem later in the day than it was. JT waved to Ali and took Toby inside to get her settled.

She saw Emerson and Jonathan in the kitchen cutting up what looked like snacks for their kids. "You guys coming?"

Emerson gave her a confused look. "Coming where?"

JT held up her phone. "We got a text and an email from the contest telling us to come to some event this afternoon. Didn't you get one? Is it a prank?"

Jonathan sighed. "Oh, you sweet summer child. Our teams were eliminated this morning based on our abysmal showing at the human dogsled race. Turns out when you nearly knock each other out and come in dead last, they eliminate you from the contest."

JT didn't understand. "But you guys killed it in the gingerbread houses."

Emerson nodded. "Yes, but apparently it's possible to be so bad in an event that they tell you don't bother coming to the next one." She laughed. "Go on. Kick some ass. No one deserves it more than you."

JT felt embarrassed by her mistake. "I'm sorry, guys. I wish you were coming."

"I'm not. We're going to go sit by the fire and probably get a little tipsier than we should while you're freezing your asses off in the snow." Jonathan raised a mug. "I'm telling Mom it's cocoa, but it's mostly bourbon."

JT, overcome by a rush of affection for her siblings, hugged them both before running out into the snow. She slid into the passenger seat and leaned over to kiss Ali on the cheek.

"Hi, aren't you freezing? Wait, why is my ass warm? Is my seat heated?"

Ali pointed to the button on the console. "Nothing but the best for your sweet, sweet ass." She grinned. "Are your siblings coming?"

JT shook her head. "They said they've been eliminated. I figured there would have been an announcement or something."

Ali pursed her lips. "That means it might be down to just us and Kyle's team."

JT frowned. "No, there must be someone else, right?"

Ali shrugged. "I don't know. I thought there would be one more event tomorrow, but obviously they pushed that up a day. And then it's New Year's Eve. So, yeah. How did Jonathan and Emerson take it?"

JT laughed. "They're cutting up cheese and apples for their kids and I'm pretty sure they are going to be drunk by the time I get home."

Ali laughed. "Judging by the snow, I think you and I might be happy to have a few drinks after to warm up."

They drove to the center of town, coming up with more and more outlandish ideas for what the task might be. JT thought it might be something artistic again after their morning athletic event. Ali wasn't sure. She listed off a few of the past final tasks, none of which she'd had to do because she and Kyle never made it that far, but nothing she listed gave them any idea of what might be coming next.

The instructions told them to park behind the Hart's Inn. There were two shovels waiting for them on either side of the walkway, and each had a note attached.

Contestants,
Congratulations on making it to the final test. This test is sponsored by the inn and by the hardware store.
Good neighbors in Hart's Landing often help each other

out in a snowstorm. You are going to shovel the sidewalk for your neighbors here in town. Your first task is to fill the forms we've set up with snow you clear from the sidewalk. We've provided you with a wheelbarrow to help you bring the snow back to the forms. When you've cleared the sidewalk on either side far enough to fill and pack the forms with snow, you can go home. Your snow should be hard packed.

Tomorrow you will return at ten to sculpt the snow that will harden overnight into snowmen or any snow creature you would like. You may consult any sources you would like tonight on the shaping, design, or any other elements you might wish, but all work on both the shoveling and sculpting must be done by your team.

Good luck to both teams, and we'll see you in the morning.

Ali and JT read the note a second time. JT grabbed a shovel. "So nice of them to give us two hard physical tasks in the same day."

Ali tucked the note in her jacket. "I bet they had some other plan, but the snow was too good not to use." She looked down the sidewalk at Kyle and Sharon. "The funniest part is that he clears snow for a living, but he never has to get out of his truck. He hasn't done this kind of manual labor for years."

JT laughed and cupped her hand around her mouth. "Sharon doesn't look too happy about shoveling, does she?"

JT and Ali got to work. They started a block or so away from the inn and worked their way back. This was JT's idea because she knew they would get progressively more tired, and by starting further away they would be saving themselves the walking by the end. The only danger was guessing wrong about how far they needed to clear, but she was willing to take that risk.

They worked in tandem to fill the wheelbarrow and then JT

was able to dump it into the forms. It wasn't easy, but she was strong and used to working hard. Ali was a champ at shoveling. She filled the wheelbarrow quickly and then smashed the snow down into the form after JT emptied it.

As they worked, they shared a few laughs, but after an hour they got more tired and their talking became more sporadic.

But when JT thought she couldn't take much more, she would look at Kyle and Sharon struggling and catch Ali's eye. They'd laugh and that was enough fuel to keep them going. Once they were satisfied they'd filled the forms as much as they could, JT did a final sweep of the sidewalk and walkway while Ali made sure the snow was pressed firmly into the mold.

Ali pulled the note out of her jacket and reread it. "You know, it says here we can carve anything we want and we can consult any sources we might have at our disposal. The only thing we have to keep in mind is that we have to carve the thing ourselves."

JT nodded along. "Yeah, I got all that."

"Did you get the part where you have four of the best artists in New England at your house right now? Including one who I believe is a world-renowned sculptor?"

"No."

Ali's eyes lit up. "Yes, JT. Your mom is a badass sculptor, and I know the two of you have a lot of stuff but if anyone can help us win this, it's her."

JT rested her butt against Ali's car. "Ali, come on. I just had a big fight with them and now you want me to go beg them to help us?"

"JT, come on," Ali said, mimicking JT's pathetic whining. "Yes, I expect you to act like an adult, make up with your family and ask them to use their world-renowned expertise to help us. Do you want to win this, or do you want Kyle and Sharon to win?"

JT groaned. "Oh my god. I hate you. Fine. Let's go ask my

mom and siblings how we can win this thing. But I swear to god, if any of them makes a crack about how my kindergarten-level skills suck, I'm walking out of there."

Ali smiled. "Deal."

JT slid into the car. "Let's hope Jonathan and Emerson aren't too hammered to help us."

Chapter Forty-Two

Ali held JT's hand as they drove up the driveway to the farmhouse she'd only visited a few times in her life. It had been a second home for Tommy, but her trips to the Coxes were usually limited to having to pick her brother up. She saw the Coxes around town but didn't know them and was slightly terrified of JT's mom. She had an eagle eye for bullshit and didn't suffer fools.

"You ready for this?" JT asked with a laugh. "They can be a lot."

"JT, my mother was trying to get me to throw the race this morning because she thought it would help me win Kyle back. There's no way anyone in that house can be as extra as my mother."

JT nodded. "Point taken. But even with me telling them earlier how much they've hurt me, you have to be prepared for them to talk to me like I'm stupid. It will probably happen. I don't expect some miraculous change in a matter of hours."

Ali hated the idea that JT's family would talk down to her or make fun of her for her lack of artistic ability. But she shoved that aside because they had a job to do, and if JT could ask her family for help with this, the least Ali could do was be supportive. Ali leaned across the car to kiss JT. "Hey, you can expect miracles. It's allowed. And besides, as a US hockey player, aren't miracles kind of what you're known for?"

JT shook her head. "Cute. But no."

Ali let JT lead the way into the house. She took her boots off in the back hall and left her snowy things to dry by the heater. JT kicked off her own boots and handed Ali a hanger from the closet and helped her balance her gloves and hat on the heater. Ali could tell she was stalling, but it didn't make her careful tending to Ali any less adorable. Ali didn't need to be doted on. She knew how to deal with wet outerwear, but JT taking care of her was incredibly sweet.

JT grabbed her hand and pulled her into the house. The kitchen was empty, the counters swept clean of any evidence of meal prep. Ali looked around and imagined how her kitchen would feel when she finished unpacking and decorating. She hoped it felt like this, inviting, calming, comfortable. "Do you want anything? Water? Beer?"

Ali shook her head. "Let's find your family and then worry about drinks."

JT squeezed her hand before dropping it as they made their way to the living room. JT's parents sat reading in stuffed chairs by a roaring fire.

"Hi, Jas— JT. And you brought Ali. How are you?"

Calling her JT was at least a step in the right direction.

"Fine, Mrs. Cox." Ali looked at JT, hoping she would speak for them.

JT poked at the fire.

"It's fine, unless you want to bring in a load of wood," her dad said, looking at her over his reading glasses.

JT put the poker back. "We just finished the first half of the final contest event."

"Mmm-hmm?" JT's mom said, barely paying attention.

JT looked at Ali, who nodded for her to go ahead. "It's us against Kyle."

Both parents looked up, first looking at JT and then at Ali.

"Kyle and Sharon, they're the other team," Ali said, adding a smile that she hoped would convince them that she was taking this seriously, but not to an unreasonable degree.

JT sat on the couch. "We need your help."

Ali almost laughed at how weird and cryptic JT seemed, but maybe after a lifetime of not asking her parents for much she was out of practice.

"The first part of the event was shoveling snow into a massive form about the size of a refrigerator."

JT nodded. "They had us shovel the sidewalks in the center of town until we filled our container with enough snow. Then we packed it down and filled it some more."

JT's mom placed her book on her lap. "Okay."

Ali sat next to JT. "What JT's trying to explain is that there's a second part. We filled the giant box and it's going to sit overnight to get set. Then tomorrow we go back and we have to carve it into a sculpture."

"Ahh," JT's parents said simultaneously.

"Yeah," JT said. "We're allowed to consult any resources we want, but we have to do the carving ourselves."

JT's dad smiled. Ali wasn't sure she'd ever seen him smile so widely or with such joy. "So you're coming to us because…?"

JT rolled her eyes. "You know why."

Her mom giggled and then stifled it. Ali had definitely never heard JT's mom giggle. It was disorienting. "We want to hear you say it."

"Fine. Because the two of you, especially you, Mom, are famously amazing sculptors known the world over for your talent, skill and artistic abilities."

"True, true." Mr. Cox was loving this.

"And if we are going to do our best in the contest, we would be very appreciative of you sharing any of your wisdom with us."

Mrs. Cox hopped out of her seat and hugged JT. "Wow, did it kill you to say all that?"

JT laughed. "No. It's the truth. But there are a lot of parents who I bet don't make their kids grovel when they ask for help."

"Fat chance. Especially if they're artists. We're famously needy."

Ali watched the scene unfold, with JT's parents bantering with her in a way Ali couldn't have imagined ten minutes ago. JT relaxed as they teased her. She transformed from the shut off, grumpy woman who acted more like a petulant teen back to the warm, caring person Ali knew. By the time her mom let go, JT was laughing along with her parents and seemed back to herself.

JT looked across the room at Ali and smiled. "Ali was the one who reminded me of what an amazing family I have."

JT's mom sobered. "I'm sorry we haven't been as amazing as we should have. But maybe we can make up for some of that?"

JT nodded, finding tears prickling at the corners of her eyes. She never expected them to apologize, she never allowed herself to hope for it, so even this mild acknowledgment of fault was an unexpected gift. "I'd like that a lot."

"Okay, what do you need from us?" her mom asked.

Ali stepped forward. "We have to take this block of snow and turn it into some kind of impressive thing—they gave us no real parameters—that the judges will like enough to give us the grand prize."

"Where is the block?" JT's mom asked, her sharp eyes focused on Ali. "Any time you make a piece of art in a location, you have to take into account your surroundings."

Ali nodded. "The two pieces are on either side of the walkway up to the inn's porch. Kyle and Sharon have one side, and we have the other."

"And we won't have an idea what they're making until it's done. So, we can't coordinate or plan based on what they're doing," JT said, anticipating her mom's question.

The Coxes exchanged some kind of telepathic conversation

with their eyes. Ali felt a pang of jealousy. She'd had that with Kyle, once. When they were teenagers. They'd been so close they'd know the jokes the other was thinking before they said anything. They'd know when it was time to go without having to say a word. They could read each other effortlessly.

She wanted that again. She wanted that easy, carefree, "we don't even need to talk to understand each other" kind of love. She was jealous of JT's parents. She was so jealous it flashed through her like anger. And then she looked at JT and it flashed through her like possibility. She could have it. The possibility was there. JT was all possibility—she even tasted like hope.

But the next two days might be all they had to test her theory. Only a few days before JT left for her new team and Ali went back to teaching and avoiding comments about her divorce in the grocery store.

But she looked at JT and she smiled back. Ali drank in all the hope and possibility and the most delicious hint of mischief in JT's eyes. And Ali knew it was love. It might have only been a few days, but if JT's parents could have a whole conversation without any words, she could know she loved this woman after a week.

"If you two are done making googly eyes at each other, what were you thinking in terms of a sculpture?" Mrs. Cox, one of the most terrifying humans Ali had ever encountered was smiling at her. It was disorienting. But Ali liked it.

"I'm not sure we'd come up with anything. We drove straight here from the center of town. We knew we needed help." Ali looked at JT to make sure she hadn't gone too far.

"Oh, she understands how to butter up a couple of artists. I like her," Mr. Cox said to JT. "Don't fuck this up, kiddo."

"Dad!"

"If you try to tell us you're just friends, I swear to god we won't help you. That would be an insult to our intelligence."

JT looked at Ali and they shared a look of mortification that turned into laughter. "Okay, Mrs. Cox." Ali giggled.

"Now that we have that settled, you better treat my kid well and you better not fuck it up, JT."

"Mom!"

Mrs. Cox held up her hand. "I love you, but your dating life is pathetic. Now, let's talk about how you two are going to carve a refrigerator-sized block of snow into something that will win you that prize."

After two hours of drawing plans, learning about tools they might want for the contest, and way more arguing from JT's parents about the proper techniques to use, Ali and JT walked into the kitchen to find something to drink.

"Do you think it's going to be good enough?"

Ali shrugged. "If I had to bet, Kyle and Sharon will come up with some wildly elaborate thing they want to carve, and he will overestimate how good he is at this and they'll end up with something terrible. But I've been wrong before. I think keeping it simple is the right choice. Not that I thought we could carve a unicorn or something like that in the time we have, but I think making it simple is smart. That way we can be sure to make what we say we're making and it's less likely to have a major fuckup."

JT held up a beer and a bottle of wine. "Drink?"

Ali pointed to the wine. "A glass of that sounds great." She waited for JT to pour it for her. "So, is there anywhere in this house where we can hang out? Or should we go freeze our asses off on your porch like a couple of teenagers?"

JT popped the cap off her beer and threw it into the trash in one fluid motion. "Are you trying to get in my pants, Porter?"

Ali struggled not to spit out her wine. "I... I wasn't, but I wouldn't be opposed to the idea. Mostly, I was hoping you'd show me your childhood bedroom or something."

JT's eyes went wide. "Oh my god, the kids! We were supposed to babysit!"

"Shit."

"Mom, are the kids here?"

"Do you hear them?" her mom called back from the living room. "When you two got called in for the contest, your brother and sister realized they had lost their babysitters and came up with someplace to go together."

"They wonder how I got to be such a smart-ass." JT took a sip of beer. "Grab your glass. I can show you my room, but it's not mine right now. I got stuck in the cellar, remember?"

They climbed the stairs to the second floor where the kids' bedrooms were. JT pointed out Jonathan's and Emerson's rooms before they got to the door for JT's room. Inside there were toys and books on the floor as well as a few piles of neatly folded clothes.

"Oh my god, those pj's are adorable," Ali said, pointing to the tiny pajamas next to the pillow on the bed.

"There's nothing cuter than little kid jammies," JT said, standing a bit awkwardly to the side. The room had a slanted ceiling, and she was too tall to stand except in the center of the room.

Ali looked at the walls. "Why are there no embarrassing posters? I want the boy bands you listened to or the cut-out magazine pages. It's too grown-up in here."

JT laughed. "When I left after college, I took most of that stuff with me and the rest of it went in the trash. Also, why would I have boy band posters? You do remember that I'm like super gay, right?"

Ali stepped closer to her and wrapped one arm around her waist. "Yes, I definitely remember that you're a sexy lesbian, but lesbians can like boy bands, too."

JT kissed Ali's cheek. "I didn't have boy band posters, but I did have *Glee* posters."

"*Glee*?" Ali asked, trying not to laugh.

JT frowned at her. "Yes, I know that show is super problematic, but I was a teenager! There were hot cheerleaders who sang and danced and made out with each other! What was I supposed to do?"

Ali wrapped both arms around JT, careful not to spill her wine. "I take it back. You're adorable. I can just imagine you with your nose pressed against the screen staring at... Okay, who was your favorite?"

JT blushed. "Obviously, I loved Santana, but Quinn..." She shook her head at the memory. "Seems like I have a thing for blonde prom queen types." She looked down at Ali, her smile so sweet and earnest.

Ali kissed her, hard. JT's hand snaked up her back and then cupped her face. She deepened the kiss and Ali pulled them together. For a minute they kissed with increasing intensity. "God, I wish I dated you in high school. It would have saved me so many years of bullshit."

JT kissed her forehead. "Ahh yes, the famously easy time of girls dating in rural New Hampshire."

Ali felt chastened. "That's not what I meant."

"I know. Teenage me wouldn't have known what to do with herself if she got to date you. I barely know what I'm doing now."

Ali wrapped her lips around JT's bottom lip and sucked it into her mouth. She felt JT lean into her before letting go of JT's lip. "I think you know exactly what you're doing." Ali held eye contact but stepped back. "But maybe I shouldn't try to seduce you in your childhood bedroom..."

"Where my nieces and nephews are sleeping this week?"

Ali nodded, keeping her eyes locked on JT. "Especially when I have a whole house to myself and an actual bedroom."

JT grabbed her hand and pulled her toward the stairs. "Now you've seen my bedroom, I think it's time you showed me yours."

Chapter Forty-Three

Ali held on to JT's hand as she pulled her up the stairs in her house. JT noticed there were the remnants of painting supplies scattered in the hallway but didn't ask about them. She was too focused on Ali's ass as they walked up the stairs. She found herself nervous the closer they got to Ali's room.

Sex on the counter in the kitchen and on the hated beige couch felt a million years away. It was different, less weighty than this walk to Ali's room. Ali's bed. Ali's space. They'd told everyone else they were just friends, but her mom had seen through it, Tommy knew and didn't care, and now this—whatever was happening between them—wasn't just a fling.

When they got to the door, JT paused. "Are you sure about this?"

Ali smiled. "Not chickening out, are you?"

JT shook her head but didn't smile. "Ali, I'm serious."

"JT, I want this. I want you. I'm not asking you to answer all the other stuff. I know there are obstacles, distance, a team that could be as far as the Midwest... But I don't care. I'm not scared of that."

JT tried to seem cool, but she *was* scared of all that. She was scared that she loved a woman who lived in a place she never could. She was scared that she'd already fallen for her and spent hours trying to figure out how they could possibly make it work when she would never ask Ali to leave Hart's Landing and she couldn't see how she could possibly live there without going insane. Even after talking to her parents, she wasn't one-hundred-percent sure she could convince the league to put her on the team in Boston after she'd made such a big deal about *not* being there.

"Stop overthinking it." Ali cupped JT's face in her hands.

"Ali, this is an impossible situation." JT's voice was urgent, pleading. She wanted Ali to tell her she was wrong, it wasn't impossible.

"Shh," Ali said. "It's not impossible. All you have to do is follow me and let me take off every single thing you're wearing." Ali grinned. Ali grabbed a handful of JT's shirt in each hand and tugged her closer. She raised herself on her tiptoes and gave JT the most mind-melting kiss of her entire life.

When she stepped away from JT and into her room, JT stood blinking for a moment. "Fuck," JT said in a low voice. She followed Ali into the room, where Ali was busy turning on a set of twinkle lights around the window. They hung around the room, casting it in a dim light.

JT scanned the space. "So where are all your posters?"

Ali wrapped her arms around JT. "If you're looking for embarrassing teenage stuff, it's mostly at my mom's house. But you're right, this room needs some art on the walls." She kissed along JT's jaw and then down her neck until she reached the collar of JT's flannel.

JT leaned her head back, allowing the feeling of Ali's lips on her skin to completely overwhelm her. She let out a breath. "It looks nice in here."

"It will be better when I get rid of this awful pink paint." Ali ran her tongue up JT's neck to her ear. "But I wanted to have it ready in case I got a chance to bring you back here."

From anyone else it might seem presumptuous or even creepy, but JT liked that Ali had a plan and that she'd been thinking about bringing JT to her bedroom for long enough to get a dresser set up and her things put away. JT kissed her, her lips opening and her tongue gently exploring Ali's lips. Ali responded immediately, one hand on JT's ass and another in her hair. She pulled them together, their thighs and hips pressing into each other.

JT cupped Ali's face, letting her fingers wander through Ali's hair while she kissed her harder and more urgently. Ali reached between them to pull JT's shirt up, exposing the skin of her stomach. She traced her fingers over JT's muscles, one by one in an excruciatingly slow line from JT's bra to the top of her jeans.

JT's nipples hardened and she could feel herself becoming impatient for more. Ali's laugh filled JT's mouth and JT's gasp filled Ali's when Ali reached her fingers inside the waistband of JT's jeans and gave a tug.

"Can I please take these off?" Ali pleaded, her hands on the buckle of JT's belt.

JT nodded and watched as Ali pulled off her belt and threw it to the side. Then she unbuttoned her fly and unzipped it to reveal JT's underwear.

Ali smiled up at JT. "I fucking love these. Did you know that?" She pulled JT's jeans down to the floor, leaving her standing with her boxer-brief-style underwear clinging to her legs. "Look at your thighs, Jesus Christ."

JT stepped out of her jeans, kicking them to the side. She pulled up her flannel with one hand and looked down at her legs. She knew she was showing off, but she was proud of her muscles. She'd worked her ass off for a long time for them and she was going to enjoy the look of absolute lust on Ali's face.

"Oh yeah?"

Ali bit her plump, kiss-swollen bottom lip. "Hell yes."

She grabbed the waistband and tugged JT closer. Her fingers lingered inside the band, whispering a touch across JT's very sensitive skin. She'd been wet since they were at her parent's house, and JT was sure her underwear were soaked at this point.

JT reached for Ali's sweater and yanked it over her head, revealing a tank top. Ali's nipples were completely visible through the thin fabric, and it made JT's mouth water thinking about wrapping her lips around them.

She took no time getting her hands on Ali's skin. She kissed down her neck toward her breasts, but Ali grabbed the side of her face.

"No way, lady."

JT was confused.

"Slow down, I'm going to fuck you, don't try to distract me with that mouth or those magic hands. I'm not falling for it."

JT smiled. "Falling for what? Are you claiming me making you scream my name is a scam?"

Ali shook her head. "I will not be distracted by your filthy mouth."

JT quirked an eyebrow. "Challenge accepted." She leaned forward, brushing her lips against the shell of Ali's ear. "I want to lick you until you beg me to stop."

Ali shook her head, her breath a little shaky. "Nope, I will not get distracted. But I might assume you're telling me exactly what you want me to do to you. So...get on the bed."

JT stood in the center of the room trying to decide if she should give in to this woman, who she very much wanted to fuck her, or if she should make her work for it a little longer. She grabbed Ali by her thighs, lifted her and plopped her onto the bed. JT loved the surprised expression on Ali's face when her back hit the soft comforter.

"Oh, you suck at doing what you're told." Ali couldn't resist pushing up into JT hovering above her. "But that's fine. I know how to keep control of a classroom. I think I can make you behave."

JT rolled her hips forward and Ali's rose to meet hers.

"Oh no, you can't just use your sexy ass and your incredible thighs to make me forget what I'm doing." Ali pushed up, rolling JT onto her back. Ali let her hips sink against JT's as she held her face above JT's. "Now, I'm not delusional enough to think I did that without your permission."

JT grinned. "I like that you think I'm fighting you for control. I like you on top." JT surged up to kiss Ali and was rewarded with Ali's hips tipping forward into JT. "But why are you wearing so many fucking clothes?"

Ali laughed. "Because I'm afraid if I take my pants off, I'll lose my focus." She giggled and JT felt herself fall a little more for this perfect woman.

"Will you take your pants off if I promise to behave? I swear to god you can top me all night long, but I really want to feel your skin against me and not your rough-ass jeans."

Ali licked her lips, and JT wanted nothing more than to suck Ali's tongue, but she held back. If Ali wanted to be in control, JT would let her be, and she would enjoy every fucking second of it.

Women usually assumed that because JT was a little masculine and built like a hockey player, she wanted to be the boss everywhere. The truth was, there wasn't much JT found sexier than a woman who knew what she wanted and wasn't afraid to boss JT around a little.

Ali hopped off the bed long enough to slide her jeans and socks off. "I'm leaving these on because it's too tempting otherwise."

JT took an exaggerated look at Ali's panties, which were lacy and gave her tiny peeks at the skin of her ass. JT let her head fall back against the bed. "You're so fucking hot."

Ali crawled up the bed until she had her legs around JT's

hips. She sat on JT's thighs and bent over to run her tongue up the center of JT's chest, higher and higher as she slowly unbuttoned JT's shirt. She pushed it open and took in the sight of JT's bra and her breasts spilling out of them.

"May I?"

JT nodded. "I told you, anything you want."

Ali gave her a wicked grin. "That's a dangerous offer."

"I trust you."

Chapter Forty-Four

If Ali didn't already love JT, hearing her say she trusted Ali to do whatever she wanted might have sealed it for her. JT looked up at Ali with her face both open and vulnerable but completely at ease. Ali knew she wanted nothing more than to prove herself worthy of that trust. Possibly for every day for the rest of her life.

But the rest of their lives weren't happening then. She took her time devouring every inch of JT's chest. Running her tongue across her nipples then replacing it with her fingers, only to go back to sucking until JT's breath grew shallow and she panted into Ali's ear.

"Ali, are you going to make me beg?"

Ali considered the question. Was she? Maybe. She hadn't planned on it but having this powerful woman begging for her release made Ali's clit throb with want.

"Do you want me to? Would that get you off?"

JT laughed. "I honestly don't know at this point. You're driving me insane with that tongue of yours." She let her head fall back and stared at the ceiling. "I'm dying, Ali, aching for you. Please fuck me."

Ali grinned but felt a flutter of nerves. She'd imagined this moment. She'd imagined it at least a dozen different ways. On her knees licking JT until she cried out. Burying her fingers deep inside JT and driving into her until she was shuddering and wrapping her legs around Ali's waist. Using any of the toys she kept next to her bed. But now that the moment had come it was like her brain was broken. How could she decide how to please this woman when all she wanted was to please her one hundred different ways until neither of them could walk? She wanted this woman spent and begging for more.

"How do you like to be fucked?" Ali felt herself blush, but not from the question. She wasn't shy about sex, but she was shy about being unsure after all her big talk.

JT held eye contact and reached behind Ali's head to hold her gently. "I like to be fucked by women who are sweet and sassy and who talk a whole lot of shit." She smiled and Ali felt like her insides were melting into a puddle. "But if you want specifics... I want to feel your weight on top of me and your fingers inside me. I want you to drive your hips into me. Does that sound okay?"

Ali kissed her and moved her legs to be between JT's. "This okay? I'm not squishing you?"

JT nodded. "You feel perfect." She wrapped her legs around Ali. "Don't be scared. You feel amazing."

Ali's heart swelled. It was all the reassurance she needed to focus. She traced her hands up JT's legs until she reached her underwear. "Look, as much as I love how these look, can you slide these off for me. They're blocking my access."

JT slid out of them, and Ali settled back on top of her, her hand poised on JT's inner thigh. "You could probably crush me with your thighs, huh?"

"I wouldn't."

Ali dipped her head to suck one of JT's nipples as her fingers explored her wetness. "It's pretty hot that you could, though."

She slid her fingers slowly along JT's slit, dying at how soaked she was. "JT, oh my god."

"You make me so fucking wet. I want you."

Ali swallowed and focused on her fingers and every single thing she could feel beneath them. She slid them lower to circle JT's opening. She teased and prolonged, watching JT's face change with every touch.

"Ali, please. I want you inside me."

Ali surged forward, pressing her fingers deep into JT and letting her hips press her hand against JT as she rocked up into the pressure. She pulled out and drove forward again and again as JT rocked against her. Ali watched the delicious way JT's face let her know what felt good. Her breathing became more frantic, and Ali struggled to keep the rhythm because she was falling apart with every touch, every thrust. She wanted JT to come, and she wanted to watch her fall apart. JT jerked and Ali felt her tighten around her fingers and she worried she was going to come just from watching.

"Ali, oh my god. Don't stop. Don't fucking stop."

Ali rocked forward again and waited. JT moaned her name, her head falling backward against the bed. Her pussy fluttered with aftershocks and Ali rode them like the best wave on the most perfect beach day of her life.

"Fuck, that was amazing," Ali said, her filter gone along with her willpower to resist this woman.

JT opened her eyes, looking slightly drunk, dazed, and so happy. "I fucking love you."

Ali's eyes widened in surprise.

JT froze. "Oh shit. I mean…" She paused, her eyes searching Ali's face.

Ali didn't know what to do. She loved this woman but she'd said it after sex, which everyone knew couldn't be trusted. Right? Ali reached for JT's face, brushing her hair off her forehead.

"Really?"

JT swallowed, her jaw and throat working up and down. She nodded. "Yeah. I'm sorry it came out like this and I'm sure you're thinking you can't trust it because I'm all sex drunk on the best sex of my life, but fuck it. I love you, Alexandra Porter. And not because you just fucked my brains out. I love you. And it's not convenient. But it's true."

Ali froze. Was she really doing this right now? She took a deep breath. "I love you, too. And not because you just said I was the best sex of your life, though thank you for that. I'm sure I have a lot to learn. But because I love you. And you're right, it isn't convenient, but I do." She kissed JT and rolled to the side so she could be beside her on the bed.

"What are we going to do?" Ali asked, her brain already moving a thousand miles an hour. Of course they couldn't do anything about the circumstances. This had to be a fling. It didn't matter that they loved each other. Their lives were impossible. They could love each other but it didn't solve the problems that physically separated them.

"Do? You mean tomorrow or the next day? Or do you mean now? Because right now, I really want to have sex with you, in your bed, in your house. And I want it to last for hours. And then if there's some stuff we have to figure out, fine. But right now, I love you, and if I'm right, you're soaking wet and you need me to do something about that. Am I right?"

Ali grinned. "You're an absolute menace. But I love you, and because you have completely ruined my underwear, I'm going to need you to make me come at least four times to make up for it."

JT smiled. "Then I better get started."

Chapter Forty-Five

JT woke up disoriented. Ali's room was a far cry from her parents' basement couch, and she forgot where she was until she felt Ali's warmth next to her. Ali's blond hair spilled across the pillow, catching the weak morning light from the window. It was still early, but if there was sunlight she really should be going home. Toby would be waiting and so would her family.

Ali stirred next to her. JT pushed a few strands of hair away from Ali's face and marveled. How was this woman with her? How had she found her way into the bedroom of the girl who made her realize she liked girls? How on earth had she been so lucky?

Ali smiled but didn't open her eyes. "I can feel you staring at me."

"Not staring, admiring."

Ali opened one eye. "Are you always this smooth? Is it your thing?"

JT laughed and kissed Ali on the forehead. "No one in the history of the world has ever thought I was smooth. Good morning, you look beautiful."

Ali snuggled into JT's shoulder. "You are smooth whether

you realize it or not." She kissed the bare skin exposed above the sheets. "This is nice, you know?"

JT nodded and stared out the window. "It really is, but I probably should go home so I can take my dog for a walk and shower before we win this final contest."

"No."

"No?"

"Stay here. Or go get Toby and come back. I'm not in favor of animal cruelty." She squinted up at JT. "I take it back. Call your brother and have him take your dog for a walk and then take a shower with me."

JT smiled and kissed Ali. "I would love to, but I don't have clean clothes and you know I can't fit into yours, you tiny gorgeous human."

"I am not tiny."

"Babe, you're like five foot two."

"Five-three! God, the slander." Ali rolled on top of JT. "But you're not nearly as curvy. I suppose you'll be more comfortable in your own clothes for the competition. And it will be satisfying to get you out of them later."

JT shook her head slowly. "Bit presumptuous of you."

Ali let her hair fall over her face, tickling JT's nose. "Are you saying you don't want to come back here after we win to have a naked celebration with me?"

JT raised herself up on her elbows so she could kiss Ali. "Definitely not saying that. But I don't want to jinx it. Maybe Sharon is secretly a master sculptor or something."

Ali held JT's face in her hands. "You are ridiculous. Sharon could be a master sculptor, but I have no doubt that Kyle is going to try to swagger his way through. Trust me, I was with that ding-dong for a decade, I know him. He's not going to be able to resist showing off. He'll say something stupid like 'landscapers are just good with their tools' or some shit and then the head will fall off the snowman."

JT laughed. "Okay, I trust you. But that doesn't change the fact that I have to go take a shower and put on clean clothes so I don't smell like sex all day." She kissed the tip of Ali's nose. "I also have to endure my family giving me shit if I can't sneak in without them noticing I was gone. So, cross your fingers for me."

Ali kissed her gently and then rolled off JT and let her escape the bed. JT didn't want to go. But every minute she stayed only made the inevitable harder. She scurried around the room, scooping up her clothes and putting them on. It was significantly colder out of the covers. Every time she looked at the bed, she had to force herself not to crawl back in with Ali.

Once she was dressed, she leaned over and kissed Ali who was still lying in the bed.

"I should walk you out," Ali said, as if the idea just dawned on her.

JT shook her head. "No. You stay there and get some more sleep if you can. I'll drive back over in time to go to the next event with every carving tool I can steal from my parents. See you in a bit." She kissed Ali again before forcing herself to leave.

Outside, the air was crisp and cold, with a light wind rustling the trees. JT kicked her boots through the snow. It was too hard to leave Ali for a few hours. How on earth was she going to leave her for good after New Year's? She wished she'd never asked the league to put her somewhere other than Boston. She knew they could do long-distance, but she wasn't sure that was fair to Ali. She was too amazing to be waiting around for JT to have a game on the East Coast, and her job wasn't exactly conducive to traveling. She had to be in the classroom every day between January and June with few exceptions. Could they make it work that way? Maybe. But would Ali want to, or would she grow bored of the travel and the distance and surviving on phone calls and texts? JT wasn't sure.

She knew how she felt about Ali. That hadn't changed much

since she was a teenager. Ali Porter had been the sun and the moon to her when she was a teenager and was again now, but relationships needed careful tending and nurturing. They might be a hardy flower, but even the hardiest needed sunlight. And if JT ended up in Minnesota, she didn't know how she'd survive for weeks or months without the sun.

She stewed for the rest of the walk home and arrived to a chaotic kitchen full of little kids, the smell of French toast, and Toby waiting expectantly for anything to fall into her mouth.

"Good morning, little sister," Emerson said with a smirk from the table, where she was cutting Brooke's French toast into sticks.

JT felt her face turning red. "Good morning, big sister." She hoped her tone was enough warning to keep her family from making jokes in front of the kids.

"Auntie JT, we're having finch toast," Brooke said, pointing to her plate.

"That looks so good. Is there any left for me?"

Jonathan handed her a plate stacked high with slices. "Oh, we sure did. I told Beth we should make extra because I thought you might have worked up quite an appetite this morning."

"Guys," JT said, her voice a low growl.

"Where were you, JT?" Mabel asked.

JT looked at her siblings, who offered zero help. She sat next to her niece. "I was at my friend Ali's house."

"Did you have a sleepover?" Harrison asked.

Jonathan sat next to his son and handed him a glass of milk. He smiled at JT and raised his eyebrows.

JT fought the urge to hold a water glass to her cheek. Her entire face felt like it was on fire. "Yes, like a sleepover."

"Cool," Harrison said and went back to his food.

Mabel looked at Beth. "Mom, I want to have a sleepover too!"

JT got up to get coffee. This was excruciating and her siblings seemed to be having way too much fun.

"Mabel, you can have a sleepover when you're a little older," Beth said. Mabel took a bite of her food but did not look at all satisfied with the answer.

JT's mom met her at the coffeepot. She handed JT a mug and poured her a full cup. "Did you have a nice time?"

"Mom." JT's voice was whiny and pleading. She wanted these people to leave her alone. "I shouldn't have come home, you guys are the worst."

Her mom laughed. "Honey, first you come home and stay longer than normal and now you've had to do the walk of shame right into breakfast. Honestly, you don't need to get us presents next year. This will more than suffice."

JT found the cream and sugar but in the process ran into her dad.

"So, Casanova…"

"Oh my god, Dad, stop it."

He and her mom laughed as they leaned against the counter. "You don't understand. Your brother and sister were always sneaking around and bringing their dates home. You never have. This is a first, and we are loving it."

JT sighed and tried to stay mad, but it was a first for her, too. She felt included and not like the weirdo outsider in her own house. She wasn't loving being made fun of in front of her nieces and nephews because it meant she couldn't truly fire back. Her family was using innuendos and cloaked language to keep the kids in the dark, but if she fought back, the kids would know something was up.

"Fine. But if you come to the final contest event you cannot act like this. Whatever I have with Ali is in the early stages. I don't even know what it is, really. And I could end up out in Minnesota next month. So, please…"

"What do you mean you could end up in Minnesota?" her

mom asked, of course seizing on the most important thing. "Why would you end up so far away? I thought established players had more say."

JT stared at a spot on the counter. No matter how much her family's indifference hurt her, she didn't want to tell them she'd asked to be anywhere but near them. They'd hurt her but she didn't want to hurt them back.

But then she didn't have to because her mom figured it out. "You asked them to."

JT nodded but didn't look at her mom. She couldn't bear to see the hurt in her eyes. "Yeah," she said.

"Why would you do that?" her dad asked.

JT looked at her siblings and their families sitting around the table. This is what she was running away from. This group of people who she loved. She was the one who was removing herself from moments like this. She was protecting her fragile heart from these people she loved not showing up for her. She'd taken that choice away from them because it was easier than getting pummeled every time they failed to show up for her.

"This is about the final game," her mom said, her voice cracking.

JT nodded. "It's about that and every other game you skipped." She turned to look at them. "I didn't want to look up in the stands at every home game in hopes you would come only to be disappointed. There's only so much I can bear."

"Does Ali know you asked the league to put you elsewhere?"

"She knows, but we're just friends."

Her mom and dad laughed right there in her face. "Oh, so it was a 'just friends' sleepover then?" her mom asked, still laughing.

JT blushed. "Come on, you know someone like Ali is never going to fall for someone like me."

"Why not?" JT's dad asked, sounding offended on her behalf.

JT sighed. "She's got her shit together. She has a real job and house and…"

JT's mom slipped her arm around JT's waist and pulled her in for a hug. "You might not believe this coming from your shitty parents, but you're an incredible woman. Ali would be lucky to be with you. We understand why you requested another team, but I'd love it if you'd consider giving us a chance to be better at showing up for you."

JT didn't want to talk about this anymore, especially not with her parents, who were both correct and the reason for the problem in the first place. "I've got to take a shower and change before the contest. Do you guys have any tools you think might help us carve that snow block?"

Her parents shared a look. "Yeah, we'll get some stuff from the barn for you."

In the shower, JT kept going over her night with Ali and her conversations with her parents. They'd been so helpful about the contest and the night with Ali had been incredible, but this morning it felt like reality was punching her in the face. Her feelings toward Hart's Landing had changed since being home. People seemed to genuinely feel happy for her, proud of her accomplishments in a way she never experienced before. And she'd talked to her parents about all the ways they'd failed to show up for her in the past. All of that was great, but was it enough to make her want to change her choice of team? Could she trust them not to break her heart again?

What if she talked to the league and they put her in Boston and everything with Ali fizzled and her parents' promises to do better were nothing more than words? Then she'd be in Boston and looking into the stands hoping to see them only to be crushed again. And what if Ali decided that dating her wasn't all that great? It had been an amazing week, but a week was nothing. Ali could change her mind or realize she was a fucking catch who deserved better than JT.

By the time she got dressed for the contest, her head was even more of a mess. No matter what came next, she had to get her ass out the door so they could make the best snow sculpture ever and win the final prize.

Regardless of what they were to each other, having an amazing romantic dinner at the inn sounded like the perfect way to end this chapter. Or maybe begin the next one, not that JT felt like she had any right to hope.

She stopped in the kitchen for another cup of coffee and some snacks to take with her. Her parents were sitting at the table, no grandkids in sight. "We loaded the tools into the back of your car. I'd suggest a few pairs of gloves in case yours get wet as you work," her dad said, nodding to a pile of gloves and mittens on the end of the table. "I pulled a bunch together in case you and Ali needed them."

"Thanks, Dad." JT wanted to say something more, but she couldn't find the right words. Not an apology, because her actions were based on her experiences and she wasn't sorry to be protecting herself. But she was sorry if that hurt her parents.

Her mom walked over to her. "We'll be there in a few hours. I know you can't ask us for help once you start, but we want to be there to see how it goes anyway. Your father tried to cook up some hand signals but I told him to knock it off. You're not a cheater, and besides, you're going to do great. You may not have chosen art as a career, but you'll do fine with Ali by your side. You two make a good pair."

"Thanks, Mom," JT said before grabbing the bundle of gloves and the rest of her cold weather gear and heading out.

She might not know how things were going to end up with Ali, but she was sure she wanted to beat Kyle's ass in this final competition. There was no way she was letting his stupid ass win the final prize.

Chapter Forty-Six

The inn had cocoa, coffee, tea and a variety of pastries waiting for them on a long, thin table inside the front hallway when they arrived to carve their snow sculptures. Ali and JT grabbed cups of coffee and scones while they waited for the judges to arrive.

"Do you really think our design is good enough?" JT asked.

Ali smiled over the lip of her cup. "Yes. We have to do a good job, obviously, but if I had to bet on one team, it would be us." She nodded in the direction of their competition. Kyle had his hands on his hips like some kind of superhero and Sharon was busy scrolling social media as he jabbered at her.

Ali knew Kyle well enough that she would have been willing to bet he would implode before lunch. He hated being outside his comfort zone, but he also overestimated his own abilities. She raised her eyebrows at JT and then walked over to Kyle.

"You must have been happy when you heard what the final contest was."

He eyed her warily. "Why would you say that?"

Ali smiled. "Isn't carving snow just like carving shrubs? You have tons of experience trimming trees and shrubs and making them look nice for people. I'm sure you're feeling confident."

Kyle blinked but recovered quickly. "Yeah, that's right. I've been doing that since I was a teenager. How hard can this be?"

Ali shook her head. "Not hard for you, I bet." She waved to Sharon. "Good luck out there!" She walked back to JT with a smile on her face.

"What are you doing?"

Ali laughed and stepped into a small room with a roaring fire. "Kyle hates being bad at things. But even worse, he hates being bad at things when people think he should be good at them. He gets embarrassed, and then he gets pissed when it's not going his way. I thought I'd remind him that everyone knows that outdoor decorating is basically his job, so…"

JT looked slightly horrified. "Oh my god you are diabolical."

Ali did her best impression of the Grinch's horrible smile. "Maybe I am. But that guy tried to shit-talk you the other day and you kicked his stupid ass. I figured it was my turn to talk some shit, in my own way. If it throws him off his game to be reminded that his job is literally to make outdoor things look good, that's not my fault."

"Were you always this competitive and I forgot?"

Ali shrugged. "Ask Tommy about how many times I kicked his butt playing soccer in the backyard."

JT laughed. "I do recall you practically knocking him out when he tried to slide into home during a family softball game."

Ali smiled. "I got in so much trouble, but he didn't score."

The inn door opened, and several middle-aged and older folks walked in. "Ah good, I see our finalists are here." A man wearing a camouflage hat stepped into the room with the fire. "Would you join us in here? I'm freezing."

Kyle and Sharon walked into the room and took the only two seats on the couch in front of the fire.

"I want to review the rules quickly before we get started and answer any questions you might have. You have until three this afternoon to finish your sculptures. At that point the judges will decide who the winner is. You may not get help in the sculpting from anyone who is not your teammate, but you may ask the judges for rule clarifications. You may take breaks whenever you like, and the inn will have food and drinks in here to keep you going.

"Finally, keep in mind that these sculptures are intended to draw interest from passersby and to bring foot traffic both to the town and to the inn—we hope you have considered that in your designs. If there are no questions, you may get started. Good luck to you all."

JT and Ali filed outside and down the steps to their giant rectangle of snow. The committee had removed the plywood forms to reveal two giant blocks of snow. They walked around theirs, inspecting the surface and pointing out areas that seemed uneven. Fortunately, Ali noted that there were no major issues with the structure. Kyle and Sharon didn't seem quite so lucky. They had a couple spots where there were chunks missing where they hadn't packed the snow in tight enough.

JT pulled a piece of paper out of her jacket and laid it flat on the table they'd been provided for their tools and food. "I think we should start by taking off these spots. I think we can safely cut off the chunks here and here. What do you think?"

Ali looked at the block and then back at the drawing. "Yeah. This whole thing makes me very nervous, but let's start with the big stuff and then work down to the stuff that takes more finesse. You want to go first?"

JT shook her head. "You're the only one of us with any kind of art background and you want to hand the tools to me?"

"I'm not sure that classroom decoration counts as an art background." Ali picked up a flat-ended shovel. "I trust you. You can do this."

JT beamed and took the shovel. She scored along the edge of the block and removed a piece. When the entire thing seemed to stay together, she looked at Ali and went back to take off another chunk. "Okay, that isn't so bad."

It only took about an hour for them to make the rough shape of their design. After talking with JT's parents, they decided to make a throne out of the snow so couples could sit on it and take cute photos for New Year's. They thought the folks at the Hart's Inn would like the way it would bring people to the front and entice them to take pictures and maybe even stay for a drink or dinner.

JT's parents had warned them about being too aggressive. "Once you cut something, it's gone for good. You can't stick it back together. Better to be careful than to have to try to repair it." Ali had felt like Mrs. Cox was speaking directly to her when she said that, like she thought she might be prone to being careless or breaking things she couldn't fix with JT.

As they worked side by side, Ali watched JT. She was careful with each bit of snow she removed. She concentrated so hard on every move she made. It was adorable how she concentrated and double-checked each piece before smoothing the edges and carving the design into the snow.

Ali peeked a few times at Kyle and Sharon and they were not having as much success. At some point, one of them made a part of the snow too narrow, and the head of the bear they were trying to carve appeared to be falling off. Kyle was barking at Sharon, who looked ready to kill him or burst into tears. Maybe both.

JT, on the other hand, hadn't said much to her. After their night together, Ali wasn't sure how to read JT's silent concentration. Was she simply trying to do her best work or was there something else going on?

"Hey," Ali said, stepping next to JT and handing her some cocoa. "Are you okay?"

JT nodded. "Yeah, why? Thanks for this." She took a sip of the cocoa.

"You seem quieter than normal, and I didn't know if I did something wrong last night…"

JT put her hand on Ali's forearm. "Definitely not. You were perfect. I just have a lot on my mind." Her serious expression disappeared quickly when she pointed to the throne. "You know, like winning this thing and making my family of famously incredible artists proud." She laughed but it sounded forced.

Ali nodded but her mind whirred with possibilities. JT wasn't usually so stiff or reserved. Ali didn't know what to think about it. Maybe this was her competition mode or maybe Ali had done something wrong, and JT didn't want to say anything in the middle of the event?

Maybe saying she loved JT was a mistake. It had only been a few days. They'd known each other forever but not like this and maybe Ali had come on too strong even when she knew they lived very different lives. Oh god, she'd really fucked this up.

Ali looked across the walkway at Kyle and Sharon. They were each working on one half of the sculpture and it wasn't matching very well. The scale of the bear was off between the two halves. Ali didn't want to feel overconfident, but she felt good about how their progress was going even if she worried about what JT might be thinking.

She took a small shovel and carefully removed some of the snow around the arms of the throne. She watched how JT was cutting the design into the other arm and tried to match it. After a few minutes, she decided it would be better for her to work on something else.

"Hey, why don't you do this arm, too and I'll work on the back." She subtly motioned to the other team. "We don't want to end up with a lopsided chair."

JT looked at Kyle and Sharon. "I don't want to get too cocky but holy shit that's a train wreck over there." She stepped to the front of the chair. "Do you want to come here and look at this for a second?"

Ali joined her. "What am I looking at?"

JT smiled. "Nothing in particular. Do you see anything that looks off? We still have time to fix it if you do. I think the back could use more decoration and I'll keep the arms as even as possible. What else?"

"What if we carve the seat to look like it has a pillow? Or is that overkill?"

JT shrugged. "I don't know." She leaned her head close to Ali's. "If those two keep fighting they're going to end up with a headless bear so I'm not too worried about winning, but I kind of want to do the best I can." Ali was charmed when she realized JT was blushing. "I know I'm not as good as my siblings, but I want this to be good, you know?"

Ali leaned her forehead against JT's and resisted the overwhelming urge to kiss her pink cheeks. "I get it. I'll do my best to make the back look like a throne. But at some point we have to stop fiddling because if we go too far we could wreck it." She held JT's eyes with her own, realizing midsentence that she wasn't only talking about the sculpture.

The hours passed and they took a break for some food and to get warm inside. JT hovered around the food and drinks table making plates for herself and for Ali while Ali sat by the fire waiting for the feet to thaw. She was used to the cold but standing on the snow all morning left her toes almost numb and her legs exhausted. The fire felt heavenly, and having JT dote on her by bringing her hot cider and a sandwich made it the perfect way to spend an afternoon. Too bad they had to go back outside to finish the throne.

Ali patted the spot next to her. JT joined her on the couch, balancing a plate of food on her thigh. "Are you okay? You seem a bit…"

JT stared at her plate. "Yeah, fine." She looked up at Ali.

"Oh god, you look so serious. I'm fine. Just a little stressed, you know?"

No, I don't know, Ali thought. "Stressed about the throne?"

JT shook her head. "No, I mean, a little maybe. But mostly thinking about what comes next." JT scowled at the floor. "Not in a pressure way. I…"

Ali put her hand on top of JT's. "There's no pressure. Other than winning, we don't have to plan anything else."

JT smiled but Ali could tell it was forced. "Right. Got it." She shoved her sandwich into her mouth and stood up. "We should keep going. I'll meet you out there."

Ali watched her go, wondering what the hell had just happened.

Chapter Forty-Seven

JT scraped at the snow as gently as she could. Of course, Ali didn't want to plan for a future with her. JT was a fun little diversion over the holiday, nothing major. If JT was ready to ask the league to put her closer to home, maybe she was the only one thinking long-term. Ali wasn't begging her to stay. She wasn't even making it seem like she cared very much about JT sticking around.

JT worked diligently to create the best snow throne she could. Ali made the back of the seat look amazingly like a real throne, complete with dimples and buttons like on a real upholstered chair. JT carved the arms carefully and then moved on to making it appear as though the chair had legs instead of a massive blob of snow. They had agreed it was stupid to try to get rid of the blob, but her parents talked to her about how she could try to create the illusion of legs.

"Excuse me, would you mind explaining your inspiration behind this piece?"

JT turned to find her parents bundled against the cold, leaning over the fence to look at the throne. "Hi! Yes, we'd love to talk about this with you art nerds. The main inspiration was making an object that wouldn't break too easily and that we thought we could carve in a few hours with minimal skill."

JT's mom cast her gaze over the entire sculpture before smiling. "You've done a good job. The arms on the chair are very even."

"Wow, your work is even? Damn, Mom, do you give such faint praise to your students?" JT asked with a laugh. She genuinely wasn't offended but wasn't going to miss an opportunity to tease her mom.

"What? No! I mean it. Snow isn't an easy material. There's a reason I don't carve ice or snow, it's a pain in the ass. Kind of like you." She peeked over her sunglasses. "Ali, you're doing a nice job with the backrest. I can see the buttons!"

Kyle yelled to the judges. "Hey! They're cheating!"

JT looked at Ali and rolled her eyes.

"I'm talking to my mom, that's not cheating."

Kyle walked closer, waving a trowel. "No, she's an artist or something. They're cheating!"

The judge stepped off the porch and walked toward them. "Mrs. Cox, nice to see you again. Are you impermissibly helping your daughter and her friend?"

JT's mom crossed her arms over her chest. "Walter, are you accusing me of cheating? No, wait. Are you accusing my daughter and her girlfriend of cheating?"

Walter blinked. "Girlfriend? I thought they were just friends."

"Mom!"

Mrs. Cox leaned over the fence. "I'm not a cheater and neither is my daughter. And yes, girlfriend. Gay people exist, Walter!"

Ali joined them. "Hi, Mrs. Cox."

"Girlfriend?" Kyle asked from his side of the walkway. "Ali, you're dating her?"

JT froze. Ali looked at Kyle and then at her. She had a panicky expression that melted into a smile. "Kyle, that's none of your business."

JT's stomach dropped. She didn't expect Ali to tell her ex they were dating when really, they were just kind of fooling around while she was home, but part of her was still disappointed.

Ali dropped her tool onto the ground. "But what if I am?"

Kyle's jaw dropped open.

Mrs. Cox nodded, a little too proud of herself, in JT's opinion.

"So you're cheating on me and in the competition?"

Ali sighed. "Kyle, we are divorced. We have been divorced for a year. I can date anyone on the planet and it would be none of your concern. Do you understand that when two people break up it's not cheating if one of them dates someone else? Or do I need to explain that to you?"

"Also, aren't you dating Sharon?" JT asked.

Kyle scowled. "It's not serious."

Sharon appeared at his side. "It's not serious? Are you kidding? You spent Christmas Eve at my house!" She threw her tools on the ground and stomped into the inn.

JT and Ali looked at each other with wide eyes.

Walter did his best to rein everyone in. "Mrs. Cox, were you helping your daughter and her… Ali?"

"No, you fool. I was complimenting them for doing a good job. So, unless cheering for my daughter is against the rules, you have nothing to worry about. God, get a life!"

Walter shrunk under her gaze. "Okay. Well, then continue, I suppose."

JT looked at Ali and then her parents. This was a mess. She didn't know if Ali would be happy to be outed to the town but she was sure the information about them dating would make the rounds by the next day.

"You okay?"

Ali shook her head. "Not really." She walked over to Mrs. Cox. "You misspoke. What you should have said was, 'Some people are bisexual, Walter.'"

JT's mom stood motionless for long enough that JT worried she was mad. But then she cracked up. Not a small laugh either. She cackled, and JT's dad joined her until they were leaning on each other to keep from falling. "Oh, JT, she's a keeper for sure." She wiped her eyes. "Try not to screw it up."

JT didn't have a chance to respond because her parents walked past them and into the inn. She and Ali stood in the front yard of the inn staring at the sculptures.

"What just happened?"

JT wasn't sure what to do with her hands. She wanted to give Ali a hug, but after her parents outed her to her ex-husband, she wasn't sure if Ali would like a hug or would tell her to fuck off. "I'm sorry about my mom, she can be kind of a lot."

Ali laughed. "That's one way to put it. Did she just tell Walter that we're dating? Or am I having a weird-ass dream?"

"No, that actually happened. I'm sorry. Did you not want people to know? I can go yell at her if that would make you feel better."

Ali shook her head. "Nah. I don't care about people knowing. Kyle's a tool, but he's known I'm bi for a long time. And I meant what I said to him. He doesn't get a say in who I'm dating…" Ali paused, looking distracted. "Are we dating?"

JT sighed. "We do stuff together, like this contest and going to Ikea, and we have a habit of making out kind of a lot. I think that qualifies as dating. At least it does for me."

Ali leaned against JT and rested her head on JT's shoulder. "Me too. I know our lives aren't set up for us to be together right now…but I meant it when I said I love you."

"I love you, too." JT sighed again. She wanted to tell Ali her plan, but if it didn't work, she didn't want to disappoint her. She knew what she wanted, but how could she ask Ali to have a long-distance relationship with her where they might only see each other a couple times each month, if they were lucky? It was unfair to Ali. It was unfair to both of them regardless of how happy she was with Ali. It didn't matter if their lives made a real relationship impossible.

"But you're here and I have no idea where I'm going to be for the season. It could be anywhere." JT's parents returned to the porch, each holding two cups of steaming drinks.

"Where do you want to be?" Ali asked, her voice quiet.

Before JT had a chance to answer, her mom handed her a cup and her dad gave one to Ali. "We thought you two might need something to warm you up." JT's mom looked at the throne. "Once the judging is over, can we sit in it?"

JT and Ali looked at each other. "Of course, but only if you agree to take a picture of us in it first."

"I suppose you've earned the right to be first." JT's dad sipped his coffee. "We'll wait over here. Walter said they're going to judge in a few minutes." He cast his eyes over Kyle and Sharon's disaster sculpture. "I don't think you have much to worry about. Those two are too busy fighting inside to even try to fix that mess."

JT's parents took a seat on a bench on the inn's front porch. JT looked down at Ali. Could she tell her she wanted to be in Boston? Was that too much or would it get her hopes up unfairly? JT didn't know if they had a future together, but she was fairly certain that if she ended up in Minnesota, any chance they might have would fizzle. She couldn't do anything about that now. But she could try to win the contest. Then, at least, she would have one more date with Ali before they both had to go back to their real worlds.

"What do you think, should we finish this thing and win the prize?"

"I can taste that fancy dinner already."

Chapter Forty-Eight

"How about a round of applause for the winners of this year's contest, JT and Ali?"

They'd won the contest, but it felt anticlimactic. They'd busted their asses to get to the final and gotten all the help they could to plan their sculpture, but in the end Kyle and Sharon weren't even there when the winners were announced because they were too busy arguing. As Walter congratulated them on their throne and accompanying picture idea to bring publicity to the inn and the rest of the town, the bear's head fell off. It landed with a thud and rolled toward the walkway.

"Lord, that's going to scare people away," the owner of the inn said a little too loudly.

Ali smiled at JT and waved to the tiny crowd gathered outside the inn as they accepted their prize from Walter and the other judges. "Thanks," she said, taking the envelope. She turned to the inn's owner. "Sorry about the sculptures. We did our best."

The woman patted Ali's shoulder. "Yours is lovely." She shook her head. "We'll have to figure out a way to deal with that one."

She turned to JT, who was accepting her prize envelope as

well. "I'd always heard that you were the one Cox who wasn't an artist. But that was clearly a lie. You did a beautiful job."

JT blushed. "Oh no, I'm not an artist at all. But hopefully I made my family proud or at least didn't embarrass them too much. This is way out of my comfort zone, but it was fun anyway." She caught Ali's eye and gave her a quick wink.

Ali waited for JT at the foot of the sculpture. "You think it will hold us?"

"Only one way to find out," JT said with a warm smile. "You need a boost?"

Ali playfully smacked JT on the stomach, or where her stomach was beneath seventeen layers of jackets and sweaters. "I'm more than capable of getting up there, thank you very much." She got on the seat and waited for JT to join her.

JT handed her phone to her mom and jumped onto the seat easily. She slung her arm around Ali's shoulder and grinned. "This thing is pretty great, you know?"

Ali nodded. "The chair or us?"

"Both," JT said with a massive grin. She gestured for Ali to look forward. "Say cheese."

Mrs. Cox took a bunch of pictures before shooing them away. "Our turn. Come on, let's show those kids how it's done." She and JT's dad climbed up on the chair and posed like royalty for JT.

JT snapped a bunch of pictures of her parents and then texted them to her family group chat.

"JT! JT!"

JT turned around and saw her nieces and nephew running toward her on the sidewalk. Jonathan, Beth, Clark, and Emerson lagged a few steps behind looking a little worse for wear.

"Hi guys!"

Ali crouched down. "Are you Brooke?"

Brooke nodded.

"What do you have there?"

"Cookies!" Brooke shouted way too loud for how close she was to Ali's ear. Ali flinched but couldn't help laughing. She stood up and said hi to Mabel and Harrison.

"Who are you?"

JT covered her smile with her hand. "This is Ali."

"Are you Auntie JT's girlfriend?" Mabel asked.

Ali looked at JT, trying to gauge her reaction. JT raised her eyebrows and gave Ali a grin.

"Yeah, Mabel. Ali's my girlfriend."

Ali's chest warmed with the realization that hearing JT call her "my girlfriend" was an unexpected comfort. After spending so much time together, Ali wanted to be able to say they were together, but circumstances made her wonder if JT would feel the same way.

"Are you going to get married?" Harrison asked with a very serious expression.

Ali opened her mouth but couldn't find the words.

JT crouched down to his level. "Would you like it if we got married?"

Harrison shrugged. "Emerson was saying she hoped you'd have a wedding soon."

JT looked over Harrison's shoulder to her sister. "Oh, she did, did she? Hey, Mrs. Bennett, why are you trying to get me married off and why are you telling your kids about it?"

Ali looked at Emerson, who was blushing. "Oh my god, JT. I'm not trying to get you married off." She looked apologetic. "All I said was I like Ali and it's about time we had another wedding in the family."

Emerson leaned closer to Ali. "I'm sorry. I'm not trying to meddle. It seems Jonathan's kids were lurking when I was talking to Clark. I really am sorry. There's nothing worse than people trying to rush you when you're first together."

Ali shook her head slowly. "This isn't pressure. You should see the kind of pressure I had to deal with after Kyle and I won prom king and queen. People would stop us on the street. It was weird how invested they were." Ali stood in the middle of this group of the Cox family and smiled. It felt nice. She was comfortable with them, even if JT's mom was still terrifying. She looked at JT for any hint of how she was feeling.

"JT! That throne looks amazing! How did you manage to make it look so good in so little time!" Jonathan walked a circle around the chair, inspecting it and pointing out things he liked to the twins.

JT grinned. "Thanks, Jon. Mom and Dad had a lot of suggestions that helped."

"Oh no, don't you try to give us credit. You two did this all on your own."

Ali wasn't sure she'd ever seen JT this joyful around her family. It made her so happy. After a week of learning all the ways the Cox family had failed her, seeing them all complimenting her work was heartwarming. But more importantly, they were there. They'd shown up to see what she had done. Ali could see they were making her feel important and loved.

Ali wished she could capture the moment and carry it around with her forever. JT's joy, the smile stretching across her face and the way her eyes crinkled at the corners, filled Ali with such a sense of happiness. She realized how much she wanted this to work out. The odds were stacked against them in so many ways, but Ali ached to spend more time being near JT and her sweet, kind, joyful heart.

That wasn't entirely up to her, though.

Chapter Forty-Nine

After the contest, JT drove Ali home and sat in the car with her. "I didn't realize how tired I am until now."

Ali sighed. "Same. All that adrenaline kept me going and now I want a nap. Do you want to come in?"

JT shook her head. "I have to take care of something first." She could hear how cryptic that sounded, but she didn't want to get Ali's hopes up if she wasn't going to be able to make this work.

Ali's face betrayed an instant of wariness before she schooled her features. "Is it serious?"

JT shook her head. "It's nothing to worry about. It's a work thing that I thought I could put off until after New Year's. I'll tell you all about it when I get it sorted out, okay?"

Ali didn't look at all placated, but she didn't ask more questions. "Okay. Will I see you later?"

JT shook her head. "Not tonight. But I'll be back in time for our prize dinner tomorrow no matter what, okay? I'm sorry. I know there's more to do on your house and now I'm bailing to go do this thing," JT said, more to herself than Ali. "But I'll tell you everything as soon as I get back. Okay?" She took Ali's hand. "You were amazing today. Sorry my mom outed you to the whole fucking town. I hope that's not going to be a problem."

Ali laughed nervously. "I don't think it matters to anyone. They were all so invested in Kyle and me and the idea of us as high school sweethearts that I'm sure our divorce was way more shocking to most of them than the idea that I'm not the straight girl they imagined." She squeezed JT's hand. "You don't have cancer or anything, do you?"

"What?" JT sputtered. "No. Nothing like that. I promise. I'm not trying to be weird. I will fill you in on everything when I get back." She sighed. "I really am sorry about the house. You should call Tommy to help you."

Ali kissed JT on the cheek. "That's a good idea. See you soon?"

JT nodded. She wanted to say *I love you* but that seemed unfair under the circumstances. If she couldn't convince the league to put her in Boston, it would be cruel to string Ali along.

Every time she thought of telling her, she remembered her parents coming to the Olympics and then skipping the final game. She had to find out after the game, in the locker room, when her siblings texted to congratulate her and she found a text from her parents saying they hoped to see her at Jonathan's show.

It had crushed her. It would have been better for them to not have come at all than to get her hopes up. She wouldn't do that to Ali. It was cruel, and even if things didn't work out with them, she would never be cruel.

JT drove the short way home and took Toby out to the yard with a tennis ball to get her some exercise and give herself some time to think. They fell into a rhythm that JT found meditative. She'd take the ball and throw it as far as she could, and Toby would sprint after it, bounding through the snow until she reached the ball, then returning to do it all over again. Between each toss, JT had time to think as she watched Toby's enthusiastic play.

Her parents had helped her last night and they'd shown up for her a few hours ago. Was it possible that they'd heard her and decided to change? Or was she setting herself up for another massive disappointment?

Footsteps crunched in the snow next to her. She launched the ball for Toby and then turned to find Jonathan standing next to her, his shoulders hunched forward against the cold.

"Mom says you're taking off?"

JT bent to give Toby a rub and to wait for her to drop the ball. "I'll be back. I'm going down to Boston in a few minutes. I'm going to talk to the team, but I'll be back tomorrow."

Jonathan watched her throw the ball. "Did something happen?"

JT didn't know how to answer that, exactly. Lots of stuff had happened. She'd finally told her parents how she felt about them bailing on her games and never valuing her accomplishments the way they valued Jonathan's and Emerson's. She'd fallen hard for Ali Porter. She'd seen her hometown in a way she'd never expected. A lot had happened.

But that wasn't how he'd meant it. "Being home this time was different."

He didn't fill the silence so she threw the ball again. Her shoulder was starting to burn a little. "Every other year, coming home felt like that time Grandma made me put on that god-awful dress for their anniversary party."

Jonathan took a minute but then cracked up. "Oh my god, I look at the pictures of you from the party at least three times a week. I've never seen an angrier seven-year-old."

"Yeah. That was the worst. And coming home always felt like putting on an itchy, too small dress with a lace collar. But everyone acted like I was insane or a bad person for not wanting to be here." She sighed and flipped the ball to Jonathan. Toby turned in her spot, waiting for him to fling it. "But this time, I don't know. The town felt okay, like I could be me here for a change."

"This doesn't have to do with you hooking up with Ali, does it?"

"Of course that's part of it. But mostly people didn't treat me like I was a freak for being good at hockey. Little girls were wearing my jersey and telling me about their teams. It felt good to be here."

"So why are you leaving tonight?"

JT stuffed her hands into her pockets. "You can't tell anyone because it might not work. I'm going to ask Boston to sign me."

"You can do that?"

JT smiled. "I don't know if you've heard, but your baby sister is pretty fucking good at hockey. So, I can ask. They might say no."

Jonathan skipped the ball over the snow, and Toby pounced on it and lay in the snow to chew it. "I thought there was going to be a draft. Didn't you tell Mom and Dad last week you didn't know where you were going to end up?"

JT nodded. "Yeah. But last week I didn't tell them I asked the league to put me on any team except for Boston. Don't worry, they know all that now." He made a confused face. "I didn't want to feel like shit every time they skipped a game. It wouldn't feel bad if they were thousands of miles away, you know?"

"Oh yeah. I get that."

JT sighed for what felt like the thousandth time. "But everything feels different now, and I know it's going to make me look stupid and flaky but I want to see if they'll put me closer to…"

"Ali. You can say it. We all know you like her."

JT chuckled. "Yeah. If I'm in Minnesota or wherever, it won't work. But if I'm in Boston, we have a fighting chance. I've never felt like this for someone, and I don't want to lose that because of geography."

Jonathan grabbed her by the shoulder and shoved her playfully. "I'm sure there's a million other ways you can fuck it up."

JT faked like she was going to tackle him into the snow. "If you weren't such an old man, I'd stuff snow down your hood." He tossed a snowball through the air, purposefully missing her. "Anyway, don't tell everyone what I'm up to. I want to know if it can work before I tell Mom and Dad or Ali."

She whistled for Toby and walked her inside. "Will you make sure she gets fed? I'll be back tomorrow, I just don't know exactly when."

Jonathan gave Toby a rub behind her ears. "Of course. Good luck with everything. We'll be here when you get back."

"Get back? I thought you were just going out for a drink?" JT's mom asked. She and her dad were sitting at the table having a cup of tea.

"I have to go to Boston overnight. I'll be back tomorrow. Jonny's going to make sure Toby is taken care of, so don't worry."

Mrs. Cox held her hand down and gave Toby the end of her cookie. "I never worry about Miss Toblerone. She's my girl, isn't that right, you sweet thing? What's happening in Boston that's so important you have to ditch us after your triumphant win?"

JT rolled her eyes. "I'll tell you all about it when I get back. Bye!" She hurried out the door before her parents could ask any more questions. With any luck, she'd be returning with good news.

Chapter Fifty

Ali was shouting at Tommy before he even got through the door.

"Tommy, she left. We won the contest and she took off!"

Tommy blinked as he entered Ali's house holding two pizzas and a six-pack of beer. "What do you mean she took off? Did she tell you where she's going?"

"Yes. She's going to Boston."

"And did she say when she'd be back?"

"Before the dinner tomorrow."

Tommy set the food down on the counter. "So why are you freaking out?"

Ali gave an exasperated grunt. "Because I told her I loved her and then she left!"

Tommy held up his hands. "Wait, you told her you loved her when?"

"Last night!"

"And like eighteen hours later she left and that has you freaking out? Maybe this is a gay thing because I'm not getting it." Ali scowled at him. "Were you hoping she would never leave your side? Because if she told you where she was going and when she'd be back and she's not missing some big important event or anything, what is the problem?"

"I'm freaking out! That's the problem!" Ali popped the top off a beer and took a swig. "She was acting so weird during the contest today and now she's left. Tommy, what if she ditches me? You said she was a flake, right?"

Tommy held up his hands. "Whoa, whoa, whoa. No way. JT has had her moments in the past, but Ali, you're not some random girl she met at a party. I know I said some stupid shit, but I was wrong." He leaned on the counter. "I'm sure you already know this, but JT had a crush on you from the time we were kids. You're her fucking dream girl."

"Then why did she leave?"

Tommy shrugged. "Why did she say?"

Ali scoffed. "Something about work and having to go meet with some people? Sounded like some bullshit, honestly." Ali walked around the kitchen, her nerves getting the better of her. Her brother's lack of worry wasn't comforting. She found it annoying because it made her seem unhinged. And she wasn't unhinged! Her girlfriend had up and fled the town after they'd spent the entire night together and had given some weird reason about a job. Ali didn't think she really had a job yet. She honestly didn't know how the whole gold medal winner thing worked.

Tommy walked over to her and wrapped her in a hug. It was annoying how big he was. He was her baby brother, but now he was big enough to wrap her in a hug and rest his chin on the top of her head. "You really like her, huh?"

Ali nodded.

"And that's what is freaking you out. Not that she left for the night, but that you're worried she's not going to come back."

Ali frowned. Was that really what she was worried about? That she was the only one out here on a limb? Was she worried that JT could walk away so easily when Ali felt so much? Even worse than Tommy being fully man-sized was him being right. She squeezed him.

"She's going to come back," Tommy said quietly. "She's not the kind of person who disappears without a warning. If she said she was coming back, she'll be back." He pushed her away. "In the meantime, are we going to finish this room?"

Ali nodded. "What if she's mad I changed the color?"

"Ali, oh my god. I will say it again. I promise you that JT Cox doesn't give a single fuck what color you paint the walls of your office or bedroom or the freaking cellar. It's yours. It's your house. It's your call. She is only going to want you to be happy. It's one of the best things about her—she wants the best for the people she loves."

Ali hoped he was right. Even more, she hoped that she was someone JT loved that way. Loved enough to keep her promises and show up when she said she would. Because Ali didn't want to be alone in this.

There was a knock on the door followed by a voice. "Hello? Ali?"

Ali looked at Tommy, already feeling her annoyance spike. "Mom?" She walked down the hall to the door, holding her beer in one hand.

"Ali, why aren't you answering your phone?"

Ali resisted the urge to roll her eyes, but just barely. "Why are you calling me?"

"Kyle and Sharon broke up."

Ali took a sip of beer and braced herself for whatever unhinged thing was about to happen. "So?"

"So, he's single again."

Tommy's footsteps creaked on the floor behind her.

Ali stopped keeping the exasperation out of her voice. "So?"

"Alexandra, don't sass me. This is your chance to get back together with him."

Ali pinched the bridge of her nose. "Mom, I don't know how many times I have to tell you this, but I have more interest in getting smallpox than I do in getting back together with Kyle."

"Don't be stupid. Of course you want to get back together with him."

Ali waved her arms, gesturing to her surroundings. "Mom, what part of me *buying* my own damn house makes you think I want to be Kyle's wife again?"

Her mom waved a hand dismissively. "You bought the house, but you haven't even finished unpacking. That tells me you don't actually want to be here. You haven't painted the walls— you barely have any furniture."

"Follow me," Ali said, doing everything in her power not to stomp the entire way to her office. She pushed open the door to show her mom. "This is the second time I'm painting it. That's why Tommy's here, to help me get it finished before school."

"You've painted it twice? You're so indecisive. Thank goodness you have me around. Call Kyle."

Ali couldn't take more of this. "Mom, I'm not indecisive. I know what I want, but you keep coming around trying to make me doubt myself. You are always in my head telling me I'm doing something wrong or making the wrong choice. And I've let you! It's how I ended up married to Kyle in the first place. It's how I ended up with the wrong color in here." Ali took a breath, trying to calm herself so her mom might listen to her instead of calling her hysterical. "Mom, I'm going to tell you this one more time, so please listen. I do not want to be with Kyle. I want to be with someone who thinks I'm amazing and supports me. I want to be with someone who makes me laugh and who shows up for me with no questions asked."

"You're blaming me for your divorce? Please, Alexandra, that was all you."

Ali looked at her brother, not because she wanted him to bail her out, simply because she needed someone to confirm this was actually happening. "Mom, I didn't say you caused our divorce. I said you caused our marriage. If everyone wasn't so invested in Kyle and me being together and getting married and having whatever storybook future you saw for us, I might have realized sooner that we weren't a good match. Instead, I didn't stick up for myself and I let it all happen. I should be the one choosing who to be with, not going along with what everyone else decided was good for me." She held her hands out and gestured to the room. "That's why I'm repainting. I did it again and listened to other people who told me yellow was a good color for my office instead of sticking to what I really wanted. It means I have to do it over again.

"Just like finding a partner. I have to do it again. But this time, I'm not listening to you or to anyone who isn't me. I know what I want, who I want, and who makes me happy, and I'm not letting you push me back toward Kyle or anyone else. Got it?"

Mrs. Porter huffed out a breath. She looked at Tommy as if he was going to offer her support. He crossed his arms over his chest. "It sounds like you have someone in mind. Are you dating someone?" she asked.

Ali sighed, suddenly hit with a wave of exhaustion. Her emotions had been too keyed up for too long and now she could feel a crash coming. "Mom, JT and I have been seeing each other this week."

"What? Tommy's JT?"

Ali almost felt bad for her mom. "Yes, Mom. She and I have gotten close this week and, look, I don't know where this is going, but I know that she makes me happy in ways no one ever has before."

Her mom sputtered. "How do you feel about this, Tommy?"

Tommy shoved away from the wall. "It took me a little by surprise. But Mom, there's a reason she's been my best friend forever. She's the best. If she and Ali want to be together, then all I want for them is to be happy." He looked at Ali and gave her a reassuring smile. "But Mom, it doesn't matter what I think. Ali gets to make her own choices, including who she wants to date."

Mrs. Porter scowled. She looked at Ali, opened her mouth, but shut it half a second later. "Have you thought about how you're going to feel when you're all alone in this house?"

Ali opened her mouth, but her mom cut her off.

"Because I can tell you, it's not easy being alone." Jean's hand fluttered next to her.

Ali realized where all her mom's rantings came from. She softened. "Mom, like I told you, I'm not alone. My friends haven't abandoned me. I don't have kids." She took her mom's hand. "I'm really sorry for how hard things were for you here. I truly am. And I'm sorry I didn't understand that until now. But Mom, I love my life." She looked at the walls. "I hate this stupid paint, but I love this house."

Her mom sniffled.

Ali pointed to Tommy and squeezed her mom's hand. "And I'm not alone. I have you and I have Tommy, and I have JT."

Jean looked at Tommy and then Ali. "I'm sorry, but I can't help worrying." She wiped her nose. "I'm your mother and I know how hard things can be…"

Ali wrapped an arm around her mom. "I know. But I'm okay. I'm better than okay. Do you understand that?"

Jean nodded and accepted hugs from both her kids. "Yeah. I'm sorry, but I won't ever stop worrying." She let go of them. "I should let you finish your painting."

She turned and headed out the door, leaving Ali and Tommy bewildered by her abrupt exit.

"You okay?" Tommy asked.

Ali nodded. "Yeah. I feel bad for what she went through, but she still drives me completely bananas."

Tommy laughed. "Yeah, that was pretty unhinged. Hopefully she heard you, though."

Ali took a deep breath. "You still up for helping me put this all back together?"

"Of course. But can we eat first? I'm starving."

Ali nodded and followed him to the kitchen. She knew she was doing the right thing. She didn't want Kyle. She didn't want her mother telling her who to date, what couch to buy or how to live her life. But she also worried that JT might not be coming back. What good would it do her to know what she wanted if she couldn't have it?

Chapter Fifty-One

JT's leg bounced up and down as she waited for her meeting. It hadn't been easy to convince the team's general manager to meet with her on New Year's Eve. Few people worked if they could help it, but with the draft coming up, there were more folks in the facility than there would have otherwise been. JT was taking advantage of that. Her agent had somehow worked her magic to get them to agree to see her on almost no notice.

JT was going in alone. Her agent couldn't get to Boston on less than twenty-four hours' notice, so it would be JT and the executives. Her leg bounced faster. She had very little hope that this would work. But she wanted to know, for herself, that she'd tried everything she could. And she wanted to be able to tell Ali that she'd gone begging. If it didn't work, she would be able to know she left it all on the ice, so to speak.

"JT? They're ready for you," an assistant said, startling JT out of her thoughts.

JT hopped out of her chair and smoothed the front of her shirt. She followed the assistant down the hallway to a glass-walled conference room. Inside, two executives sat at a giant table overlooking a view of the city.

A woman, probably in her mid-forties, stood up and walked

to the door to shake JT's hand. The man next to her stood and held out his hand.

"I'm Emmett. I'm the assistant GM."

"I'm Jess, I'm the general manager. Sorry for the light crew here today. Would you like some water or anything?"

JT nodded and filled a glass with water from the pitcher on the table. "Thank you so much for agreeing to meet with me on such short notice. I'm sure you had plenty of other things to do today, and I truly can't thank you enough."

Jess laughed. "Don't thank us yet."

JT's nerves spiked. "Right." She nodded and reached for her water. "So, the reason I'm here is to let you know that I would love to play in Boston." She exhaled, and her heart raced.

Emmett and Jess exchanged a look. "That's not…"

"I know. I know I asked to be anywhere but here. But I wanted a chance to explain myself and ask you to consider taking me in the draft." Her hands were shaking. Before games she got nervous, but nothing like this. There were warm-ups and routines and plenty of time to get her nerves out before they dropped the puck. But this was her and two executives that possibly held her future in their hands, and she'd had no time to prepare for this.

"I've been home with my family in New Hampshire all week. They were the reason I asked not to be in Boston."

Jess's eyebrows shot toward her hairline.

"They're not horrible or anything. They are into art. They're all professional artists and professors, so my whole sports thing isn't their world. And in the past, they've shown an inability to, um, be there for me even for big events. So, the truth is, I didn't want to be close to them because I thought they wouldn't show up and it would be too hard.

"But I don't think that's the case anymore." JT fiddled with her Olympic champion ring. "And maybe that won't be true and maybe it won't be any better, but I have hope that if I'm close by I might see them more. And I have nieces and nephews who like hockey and…" She took a deep breath. "Sorry, I'm rambling a little."

Jess rested her hands on the table. "So, you had some kind of reset with your family and now you want us to draft you?"

JT nodded. "I know it's ridiculous. I know it's a big ask. I asked to be somewhere far away when I thought I would be better off away from my hometown. But that's not the case. I have a lot of reasons to want to live and play for a team as close to home as possible.

"I understand if you have already made your choices and I'm not in your plans. Asking for this was certainly not in mine. But sometimes life surprises you in really good ways. And I wanted to tell you that if you draft me, I will work my ass off for you and this team and the city of Boston. I was born and raised less than two hours from here, and I want to show the little girls in my hometown that not only do they not have to play on the boys' team, but they can play pro and be near their families and the town they love."

JT took another sip. "And, like I said, if choosing me for your team isn't in the cards, I totally get that. But I've never been afraid to take a big swing. I took one when I tried out for the boys' team in high school and when they made me captain the year we won states. I'm a player who is always going to give you everything I have. Which means I came down here on what was supposed to be my vacation and asked you to consider me."

She stood up. "Thanks for your time. I really appreciate it."

Jess motioned for her to sit. "Hold on, you can't leave yet."

Emmett laughed. "Yeah, that was like a sports movie level speech and you're just going to leave?"

JT sat and laughed nervously. She hoped this was a good sign, but she couldn't tell from their faces. Maybe they just wanted a chance to talk, too. Maybe they were going to tell her off for wasting their time. Maybe a lot of things.

But one thing was for sure, she'd given it her best shot. She could go home and have her date with Ali knowing she'd done everything she could to give their relationship a fighting chance.

Chapter Fifty-Two

On my way

JT had sent the text, but Ali was still sweating over whether she'd get back in time for their date. The dinner was at seven and it was already six, and she hadn't heard from JT again to say she'd made it. There was no text saying she was on her way to meet her or to pick her up, and Ali's brain was getting the better of her.

She checked the temperature for the second time in ten minutes. It hadn't changed from epically freezing. She stared at her closet. A lot of her house might still be in boxes, but her clothes were put away, thanks to the new dresser JT had assembled for her. She paused with her hand on the drawer pull. Everywhere she looked in the room she saw reminders of JT. From the furniture she'd driven Ali to buy in her parents' van, to the dresser she'd assembled, to the bed where they'd spent the night together. Every single thing had JT attached to it.

If JT didn't show up to their date she would be surrounded by reminders of her. What a stupid thing, to have allowed JT to worm her way into Ali's home and heart. When JT went back to her normal life, wherever that was, Ali would be stuck staring at walls and furniture and her own bed, and all of it would make her think of JT.

She flipped through her closet, looking for the perfect thing to wear. The inn was fancy, but New-Hampshire-in-December fancy. People looked nice, like they made an effort, but still understood it was nineteen degrees outside and would be colder later. Ali wanted to look amazing. She and JT hadn't had a real date yet and she wanted to make an impression.

But that sounded increasingly stupid the longer she went without hearing from JT. What if she got all dressed up and JT got stuck in traffic or bailed on her completely? People at the inn would know. They'd see that she was there alone, and they'd feel bad for her or text their friends about it. It would be completely embarrassing.

No. She wasn't going to think like that. She was going to get dressed up however she fucking wanted and eat amazing food and not think about the possibility that JT would stand her up. Other than being a little weird during the snow sculpture event, JT hadn't given her any reasons to doubt her. Ali was being insecure for no reason.

She selected a dress that made her feel good. No, not good, she felt hot and sexy, and if people were going to stare at her with JT, she was going to give them a damn good reason. She'd worn her hair up in most of the contests to keep it out of the food or to make it easier to tuck under a hat, so she left it down. She let it fall in soft waves around her face and admitted that she looked amazing.

She wasn't the homecoming queen anymore. She wasn't the town's golden girl married to the golden boy. She was something else. Not worse—different.

Chapter Fifty-Three

JT already knew that she was cutting it close when she left Boston. She'd wanted to stay and talk with the folks at the team for as long as she could. It might've given her a better chance of having them pick her when the draft started. And she was willing to do just about anything to make that happen.

The meeting made it clear they weren't sure what to make of her after her complete one-eighty on where she did and did not want to play in the upcoming season. She couldn't blame them. She'd been shocked by the change in her family and the way her hometown embraced her. She'd been delightedly surprised by that. She had always hoped her family might find a way to support her, even if they didn't fully understand her, and she was hopeful they had. But falling for Ali wasn't something she'd ever expected.

Unfortunately, that extra time with the team execs trying to get them to see why it would be worth taking a chance on her meant one thing: She was going to be late. She was going to be late, and her phone was dead. She'd sent the text that she was on her way when she left Boston, but then traffic got bad and the cord in her car crapped out and she was following directions that were supposed to take her around some big accident on the main highway only to have her phone go into power save mode and die.

She arrived at her parents' house at quarter to seven needing a shower, an outfit for dinner and a way to tell Ali she would meet her at the inn. Oh, and her dog would need a walk, too. There was no way she could get it all done in fifteen minutes.

"Mom? Can you call the inn?" JT asked as she walked in the door to the kitchen.

Mrs. Cox walked into the kitchen. "Why are you yelling at me?"

JT rushed in, gave Toby a pat and skidded to a stop at the counter. "Hi. Sorry. Can you call the inn and ask them to tell Ali I'm running late?"

"Why don't you call her yourself?"

JT held up her phone. "My phone died and I don't know her number by heart. Please, Mom. I have to get ready as fast as I can, but can you get the inn to tell her I'm coming?" JT was freaking out. She could imagine Ali sitting there waiting for her and worrying when she was late.

What if she left? What if she thought JT had blown her off or stood her up? Shit. She had to hurry. She raced to the basement to grab her clothes. She didn't have time to think about what she was going to wear. She'd brought one nice outfit for Christmas, a pair of nice pants to go with a blazer and a button-down, but then she'd spilled on them when she was messing around at the table making the kids laugh. Shit.

The suit-adjacent outfit she'd worn to meet the executives was more professional than date night, but it would have to do. Thankfully she had one more clean dress shirt. After the quickest shower of her life, she dressed as fast as possible, and hurried upstairs to talk to her parents.

"Did the inn say they'd tell her?"

Her mom nodded but her face betrayed skepticism. "I talked to some kid at the front desk, but I don't have much confidence he'll tell her so you better hurry. I swear if you screw this up because you got lost..."

"I didn't get lost! There was traffic!" JT's voice was a shriek.

Her mom laughed. "Oh my god. I can't remember seeing you like this about a girl. It's kind of fun. Go, I'm sure she's waiting for you. Hopefully you have good news to tell her about today." She raised her eyebrows. "And maybe you'll tell us later?"

JT laughed. "I'll tell you, but don't wait up." Toby whined. "Shit, can you guys take care of her?"

JT's dad laughed. "Oh, because that would be a change from what we've been doing for the last several weeks? Of course we'll care for Miss Toblerone in your absence. Though if you keep ditching her, she might be our dog soon."

JT gasped. "You wouldn't!"

"I might!" her mom said, letting Toby give her kisses. "Get your ass out of here!"

JT drove as fast as she dared to the center of town. There was usually only one cop in town on duty at any time but on New Year's Eve she thought they might have a second one working. She parked in front of the inn, checked her hair in the rearview mirror and stepped into the freezing air. If she didn't hurry, her hair would be frozen when she got to the door.

On the way, she admired their sculpture. It looked good with the lights trained on it. She saw a couple walking up to it and considered offering to take their picture, but she was too late to be nice.

She ran up the stairs and opened the door to the entryway. Inside, the lights were bright and there was music playing. She shrugged out of her coat and hung it on the coatrack and then made her way into the side room with a roaring fire. She didn't see Ali at first. She was blocked by a tall man with his back to JT.

She stepped through the room, trying to get to the restaurant but stopped when she saw Ali. She looked stunning. Her blond hair framed her face and her dress displayed a tasteful but glorious amount of cleavage. JT's face broke into a massive grin.

How could she get so lucky?

"JT," Ali said, her voice strained.

The man turned around. Kyle. He straightened his shoulders and made himself seem larger than he was. He was dressed up in a flannel and a jacket.

JT's heart fell. "I'm sorry I'm late. Traffic was terrible and my phone died…" It sounded so weak even as she said it. Ali's face was unreadable.

"What did your brother say? That she's a flake?"

Ali's eyes blazed with anger. "Shut up, Kyle." She walked to JT and wrapped her in a hug. "I'm glad you're here," she whispered in JT's ear.

JT exhaled but she kept her eyes on Kyle. "What's he doing here?"

Ali stepped back. "Apparently, my mom gave him the impression the other day that he should meet me here. But that that was before I talked to her, and I guess she never told him not to come." JT made a face of disbelief. "Exactly. Kyle, I'm sorry my mom gave you the impression I have any interest in seeing you. I do not."

Kyle scoffed. "Your mom made it pretty clear that you wanted to get back together with me." He preened like he thought that might work.

Ali closed her eyes and took a deep breath. "Kyle, regardless of what my mom might have said to you, we are divorced. I have no interest in changing that. At. All."

Kyle's face reddened as people walked through and took in the scene. JT feared he might get angry so she stepped closer to Ali. She wasn't as big as Kyle, but she was still much larger than Ali.

He seemed to deflate. "I thought you and I were forever, Ali." He looked like he might cry. "We were something special."

JT watched Ali's face for signs she was buying this. "Kyle, I'm sorry, but if you'll excuse us, we have a dinner reservation."

Kyle blinked but didn't move.

Ali grabbed JT's hand and pulled her toward the dining room. JT looked back long enough to see Kyle being herded to the door by a teenager who was probably the kid her mom talked to on the phone. He looked maybe seventeen, but he didn't appear intimidated by Kyle.

Ali led JT to a beautiful table set with white linens and candles. "I'm glad you made it."

JT waited for Ali to sit before she took her seat. "I'm sorry. Did they give you the message?"

Ali nodded. "Yeah, after I'd been waiting for ten minutes. What the hell happened to you?"

JT took a sip of water. "I'm sorry. I got redirected around this huge accident on the highway and then the cord stopped charging my phone so it died and I had no way to get in touch until I got home. I don't have your number memorized so I had my mom call here while I rushed to get ready. I'm so sorry. I didn't mean to make you worry or think I stood you up." She reached across the table and took Ali's hand.

Ali flicked her eyes around the room. JT pulled back but Ali gripped her hand with her fingers.

"I was worried," Ali said in a low voice. "I was scared you decided you didn't want this and didn't know how to tell me. I freaked out a little."

JT's chest ached. "I'm sorry. I never meant for that to happen. I went to Boston to try to fix everything and then I fucked it up."

The waiter arrived with a glass of champagne for each of them and offered them a look at the menu for the night. The New Year's Eve menu had only a few options, so they sent him away quickly with their choices.

"You didn't mess anything up." Ali smiled across the table and offered her glass to clink JT's. "Cheers."

"To us?" JT said, unable to keep the doubt out of her voice.

Ali took a sip and smiled. "That sounds good. So, will you finally tell me what you were doing in Boston or am I going to have to torture it out of you?"

JT drank half her glass, considered it for a second and then finished the rest. "Okay, I went to talk to the Boston team's executives." JT watched Ali's reaction, but she mostly looked confused. "I asked them to consider drafting me."

Ali's face brightened. "Is that something you normally have to do? I mean, you're a star and I would think all the teams want you."

JT blushed. "That would be nice. But I had already asked the league to put me anywhere but Boston. I didn't want my family to be so close and never come. I thought it would hurt too much. But after spending this week…"

"With me."

"Yes, with you." JT nodded as she spoke. "And also seeing that maybe my family could change and could find a way to support me, I wanted Boston to know that I want to be on their team if they are willing to pick me."

"So, this thing between us?"

JT nodded. "I don't mean this to put any pressure on you or our relationship. I didn't tell you what I was doing in case they laughed in my face and told me they didn't want someone so indecisive on their team. If it was impossible, I didn't want to get your hopes up. Or mine." JT stared into Ali's eyes, not sure she was seeing things or if Ali looked happy.

"We have a fighting chance," Ali said in a low voice.

JT nodded. "If you want us to, we do. If this is really a vacation thing for you, I understand, but I wanted to be able to try. If you want me, I'm all yours."

Ali smiled warily. "Now I know what you've been up to, I think I should tell you what I did while you were gone."

JT's stomach dropped. Had she screwed this up completely? Had Ali given up on her in a day?

"First, I freaked out a little about you leaving."

"I'm sorry."

Ali laughed. "I was freaking out, for no reason, so I called Tommy to come over and he helped me finish a project at the house and calmed me down."

"What project?"

Ali shook her head. "I'll tell you in a minute. Then my mom showed up and went off about how I should get back with Kyle, so I yelled at her and told her I was never getting back together with him. You can imagine my surprise to see him here when I was looking for you."

Ali's voice climbed as she spoke, and JT grew more worried. "Don't look so scared. I'm fine. I think I have a better understanding of why my mom keeps pushing me toward him. Talking with her seems like in a scary movie when you have to keep defeating the bad guy. Kyle showing up here was like the bad guy sitting up that one last time before you smack him with a shovel." Ali laughed.

JT reached across the table, but Ali grabbed her hand first. "I'm sorry you went through all of that and I wasn't here."

"Oh, I was mad about that, too. You could have told me what you were doing."

JT sighed. "I didn't want to let you down if they said no way. I think my chances for Boston are better than zero now, and if they take me we can figure out if we have a future together on our timeline, not in a week."

The waiter arrived with their salad course but disappeared quickly after they thanked him.

JT fiddled with her fork. "I want a chance with you. I want to find out if we fit together in real life and not only over Christmas vacation. I want to know your friends and meet the people you work with and help you finish your house. I want to wake up with you and fall asleep with you. I want all of that."

Ali looked around the room. Other couples were having their meals, and at one larger table there was what looked like a family sitting together and laughing. "You want that even if it means having to deal with this town?"

JT nodded and smiled. "I was wrong about the town. Wait, no. I wasn't wrong about the town as it was when I was a kid. I was wrong that it hadn't changed in a decade. I love this place—it was the people who were a problem. But this week, I've met a lot of people who are amazing and kind and welcoming."

Ali smiled. "I'm glad to hear that, because I bought a house here and my job's here and it would be really annoying to have to sell everything and start over because the woman I love doesn't like it here."

JT's cheeks hurt from smiling. "Really?" JT looked around the room to see if anyone was paying attention to them.

Ali nodded. "I love you. And I don't care if everyone in this inn knows it. They probably will get the idea if you come up to the room with me later." Ali quirked an eyebrow and smiled suggestively.

It was so over the top JT had to laugh, even if her stomach flipped at the idea of spending the night with Ali.

"But I also have a confession." Ali twisted her napkin in her hands.

JT's heart kicked into a higher gear. "What?"

Ali looked away for a second and JT felt her panic rising. "You know the paint we picked out together for my office?" JT nodded, completely confused. "I hated it."

"What?" JT asked with a laugh. "Why didn't you say something before?"

Ali blushed. "I didn't want to hurt your feelings." JT protested but Ali stopped her. "No, this isn't your fault. I was so used to getting along with everyone—my mom, Kyle—I just went along with the color, and then over the last few days I've been staring at it and hating it. Finally, I called Tommy and asked him to help me repaint."

"Why didn't you call me? I would have helped."

Ali sighed. "Because I was afraid I would hurt your feelings and I didn't want that. You didn't do anything wrong. I agreed to the yellow when I really wanted something darker and richer. I took the gift certificate we won and I bought the paint and Tommy and I redid the whole room." She smiled, her eyes wet. "It looks amazing now. The bookcases you built really stand out."

JT got up and walked around the table and wrapped Ali in a hug. It was awkward to kneel next to her chair and hug her, but JT didn't care if the entire place stared at them. She wanted to offer whatever comfort she could.

"Babe, it's your house and I want you to love it. Who the fuck cares what I think? I'm just some random hockey star."

Ali laughed and wiped her tears. "No, you're not. You're my girlfriend and I care about you and what you think. But I had to do this for me. Do you get that?"

JT sat back on her feet, still at the side of Ali's chair. "Of course I do! Do you know the number of things I've had to do just for me?" Ali laughed. "I want you to do whatever you need to do for yourself. But I also want you to know that I will help you if you want it. I'm not going to break if you tell me you hate a paint color. You don't have to appease me." She stood up and took her seat. "I'm so happy you love your office. Will you show it to me?"

Ali grinned. "I'd love to. I need a new desk though, something sturdy." Her eyes flashed with lust and mischief and JT felt like she might fall out of her seat.

"Is that so? Maybe you could tell me about it later."

Ali shook her head. "Forget telling, I'm going to show you."

Chapter Fifty-Four

After their meal of delicious food and more honesty than Ali had expected, she grabbed JT's hand and led her up the stairs to their room. She caught JT looking at their hands and then around the room.

"What's the matter, scared to have people see us together?" Ali said with a smile.

JT shook her head. "Overwhelmed. How many times in your life do you get to have a dream come true?"

Ali stopped and looked at JT's face. She reached up and cupped her cheek. "You've already seen me naked."

JT smiled. "I'm not talking about seeing you naked, although that was a transcendent experience. I'm talking about you, Ali Porter, choosing me. I dreamed of this from the time I was a kid and never in my life did I think it would happen. So don't make fun of me for savoring it."

Ali shoved her against the wall of the empty hallway and kissed her until she felt like she might explode. Then she dragged JT to the suite the inn had set aside for the contest winners. Inside, the bed was festooned with rose petals and two robes. There was an ice bucket with a bottle of champagne as well as a platter of chocolate-covered strawberries on a side table.

"Wow," JT said, taking in the sight. "They really went all out."

Ali walked to the side table and inspected the offerings. "Looks like there are things from all the places we did the contest. Cocoa bombs, pastries, some candy, and obviously the strawberries look amazing." When she turned back to JT, she discovered her looking hungrily at her.

Ali felt a wave of overwhelming desire. She had been such a bundle of nervous energy as she waited for JT to come back for their date, and then during everything with her mom and Kyle, she hadn't spent enough time thinking about how gorgeous JT was.

JT cocked her head to the side as if she understood everything going on in Ali's brain. "Come here," she said, crooking a finger in a way that would have been cheesy from anyone else. From her, it made Ali so turned on, JT's finger might as well have been inside her already.

Ali strutted over to her feeling more confident than she could remember ever feeling in her life. This hot, muscular woman wanted her. She wanted her so much that she was willing to rearrange her entire life simply for the *possibility* of being with her. Was there anything sexier than knowing someone would actually move mountains for you?

As Ali got closer, she held eye contact with JT and slipped out of her dress, revealing the brand-new lingerie she'd been saving for a special occasion. She'd ordered it when her divorce was finalized and was thrilled to have a reason to put it on.

JT looked ready to rip it off with her teeth. "Ali, you look so fucking unbelievable. Jesus, you're killing me."

"Good," Ali breathed.

JT's jaw slackened. "You said you had plans for me?"

Ali nodded slowly. She slipped her hands under JT's jacket and slipped it off her shoulders. Ali let her hands feel every bit of JT's shoulder muscles and then her arms, and she slid the jacket off and threw it on a chair.

Then she started on the buttons on the front of JT's shirt. She teased and took her time and watched as JT's pupils blew wide. She dragged a finger down JT's front from her chest to the top of her pants. She kept her eyes on JT, and her fingers moved to her zipper. She opened JT's pants and slid a hand around to grab her ass.

She tipped her chin up to look into JT's eyes and waited for her to lean down. "Kiss me."

JT dipped her head to bring their lips together. Ali squeezed her ass with one hand and pulled JT's head down with a hand gripped in her hair. The kiss was searing. Ali slid her tongue against JT's, teasing her until JT's hips tipped forward against Ali's.

JT reached for her, her hands roaming all over Ali's skin, her fingers skimming along Ali's lacy lingerie. Ali hissed at the feeling of JT's palm on her nipple. She wasn't going to get distracted from what she planned to do. She'd been thinking about it for days and every time she pictured the scene in her head she got so wet she had to change her underwear.

"What do you want, Ali?"

Ali moaned. "I want to bend you over that bed and fuck you from behind."

JT pulled back, looking stunned.

Ali froze. "I'm sorry. I said the wrong thing. Sorry, sorry…"

JT put one finger under Ali's chin and tipped her face up. She gently kissed her. "Don't apologize. You don't have to apologize for wanting things." She kissed Ali harder. "You want to fuck me?"

Ali nodded, feeling drunk but powerful. "Yes. You're so hot. I've been imagining you bent over a desk." She nodded to the bed. "But that will work, too."

JT shrugged out of her shirt and let her pants fall to the floor.

She tossed her shirt onto a chair and ran a hand through her hair, never taking her eyes off Ali. "So, you've been thinking about me?" JT sat on the edge of the bed and motioned for Ali to stand between her legs.

Ali obliged, her hands exploring JT's thighs. "You're really hot, and honestly, I'm not sure we've spent enough time together without our clothes on." Her hands explored every bit of JT's skin she had access to. "When you're not around it's all I can think about. My hands ache to touch you, and my mouth craves you. I don't know how else to explain it."

JT captured Ali's bottom lip with her teeth and gently pulled back before letting go. Ali felt like she'd been lit on fire. She pushed JT backward and hovered on top of her.

"Is this okay?"

JT nodded and sucked Ali's lip into her mouth again. "I like you on top of me."

Ali ground her hips into JT and they both moaned at the contact. "Do you know how hot it is that you let me be in control? I know you could probably pick me up and carry me over your shoulder with ease, but instead you give yourself to me." Ali exhaled, overcome for a moment. "Seriously. Do you know how hot that is?"

JT laughed. "Why don't you show me?"

If Ali needed encouragement, that was more than enough. She set to work, her tongue roving over every inch of skin she could find. When she ran into JT's bra, she took only a second to take it off before wrapping her lips around JT's nipple and sucking and licking until JT's back arched off the bed.

From there she worked her mouth down JT's stomach to her underwear which she removed by hooking her fingers under the band and practically throwing them across the room. Ali got on her knees and licked a line along the inside of JT's muscular thighs from one knee to the other, leaving JT gasping.

"Ali, please. I'm dying."

Ali looked up, her mouth covered in wetness, and grinned. "Turn over."

JT did as she was told. Ali couldn't believe her luck as she stared at the shifting topography of JT's back and her muscles shifted under her skin. Ali reached out, running her hands over JT's shoulders and back all the way down until her hands cupped JT's ass. Ali pressed her hips forward, leaning into JT and letting her weight settle against her.

JT arched into the pressure as she steadied herself on her elbows. Ali reached around to take JT's breasts in her hands. She teased and stroked her nipples until JT was panting again and shoving herself back into Ali.

"Ali, please," JT said between ragged breaths. She turned her head. "I swear to god, I need you to make me come or I'm going to do it myself."

Ali laughed but followed JT's instructions. One of her hands traveled to JT's clit and stroked it slowly to match JT's own thrusts. The other hand stayed on JT's nipple, the pad of her finger rubbing back and forth in a matched rhythm.

"Inside," JT gasped. "I want you inside me."

Ali moved her fingers lower, thrusting them into JT's swollen, soaked pussy. "Fuck," Ali breathed, unable to hold back her own arousal at the feel of JT clenching around her. Their pace picked up and she pressed into JT and she rocked back against Ali's hand.

"Harder," JT said, her voice pleading and raw.

Ali obliged, her heart hammering in her chest, her own breath becoming ragged as they moved together. Suddenly, JT jerked forward, her insides seeming to grab Ali's fingers tighter and tighter before JT released and fell forward against the bed, her arms giving out.

Ali stroked her through the aftershocks and then lay on the bed next to JT. JT rolled on her side so she could look at Ali. Ali let her eyes travel over her naked body. "God, you're so hot."

JT laughed. "How the fuck are you still wearing all of that? What kind of girlfriend am I?"

"The perfect one, if you ask me."

JT shook her head. "Impossible. Please don't expect perfection from me. You'll be disappointed."

Ali sighed. "I don't think I will." She inched closer and wrapped herself around JT. JT took the chance to unhook Ali's bra. Ali pulled her head back. "What are you doing?"

"You're wearing too much. I want access to your boobs, Porter. I have plans."

"Oh yeah?"

JT nodded. "Unless you have any requests. I'm very accommodating if you have anything else you've been thinking about while I was gone."

Ali's mind went blank at the stunning amount of possible answers to that question. It was like JT asking made her lose all ability to communicate any more of her fantasies.

"You don't happen to have a hockey jersey with you, do you?"

JT grinned. "No, but you're into that?"

Ali nodded. "I want to wear your jersey while you go down on me."

JT's mouth hung open. "I—I can get to work on that. But for now?"

Ali smirked. "Be creative."

JT moved closer, her eyes focused on Ali's chest. Her intensity and the anticipation of JT's tongue on her made Ali's heart pound and her breath grow shallow. JT ran her tongue in a circle around Ali's nipple, teasing without touching it. She did this until Ali thought she would scream of frustration. JT let her tongue travel over her nipple in a gentle, then firmer swipe.

Ali didn't know how long it lasted but JT did to her nipple what she'd done to Ali's clit days before. Somewhere in the recesses of her mind, Ali remembered reading that nipple orgasms were possible even if she'd never had one. The longer JT's mouth moved in slow, firm circles and flicked across the stiff peak of her hardened nipples, the closer Ali came to release.

"Jesus Christ, don't stop."

JT hummed happily and continued with her mouth moving between both breasts and her slowly moving to grab the back of Ali's thigh. She let her fingers work closer and closer to the hem of Ali's underwear until she touched them at Ali's soaking center.

"Can I take these off?"

Ali nodded and moved to take them off herself. JT stopped her.

"Let me, please." She gently tugged them off, being so careful to slide them down Ali's thighs.

Ali let her legs fall open, practically begging JT to touch her. JT went back to sucking on her nipples, leaving Ali frustrated.

"JT, please. I want to come. I'm so close."

JT's hand slid up the inside of Ali's thigh and quickly found her clit. Her fingers slid back and forth over it, and Ali felt herself winding tighter and tighter.

"Right there, I'm so close!"

JT smiled around Ali's nipple and increased the speed of her licking and the rhythm of her fingers gliding through Ali's soaked pussy. All that nipple play had brought Ali to the edge and it took no time at all for her to fall apart completely with JT's fingers stroking her.

"Fuck, JT." Ali cried out and then stilled. She rolled closer to JT, wrapping her as tight as she could as she came down from the intense waves of orgasms washing over her. After a minute she had the most intense urge to laugh. It started as a giggle and then grew.

JT picked her head up and looked down at her. "Are you okay?"

Ali laughed harder. "I can't believe we can do that anytime we want."

JT looked at her like she'd lost her mind.

"You asked to stay! You asked them to pick you so I get to keep having un-fucking-believable orgasms!" Ali laughed harder until she was wiping tears from her eyes. "How did I get so lucky?"

JT gave a wary smile. "Are you sure you're okay?"

Ali wrapped her in a tight hug and threw one leg over JT's hips. "Yes! I'm great. You want to stay! I get to have you." Ali gestured at JT. "I get all of you. How on earth did that happen?"

JT laughed. "Oh my god, I thought you were losing your mind." This only made them both laugh harder. "But yes, I asked to be near enough that I can keep being your girlfriend, if you'll have me."

Ali cackled. "Have you? I plan to have you at least eighty-seven times a week. I'm going to have you all over my house."

JT laughed and, after a few minutes, the two of them finally wore themselves out laughing and had to wipe away their tears. "You can have me as many times and for as long as you like. I love you, Ali."

Ali smiled. "I love you, too. I really, really love you."

Epilogue

Nine Months Later

JT sat in a studio, waiting for Darcy LaCroix to ask her first question, and hoping to god that no one could tell how much she was sweating. She'd met Darcy before, of course, at the Olympics when she'd made a complete ass of herself, and now she was wishing she'd told her team publicist she was sick so she didn't have to do the interview.

JT saw movement in her peripheral vision. Natalie Carpenter walked toward Darcy. "Carpenter?" she asked.

Natalie smiled and leaned in to give Darcy a kiss on her cheek. "Did you think I was going to let you come in here and flirt with my fiancée without stopping by?"

JT's mouth dropped open and her face burned.

Darcy laughed and swatted Natalie's leg. "Go on, I have work to do."

Natalie grinned and walked off the set. "I'm watching you, Coxie," she said over her shoulder. Coxie looked at her lap and twisted her fingers together. She tried taking a deep breath.

"Cox, it's going to be okay."

JT looked up and found Darcy smiling at her. "What?"

"You look a little nervous, that's all. Forget Nat, you know how she is. I'm not going to give you a hard time, you know that, right?"

JT nodded shakily. "Right. Yeah. Just, you know."

Darcy laughed. "I'm not exactly sure what you mean by that, but I think I get you anyway." Darcy touched her earpiece. "Okay. You ready?"

JT nodded and adjusted her jacket for the seven hundredth time.

"JT Cox, reigning league MVP. Thanks for joining us today."

JT nodded and tried not to fiddle with her hands. "Thanks for having me."

"The last time I saw you was the winter games where you and Team USA won gold. Now you're sitting here with a league championship and a league MVP to your name. You've had quite a year."

JT blushed. "Never in my wildest dreams would I have imagined all of that in one year. Of course, I grew up dreaming of those kinds of accomplishments, but to have them so early in my career and all in the same year is honestly overwhelming."

"I can imagine. Now you're getting ready for your second year in Boston. How are you hoping this year will go?"

"You know, I'm hoping we can build on what we did last year, bring our new folks into the fold, and hopefully give our fans a lot to cheer about. We've got the best fans here in Boston, and we want to make sure we put on a good show for them." She put her palm on her thigh, trying not to be too obvious about the fact her hands were sweaty.

Darcy smiled. "And your fans love you and your personality on and off the ice. Can you tell me some highlights from the past season?"

JT relaxed as joyful thoughts flooded her brain. "Honestly, there's nothing better than meeting all the kids who come to watch us. No slight to the adult fans, I love you all, too. But when I was a little girl playing hockey, I didn't have a girls' team to play on until I got to college. And being close enough for my family to come to games has been incredible now my nieces and nephew are all learning to play. It's all a dream come true."

"You were the captain of your high school team, right?"

JT nodded. "Yeah. The guys I played with were amazing, but not everyone was happy to see a girl out there. To have little girls in my hometown have places to play and get to see us big girls compete professionally has been a dream come true." JT was not going to cry, but tears threatened the corners of her eyes. She blinked them away as fast as she could.

"Anything else that's brought you happiness this past year?"

JT heard the sound of paws on the hard floor and turned to find Toby running at her. "Oh my god. Toby, what are you doing?"

Darcy laughed. "Who is this?"

JT bent over and grabbed for Toby's collar. "This is my girl, Toby. I got her after the Olympics. Since she's yellow, I named her after the chocolate bars I ate in Switzerland. She's always there for me and she's always so happy to see me when I come home from a road trip. She's the best."

Darcy smiled and looked off camera. "Where does Toby go when you're on the road?"

JT froze. Was Darcy asking about Ali on camera? She had not prepared for this. She heard footsteps rushing toward them and saw Ali with a huge grin.

A chair materialized next to JT, and Ali sat down.

"I'm the dogsitter," Ali said cheekily. "When JT's away, Toby and I hang out."

Darcy held out her hand. "Nice to meet you, dogsitter."

JT scowled. "What are you doing? You're not the dogsitter, you're—" She stopped, looking around at all the cameras.

Darcy laughed. "Should we tell her?"

Ali smiled. "Babe, I'm here to ask you a question."

JT shook her head. "No."

Ali laughed. "I haven't even said anything and you're telling me no? Please."

JT was freaking out. "Ali, what are you doing?"

Ali held out her hand and opened it to show her palm. "I'm seeing if you might like to move in with me." She looked at Darcy. "And no, the cameras are not rolling. What kind of asshole do you think I am? I'm not asking you to marry me. I'm not sure I'm up for another marriage at this point, but I love you and I want you to move in with me and Toby."

"With you and Toby? She's my dog!"

"Bullshit, she loves me more. Deal with it." Ali's face softened. "So, what do you think? Can you handle living next door to your parents?"

JT smiled. "The next-door thing wouldn't be my first choice, but...nothing would make me happier than to live with you." She kissed Ali and then pulled back to look at Darcy. "You swear no one's taping this?"

Darcy nodded. "Look, I know a thing or two about being on camera with the woman you love. I swear they're off. But if you don't mind introducing Ali to our viewers, I have a couple questions."

JT looked at Ali. "You up for it?"

Ali gestured to her outfit. "Why do you think I look so hot?"

"Born that way?"

Darcy laughed. "God, Nat did say you've always got a line ready."

After they got Ali a mic, they restarted the interview.

"JT, rumor has it you have a thing for goalies. Ali, does that mean you play in goal?"

Ali shook her head. "My playing days ended a long time ago, and I was never a goalie. I'm too short for soccer goalie anyway."

JT blushed deep red. "But you did play catcher." She looked at Darcy. "I have to confess that I first fell for Ali when I was a teenager. And part of what drew me to her was the fact that she was a catcher in softball. There's something about the intensity behind the mask." She looked at Ali. "Completely irresistible."

Ali smiled. "Really? I never knew that."

"Yeah, whatever thing I had for goalies came from my teenage crush on you. When it comes to who I love, it's always been you."

★ ★ ★ ★ ★

Acknowledgments

Nothing I have ever done, writing this book included, has been a solo endeavor. I want to thank my brilliant agent, Paige Terlip, for her support, guidance, sense of humor and ability to talk through any writing issue with soft kindness and sharp insight.

Thank you to Errin Toma for helping me to craft this story from a tiny idea into a fully-fledged novel. I'm glad both you and Paige asked, "What if Coxie had her own book?" I so enjoyed working with you on JT and Ali's story.

Thank you to everyone at Carina Adores who made this book possible: Stephanie Doig, Shana Mongroo, Maya Price-Baker, Katixa Espinoza, Eugénie Szwalek and Amy Wetton.

I grew up in a very small town in rural New Hampshire and share some of Coxie's reticence about the place that wasn't always sure what to do with an obviously queer kid. But, like Coxie, I love where I grew up—the trees and fields, the snow and mountains, the bumpy, frost heave–addled roads and the way people can be kind even when they're not always nice. I had a hard time, as many adolescents do, but I also had teachers and coaches who got me and nurtured me and supported me. I hope they know how much of a difference they made in my life and how much I have carried them with me everywhere I go.

I hope every teacher, coach, music and art director who nurtures kids in places that don't always understand them knows that you are changing the world one kid at a time. Things can be very bleak, especially for the queer kids, but having adults in their lives who care for them is life-changing. Please keep doing what you do. You are all my heroes.

Unlike Coxie, I have parents who showed up to every single one of my games, plays and performances. I could always look to the sidelines or the stands and find them there, cheering me on (sometimes at an embarrassing decibel level). Thank you, Mom and Dad, for showing up for me over and over. I love you very much.

My siblings are a constant source of joy and laughter to me. Like Coxie, I am third in my family. And I am the weirdo jock in a family full of artist types, but that has never hampered our ability to speak in inside jokes, movie quotes and memories drawn from years of being together. I love you all.

I have been lucky to have friends who have been lovely to me and generous with the use of their names for characters in this book and others. I hope you all know I have borrowed your names out of love and affection. JT, Jen, Ali, Brooke, Isla (who was in the last book) and everyone else whose name I have finagled into my stories, I can't tell you how much your friendship means to me. I hope you'll accept this token of my gratitude. This book is for you.

Finally, to my own little family—I couldn't do this without your love and support. Gusty and Beatrix, being your mom remains one of the most stunning miracles of my life. You bring me nothing short of a hundred joy. Thank you for tolerating my silly songs, interminable stories and bad puns. I love you to the moon and back.

Thank you to my wife, Jennifer. My imagination wasn't equipped to dream up someone as spectacular as you are, let alone to dare to think I would get to be your wife. I could not write these stories without you. I love you.

And lastly, to our dogs, Bear and Puck. Bear, you remain the perfect dowager Labrador of our household, content to cast judgment on all of us while sleeping soundly on couches. Puck, you are a sweet but horrid little beast. I do not thank you for your help writing this book, however, because I surely would have written much faster without you trying to steal every shoe, sock, scrap of paper or remote control you could find. I love you, you infuriating chaos demon.